William Alexander Hammond

**Doctor Grattan**

William Alexander Hammond

**Doctor Grattan**

ISBN/EAN: 9783337039653

Printed in Europe, USA, Canada, Australia, Japan

Cover: Foto ©Andreas Hilbeck / pixelio.de

More available books at **www.hansebooks.com**

# DOCTOR GRATTAN.

*A NOVEL.*

BY

WILLIAM A. HAMMOND,

AUTHOR OF "LAL."

NEW YORK:

D. APPLETON AND COMPANY,

1, 3, AND 5 BOND STREET.

1885.

# CONTENTS.

# DOCTOR GRATTAN.

## CHAPTER I.

EVERYBODY in Plato wondered who Mr. Lamar was. Not Crito, or Phædo, or Apollodorus, or Socrates, or other of the disputants whose questions and answers, whose affirmations and denials, whose speculations and assertions are set forth by the immortal philosopher, but the inhabitants of the little town in the State of New York, so named by the surveyor who ran the lines of the counties and their subdivisions a hundred years ago. This learned person, having a contempt for the aborigines and their nomenclature, and armed with a classical dictionary, went through the wilderness with a heart untouched by the hills, the valleys, the rivers, and their significant and musical names that the Iroquois, the Mohawks, and the Senecas had given them, and scattered broadcast the designations that ancient Greece and Rome had bestowed upon their cities and great men.

Plato, which ought to have been called Canemanga, from the little river upon the bank of which it was built, could have boasted, had it been disposed to indulge in self-glorification, of about twelve hundred and fifty men, women, and children of the Caucasian—or, as we now call it, the Aryan—race, besides ten Indians and five negroes, the latter all belonging to one family. These three integral parts of the village population showed no tendency to miscegenation or even to social intercourse. The Aryans lived in the center of the town, and, being all well-to-do people for that section of the country, occupied the best houses. The Indians, keeping up their nomadic habits, moved off into the Adirondack region as soon as the snow had disappeared from the ground, and did not return till the cold weather drove them into the miserable huts that they had been permitted to construct on the outskirts of the village. As to the negroes, they had no autonomy, but were scattered among the inhabitants as servants—the clergyman, the doctor, the lawyer, a literary lady named Hadden, and Mr. Hicks, the village storekeeper, having each one. It need scarcely be said that the wives and daughters of all the other householders did their own domestic work, not altogether because they could not help themselves, but partly because they liked occupation, and partly, again, because they did not care to give themselves airs and set up for being above honest labor. At least, that was the way Mrs. Spill, the wife of the carpenter, put it in an animated discussion with Mrs. Bishop, whose husband kept a little book-store and circulating library, and who had been complaining of a pain in her back, which she alleged was the result of a prolonged series of house-cleaning operations.

Plato was situated on the very edge of the Adirondack forest, and at the foot of one of the highest mountain-peaks of the region. The Canemanga, a little stream that connected a lake of the same name with Cold River, ran along its eastern boundary; while facing it to the south was "The Giant," a lofty peak that rose abruptly out of the plain, and on the north "Hurricane Mountain," of almost as great an altitude. On the east and on the west were high hills and mountains—"Cobble Hill" and "Pitchoff Mountain," and "Green Hill" and "Mount Mary"; while

to the southwest was the loftiest of them all, "Dix Peak."
Surrounded as it was by these mountain-ridges and isolated
crags, which cast their shadows far into the valley below,
it was late before the sun rising over their summits lit up
the little village, and early when, sinking below the high
range at the foot of which lay the Au Sable Lakes, it left
it in half twilight long before the hour agreed upon by the
almanac-makers.   Hence it happened that Plato was not a
particularly cheerful place, and that many of the inhabitants, except, of course, the two sets of colored contingents,
were very much in the condition of the dwellers in the
mines in England and the people that live in the deep valleys of Switzerland and the Tyrol.   They were blanched
by being deprived of light just as celery is blanched by
heaping up the earth around its roots so as to shut off the
direct rays of the sun.   Indeed, Doctor Grattan, who had
lived in Plato for nearly twenty years, ever in fact since he
began the practice of medicine, declared that the process
of etiolation was going on in the Indians and negroes, and
that the first were not so red nor the latter so black as their
progenitors.   There were not wanting skeptics, however,
who alleged a more obvious cause for the lighting up of the
complexions of the sons and daughters of Shem and Ham.

The "Platonians," as they delighted to call themselves,
not only wondered who Mr. Lamar was, but, not knowing
anything about his antecedents, they proceeded to form
surmises more injurious than complimentary to that gentleman.   There appears to be an almost universal provision
of nature that mankind shall denounce the man or woman
that presumes to set up for himself or herself a type different from that established by the people of any particular
locality, or that prefers to be guided by his or her ideas
rather than by those of other persons.   The greatest insult
that can be given to narrow-minded individuals is to differ
from them—not in words, verbal differences make little

impression ; but the difference in manner, in custom, in
conduct, in modes of life generally, excites their direst ire.
When the inhabitants of a village dine at twelve o'clock,
and a person moves into their midst and, regardless of the
custom of the place, takes his dinner at six, it were better
for that man's reputation that he should have stolen a
sheep or picked a pocket than that he should persist in his
nefarious prandial habit.   Mr. Lamar not only dined at
six, but he breakfasted at ten, and did sundry other things
which convinced the Platonians that there was something
radically wicked in his antecedents and mental organization.

Thus Mr. Hicks, who kept the one "store" in the village, at which, as he said, could be bought anything "from
a plow to a spool of cotton," declared, with many noddings
and shakings of his head that were intended by him to
express the wisdom with which his cranium was stuffed,
that Mr. Lamar was "no better than he should be"—as if
anybody ever was !   He further asserted that he had indubitable evidence that the person in question had been an
officer in the Cuban army, and had been obliged to leave
the country "between two days," as he expressed it, in
order to prevent his body being riddled with musket-bul-
lets or his neck broken by the garrote, when the Spaniards
had finally succeeded in suppressing the rebellion.

"Of course," continued Mr. Hicks, after delivering this
opinion, which he did daily to the loungers in his store,
"he took mighty good care to feather his nest before he
got away.   I shouldn't be at all surprised if he robbed a
plantation, or even a bank.   You see, they ain't much
down there for police, and things was pretty well turned
topsy-turvy at the end."   Then the village merchant would
stop and look sapiently at the listeners who, with staring
eyes and open mouths, sat around the stove, taking in his
gossip as though it were so much "gospel truth."

It almost invariably happened that some one of the

attentive group would inquire of Mr. Hicks the reasons for
his suspicions. This was the opportunity for which he
thirsted, and he was always ready for the emergency.

"Why do I think so!" he would exclaim. "Every
one who knows Joshua Hicks knows that he ain't the man
to go round slandering his neighbor, even if he does take
his dinner at an outlandish hour, and go about with a Spanish cloak over his shoulders, besides doing many other
things which, if they ain't unlawful, are contrary to the
peace of the people of the State of New York—no, not if
he does look as black as Satan, and never has a good word
for no one ; not even so much as passing the time o' day—
Joshua Hicks ain't that kind of a man. He has reasons
for the faith that's into him every time. Well, now, touch-
in' this particular case, I'll only say that whenever he's
bought anything in this store—which I'm free to admit
ain't been often, for I guess he sends to New York for
a'most everything he wants, instead of patronizing his fel-
low-citizens of Plato—he's always paid for it in Cuban gold
—doubloons and such like. That's one reason, and I guess
it'll be granted all around that it's a good one."

"As if having doubloons made a man a captain in the
Cuban army," said young Hadden, contemptuously, on
one occasion. "You might as well say that because a man
wears moccasins he's an Indian."

"I never said a man that wore moccasins was an Indian," rejoined Mr. Hicks, somewhat irresponsively. "I
was talking of Mr. Lamar and his doubloons. Perhaps,
Mr. William Hadden," he went on, assuming the most sar-
castic tone of which he was capable, "if you was to attend to what was bein' said, you wouldn't get your brains
muddled."

Hadden looked at his antagonist with an expression that
was meant to be both defiant and supercilious, but did not
deign a reply in words.

"Well, perhaps now that we've heard from Mr. William Hadden," continued Hicks, not yet appeased, "and got his views on the subject, I'll be allowed, seein' as it's my own store I'm a-talkin' in, to go on." He looked round the group; but, as no one interposed any further objection, he resumed the declaration of his opinions.

"But that ain't all. He dropped a piece of paper here one day, and I picked it up after he'd gone away, and what do you think it was? Them as don't know already couldn't guess in a month o' Sundays. It was the back of a letter, and it was directed to 'Captain Juan Lamarez, Matanzas, Cuba.' 'Juan Lamarez' is the Spanish for 'John Lamar,' I guess. Now, it strikes me that them two things put together make out a pretty strong case. Of course, there ain't no absolute certainty about it, for there ain't many things in this world that a man can be certain about outside of religion and death, but many a feller's been hung on less evidence than that. Gentlemen," looking triumphantly around the group, "I guess he's a filibuster."

"Well, if his money is Cuban money, it's good enough for me," said Mr. Spill, the carpenter, upon the occasion in question; "but he ain't no military man. He's a sea-farin' man. That's what he is. Now, you just listen to me, and you'll all agree that I'm right, and consequently that Hicks is wrong. You see," he went on, speaking very low and with an air of mystery, "this is a serious matter, and you've all got to give me your Bible oath that you don't let what I'm goin' to tell you go any further—and I mean you specially, Bill Hadden," looking, as he spoke, at that young gentleman, who was cutting a dog's head on a hazel-rod, evidently with the intention of using the stick as a cane; "for the last time I told you a secret it wasn't an hour before it was all over the village."

"That isn't true!" exclaimed Hadden, with some excitement of manner and voice; "you told a foolish story of a man being cured of hydrophobia by a mad-stone, as you called it, and I made fun of you to Lucy Craig and Cynthia Grattan. That's all there is in it."

"Well, you ain't got no right to make fun o' me to any one ; and, as to bein' a fool, I guess a fellow that don't believe the truth is as big a one as the man that does believe it."

"Come, now, gentlemen !" said Mr. Hicks, "this ain't the place for bad blood to be spilt. If there's anything between you two, you can settle it outside o' these premises. And there's another thing, too," he continued, looking at Hadden somewhat menacingly. "What's said around this stove ain't to be told all over the town to a lot of giddy girls. So, with that understanding, we'll hear what Mr. Spill has to say."

"I don't want to hear any of his nonsense," said Hadden, angrily, rising as he spoke and going toward the door. "The man that's fool enough to believe that what he calls a mad-stone can cure hydrophobia isn't likely to say anything sensible about Mr. Lamar. So you'll please excuse me. I've better things to do than to listen to his twaddle. But you'd better mind what you say," he continued, looking defiantly at Spill. "Mr. Lamar isn't the man to let riff-raff like you talk about him. If you don't look out, he'll punch your head." With which words he went out, shutting the door with a bang that gave some idea of the state of his feelings.

"What's made Hadden so touchy ?" inquired Mr. Bishop, who kept the little book-shop and circulating library. "He's taken to reading the queerest books lately. You know, when old Dr. Robinson died, I bought a lot of his odd books. Nobody else wanted them, and they went for a song. I put them in the library ; but not a soul ever took any of them out, till a few months ago Hadden began to go through them, till now I guess he's about finished the whole of them."

"Oh, well, never mind Hadden," said Mr. Hicks, giving the fire in the big, red-hot stove a punch with a broomstick that did duty for a poker. "He's got the run of the house on the hill, I guess," he added, giving a wink which, as he revolved his head in a circle, was intended to act upon the whole company; "there's more attraction up there for Mr. William Hadden, Esq., than you'd think for."

"If you mean the daughter," exclaimed Spill, "she wouldn't look at him. Lord bless you! she's a mighty sight more stuck up than her father, though I'm bound to say she never give me a sassy word, but was always fair-spoken. But she wouldn't think of Bill Hadden. And if she'd like to, the old man wouldn't let her. She's meant for a member of Congress at least."

"Well, go on," resumed Mr. Hicks, "and tell us what you know about this man Lamar, who's built a house fit for the President of the United States to live in, and only him and his daughter. It's a wastin' of the gifts of Providence, that's what it is. Twenty-two rooms for two people!"

"Twenty-three," interrupted Spill; "I ought to know, for I helped to make 'em. But then there's seven help—servants they call 'em. They've got four of the rooms."

"Seven help for two people!" exclaimed Mr. Hicks, indignantly. "It's downright sinful; such pride is bound to have a fall some time or other. It may be postponed, but it can't be prevented. But go on, Spill."

"Well, one day when I was fixin' them window-casings on the first floor—them as was made in New York, and wouldn't fit after they got 'em here—Mr. Lamar was loungin' around, when, says he, 'Mr. Spill, I ain't feelin' uncommon bright to-day, and I think a little exercise would do me a power o' good. If you want some boards sawed, point 'em out to me, and I'll do the work.' Well, I showed him some rough boards, and give him a saw, and told him to go ahead. He offs with his coat and ups with his shirt-

sleeves, and there just below his elbow on his right arm was
a skull and cross-bones tattooed. Right on the naked skin
they was, and done in sky-blue and blood-red! You see he
forgot himself; but it wasn't only for a twinkling of an eye,
for as soon as he saw me looking at him he rolled down his
sleeves as if nothing had happened. Notwithstandin', I saw
'em as plain as I see the nose on Mr. Hicks's face."

"And you can't help seein' that," laughed Hicks, "for
it's twice as big as any common nose."

"Not carin' to flatter you, which is contrary to my
principles," rejoined Spill, "it's a good enough nose for all
the things as a nose is needed for, and the Lord knows
beauty ain't one of 'em. But to go on : of course I was
taken aback at such a horrid sight; but there wasn't only
the one conclusion to come to, and that was that Mr. Lamar's been a pirate-captain."

"I'll tell you what I think," exclaimed a tall, stout, and
big-whiskered man, who had entered the store while Spill
was speaking, but had remained standing behind him till
the carpenter had finished his story, and had expressed his
opinion of Mr. Lamar's antecedents—"I think that you
are a lot of blockheads, every one of you! You, Hicks
and Spill, are the worst, for you've been slandering the man
that's spending his money right and left among you, and
who will probably continue to spend it for many years to
come; and you" glaring around at the others, every man of
whom hung his head as though afraid to face the intruder,
"for sitting here and listening to the abuse of the man
that's putting bread into your mouths and who in the last
six months has done more for Plato than all the rest of the
inhabitants have done for it since old Scully laid it out.
Will Hadden told me what was going on here, and I came
to see for myself, and I've seen enough and heard enough
to convince me that you're a lot of blockheads, and that
you ought to be ashamed of yourselves."

"Don't call no names, doctor," said Spill, as the indignant gentleman stopped for a moment to take breath. "It ain't seemly, and it's dead ag'in Scripter, too."

"You arrant old humbug!" exclaimed the doctor, shaking his fist at the protesting carpenter, "how dare you call me to account, when you have been calling a gentleman a pirate? Do you know, Tim Spill, that you've been guilty of slander, and that you've laid yourself open to criminal prosecution that might end in your getting a year in jail and a fine of five hundred dollars?"

"*I* only said he was a captain in the Cuban army," said Hicks, apologetically. "There ain't any slander in that, I guess."

"That wasn't all you said," rejoined the irate doctor; "you've been throwing out hints for the last week that Mr. Lamar had got his wealth by some foul means. You're worse than Spill, for you have a little education and you set yourself up as a well-informed man, while he is an ignoramus, and doesn't pretend to having any knowledge beyond his jack-plane and auger."

"I'd like to know what a respectable man's doing with a raw-head and bloody-bones printed on his arm," said Spill, gathering courage as he thought of the tangible fact he had discovered, and not heeding the attack made on his acquirements. "Every one knows that them are the pirate's emblems, and that they are on the pirate's flag. If it didn't amount to anything, what did he hide 'em for when he saw me looking at 'em?"

"Oh, you sapient ass!" exclaimed the combatant intruder, taking off his coat and approaching Spill, while that individual hastily jumped over the counter under the impression that an attack *vi et armis* was about to be made upon him. "Don't be a fool—I'm not thinking of soiling my hands by touching you. Look at this," he continued, rolling up his shirt-sleeve, and exhibiting a skull and cross-bones tattooed on his arm. "Perhaps you'll go about the village accusing *me* of having once been a pirate."

"I guess," said Spill, from behind the counter, where he felt safe from any assault that might be attempted, "that a death's-head and cross-bones is about as good a sign for a doctor as it is for a pirate."

"Ha, ha, ha!" laughed the doctor. "You're not quite such a fool as I took you to be. Under proper supervision you might do tolerably well. At any rate, I beg your pardon for placing you below Hicks. You're more intelligent than Hicks, and ought to be encouraged. Miss Grattan has a job for you. Go up to the house and see her; she wants a lot of boxes made.—Hicks," he continued, addressing that rather crest-fallen individual, "if ever I hear of you daring to utter a word against my friend Mr. Lamar, or any member of his family, I'll"—here he approached Hicks, and whispered something in his ear. The man turned as pale as death, and slunk away, and the doctor, without a word to the rest of the company, stalked out of the store.

# CHAPTER II.

## A VILLAGE DOCTOR.

DOCTOR GRATTAN was the only medical practitioner in Plato, or within ten miles of it in any direction, and, though the region was considered a healthy one—that is, it was not subject to any special causes of disease—the ordinary ills to which flesh is heir the world over kept him pretty busy. Some five or six years previously there had been another physician, who, however, was in no sense a rival, for he had retired from the practice of his profession when Doctor Grattan took up his residence in the village. Indeed, Doctor Robinson had invited Grattan, who had just received his diploma, to come to Plato, and relieve him from duties that had become irksome to him, and that he had long been desirous of giving up. Young Grattan was the son of his dearest friend, and had begun the study of medicine at the old doctor's request, with the intention of succeeding him. All this was twenty years ago. Doctor Robinson, on retiring from practice, had given himself up to scientific studies, altogether outside the pale of medicine, and had lived on to advanced old age, scarcely ever being seen out of his own house, and rarely allowing visitors to approach him. It was said by the neighbors that he lived entirely in one room—his library and laboratory—spending the whole day there, and sleeping in it at night, though they declared that they did not believe he lost much time in sleep ; for it was rarely the case that a

light was not seen burning in this room far into the small
hours of the morning. The windows were furnished with
inside solid oaken shutters in two sections. The lower one
was always kept shut, so that it was impossible for the most
curious observer, night or day, to get a glimpse of what
was going on inside; while the upper section was allowed
to be open so as to permit light to enter. There was a
story prevalent, at the time the old doctor was living, that
a boy had climbed up the side of the house and had looked
in through the upper and unobstructed sash, but that what
he saw had so frightened him that he had lost his hold and
fallen to the ground, where he had remained for several
hours in an unconscious state. Then he had walked home,
and found, on attempting to describe what he had seen, that
he had lost the faculty of speech. Most of the wise men
and women of the village declared that the old doctor had
struck the boy dumb as a punishment for his unwarrantable
inquisitiveness; but Doctor Grattan, who had about that
period arrived at Plato, said they were a pack of fools, and
that the boy was the subject of the condition known as
aphasia, which was just then beginning to be very much
discussed in Paris and in New York, and that it had been
induced by the fall. However that might have been, certain it is that the boy had never spoken a word since that
day; and, not having been able to write, had never revealed what he saw in the mysterious room. It was supposed, however, from the grimaces and gestures that he
made, whenever the matter was discussed in his presence,
that something horrible was being done; but no one had
ever been able to make out distinctly what the signs indicated, unless, as was supposed by some, they referred to
the dissection of a dead body. Doctor Grattan declared,
with much emphasis, that his old friend had certain views
relative to the association of the brain with the mind, and
that, having obtained a number of human brains from New

York, he was engaged in examining them when the boy
looked in through the upper sash of his window. Others,
however, went so far as to express their suspicions that the
body that was being examined was not that of a dead
man; for when they asked the boy whether or not there
were any sounds from the room, he groaned and cried as
though such were the noises he had heard, and made signs
that were regarded as being intended to declare that a person in the room was undergoing great suffering.

Doctor Grattan, however, on the death of his old friend,
had moved into his residence, a fine old stone house, not
very large, but yet built with that regard for permanence
which the people of colonial times seem to have had. It
stood on the north side of the village, beyond all the other
dwellings, and, from the height of the little knoll on which
it was placed, overlooked the town as well as the surround-
ing country. The Canemanga, in the course of its meanderings, came to the very foot of the hill, so that it would
have been possible for any one to have stood on the front
porch of the doctor's house and throw a stone into the
turbulent stream which, in certain seasons of the year, was
a roaring torrent. This porch commanded a fine view of
the high range of mountains, which prevented the rays of
the sun reaching the village of Plato for an hour after they
would have warmed the place, had the black, frowning
peaks been out of the way, and the doctor was accustomed
to sit for hour after hour with his pipe in his mouth and
with his daughter Cynthia near at hand, thinking of what
interested him at the time, and every now and then addressing a word to the girl at his side.

Doctor Grattan was of a contemplative disposition. He
had many opportunities for thought as he drove around in
his buggy, making his visits to the sick under his care; but
he had always asserted that there was no place for thinking
equal to his front porch. He even went so far as to declare

that the different mountains were associated in his mind with different lines of thought : that, for instance, when he was troubled over a patient that was seriously ill, he always obtained a clearer insight into the character of the disease, and more definite ideas of treatment, by letting his eyes rest on the Giant while he puffed away at his pipe. Again, when he got to thinking of his daughter and of her future life, which he did very often, nothing soothed his anxiety so much as a good long look at Mount Mary ; and when he was angry, which, it must be confessed, was frequently the case, a long, contemplative gaze at Mount Pitchoff acted more potently as a calmant than any nervine in his pharmacopœia. Cynthia laughed when he spoke to her of the different influences that these mountains exercised over his mental processes and emotional moods, and expressed her belief that it was the pipe that allayed his excitement or caused him to look more philosophically at the real or imaginary ills that bore upon him ; but he stoutly maintained that as the mountains were different from each other in size, in form, and in coloring, so the effect upon his mind must be different according as the image of one or the other impinged upon his retinæ.

"You argue just like a woman, my dear," he would say. "That is, you form your opinions first, and then you ransack your little head for what you innocently think are facts to bring forward in their support. Don't you see that, if tobacco were the factor, it would make no difference in the result which mountains I looked at, or whether or not I looked at any mountain ? But experience teaches me that it *does* make a difference. If, for instance, when I am puzzled over Mrs. Smith's baby, I turn my eyes toward old Pitchoff, I immediately get into a frame of mind that makes me absolutely indifferent to the pathological condition of that unfortunate infant. My sensibilities are blunted, and I don't care a sixpence what its disease is,

or whether it lives or dies. I am firmly convinced that
long and uninterrupted contemplation of Pitchoff would
reduce me to a state of apathy, compared to which the condition of an oyster would be soul-stirring hilariousness.
There is something about the dark blue of Pitchoff that
blunts the sensibilities. I shall have to write a memoir
on the influence of colors on the mind. We have familiar
examples in the fact that red irritates many animals, as
the bull and the turkey-gobbler, and that others, as the
bull-frog, for instance, are pleased with a piece of red flan-
nel. I know a man that always sheds tears at the sight of
any purple object. And we know that yellow light is exceedingly irritating to some persons. No! no! don't attempt to shake my faith in the mountains. You can do
almost anything with me, I admit, you minx; but that's
entirely beyond your powers." And so he held to his belief and lived up to it.

Take him all in all, Doctor Arthur Grattan was a singular compound. In the sick-room he was all gentleness
and kindness; out of it, except with his daughter and one
or two friends, he was often ill-nature personified. And
yet, with all his harshness and roughness and cutting sar-
casm, there was a vein of honesty and humanity that showed
that at heart he was good and true, and that caused his influence, brutally manifested as it often was, to be exercised
on the right side. But should the boy whom he had un-
mercifully kicked and cuffed for maltreating a dog or a cat
happen to be taken sick the next day, Doctor Grattan was
unwearying in his attentions so long as there was necessity
for his interference. Upon one occasion he saw a disrepu-
table fellow named Tim Maddox torturing a crow that he
had caught with a fish-hook baited with a grain of corn.
To seize the wretch and belabor him well with a stout cane
was a matter of course. The next day he was informed
that he had broken Tim's arm, and that the man had no

medical attendance other than that given by one of the Indians, who professed to cure such injuries with roots and herbs. Not only did the doctor set the arm, but he took the fellow to his house and kept him there till the bones had entirely united. Then he gave him fifty dollars and sent him off.

"Now," he said, "go; and if ever I again hear of your treating a dumb animal cruelly, I'll break your other arm!" The effect upon Tim was so beneficial that he afterward acted as a sort of detective and constable for the doctor in the cause of humanity, and was encouraged in this good work by a small salary that his instructor paid him.

For the Platonians generally the doctor entertained the most undisguised contempt. Like the average dwellers in small towns, they were narrow-minded and ignorant. Up to the time of the arrival of the Lamars, he had had but two intimacies—one with the Rev. Mr. Craig and his family, and the other with Mr. Ellis, an old bachelor, and the only lawyer in the place. Doctor Grattan hated ignorance in all its forms, and, worse than all, he hated the smallness of mind and the mean emotions that so generally accompany ignorance. His own ideas were large and liberal; he detested intolerance in everything; and one reason why he liked Mr. Craig, the parson, was that he had always found him ready to see good where there was good, even though there was evil mingled with it. Soon after the doctor's arrival in Plato, the reverend gentleman had preached a sermon which the physician had heard. In this address the ground was taken that there is some good in almost every one of God's creatures, and that it is the height of presumption in us to determine for him how far the good shall weigh against the bad. "When we reflect," said the preacher, "upon the immense benefit that the teachings of Voltaire have conferred upon the world—how the spirit of liberty pervades his writings, and how statesmen and nations have had their ideas of independence formed and strengthened by his utterances—who shall dare to say that Almighty God in his infinite wisdom and beneficence will not regard the good done to his people as far outweighing the doubts and slurs cast upon him, who is above injury?"

From that time Doctor Grattan and Mr. Craig became intimate friends. The doctor, though not an atheist or even an infidel, was to some extent a freethinker. He rejected altogether the right of any church or body of men to tell him what he should or should not believe. He had taken the Bible and studied it with the light of his own reason and from his own stand-point, and had arrived at the conclusion that it was essentially true, and to be regarded as the word of God. But he did not believe these things because a body of churchmen, called the Council of Laodicea, had met four hundred years after the death of Christ and had adopted certain books as the Bible, voting on them one by one as a Legislature might vote on the several sections of a code of laws submitted for its action, and adopting some by a large vote, others by a small vote, and one by a majority of a single vote.

"I've just as much right," he said, "to determine what shall be the word of God as had the gentleman who, by his vote, succeeded in having the book of Revelation incorporated into Scripture. Some of the books I accept, others I reject. In either case I act from the reason that God gave me for my guidance. If I am wrong, he will be my helper when the time for help comes."

Nevertheless, although the doctor and the parson were very intimate, being often seen walking together, and frequenting each other's houses, the former was generally regarded as being unsound in his theology, and some of the stricter members of the church did not hesitate to denounce him as an atheist. Mrs. Bishop had frequently declared with great vehemence that he should never darken her doors, even though every member of her family should be taken ill. When she herself was visited by a severe attack of typhoid fever, she resisted all importunities that Doctor Grattan should be called in, till finally when she became delirious, and was no longer capable of determining for herself, her husband, who was a man of some sense and education, regardless of her lately expressed wishes, sent for the doctor, and put him in charge of the case—which from that time on went forward to a successful termination. After that, Mrs. Bishop was a little more careful how she hurled her denunciations at the physician, but she never quite got over her prejudices.

The doctor's friendship for Mr. Ellis, the lawyer, rested upon an entirely different basis. They were never known to agree upon any subject. Now, if the doctor liked any kind of an individual better than he did one whose ideas were in harmony with his own, it was an intelligent, well-educated person, whose views were diametrically different from those that he himself entertained, and who knew how to give and take good, strong dialectical blows. Such a man was Mr. Ellis. Of about the doctor's own age—forty-five; he had, like him, turned his attention to some extent in the direction of theological studies, but, unlike him, had succeeded in arriving at the conviction that man had no right to set himself up as an interpreter of Scripture, and that there was only one authorized guide for his reason, and that was the Church. Further, he contended, that there was but the one true and apostolic church, and that was the Roman Catholic—all the rest being heretical and devoid of all claims to be regarded as instituted by Christ. When asked by his friend the doctor why, holding such views, he did not at once unite himself with that church, he would reply that he had good and sufficient reasons for not doing so, and that what they were was nobody's business but his own. And then, when taunted with inconsistency, his reply was, that abuse and misrepresentation would not make him disclose his reasons. Then the doctor would accuse him of being a pretender, and of talking merely for the sake of argument. "You know, Ellis," he had said upon several occasions, "that at heart you're an old pagan, and that you don't believe in anything. You want to obtain a reputation for sanctity among the people of this benighted region, and hence you take high ground, and throw upon me the odium of being an atheist or infidel, when in fact it is you who are a total unbeliever. You're a wicked man, Ellis, and, although you are what they call about here a 'smart lawyer,' you won't be able to get out of the difficulties that will encompass you when you stand before the judgment-seat. You'll find out then that all your deep arts and special pleading will not avail you." To all of which Mr. Ellis made no reply other than such as could be conveyed through his expressive face, which clearly indicated that the predominant emotion excited by the doctor's charge was contempt.

Then the Lamars had come—first Mr. Lamar, bringing no letters of introduction, but apparently relying solely on his personal characteristics and wealth to obtain recognition from the best people in the little place that he had selected as the future home of himself and daughter. The doctor had such an exalted opinion of his powers of perception and knowledge of human nature, besides being remarkably independent of the opinions of other persons, that he formed his judgment of Mr. Lamar and began to act upon it as soon as that gentleman and himself came in contact. The little tavern of the village was the only place to which the new-comer could go on his first visit to Plato, unacquainted as he was with a single one of the inhabitants. It was an exceedingly uncomfortable hostelry, even for the non-exacting travelers that formed the majority of its guests. For a man, such as was Mr. Lamar, one evidently accustomed to every luxury that wealth could obtain, it was almost insupportable. But, on the night of his arrival, he was suddenly taken ill with a severe pain in his head, to which he had been subject for several years, and which this time refused to yield to the simple remedy he was in the habit of employing. He was forced, therefore, to send for Doctor Grattan, in the hope that medical science might suggest something that would relieve him of the agony that had become unendurable. The doctor was a bold practitioner. He found his patient walking the floor, his hands pressed to his head, and uttering disjointed exclamations that the pain forced from him. He saw at once that there was danger of serious complications unless relief was instantly afforded. He, therefore, directed the sufferer to lie down, and then, pouring some chloroform on a towel, held it to the patient's mouth till he had inhaled enough of the potent agent to produce insensibility. Then he sat by the bedside with his fingers on the pulse of the now lethalized man till sensibility returned. A few minutes only were necessary, and then it was found that the pain had gone.

He stayed a half an hour talking with his patient, and was delighted to find in him a man of superior education, of vast information, and pleasing address. On being told that it was his intention to make Plato his residence, and that his visit was for the purpose of examining a tract of land that had been offered for sale, the doctor could not conceal his surprise.

"It's all very well for me to live here," he said, "for I can't help myself. If I went anywhere else, I should starve. But for you to voluntarily put yourself outside of the pale of life, as you would should you come to Plato to reside, is to me incomprehensible."

"Ah, that is because you are as yet unacquainted with my motives," said Mr. Lamar. "I have beaten around the world all my life, and have received many hard blows in

2

my career that have left their scars. I want rest. Nothing to me is so pleasant as absolute repose. I can understand the longing that the Buddhist has for that stage of entire forgetfulness into which he hopes to pass when his life on this earth is ended. And you know that Buddha taught that Nirvana might be attained even in this life. May I not hope to get something like it here in Plato, amid these mountains, far from the busy centers of commerce and excitement, and where there is almost nothing to contemplate but Nature in her grandeur and repose? There are only my daughter and myself. We are alone—absolutely alone, in the world. We want to live solely for each other, and I want forgetfulness. As for her, dear child that she is, she has nothing to forget. But she is quiet by nature, a great student, an artist, my companion. Here we expect to be happy. Is it likely, think you, we shall succeed in our desires?"

"That, of course, I can't tell you," replied the doctor; "but, so far as the opportunities for getting rest are concerned, I am disposed to think that Plato affords better facilities than the middle of the Sahara Desert or the top of the Rocky Mountains. During the winter no one comes here, and through the summer the few people that visit the place stay no longer than they can help, but hurry off to their destinations in some part of the Wilderness."

"Then it will suit us admirably; and one reason additional is given in the assurance that we shall have an excellent physician to care for us when we are ill. My daughter, thank God! enjoys excellent health; but I not only suffer with my head, but with a complication of other disorders for which I am constantly requiring medical assistance. If I had found no good physician here, I should have been obliged to renounce all idea of making it our residence. I have never been relieved so promptly and thoroughly as by you."

The doctor was delighted. Here was a man that could talk to him of Buddhism, to which form of religion he had great predilections—and doubtless of all the other theological systems of the world. Ellis did very well within a certain range of subjects, but that range was limited ; whereas there were indications that Mr. Lamar's was one of those omnivorous minds that imbibe nourishment of all kinds and from all sources. He had ample room in his house. There were only himself and daughter. "Why not," he asked himself, "invite the stranger to take up his residence with us till his house is finished?" An idea once conceived by the doctor did not remain long unacted upon.

"I have a larger house," he said, "than I can fill, and should be happy to have you occupy a part of it, as my guests, till your own is finished. I have a daughter who will unite with me in trying to make your stay with us pleasant. I mean, of course, you and your daughter."

"You are very kind. You overwhelm me, in fact, with your goodness, but I could never consent to burden you and your daughter with such an unmitigated nuisance as I am, especially when I am seized with some one or more of my numerous ailments."

"But this hotel, as they call it, is a wretched place. You could never be comfortable here, especially if you have to stay any length of time and are ill. Come to us, I beg of you. We—that is, Cynthia and I—want company, especially that of sensible people ; but you shall be as free as the air while you are with us, and shall go and come when you please, and see as much or as little of us as you may think desirable."

"No, my friend," said Mr. Lamar, "if you will permit me to call you such, I can not consent for myself, but I shall be glad to compromise the matter with you, and send my daughter to you if you will kindly receive her. She is a good girl ; you will like her, and I trust Miss Grattan will like her also. As for me, I shall take one of these rooms, and, with a little work on it and some additional furniture, I shall be very comfortable. I shall be here off and on during the ensuing year, and then I shall bring my daughter to you, if you will kindly look after her for the month or two during which our house is being finished and furnished."

So it was agreed that Miss Lamar should stay with the Grattans till her own house was ready for her. Mr. Lamar bought the land he had come to examine, and in due time began the construction of a large house. For more than a year he was in Plato at intervals of every two or three weeks, remaining for several days at a time, and giving his personal supervision to the building operations that were going on. Then, when the house was nearly completed, requiring only something in the way of decoration to fit it for immediate use, Miss Lamar arrived and was duly installed at Doctor Grattan's, her father continuing to occupy the room at the hotel that he had had fitted up for his use. On the very day that the doctor had delivered his sentiments so emphatically to the assembled wisdom around the stove in Mr. Hicks's store, the Lamars had taken possession of their new home.

The doctor was a widower. He had come to Plato a married man, but his wife had died soon after giving birth to a first child, a daughter, and the husband had never again entered into the marriage state, though he had not arrived at the determination to remain single with that mature consideration of the subject which he gave to every matter of any importance. Had he consulted his own inclinations only, he would probably have married again. He was, by nature, sociable in his habits, but his taste in the matter of companions was exacting, and there were very few that he admitted to his friendship. There was no woman in Plato, or its vicinity, that he would have mar-

ried, and he did not know where to go to find one. Had
he been very anxious on the subject, doubtless he would
have gotten over the difficulty ; but then the relation which
a new wife would bear to his daughter, that was not hers,
caused him to think with greater hesitation, in regard to
the course to be pursued, than would otherwise have been
the case ; and so the matter was allowed to rest, every year
seeing him less disposed to change the situation, for Cynthia was growing up into womanhood and daily becoming
more and more of a companion to him. Her education
had been the chief delight of his life, and though, when
this story begins, she had attained the age of eighteen, he
still continued instructions that it was as much a pleasure for her to receive as it was for him to give. But here
he was in a little country village, at the age of forty-five,
a widower still, with a lovely daughter, and fit in every respect to fill a much higher *rôle* among earth's actors than
that which he was called upon to perform in Plato. But
he was happy. He was not rich, but he had enough, independent of his practice, to give him and his daughter most
of the comforts of life that they required, and in her society, and that of the couple of friends he had made, he found
all the companionship he desired.

Still, there was a degree of isolation, and the other people were so measurably below those to whom he was attached that he had acquired a habit of, treating them
with a kind of imperiousness and dogmatism sometimes out
of place, though often warranted by their narrow-minded-
ness, their ignorance, and their many acts of petty malice.
It had often been a puzzle to him to account for the fact
that the inhabitants of Plato were of a meaner type than
those of many other small places. It could not be due to
the geographical features of the situation, for they were of
a character to develop the nobler impulses of human nature ; nor to the belittling influences of trade, for there was

no trade worth mentioning, and those that indulged in it
were no worse than their neighbors ; nor even to the comparative sequestration of the village, for, although isolation
contracts the mentality in some respects, it enlarges it in
others, and the effect upon the whole is not bad.  So he
could not account for the circumstance that, of all the people he had ever known, those of Plato were the most insignificant and unpleasant, till one day his daughter Cynthia,
who stood in no more awe of him than if he had been only
a friend of mature age, and not her father—a frame of
mind into which he had constantly endeavored to bring
her—asked him if it was not just possible that the disagreeableness of the Platonians was due, not so much to any peculiarity inherent in them, as to a certain form of mental
organization belonging to him, and which caused him to
view, with disgust, traits that others differently formed in
this respect would have admired.  He knew the Platonians better than he knew the inhabitants of any other town,
and hence he disliked them more.  This set him to thinking, and the end of his cogitations was that mankind as a
whole were exceedingly unpleasant features of a world which,
but for the majority of them, would be a tolerably good
sort of an abiding-place for a few years, and that the people
of Plato were neither better nor worse than their fellows of
like position in life, in other parts of the earth.

Thus matters stood at Plato when Doctor Grattan
pounced in on the malcontents in Mr. Hicks's store, and
delivered his invective with such effect as to silence the two
principals, and to make the listeners feel a portion of the
mortification that he had endeavored to cause them to experience.

# CHAPTER III.

THE doctor left Mr. Hicks's store, feeling that he had gained a victory over the calumniators of his friend, and that in all probability they would cease to form surmises and invent tales to his disadvantage. It was not that what they said amounted to anything in itself, but the summer was approaching, visitors from New York and other parts of the country would soon be making their appearance, and the doctor knew enough of human nature to be aware of the fact that men's reputations are often seriously damaged by just such stories as those told by Hicks and Spill being allowed to remain uncontradicted, and kept going from one to another till the very fact of their repetition gives them some standing even among respectable people.

He went on down the long, straggling street with its little white wooden houses on each side of it, some of them with neat flower-gardens in front of and around them, and looking as though their owners had some idea of neatness and beauty, but the most of them presenting an unkempt and dilapidated appearance that from its obtrusiveness gave a predominance of slovenliness to the whole, that was far from being attractive either to the eye or the nostrils. He had about a half a mile to go to reach his house, and about a quarter of an hour in which to walk that distance and get ready for a two-o'clock dinner. He and Cynthia were alone again, for that very morning Miss Lamar had departed for her own home at the other end of the village, after remaining nearly two months under his roof.

The visit had, he thought, been pleasant to all concerned. Certainly he had enjoyed it very much, and he was quite sure, from many indubitable signs, that the young lady that had recently come among them had taken pleasure in the society of himself and his daughter. It would have been strange, indeed, had such not been the case, for he was conscious that he and Cynthia had done all in their power to make their visitor feel at home, which, after all, is the best way to entertain a guest. Now that she had gone, he was quite sure that he should miss her, for he had got to the point of regarding her as one of the family—almost, in fact, as a second daughter, and that was a great deal for him to do—an event that could not possibly have been brought about if there had been a single disagreeable feature of disposition, or of mental development, or of physical conformation in his visitor.

It was not, however, as though she had gone away from them altogether. The distance between his house and hers was not much over a mile, and doubtless there would be many occasions for their meeting and for continuing the agreeable relations that had been established between him and his daughter on the one hand, and Louise Lamar and her father on the other. Yes, he could surely include Mr. Lamar in his agreeable cogitations, relative to the past and future, for the more thoroughly he had become acquainted with that gentleman the more he had found for admiration and astonishment. For here was a man that had evidently been engaged in extensive business operations of such a character as one would think must necessarily have taken his thoughts out of the line of science, literature, and art into that lower one, to follow which with success, requires all the energy of an active brain, and yet who appeared to be entirely at home with any subject brought to his notice.

He had himself often wondered who Mr. Lamar was, but he had done so with a far different spirit from that which actuated the envious and unappreciative villagers. That the stranger was a gentleman was undoubted. In all the time that he had been acquainted with him he had never heard him say an ungentlemanly word, or known him to commit an ungentlemanly act. But, notwithstanding the explanation that his new friend had given relative to his selection of Plato as a residence for himself and daughter, there was much in the affair that the explanation did not cover, or at least did not explain. He was very far from suspecting the existence of any unworthy motive for the desire to bury himself from the world that Mr. Lamar exhibited, but he could not avoid entertaining the idea that, in some way or other, his friend had passed through a stormy life, or had endured an amount of suffering far greater than that which ordinarily falls to the lot of mortals. There was a seriousness in his demeanor upon all occasions that was, under the circumstances, apparently unnatural. He did not appear to be unhappy, but he did seem to be restrained by some solemn and ever-present thought from departing, even for a moment, from the habitual gravity that characterized every word and action. Occasionally, at some quaint remark of the doctor's, or some witty speech of Louise's or Cynthia's, his face would light up for a moment, but it never relaxed into a smile ; and as to a laugh, it only required a short acquaintance with him for the doctor to perceive that nothing could be more improbable than that such a manifestation of emotion should be exhibited by a person whose facial expression showed him to be a man to whom merriment had long been an unfamiliar demonstration.

The doctor thought over these and many other correlative matters, till he arrived at his own premises. He crossed the little bridge over the Canemanga and ascended the

winding road that led to the summit of the hill on which
his house was built. Then he stood for a moment on the
front porch where he was wont to sit on summer evenings
and meditate, while looking at his friends the mountains,
which reared their dark summits before him. He turned
now and surveyed them all in turn; but the disquietude that
had taken hold of him was altogether different from any
that had hitherto affected him, and it was not to be ban-
ished by a glance at a mountain, no matter how stern might
be his determination to get rid of it. "It requires a special mountain of its own," he said ; "I'll try the Hurricane
to-night." Then he grasped the knob of the door, but
found that the key had been turned on the inside, and
that he was locked out. He rang the bell, and almost instantly the door was opened as far as a check-chain would
allow, and the sunny face of a young girl appeared at the
narrow opening.

"We haven't any cold victuals," she said, trying to
look severe. "You'll find some down at Mr. Craig's, the
clergyman's. They're very kind to tramps there."

"You baggage ! open the door instantly and give me
my dinner."

"Hey !" putting her hand up to her ear, as though
she were deaf.

"I say I want my dinner !"

"Oh, you say you are an old sinner ? Yes, I've known
it for some time."

"Will you open the door, you minx, or must I batter it
down ?"

"Well, really, I think you had better batter it down.
It's about the only batter you'll get. I made a pudding
for dinner, but it's quite spoiled by your being so late !"

"I'll pay you for this !"

"Will you, indeed ? Thanks ! It will be the only
thing you ever paid me for yet. I've been your housekeep-

er for ten years, beginning at the tender age of eight. I'll
take my wages, please." She put her hand through the
opening, when instantly the doctor seized it.

"Now !" he exclaimed, "will you open the door ? I'll
hold you fast till you do."

Instantly the chain was disengaged, and in a moment
the doctor stood within his own walls.

"How dare you treat your old father in that way ?" he
exclaimed, speaking with assumed sternness, but, with characteristic inconsistency, putting his arm around her as they
walked together through the wide hall. "Here am I dying
with hunger, and you doing your utmost to hasten the
starvation process !"

"Oh, yes, your sufferings must be very awful ! I've
been watching you for the last half-hour, while you've been
loitering—yes, sir, loitering—along the street like a school-
boy on his way to say a lesson that he had not half learned.
I saw you stop several times and hang your head as though
you were ashamed of yourself. No wonder your dinner's
cold !"

"Oh, you contradictory and perverse-minded young
woman ! Didn't you just now tell me that there were no
cold victuals ? And now you have the brazen effrontery
to say that they're all cold ! No wonder I can't place any
confidence in a woman that blows hot and cold with the
same breath."

"Well, now, go up-stairs and take some of the dust off,
and then hurry down to eat what you can get. You're
really not so bad as you look," she continued, standing off
at a little distance and looking at him admiringly, "and
in recognition of that remarkable fact—the only instance
within my knowledge—I've made something nice for you.
But, if you go on calling me names, you sha'n't have any."

He laughed and went to his room, while she waited for
him in the hall.

Cynthia Grattan, whom I now formally introduce to the reader, is destined to play an important part in this history, and hence her personality should be brought out as distinctly as may be before those who may deign to take an interest in the circumstances about to be related, and the characters with whom she will be associated.

She was a little over eighteen years old, and had, as the reader already knows, been deprived at an early age of her mother's care. During her infancy and childhood she had been looked after by a maiden sister of her father's ; but, when Cynthia was only about twelve years of age, this lady, though advanced in life, was married to a gentleman to whom she had been betrothed while she was a young girl, but who, being poor, had gone to Australia to make his fortune. It was many years before he succeeded in accordance with his desires, and then, true to his promise, he had returned to claim his bride, when she was nearly forty years of age and he not far from fifty. The doctor, her brother, was of the opinion that they had wasted the best years of their lives in order to be able to enjoy those that remained, and when the keen relish of youth had disappeared from them forever.

From that time on Cynthia had had no other guide or instructor than her father, and he gave himself up to the duties that thus fell upon him with a zest and a degree of interest such as he had never before experienced for any work, although into everything he did he threw more energy and constancy than are generally exhibited by laborers of any kind.

She had always shown an aptitude for learning, so that the father's tasks were not irksome. Indeed, he was often surprised at the assiduity with which she imbibed knowledge, even when the subject was one that he had not thought would interest her. He took her through English literature, taught her Latin and German and French, the only languages, besides his own, that he knew, and would have had her taught Spanish and Italian, for he believed greatly in the modern languages, not only for their uses as aids in acquiring other knowledge, but as exercises in the way of mental development ; but there were no teachers of these languages in Plato, and he could not make up his mind to send her away to where competent instructors were to be found—which was not nearer than Albany.

She had made with her father two or three visits to New York, and, while in that city, had seen all that was to be seen in the way of theatres, museums, libraries, and shops, and had spent with him part of a summer at Long Branch—and this was all. The rest of her life had been passed quietly at Plato, though it was a frequent event for her and her father to make little excursions to the mountains for a day at a time, during which they beat the streams for trout, with which all the waters at a little distance from the village were well stocked ; or made collections in natural history, a pastime of which the doctor was especially fond, and with a love for which he had succeeded in imbuing his daughter. Then they would return—sometimes not till after nightfall—with their baskets well filled with a goodly supply of speckled beauties, fresh from their mountain-brooks, and with other receptacles stocked with plants, insects, reptiles, and other specimens of the flora and fauna of that region, then almost as unexplored by the naturalist as any part of the Rocky Mountains.

As a consequence of the intimate friendship that existed between Cynthia and her father, more probably than from the influences of the mere relationship, the two were devotedly attached to each other. They were more like companions standing upon the same social plane, between whom there is a perfect reciprocity of sentiment, than like father and daughter as ordinarily seen in every-day life. There was no restraint on her part in her conduct toward him, for she felt no fear of him. She knew he was the best friend she had in the world, and she did her duty by him faithfully, yielding obedience to every wish, and seeking by every means in her power to secure his happiness. But she had two apparently very different ways of conducting herself toward him; and he, quick to perceive the vein that prevailed with her, met her in like mood. One of these was serious, the other jocular or bantering. She seemed to know intuitively just which one to use with him. She never once made a mistake on this point, and she never misplaced them with reference to her own feelings. In her serious humor she was all sedateness and demonstrative tenderness. Then she was the loving daughter, whose whole object in life appeared to be to render respect and devotion to the father whom she adored. But in her merry mood she was changed. She was still tender, as one might easily perceive by the loving glances of her eyes, her joyous laugh, and her quaint, incongruous terms of endearment; but her words were as free and as outspoken as though she were addressing a boy on whom she was playing her pranks or teasing, in the way that bright and light-hearted girls sometimes employ with callow members of the opposite sex.

And thus they had gone on together, these two, with nothing to disturb the joy of their lives; the one reaching to the verge of early old age, the other budding into womanhood. The doctor had his two friends, the clergyman and the lawyer, whom occasionally he invited to dinner, and who often sat with him on his front porch, while he smoked and talked of his beloved mountains and his theological notions. Cynthia had a few more acquaintances, but none that could be called very intimate, unless it was Mrs. Hadden, a widow who had made enough money to live on in a quiet way, and who was still busily engaged writing children's story-books and contributions to a couple of children's magazines. She was very fond of Cynthia, as was also Will Hadden, her son—the same who, as we have seen, gave Mr. Hicks a piece of his mind when the latter was telling scandalous tales about Mr. Lamar. Cynthia liked Mrs. Hadden, and she liked Will also, or rather she would have liked him had he been content with her friendship. But he was very far from being satisfied with a relation so mild as that. He was very much in love, and he made the state of his feelings so evident whenever he was thrown into her company that she avoided him as much as she could without slighting his mother. He did not make himself oppressively obtrusive. He had told her once that he loved her, and she had answered him by saying that she could never be his wife, or indeed any man's wife, as she preferred to stay with her father. Then he had begged her to wait before giving him his final answer—to wait till she had known him better, and till she had discovered for herself how earnest he was. But she had very gently but yet firmly told him that it was impossible she could ever love him, that she was ready to be his friend, as she had always been, but that loving him and being his wife were altogether out of the question. Sadly, but yet not reconciled to giving her up, he had desisted from further importunity, and he had never subsequently alluded to the matter in words; but she saw from his manner whenever they met that the passion was still there, and the fact acted as a deterrent, by causing her to make her visits to Mrs. Hadden less frequent, and to select times for them when she was tolerably sure Will would not be at home.

Then there was Lucy Craig, the clergyman's daughter, a girl whom she also liked, for she was gentle and refined, and very loving in her disposition. As to the rest of the people of the village, all of whom she knew more or less, though she did not actually dislike them, as did her father, they were objects of indifference to her. Some were, of course, a little more agreeable than others, but not one of

them interested her. There was nothing between them
and herself calculated to arouse any feeling, unless occasionally that of mirth over some of their absurd sayings or
doings, or a transient emotion of anger when she heard of
some particularly spiteful or mean act on the part of some
one of them.

Finally, the Lamars had come. Then, as she was, by
the force of circumstances, thrown into close relations with
Louise, it was not to have been expected that a girl as quick
and accurate in her perceptions as was Cynthia Grattan
could have failed to appreciate her visitor at her true value.
There was scarcely a day that some new point of excellence
or some charming trait of character was not discovered.
Cynthia was not effusive, there was nothing like "gush"
about her, she was not even demonstrative in the ordinary
sense in which the word is used, though she was not lacking in emotional manifestations toward those she really
loved. She kept her feelings, therefore, so far as Louise
Lamar was concerned, well in hand, till she knew her so
well that there could be but little, if any, risk of her being
deceived, and then she yielded her heart freely and fully
without reserve, and with the consciousness that she had
found a life-long friend.

Cynthia would have passed for a beautiful woman in
any part of the civilized globe. She was above the medium
height of women, and as graceful in her movements as—
well, as the most graceful woman—nothing is more graceful.
Her long walks over hill and dale had made her strong of
limb, and had given her muscles that power of co-ordinate
action and strength without which muscular movement is
a clumsy exhibition. As she waited in the hall for her
father, she felt that exuberance of spirits that comes from
sound physical and mental health. She walked up and
down the floor for a moment or two, but the exercise did
not appear to be sufficiently active to enable her to get rid

of her superabundance of vital force ; for with a smile on
her face she began to dance after the manner of the peasant
maidens of Brittany, moving her arms in unison with her
feet and humming a lively air, to which she kept time.
She was so deeply interested in this amusement that she
did not see her father standing on the steps half-way down
the staircase, and regarding her with an expression of the
greatest admiration depicted on his countenance. For several minutes he stood watching her, while she, unconscious
of his presence, continued her graceful movements with an
*abandon* that would have astonished some of the prudish
women of Plato had they been there to see. Then suddenly
seeing him, she stopped, and a warm blush suffused her
face.

"I couldn't help it, dear," she said ; "I felt so happy
that if I hadn't danced I should have run away, and then
what would you have done ?"

"The Lord only knows ! But I think I should have
run away too. Where did you learn that beautiful step ?
I have never quite understood the 'poetry of motion'
before."

"Was it so very graceful ?" she replied, putting her
arm within his and going with him toward the dining-
room at the end of the hall. "I was reading about the
*trioris*, the national dance of Brittany, and I thought I
would try and do it. The next time I attempt it you shall
assist. Etienne Tabourot says it is 'an ancient, honorable,
and profitable amusement,' and that in his day the 'old
men'—such as you—'and the young ladies'—such as I—
'liked to display their agility and to find therein a temper-
ate exercise calculated to contribute to their health as well
as to their diversion.' "

"What is the girl talking about ?" exclaimed the doctor. "Where did you ever hear of Etienne Tabourot ?"

"Oh, I can tell you all about him if you want to know,

but at present I'll merely inform you that I've been reading
his book of 'Bigarrures,' which, as he says, he wrote for
the purpose of making first himself and then everybody else
laugh."

"You're a very wise young woman, in your own estimation. But you dance like Terpsichore, 'the sprightly,'
and you only require the cithara in your hand to complete
the illusion. May I ask how you got hold of Tabourot's
'Bigarrures'?"

"I found it."

"In the street, I suppose! It's quite a common thing
to pick up rare French books, three hundred years old, in
the streets of Plato!"

"No, it isn't, and I didn't find it in the street," seating herself at one end of the table, while the doctor took
the chair opposite. "It was among a lot of Dr. Robinson's
books that you seem to have overlooked."

"Ah! he had a rare collection, and I lost some of
the best of them by being called out of the auction-room
while the sale was going on. That wretch Bishop got
them."

"Yes, and Will Hadden's been reading them all, and
he loaned me Tabourot."

"Will's a good fellow, and he comes of good stock. I
suppose some of these days you'll be going off, and I don't
know a man I'd be willing to give you to except Will
Hadden."

"I shall never leave you, father," said Cynthia, gravely.

"So they all say till some man they love comes along,
and then the old father doesn't count for much."

"You don't think that of me, father; you know there
isn't the man in all the world I'd leave you for."

"Yes, you're a good girl, the very joy of my life; but
I think every woman ought to be married, and I've long
looked forward to the time when you will fulfill your des-

tiny. And I am reconciled, for I know that a good husband is the best thing a woman can have."

"I shall never leave you, unless you drive me out of the house. But what put Will Hadden into your head?"

"What put Will Hadden into my head? Well, of all the shameless impertinence I have known of in all my life, that excels! Didn't you tell me you had borrowed a book from him?"

"Oh, yes, I had forgotten! I believe I did," said Cynthia, in some confusion.

"You believe you did!" rejoined her father, laughing. "Your memory is short to-day, my dear."

"I think so rarely of Will Hadden that it's quite a surprise to me when his name is mentioned."

"Or when you mention it yourself?" interrupted her father, laughing again. "Come now, Cynthia, admit that the introduction of Will Hadden's name has disturbed you."

"Yes, it has," she said, dropping her eyes on the table, while a faint blush suffused her cheeks. "I like Will Hadden as a friend, but I can never, under any circumstances, be his wife."

"I think I understand," said the doctor; "of course, my dear, you will do as you please about the matter, but if you don't take Will, I'm afraid you will remain in single blessedness all your life, unless I take you away from Plato. There's no one else here that I would be willing to accept as a son-in-law, or you to choose as a husband."

"No," she answered, still with downcast eyes, "there is no one—and that's why I said I shall always remain with you."

"Hadden did a good thing to-day," said the doctor, changing the subject. "He gave Hicks and Spill a piece of his mind in regard to their suspicions against Mr. Lamar, in which they were freely indulging. And I arrived at

Hicks's store in time to finish the good work. I think they'll be silent after this."

"It is strange that everybody in Plato should be wondering who Mr. Lamar is," said Cynthia, reflectively. "I've even wondered myself."

"Then, my dear, you do not possess the discriminating power that I have hitherto awarded you. To have known a gentleman as intimately for a year as you have known Mr. Lamar, and then to wonder who he is, strikes me as being a little remarkable. I know who and what he is. He is a gentleman—educated, refined, intelligent, honorable. That is what he *is*. As to what he *was*, which I suppose is what you meant, it's none of our business; and, besides, it's a matter of no consequence."

"Spill was here just before you came in; he couldn't keep his tongue quiet, and he told me that you and Mr. Lamar had the same sign on your arms, and that either Mr. Lamar was a disguised doctor, or you were a disguised pirate. He seemed to be in great glee over the matter."

"Yes, we both have a skull and cross-bones tattooed on our arms. Mine was done when I was a medical student, and I suppose Mr. Lamar's was also the result of boyish bravado. When I showed my arm to Spill, he said the sign is as good for a doctor as it is for a pirate, which, considering what an ass Spill generally is, was not bad."

"It was a piece of impertinence for Spill to speak in that manner to you—a great liberty!"

"Oh, my dear, there's no such thing as impertinence in Plato. One man's as good as another here. Besides, I spoke my mind to him with sufficient freedom."

"I wonder why they dislike Mr. Lamar so much? I never heard him say an unkind word of anybody."

"Nor I; but he is reserved, he does not go to Hicks's store and whittle sticks, and spit tobacco-juice on the stove, and abuse his neighbors. Then, besides, he has committed the great fault of getting rich, and the still greater one of not telling the gossips how he made his money."

" But you don't go to Hicks's, or spit tobacco-juice on the stove, or abuse your neighbors."

" No," laughed the doctor, " I don't go to Hicks's very often, and I don't spit tobacco-juice either ; but, as to abusing my neighbors—well, if the meek Moses lived among such a lot of asses and malignants as I do, he'd abuse them too ! But they know better than to slander me. I'm the only physician within ten miles of them, and they can't get along without me. If they could, they'd lie about me just as they do about Lamar."

" It's all very shocking," exclaimed Cynthia. Then, after a little pause : " Next to you, I think he knows more than any person I ever met. He appears to be ignorant of nothing."

" He has accumulated a vast amount of knowledge, and how he ever managed to do it I can't imagine. He couldn't have done it, and at the same time have followed any money-making business."

" He may have inherited his fortune."

" Yes, but he has often spoken to me of his travels and his troubles, and somehow or other I got the idea that the two were connected, and that they were both of a business nature."

" I miss Louise very much. She is like her father in many things, but I think she has even a higher nature than his."

" Perhaps so, and then she is much better-tempered."

" Ah ! but she does not suffer from disease as he does, and then she has evidently never had much to grieve her."

" You would not know it if she had. She has a wonderful degree of command over herself. I saw her one day receive a letter which she read without the change of a muscle, and which she then handed to her father with a smile, as though it contained the most pleasing intelligence. He read it, and was instantly seized with one of his agonizing headaches."

"They want us to come over there this evening. Shall we go after tea?"

"Yes, of course."

"Now see what an unappreciative man you are! You've eaten my new dish, and you've never given me a word of praise for it. Much encouragement there is for me to addle my brains over the kitchen-fire concocting delicacies for you! Hereafter I'll let Martha cook your dinners for you."

"I thought that *pâté* was wonderfully good; but, to tell the truth, I was afraid to ask what it was made of. It tasted like calves' brains, and somehow I have a prejudice against eating the brains of an animal, although I like them. I preferred, therefore, remaining in ignorance of its composition."

"It *was* the *pâté*, but it was not made of brains, but of something Mr. Lamar gave me this morning."

"Something Mr. Lamar gave you? What?"

"Yes, and he gave me the recipe for cooking them, for there were a dozen."

"Well, don't keep me in ignorance any longer, or I shall begin to think I have eaten something horrible."

"Sir! you have eaten *escargots à la Toulouse*, prepared by the fair hands—somewhat sunburnt—of your only daughter."

"Snails!"

"Even so, most dread—or rather dreadful—sovereign. Mr. Lamar is very fond of them, and imports them from France."

"Well, I'm glad I didn't know what the thing was till I had finished my dinner. It was good, that I'll say without reservation; and I think, after a while, I might be tempted to try another *pâté d'escargots à la Toulouse*, if you'll make it. As it is, I'm much obliged. Come, kiss me before I go to see old Mrs. Withers. Let me have something pleasant to think of while I am listening to that aggravating old woman. Good-by, dear, and to-night we'll walk over to see the Lamars in their new house."

# CHAPTER IV.

MR. LAMAR had been very wise in the selection he had made of land on which to build his house. The tract he had purchased comprised about two thousand acres, and extended from the north boundary of the village to the foot of Hurricane Mountain. There were hill and dale, meadow and upland, two beautiful lakes, not very large of course, but with steep, craggy sides and rocky islets, besides the Canemanga, which, in its devious turnings and meanderings, appeared and reappeared several times on Mr. Lamar's estate, as it babbled on to its junction with Cold River.

The house, like that of Doctor Grattan at the other end of the village, stood on a hill, and, like it, was approached by means of a bridge across the river. But here all resemblance ceased, for Mr. Lamar had built what in Europe would have been called a "château" or a "Schloss," and which, with its battlements and towers, reminded the observer of a feudal castle; while the doctor's house was a plain square stone structure, in which there was an absence of all style, most painful to one with any taste for the beautiful in architecture.

Like the builder of "Mountain View," as the doctor's residence was called, Mr. Lamar had used the stone of the country as the material for the walls of his castle, laid in what is called "rubble-work," and had thus succeeded in greatly enhancing the beauty of the structure. For some time he had hesitated whether or not to accept the opinion of his architect and use red brick, which, on several accounts, would have been more appropriate ; but finally his æsthetic ideas prevailed over those based on mere expediency, and stone was chosen.

It was a very imposing edifice, but it certainly would have been more comfortable had a different style of architecture been adopted, and had the wishes of the architect relative to brick been acceded to. It was grand inside and out, but it was damp and dark, for the walls were thick, and the rooms, to allow for the turrets, the towers, and the barbacans, were necessarily arranged without a compliance with those laws of health which the recent developments of sanitary science have shown are of imperative force.

After entering a tower, the lower story of which was the vestibule, the visitor passed into a large hall, at one end of which was a triple stained-glass window, and which was open to the top, a gallery giving access to the rooms on the second floor. This hall Mr. Lamar and his daughter intended to use as a sitting-room in the evenings, especially in those of the summer months ; but as it had an immense fireplace at one end, besides being heated by steam, it would, they thought, prove to be a not unagreeable place even during the long and cold winter nights that were now approaching.

It was late in October when they got into the house as permanent residents. Mr. Lamar had had a room in the second story fitted up for himself several months previously, thus enabling him to leave the wretched inn at which he stopped during his visits to Plato ; but Louise had, as the reader knows, remained with the Grattans, and had not moved over to "Hurricane Castle," the name which, in accordance with Doctor Grattan's suggestion, based on the fact that it faced the mountain so called, Mr. Lamar had

3

given his residence. "Besides," he added, after agreeing to the doctor's proposition, "it may be even a more suitable designation than we now think. It may be a stormy enough place before we are done with it."

Everything that good taste and apparently boundless wealth could do to make Hurricane Castle beautiful had been done, and it had been. stocked with works of art and books to an extent not then exhibited in the State of New York outside of its chief city. In the arrangement of these, both Mr. Lamar and his daughter had taken the greatest interest; and, ever since Louise's arrival at Plato, the two had spent a great part of each day in classifying the books and articles of *vertu*, and in assigning them to their proper places on the shelves, the walls, and the cabinets. In this work they appeared to be perfectly at home, though they frequently appealed to the doctor or to Cynthia, when some question of taste was involved. Louise had got the idea that, upon questions of the harmony or contrast of colors, Cynthia's opinion was infallible.

"You are a natural-born judge of colors," she had said upon one occasion, when a point relative to the hanging of a piece of tapestry in one place or another of differently tinted backgrounds was being discussed. "Your eye is as true in such matters as that of a Persian or an East Indian. I watched you the other day when you were sorting a basket of worsteds, and you were simply wonderful."

"The best combiners of colors I have ever seen," said Mr. Lamar, "are the Japanese, and the people that have the most exact perception of tints are the rug-makers in a little town on the Persian shore of the Amoo, called Hazaat. I have seen a woman there arrange in perfect sequence sixty-nine shades of blue and eighty of red. After they were in order everybody could see the regular gradation; but as the different colored wools lay in a pile together, they looked as though they were nearly all of one tint."

"Where is it you have not been?" laughed the doctor. "I shall expect next to have you tell us that the people of Timbuctoo do not eat their peas with a fork, or that King Bugaboo, of Ashantee, prefers to pound his prisoners of war in a mortar to selling them into slavery, as did his predecessors."

Mr. Lamar was at this instant engaged in hanging a rare Kaga plaque on the wall, but, as the doctor finished his observation, it fell from his hand and was broken into a dozen pieces.

"I am afraid I shall want your services very soon, Grattan," he said, in a tremulous voice; "I feel my headache coming on, and one of the first evidences of the approaching storm—nerve-storms I believe you call them—is weakness of the muscles of my arms. I can't hold anything in my hands. That plaque I can not replace. It was given to me by Prince Samobata, in reward for allowing him to save my life. Some of these days I will tell you the story."

Strange to say, however, the headache did not come this time, in spite of the positive signs of its approach, so confidently relied upon by Mr. Lamar.

After making his visit to old Mrs. Withers, and listening with as much patience as he could command to her complaints, mingled as they were with gossip about the neighbors and sundry reflections on the fact that, as yet, neither Mr. Lamar nor his daughter had set foot inside of the village church, Doctor Grattan returned home, and after tea lighted his pipe, and, with Cynthia by his side, strolled along the street toward Hurricane Castle. The western heavens were still aglow with light, though the sun was below the mountain-range that frowned up black and gloomy on their left. Neither the doctor nor Cynthia appeared to be much inclined at the moment to talk. He was puffing away slowly at his pipe, and she was looking

intently at the sharply defined outline of Mount Mary as
it stood out against the bright background of yellow and
red that tinted the autumn sky.

"Why don't you say something?" at last demanded
the doctor, stopping for the moment to turn round and
look at Pitchoff, the top of which was bathed in light,
while all the rest of the huge mass of rock and earth and
trees was in deep shadow.  "I've been waiting to see, as a
mere matter of curiosity, how long you could keep your
tongue from wagging; but I can't stand it any longer. It's
been just six minutes and twenty-two seconds since you
spoke a word."

Cynthia laughed.  "I was thinking," she said, "whether
or not it is quite certain that the sun will ever rise again."

"And may I ask, great inquisitor, at what conclusion
you arrived?"

"I was thinking that I did not know."

"A most wise conclusion, but a most unprofitable one.
Now, if you had determined in your own mind that it
would not, you would probably by to-morrow morning
have learned something."

"Yes, but you can not tell me what I should have
learned—I have often heard you say that certain knowledge is not attainable in this world, and that the only thing
you know is that you know nothing."

"True, but this, allow me to suggest, is not the time
for metaphysical disquisitions about things of which you
confess yourself to be profoundly ignorant. Here we are,
blocking up the path. If anybody came along, we should
have to get out of the way, and it irritates me to have to get
out of any one's way."

"Then, perhaps, we had better move on. Fortunately
for us, there is no policeman here to compel us to go forward."

"But where shall we go?"

" Are you losing your senses ? Didn't we propose to go to Hurricane Castle to see the Lamars ? "

" Oh, yes, so we did ! "

" You old humbug ! " exclaimed Cynthia, laughing, while she laid her hand on his arm. " You know perfectly well that you have thought of nothing else all day but of this visit to Hurricane Castle."

" And now I think I'll turn round and go home, ere it is too late."

" Too late ! Why, what has got into the man ? One would think you were on the way to commit a burglary ! "

" It's a good deal worse than that, I'm afraid. However," he continued, taking hold of Cynthia's hand, which still lay within his arm, " come along—never mind me. I'm only an old *heautontimorumenos*."

" Good gracious ! " exclaimed Cynthia, in affected astonishment. " Is that worse than a burglar ? "

" Infinitely. In fact, there's no comparison. I should say that a burglar, although he usually likes night better than day for his work, is a child of light in comparison with a *heautontimorumenos* ; for he is only a nuisance to other people, but the *heautontimorumenos* torments himself. Read Menander's play."

" Never ! I prefer more cheerful literature. But tell me," she continued, very gravely, " why do you torment yourself ? I thought you were always happy. You have always been so until now."

" Yes, through you. But for you, I should have been miserable enough. My temperament is melancholic, and I am therefore naturally morbid ; but your cheerfulness and sunny disposition, under all circumstances, have probably been the means of saving me from suicide. I have not felt so happy in years as when I watched you dancing in the hall this afternoon."

" Was my mother cheerful ? "

" As a bird," answered the doctor. " She was too good for me. We were most unequally matched, but I tried to make her happy."

" And you did, for I came across a letter she wrote you during a short absence and just before she died ; she loved you dearly."

" Yes, and you are like her."

By this time they had reached the bridge that Mr. Lamar had built over the Canemanga, and that it was necessary to cross in order to reach Hurricane Castle. In front of them stood the imposing building that he had erected, and to which a broad, well-rolled gravel road led. Again the doctor paused. The little stream was wider than the Rubicon, on the bank of which, more than eighteen hundred years ago, Cæsar had stood and reflected. He felt that this was the critical moment of his life. He looked down at the fair young girl so dear to him, who stood by his side, her little hand resting on his arm, all unconscious that her fate also probably depended upon the determination at which he should arrive. Evidently she did not comprehend the reasons for his hesitation. If she had, he thought, would she not also waver, or, rather, would she not try to draw him away from a spot that she would know was fraught with danger to the permanency of her happiness ? Evidently she was ignorant and unsuspicious.

" Come," she said ; " now that you have studied the general effect of the exterior of the building, you must be anxious to see something of the inside. I see Mr. Lamar and Louise on the steps, and they have observed us. They are coming toward us. Come ! "

Mechanically he allowed her to lead him, and in a few moments they were face to face with the owner of Hurricane Castle and his daughter.

"It is kind of you to keep your promise," said Louise,
holding out a hand to each, while her father, after her
greetings, followed her example. "Papa was not feeling
well this evening. He has been expecting you, and so have
I, for the last half-hour; and then he got fidgety, and
nothing would do but that he must come out here in the
cold night air and look for you. I believe, if we had not
seen you, he would have insisted on going over to Mountain
View. It was clearly another exemplification of the prov-
erb that, as the mountain would not come to Mohammed,
Mohammed must go to the mountain. But for once the
mountain has come to Mohammed."

Doctor Grattan answered with what he intended for a
polite speech, but exactly what he was saying he scarcely
knew. Then Mr. Lamar drew Cynthia's arm within his,
the doctor gave his to Louise, and they walked slowly
toward the house.

Louise Lamar was what Balzac would have called *une
femme glorieuse*. She could have worn the robes of an em-
press and have done honor to them in the eyes of all be-
holders. She was grand in figure, grand in mind, and yet
a very woman in all her thoughts, her emotions, her impulses. With all her sedateness of demeanor and intellectual strength, there was at the same time a degree of effemi-
nacy of the higher kind that charmed with irresistible
power those, especially men, who were thrown into association with her. Her face was beautiful even when in repose,
but when she was engaged in earnest conversation, or when
some passing thought interested her, then it was that the
full splendor of her Zenobia-like features was at its height.
The shape of her nose or mouth, even the color of her eyes, I
can not give. I only know that the entirety of her face was
so charmingly harmonious that I never cared to study the
individual features. Certainly, however, there was nothing
mean or insignificant or redundant in her countenance.

Her nose could not have been either too small or too large; her mouth too narrow or too wide; her teeth could not have been in the slightest degree imperfect; her eyes—well, I *do* know that they were large and very soft in their expression; her hair—yes! I also know that her hair was all her own in its luxuriance and rich umber-brown color. As to the faults I have specified, they did not exist. If they had, I should have seen them. But describing her *physique* in detail, as one would specify the points in a blooded mare, is simply impossible. Something must be left to the imagination of the reader. He or she may fill the *lacunæ* as he or she pleases.

"Do you miss me at Mountain View?" she said, after they had walked a few steps in silence—"you and Cynthia, I mean. Perhaps I should inquire as to Cynthia alone, for you were always so busy with your books, your patients, and your dear mountains, that I can scarcely flatter myself that you were aware of my presence."

"One like you," he answered, "can not go out of a quiet household like ours without being missed by those that remain."

"Ah, but that is a general statement. I want to know specifically whether or not I, Louise Lamar, am missed by you, Doctor Grattan—and you, Cynthia Grattan. Do I make myself sufficiently plain," she continued, laughing low and melodiously, "or must I be still more direct?—though how to be more explicit I have not the slightest idea."

"Cynthia has several times expressed to me her regret at your departure. How could she help missing you, when you and she were so intimately associated for more than two months? Yes, I think she feels that a light has gone out of the house, and that it will take her long to get accustomed to the dimness that now exists. I am quite sure that she must be getting tired of living alone with an old

fellow like me, though she is good enough not to show her
weariness."

"She will never show it because she will never feel it.
You are almost a part of herself. She lives and moves and
has her being in you."

"Yes, I am afraid I have been very selfish. I ought to
have carried her out into the world, so that she should
have seen more of society than she does in this horrid little
village. All the young life will be killed in her before she
is half a dozen years older."

"Cynthia will never feel old if she lives to be a hundred. She is far happier here with you than she would be
away from you in any relation in which she might be
placed."

"She has a rich and fashionable aunt, living in New
York, who has several times written, to request that I
would allow her to bring Cynthia 'out,' and to establish
her in life, which I suppose means getting a husband for
her ; but I have selfishly refused to allow her to go."

"Did Cynthia wish to go ?"

"No, I am bound to say that she strenuously resisted
all the inducements held out."

"You urged her to go ?"

"Well, I pointed out to her in hypocritical accents that
there would be many advantages accruing to her from a
couple of years' residence in New York ; but of course she
saw that my words did not express my real feelings."

Louise laughed. "Are you noted for your insincerity ?"
she inquired, turning round to look into his face. "You
don't look like a double-dealing man ; and yet I begin to
have my suspicions, for you have not yet answered my
question whether or not you missed me at Mountain View.
You have very minutely explained Cynthia's feelings to my
entire satisfaction, but not a word of your own. Come,
sir, I insist on a categorical answer."

"Miss Lamar, are you superstitious?"

They entered the house at this moment, and amid the new surroundings Louise was prevented giving an immediate answer to this question. She and Mr. Lamar were indefatigable in explaining all the details of the arrangements to their inquiring guests. The large hall had been lighted up expressly on account of the visitors, and its magnificent proportions, as well as the works of art, statues, pictures, pottery, were thus seen to the fullest advantage. At one end was the large fireplace, built from an original design by a young American artist, elaborate, massive, and in perfect keeping with the other architectural features, and around this were placed all kinds of luxurious chairs, with a couple of sofas and *tête-à-têtes*, so that the convenience or the precise state of fatigue one might experience should be exactly suited.

"Shall we go into the drawing-room, or shall we stay here?" inquired Louise.

"Oh, let us stay here by all means!" exclaimed Grattan. "This is the kind of a room for which my soul has been athirst for years. I should like to sit here alone for hours, and look into that fire or at that wall opposite, with that picture of a Roman amphitheatre on it, and think."

"Did you ever hear such a rude man?" said Cynthia, laughing. "Come, Louise! come, Mr. Lamar! let us leave him to his reflections *à propos* of the fire and the Roman amphitheatre. But I must say that the man, even though he be my father, who is capable of preferring such society to that of two pretty women, who, I may say, with all humility, are not fools, is 'fit for treasons, stratagems, and spoils.'"

"I meant at some other time," rejoined Grattan. "Now I would rather listen to the prattling of the two pretty women than do anything else. I think I asked one of them a question just now that has not been answered."

" Yes," said Louise, " you did ; and if you will all sit
down in whichever chairs you like best and give me two
minutes in which to collect my thoughts, I will endeavor
to expound my views on superstition."

" Such a reasonable request should, of course, be
granted," assented Grattan, selecting a wide and deep
leather-cushioned chair, and dropping his massive form
into it. " If you would, Miss Lamar, kindly teach a young
woman who, for the present, shall be nameless, how to collect her thoughts in two minutes, she and I will be under
eternal obligations to you."

" He means me," said Cynthia, " but don't mind him,
please. He told me, as we were coming over here, that he
was a chrononhotonthologos, or something of the kind.
What can you expect from a creature like that ? But you
were about to answer a question."

" Yes, your father asks me if I am superstitious, and
I am afraid I shall require more than the two minutes I
requested, in order to give an answer. Still, I think I
may say that if, by superstition, he means a belief in omens,
supernatural signs, dreams, portents, or the direct interven-
tion of superior powers in our affairs, that there is not a
vestige of it in my organization."

" Superstition," said Mr. Lamar, who had been attentively listening to Louise's declaration of principles, " results from man's weakness. If he could always accomplish
his ends by the means at his command, he would not be
superstitious ; but, often finding that circumstances are too
strong for him, he appeals to the supernatural."

" I have often seen that fact exemplified in my practice," said the doctor. " So long as a patient has faith in
his physician, he is willing to be guided by the results of
experience ; but should he lose faith, or his doctor tell him
that there is no hope, he takes to clairvoyance, quack medicines, and all sorts of humbug."

"The world is becoming less superstitious every day," observed Mr. Lamar, "and, as the domain of science increases in extent, that of superstition becomes smaller. Many things that were once thought to be supernatural, simply because they were unexplainable, are now known to be within the operation of natural law. The savage, seeing a lucifer-match lighted for the first time, regards the act as a supernatural performance; but the civilized man, who knows its *rationale*, takes it at its true value, though perhaps something else which he does not understand he regards as miraculous."

"May I ask, Miss Lamar," inquired the doctor, "if you have no lingering idea that certain days are unlucky, or that looking at the new moon over your right shoulder is a sign of good luck, or something of that sort, hanging about you?"

"No," she answered, "I think not. I have likes and dislikes that are as it were instinctive, and for which I can not account, and which are often contrary to my reason. I try sometimes to combat them, but I have never yet succeeded in conquering one; they seem to be implanted in me as parts of my being."

While she was speaking, Mr. Lamar rose from his chair and appeared to be anxiously waiting for her to finish what she was saying. His fingers twitched nervously, and once or twice he put his hand to his head as though he were suffering pain. When she had concluded, he drew a long breath, as though he had escaped a danger he had expected. Then, before any one else could speak, he turned to Cynthia, who was sitting by his side, and said:

"The conversation is getting to be quite pathological, is it not? I want to show you a picture that I received a few days since from a dealer in St. Petersburg. He was not allowed to exhibit it there, and sold it to me in order to prevent its being destroyed by the police.—Will you join

us?" he added, addressing Grattan and Louise. "You, my
child, know all its points, and you will help to make them
evident to our friends—who, however, do not really need
any suggestions from us when it comes to matters of art or
taste."

He talked somewhat confusedly, and Grattan attributed
the circumstance to his not feeling well. He remembered
that Louise had said as much when she had joined them at
the foot of the hill, and then he too had observed the look
of pain and the hand carried to the forehead a moment before. He looked at his host closely ; but he could see no evidence of suffering on his handsome face, and he seemed to
have entirely recovered his equanimity, if indeed it had
been disturbed. "Doubtless," thought the doctor, "he
was on the verge of one of his 'nerve-storms,' which come
over him in the most unexpected manner. I shall have to
submit him some day to a very thorough examination.
Perhaps the cause can be discovered, and that is half the
cure."

The picture to which Mr. Lamar led them hung on the
wall at the other end of the hall. It represented a snowy
waste, in the midst of which stood a man, the only living
being depicted. Broken chains were hanging on his wrists
and ankles, and his garb was one of those peculiar ones that
prisoners are forced to wear. His hair was in disorder,
and his eyes were sunken deep in his head, where they
shone like two stars with an unnatural brightness. His
wan cheeks and skeleton-like hands showed that he was
suffering for want of food. Behind him was the sun, like
a red ball of fire, just above the horizon, below which it
would sink in a few minutes. The man's bony hands were
clasped together, the severed fetters dangling from his wrists.
His knees were bent, as though he were about to sink exhausted upon the snow-covered earth, never to rise again
till the trump of the archangel should call his emaciated

form to another world. But his eyes were bright, his head
was erect, and an expression of defiance of the desolation
and the dangers that surrounded him shone in his face
—the evidence that his soul was still stronger than his
body.

For several minutes they stood in silence studying the
remarkable painting, which told its own story without the
need of an interpreter.

"I should like to know," said Cynthia at last, "whether
this is altogether a conception of the artist, or if there is a
basis of fact which he has used as a starting-point for his
imagination—it seems to me so real."

"It represents a real event," said Louise—"the escape
of Vladimir Brolaski from the mines of Siberia, to which he
had been condemned for conspiring against the government
of the Czar."

"And did he really escape?"

"Yes; a wandering band of Tartars came across him
and rescued him on the fifth day after his flight. The
painting is intended to represent him when, on the fourth
day, he stopped just before nightfall to consider whether
he had not better lie down and die than to continue on, in
what appeared to him to be an almost hopeless attempt to
regain his liberty."

"How he must have suffered!" said Cynthia, gazing
intently at the picture as she spoke. "How haggard and
worn his face is, and yet what a spirit of determination it
exhibits! It almost seems as though in the far distance he
saw the Tartars that were to save him."

"You are right," observed Louise. "I see you know
how to read a picture painted by an artist who thoroughly
understands human nature and the expression of the emotions. He did see the Tartars."

"And is not quite sure that they may not be the sol-
diers in pursuit of him."

"Yes ; you are again correct.—Papa," she continued, "do you—" She stopped, for, as she turned toward the place a little behind the others where Mr. Lamar had stood, she saw that he had disappeared.

"Papa is not well to-day. In truth, he seems to me to be suffering more with his head than usual. I wish, doctor, you would take him under your special care. Last night I do not think he slept well. I heard some one walking in the upper hall very late. I got up and opened my door, and then I saw him in his dressing-gown, and with a candle in his hand, walking up and down the floor and talking to himself. I spoke to him, but he did not seem to hear me till I had called to him several times. Then he said that his room was too warm—there is no fire in it—and that he had come out into the hall to get cool. He went back to his room ; but this morning he confessed to me that he had not slept, and his looks amply confirmed his words."

"He has seemed absent-minded all the evening," said the doctor, "and yet at times it has struck me that he has been painfully vigilant, as though he expected a surprise of some kind."

"I think, if you will excuse me," interrupted Louise, "I will go and see if anything is the matter." She left the hall as she spoke.

"He is unhappy and terrified," said the doctor to Cynthia. "There is no mistaking the expression of his face. I never saw the emotions of grief and fear more distinctly exhibited, and my experience in such matters has not been small."

"What can make him sad or afraid ? He has everything to give happiness and peace."

"Ah ! my dear, who can tell ? How many men and women wear a peaceful exterior, whose hearts are torn by ravening wolves ! Our friend can not even present the externals of repose.    He shows what a storm there is raging within."

"It is as I expected," said Louise, as she rejoined them ; "papa has one of his intense headaches, and he begs, doctor, that you will kindly call to see him to-morrow."

After that the conversation languished, and in a few minutes the doctor and his daughter took their leave.

# CHAPTER V.

AFTER Doctor Grattan and Cynthia had gone, Louise, instead of retiring to her own apartment, sat down in front of the fire which still burned brightly on the hearth. The day had been an uncomfortable one for her, for she saw that there was something wrong with her father—something obviously much beyond any disease from which, so far as she knew, he had yet suffered. She had not seen him since she was eight years old till she was twenty-two, now less than three years ago. In all those fourteen years she had not even had direct communication with him, and very rarely any at all. Shortly after the death of her mother, which had occurred when Louise was scarcely four years old, her father had committed her to the care of a sister, an American like himself, but living in Italy, and spending her winters in Rome and Naples and her summers near the little village of Pisogne, at the northern end of the Lago di Iseo, where she had a villa beautifully situated amid mountain and water scenery, and which was full even to the matter of what are called nice people, with everything that wealth and refinement could provide.

The Lamars were of Spanish descent—Don Fernando Cleofonte Lamar having been an officer of high rank in the little army of Ponce de Leon, when this adventurous soldier discovered Florida. He did not find the fountain of perpetual youth, of which he was in search, nor did he dis-

cover much else tending to reconcile him and his followers
to staying in the country. Don Fernando Cleofonte, who
appears to have been a brave and good-hearted gentleman,
instead of returning to Spain, went over to Cuba, where he
married. One of his descendants, Don Bernardino Lamar,
settled in Charleston, South Carolina, shortly before the
Revolutionary war, and there married an American lady of
French descent, a Mademoiselle Louise de Vaux, daughter
of the Marquis Achille de Vaux, a Huguenot, who, on the
revocation of the Edict of Nantes by Louis XIV in 1685,
left France forever, and with his family took refuge under
the British flag in South Carolina.

During the War of Independence Don Bernardino Lamar,
his name now Americanized to Mr. Bernard Lamar, was
active on the side of the patriots, participating in several of
the battles, and eventually being killed at Yorktown just
as the contest was coming to its end. He, however, left
several sons and daughters, the former of whom all married, thus doing their part toward perpetuating the name
and the blood. Eventually, however, as often happens in
families in which marriage is restricted to a particular class,
a tendency to extinction began to be exhibited, for only
one male representative was left, and that was Francis, the
father of John, the owner of Hurricane Castle.

Francis Lamar was a merchant of Charleston, and was
for many years engaged in the importation of French and
Spanish wines into the United States. To this day the
Lamar madeira, imported in 1828, is prized above all other
wines, not only in Charleston, but even in New York, by
the very few in the latter city who are able to appreciate
its excellence. Happy is the Charlestonian who can bring
on a bottle of the Lamar madeira with his dessert! How
carefully is it handled even after he has, several hours before dinner, taken the pains to decant it himself! The individual that leaves a drop of it in his glass falls immeas-

urably in his estimation. He feels that he has been casting his pearls before swine, and he makes a vow never again
to offer the precious liquor to the offending person.

Mr. Francis Lamar remained a bachelor till he had arrived at the age of fifty years. He then suddenly seemed
to awaken to a knowledge of the fact that he was the last
of his name, and that he had been negligent of his duty to
provide for the continuance of the excellent stock from
which he had sprung. To be sure, he had two married
sisters, one a Robinson and the other a Chever. They had
the same blood that he had, but they were not Lamars
now, and never again would the name reappear through
them, though they might be blessed each with a hundred
children. He, therefore, after much weighty consideration,
determined to marry.

It is perhaps easier for a man of fifty to get married than
one of twenty-five, and if the man of fifty is blessed with a
large fortune and is in every respect a gentleman, besides
being fine-looking and endowed with good sense, the proceeding is ridiculously easy. He can very generally have
his pick of the eligible women, young and old, with whom
he may chance to come into association, and the young
sprig of twenty to twenty-five, with his callow development,
his assurance based, as it generally is, on nothing, his stu-
pid bashfulness, and his ignorance of the feminine mind,
has no chance against the courtly, deferent, tactful, mature gentleman, who knows what he wants and who sets
out in a business-like way to obtain it. The young woman
to whom he may pay attention, at once, if only on account
of his years, yields him respect, and her confidence soon follows. She begins by looking upon him somewhat in the
light of a father, and she is more free with him and allows
him greater liberties than she would dream of permitting
to the very bold or the very diffident youth. She perhaps
does not at first suspect that he has any deeper emotion

than that which all middle-aged or elderly men have for
pretty young girls, a sort of paternal or protective feeling
most pleasant both to the giver and the recipient, and
which under favorable circumstances almost invariably
ripens into love.  Again, perhaps, it will not be thought
malicious if I mention the fact that it is just possible that
in the mind of the rich "old man's darling" there is the
faintest scintillation of the idea that there is a good chance
of her being, ere very long, a blooming young widow, with
a fair stock of this world's goods to bestow on some younger
man.

Mr. Francis Lamar might readily have married in
Charleston had he been so disposed.  He was the favorite
of all the young society girls in that city; but he had been
in the habit of spending his summers at Saratoga, and there
he had met a lady twenty-five years younger than himself,
to whom he had offered his hand and heart, with the result
that he was accepted and in due time married.

Miss Alicia Stevenson could not have been justly accused of marrying Mr. Francis Lamar for his wealth, for
she had enough of her own and to spare.  What was more,
she had it in her own right, not prospectively, but actually,
and it consisted mainly of "lots," located in the best business centers of the city of New York.  After his marriage,
Mr. Lamar relinquished his business in Charleston and settled in the metropolis of the country, prepared to enjoy
himself in a manner befitting his high social position, his
refined tastes, and his great wealth.  This course was
adopted chiefly out of regard to his wife's predilections.
She had been accustomed to life in a large city, and looked
forward with very vivid anticipations to the influence
which, as the mistress of an elegant establishment, she
should exercise in society.

At last, therefore, the desire relative to the transmission
of his name, which Mr. Lamar had entertained for several

years, and which had finally forced him into the only procedure by which it could be realized, was apparently likely
to be gratified. He accordingly received with great satisfaction the intelligence that his wife was in that condition
in which ladies who love their lords like to be. In due
time a child was born ; but, to his intense disappointment,
almost amounting to displeasure, it was a girl. He looked
at the immature object with no loving glances in his eyes.
Then he kissed his wife. "My dear," he said, "I hope
this will not occur again." It did not occur again, nor for
several years was there any occurrence of a similar nature.
Then another child was born, and to the great relief of both
father and mother this one was a boy. He was christened
John, and he was the John Lamar who built Hurricane
Castle in the little village of Plato.

Francis Lamar did not live long enough to see his children attain to adult age. At sixty-five he died, leaving his
wife a widow of forty, his daughter fourteen, and his son
eight years of age. Soon after his death Mrs. Lamar took
up her residence in Paris, tutors and governesses being provided for all the educational wants of the two children.
She had liberal ideas in regard to education, and she carried
them out with the utmost thoroughness. At the age of
twenty her daughter Alicia married an English peer, Lord
Compton, and at almost the same age John went to Oxford,
where he applied himself so diligently that he took a
double first, and might have had a fellowship had he desired it. He preferred, however, to travel as his own master ; so he set out on a tour around the world, but had
got no farther than Rome, when he was introduced, at a
dinner at the American minister's, to the Contessa Frances-
ca di Bracciolini, whom he shortly afterward married.

In the mean time his mother had died, and John Lamar
and his sister, Lady Compton, found themselves each the
possessor of about two million dollars. John at once re-

turned to the United States, from which he had been continuously absent for nearly seventeen years. His wife, to whom he was devotedly attached, accompanied him, and soon after her arrival in New York a daughter, Louise, was born.

There was no other child, and consequently Louise received the undivided attention of her father and mother. Mrs. Lamar was not specially devoted to society, and Mr. Lamar preferred his library and other home features to those afforded by clubs or other places of exoteric amusement. But when the child was yet an infant the mother died, and then his whole nature seemed to undergo a great change. He shut himself up more than ever, would scarcely allow his daughter to be a moment out of his sight, and appeared to have determined to assume personally all the care of her education. This went on for three or four years, till in fact Louise was eight years old. Then another alteration occurred. He wrote to his sister, Lady Compton, who was then a widow, residing in Italy, stating that he had resolved to carry out the idea which he had formed many years ago, and to make a tour around the world. He requested that she would so far aid him in his plans as to take the entire charge of Louise during his absence, and that, should she consent, he would himself bring the child to her as soon as possible after receiving information that she would accede to his wish. Lady Compton was childless and lonely, and it therefore suited her exactly to write to her brother a glad acceptance of the charge he desired to have her assume. At the time, she was living in elegant apartments in the Piazza di Espagna in Rome, endeavoring to get what satisfaction she could out of life by studying the antiquities and works of art with which the Eternal City abounds. She cared little for society, but she nevertheless kept her place in it by giving a sufficient number of quiet little dinners every winter to embrace in turn all those whose friendship she valued. In due season her brother and niece arrived, and in a few days thereafter he set out for India, with the expressed intention of seeing before his return every part of the earth that was worth his notice. It was fourteen years before either his sister or daughter saw him again.

At first, letters came regularly to Lady Compton, all containing messages of love for his daughter, then they began to grow less frequent, and finally they ceased altogether. It was then supposed that he was dead. The last that had been heard from him was by a letter dated at Mombasa, in Zanzibar, and announcing that he was about to attempt to cross the Continent of Africa. This was sent by a private hand. The gentleman, an Englishman, who brought it, said that he had seen Mr. Lamar on the day that the letter was written, and that he was at the time in excellent health and spirits. He had, in conjunction with a half-dozen other adventurous beings, organized an expedition for exploring the course of the river Congo, from its source to its mouth, and expected to be at least two years in making the journey.

When this letter was received he had already been absent about three years, and Louise was consequently eleven years of age. As time went on, and no further intelligence was received of her father, she, as well as her aunt, believed him to be dead. She had been informed of the probable course he would follow, and used to try to trace it out on the map, and to imagine that he was at this or that point. Still less was known then of the interior of Africa than is now known, but she was aware of the general direction he would take, and it was some satisfaction to her to picture to herself her father going on successfully day by day toward the end of his journey at the Atlantic Ocean.

But when four years had elapsed and no letter or other information was received from the party, it seemed to be

the general impression all over the civilized world that dis-
aster either from the natives or the climate had overtaken
them. Learned travelers and geographers wrote elaborate
essays to prove that it was impossible that a single one of
the party could have escaped. "No person of European
descent," wrote Professor Gottlieb von Berghaus, of the
University of Steyermark, "has ever yet succeeded in resisting for longer than four months the pestilential exhala-
tions of the interior of Africa. We can recall many in-
stances of individuals as eager in the effort to unravel the
mysteries of the 'Dark Continent' as Mr. Lamar and his
party, who perished miserably before they had traversed a
tenth part of the distance between the two oceans. That
this has been the fate of this last devoted band of explorers
there is scarcely a doubt. Indeed, bearing in mind the circumstance that it is now four years since any intelligence
of them has been received, we may assume it to be an actual
fact that not a soul of them has escaped."

Professor von Berghaus's essay was read by Lady Compton and Louise. They consulted with several eminent Italian, English, and American scientists on the subject, and
there was such a uniformity of opinion in favor of the view
that there was no hope, that they went into mourning,
with the certainty that the brother and father was dead.
They waited two additional years, and then, in accordance
with eminent legal advice, proceedings were taken in the
courts of New York, of which State he was a citizen. He
was declared legally dead, and Louise as his heiress was
decreed to be entitled to take possession of his estate on
her attaining the age of twenty-one. A month before this
period was reached, John Lamar returned home, having
been absent fourteen years to a day.

Of course, time, hardship, and anxiety had made terrific
inroads on his constitution, and had caused great changes in
his mental and physical organization. He had become quite

gray ; his complexion, which previously had been fresh,
almost what is called blooming, was now sallow ; his face
was haggard ; his cheeks were hollow ; he was melancholy
almost to moroseness ; he appeared to be prematurely old,
and to have met with some great sorrow that had embit-
tered him against life. One singular feature of his conduct
was, that he declined positively to speak of his adventures,
or of the fate that had overtaken his companions. It was
only known that he had arrived at Leghorn in a sailing-ves-
sel, which a month previously had cleared from Matanzas in
the Island of Cuba.

Finally, however, it became absolutely necessary for
him to make some explanation. Most of those who had
accompanied him on his expedition were men who had for
several years been on the outskirts of civilization, and who
had lost their identity as members of any particular families. But among them was a young Neapolitan, who had
friends, and they insisted that information should be given
of the fate that had befallen him. Lamar at first would
say nothing more than that all but himself had died from
the effects of disease, and that the subject was altogether
too painful for him in his precarious state of health to reflect upon sufficiently to give the details of their sufferings.
But when the young man's mother came to see him and
implored him to tell her how her son had died, he, with
every appearance of distress at the recollections evoked,
stated that they had been kept in captivity for five years
by the King of Uregga, during which time all but himself
and the young man in question had died of fever and starvation, and that at last he alone was left, his companion
having been drowned in Lake Tanganyika while suffering
from the delirium of fever. The mere recital of these
events was sufficient to produce such a severe headache
that it was several days before he was able to leave his bed.
Then he demanded a promise from his sister and daughter

4

that they would never again ask him for any account of his fourteen years' absence, declaring that, if his wish were not complied with, he would go away, never to return. After that the matter was allowed to remain a forbidden topic of conversation in his presence.

It was not long, however, before Lamar began to recover something of his former appearance and manner. The indifference that he had at first manifested in regard to everything and everybody except his daughter, for whom he had evinced, from the very moment of their meeting, all his old affection, gradually disappeared. He began to ask questions that indicated his renewed interest in the affairs of every-day life, and to make comments on matters that were occurring about him. Nothing, however, gave him so much pleasure as Louise's society, and she appeared to be entirely willing to give up everything for him. As a consequence, the two were almost constantly together, and through her influence he little by little relaxed the severity of silence he had imposed upon himself, and would occasionally speak of the places he had visited, the persons he had met, and the adventures that had befallen him. Africa, however, was still a sealed book, which he never by any chance opened even for her instruction. He spoke of India, of China, of Japan, of his wanderings among the Buddhists of Thibet, of his narrow escapes from death in Burmah and Siberia, but never once did he allude to anything that had occurred to him in Africa; and she, respecting motives that she did not doubt were worthy, kept clear of all inquiries relative to a subject that she perceived was at least painful to him, whatever else it might be.

Thus the affection, that had been left to slumber, was reawakened. He often reproached himself for the neglect that, for fourteen years, he had exhibited toward her, and she, under the influence of his tenderness, soon found that the old filial love was returning with tenfold force.

And yet he was not demonstrative. All his emotions seemed to be subdued in intensity, so far at least as their manifestation was concerned, though it was easily to be seen that there was no diminution in the fervency with which they were felt. He never once told her how dear she was to him, or gave her any of those caresses that a father may give to his daughter, but he showed that he was not happy out of her presence. He would invite her to take long walks up the ravines and over the hills with which the country abounded, and on several occasions had made excursions with her far into the mountains. Then in the evening the two would take to the little boat on the lake, and while he rowed she would read to him extracts from the last new book, and these would call up recollections that generally brought from him the account of some adventure of his own, having some relation to that of which she had read.

This life was apparently exactly suited to him. There was a quiet happiness about it of which he never seemed to weary. At times, however, he would become depressed and even morose, would shut himself up all day in his rooms and see no one but his daughter. "You must bear with me," he would sometimes say to her when these moods were on him. "I can not control these paroxysms. They come without warning and they go just as suddenly. When they are on me, I feel an overpowering melancholy which bears me down to the very dust. Life seems to be entirely without hope, and, were it not for the one single fact that you are near me, I think I should commit self-destruction."

Sometimes they lasted only an hour or two, at others a whole day. During their continuance he walked the floor, wringing his hands together, but never shedding a tear or uttering a moan or an exclamation of any kind. Notwithstanding the fact that his general condition was constantly undergoing amelioration, it was undoubtedly the case that these periods of mental depression were becoming more frequent and more severe. He would not consent to a physician being called in, although Lady Compton and Louise implored him to take medical advice. "No," he would say, "it is out of the question ; I can not open my heart to a stranger, even though he be a physician. If I placed myself in his hands he could do me no good, unless I made him acquainted with circumstances of which I can not bear to think. The mere speaking of them would make me worse, and even the distant allusion which I am now making to them give me an atrocious pain in my head." So he suffered.

It was evident, however, that something would have to be done, and finally the idea suggested itself to him that he would return to America, taking his daughter with him, and making it their future home. He had lost little of his energy and quickness to act, after he had once formed a determination. The fact that he was not dead had already been judicially established, and he had reacquired the possession of his property. "I will not keep you much longer out of it," he had said to Louise. "It will be yours almost as soon as though I had never come back." Then the girl had thrown herself sobbing into his arms, and he had cursed himself for having caused her a moment's pain.

So they went back to the United States, where they found that the fortune of a million which he had inherited from his father and mother had simply, by being let alone, increased to nearly three millions, if it was not, as some good judges supposed, over that sum. Then through accident he had heard of Plato. The place suited him. It was as much out of the world as any he would be likely to find anywhere else, and it was sufficiently in it to admit of existence being made comfortable and even luxurious.

Louise was troubled. Her loving and watchful eye saw

that things were not right with her father. He was tremulous and weak—objects had fallen from his hands several
times that day when he had been startled, just as the Kaga
plaque had dropped when Doctor Grattan had said something about Africa. He had repeatedly put his hand to his
head as though suffering pain, but when she had asked him
if his head ached he had answered rather dreamily in the
negative, as though not quite certain whether it did or not.

Then she had observed that all day his manner had been
absent, as though his thoughts were far away. When she
had spoken to him, he had appeared not to hear her, and
even when her remarks had been repeated he had looked at
her for a moment or two in a half-stupid sort of a way before answering, and then, that which he said was far from
being so clear as was his ordinary speech.

As to his conduct that evening, how was it to be explained ? What hidden relation was there between the picture of the escaped Polish convict and the fact of his sudden disappearance and the nervous agitation which she had
perceived when she had gone to his room ? It was all a
mystery to her, but it was one she felt sure that was weigh-
ing heavily on her father, and that was, she feared, slowly
perhaps, but nevertheless very surely, dragging him down
to the grave.

She rose from her chair and began to pace the long, tiled
hall. Her anxiety for her father was such that she could
not sit down quietly and think, much as she desired to do
so. There were many subjects crowding themselves upon
her mind, but they were all put aside by the predominance
of the thought of her father's illness. What was she to do ?
Could she do anything ? Oh ! if he would but give her
his confidence, then she might be of assistance to him ; but
as it was, she must wait supinely, while what she felt was
the secret of his life was slowly sapping the foundations of
his body and mind. She went to the door, opened it, and

looked out. The night was cool, and she shivered a little
as the wind from the north, coming over Pitchoff Mountain, struck against her lightly clad form. Here and there
in the village a dim light could be seen. That one to the
left, a few hundred yards distant, was at Mrs. Hadden's.
Doubtless the widow was busy at her literary work, for she
was obliged to labor day and night in order to finish a book
she had engaged should be ready by the first of the coming
year. That one a little farther off was at Mr. Craig's. To-
morrow was Sunday. The parson was probably deep in the
composition of a sermon that in the morning would remind
the Platonians of their sins and point out to them the way
of salvation, and be received with the same degree of indifference that hundreds of others of like import had encountered. These were all. As to the other houses, only
their dim, shadowy outlines could be seen as the faint light
of the crescent moon and of the stars fell upon them. The
stillness was oppressive. There was not even the baying of
a dog at the moon. She turned to go in. Ah! there was
another light. Certainly it had not been there a moment
before, for her eyes had swept the narrow valley in all its
extent, and she would have seen it. It was brighter than
either of the others, though much more distant, and it was
in one of the windows of Doctor Grattan's house. Which?
she asked herself. She stopped to think, while she still
kept her eyes fixed upon it. She could not tell, for she
could not distinguish any point about the house that would
have served as a guide. There was nothing visible but the
light. Well! what did it matter? It was either in Cynthia's or the doctor's room—and they were situated in opposite ends of the house. Still, for curiosity's sake, she
would like to know in whose room was this light that shone
so brightly at the distance of a mile. It was directly in a
line with a cedar that grew on the lawn, a few feet from
her, so that to-morrow she would be able to determine.

Then she should not care anything about it. But to-night she would like to know.

Perhaps it was in the doctor's room. For an instant the idea occurred to her that she would ask his advice about her father and tell him all she knew, little as it was, of his life and sufferings. Why not go now? She was not afraid. It was not at all likely that on the way she would meet a single soul. There was no one else in whom she could confide—no one to whom she could appeal for aid that she felt was every day becoming more and more necessary. Yes, she would go!

She went in to get a cloak or a shawl to throw over her shoulders. As she crossed the hall she glanced at the clock that stood at the end opposite the fireplace. It was just about to strike the hour of ten. A shawl lay on a chair, and she threw it over her shoulders, preparatory to going on her mission, when a servant—Mr. Lamar's valet—approached her.

"If you please, miss," said the man, "Mr. Lamar would like to see you before you retire."

"Is anything the matter?" she inquired, anxiously.

"Nothing special, I think, miss, but he seems restless and is unable to get to sleep."

"Tell Thomas to shut up the house," she said, removing the shawl.

She ascended the broad staircase and went toward her father's room. The door was ajar. She entered quietly and stood by the side of his bed. He was asleep, but breathing heavily and irregularly. She had never before seen her father asleep, and she did not now perceive him distinctly, for the light was turned down low and shaded so that it should not fall on his face. But she saw that his countenance was distorted, as though he were still suffering either bodily or mental pain. It was better that he should sleep, she thought; so she turned away, and had got half-way to the door, when a groan from the sleeping man caused her to return to his side. A few words escaped him, but they were uttered so indistinctly that she could not make them out. But in a little while he appeared to grow calmer, and she was able to distinguish every now and then a word of the sentences, mostly incoherent, that he muttered. "Chains, fetters—only these!" he said. "Nothing but chains and manacles and—and—death, only these—manacles and death!"

He stopped speaking, and his breathing became easier. Then she left him. But what could be this mystery in which chains and fetters and death blended; and why had he disappeared so suddenly from before the picture of the Polish convict with the broken manacles hanging from his arms and legs?

# CHAPTER VI.

"My dear," said Doctor Grattan at the breakfast-table a few mornings after the visit to Hurricane Castle, "I used to think that you were a very intelligent young woman, but I am gradually becoming undeceived. I have asked you eleven questions since we sat down to this frugal meal— frugal *meal* very decidedly, seeing that it consists mainly of the flour of the grain that Dr. Johnson said is not fit for a man to eat—and you have not answered a single one of them. Now, Miss Grattan, I should like to know what has been the use of my spending fabulous sums on your education, and you to be ignorant at this period of your life of the simplest facts in anthropology?"

"You may well say *fabulous* sums," laughed Cynthia. "Nothing could be more fabulous than the sums you have spent on my education. As to the meal and your shocking attempt at that lowest of all kinds of wit, a pun, it's as good as you've ever been accustomed to since I have had the honor of your acquaintance : and the eleven questions ! You asked me who the strange man was that passed the house yesterday morning, and I told you I didn't know."

"Worse than that, you incarnation of ignorance ! You said you didn't want to know. Under some circumstances ignorance is excusable, but the expression of a desire not to wish for knowledge is simply horrible."

"Don't interrupt me, please. Then you asked me

where he came from, and again I answered that I didn't
know."

"And, with a degree of self-sufficiency that I think I
can never forget, you added that you didn't care."

"Then," resumed Cynthia, "you wanted to know where
he was going."

"Yes, and you impertinently told me that I had better
go and ask him."

"Did you take my advice?" inquired Cynthia, her face
beaming with mirth.

"Oh, now it is you who are asking questions! No, I
did not. But I know all about him nevertheless."

"Trust a doctor for picking up gossip! Well, you are
dying to tell me what you have discovered; so go on."

"And you are dying to be told; but I will be merciful
and will enlighten you. He is Mr. George Frazier, a rich
young gentleman from Pittsburg. He owns a large factory
or rolling-mill or something of the kind. He is an orphan,
and is twenty-six years of age, is rather good-looking, has
pleasing manners, is a graduate of the School of Mines of
Columbia College, is married or unmarried, I don't know
which, came here on a hunting expedition with his friend
Mr. Digby Wyant, and proposed to stay two weeks. But
man proposes and God disposes : instead of remaining two
weeks, he will probably stay a dozen or more."

"How in the world did you pick up all that?" inquired Cynthia. "And why should he stay so much
longer than he desires?"

"I 'picked it up,' to use your rather slangy expression,
in the exercise of my profession, and he will probably stop
here two or three months, because yesterday afternoon he
fell from a rock on Dix Peak and broke his thigh."

"And you never told me till now!"

"How could I tell you before, when this is the first time
I have had the pleasure of seeing you since I knew of it

myself ? I was called up in the middle of the night, and I did not think it necessary or proper to inform you of the fact at two o'clock in the morning."

"Poor fellow, and he lay on the mountain all that time ! How he must have suffered !"

"Yes, he was almost exhausted by the time his friend returned with assistance. They had to bring him by a roundabout road nearly two miles on a stretcher, and he fainted several times on the way."

Cynthia was of a kindly, sympathizing nature, and she felt an interest in the young man, now that he was seriously injured, that would never, probably, have been aroused under other circumstances. There was not much that she could do beyond the expression of her sympathy ; but even a little, as she well knew, done by kind hands, comes with grateful force to the sick and miserable. A few flowers have been known to turn the scale in favor of life, and she could at least, as the daughter of his physician, send Mr. Frazier a bunch of roses from the greenhouse, which was her and her father's greatest delight. She thought all this out in a moment, and then she said in a manner which she did not mean should show too much interest :

"I suppose there is nothing I could do to make him more comfortable ?" pouring out a second cup of coffee as she spoke, and handing it across the table to her father.

He looked at her for a moment with a quizzical expression on his face before answering her question. "I think," he said at last, "that if you simply sat at his bedside and handed things to him, you would make him a great deal more comfortable than he is likely to be when his hand-maiden is Mrs. Ruggles. She isn't unkind, but her hand and arm are those of a stone-cutter, and yours—well, never mind. Yes, I think you might do something for him ; send him something good to eat. 'The Bear' is not famous for its *cuisine:* and then two or three roses every morning—not my Noisettes—put on the table by his side will give him some little notion of our not being a community of barbarians."

" Is his leg badly broken ? "

" It's a bad double fracture, and he may be lame all the rest of his life, unless I succeed to perfection in the permanent setting which I shall give it to-day or to-morrow. This morning I could do nothing but put on a temporary dressing, as he was too much exhausted to stand the fatigue of adjusting the broken bones for the fixed apparatus; and, besides, the leg was terribly swollen."

" How did it happen ? "

" You recollect that big mass of granite on the north side of Dix, about half-way up to the summit ?   Well, he and his friend Wyant were standing on the very edge of it, looking down into the valley, when somehow or other his foot slipped—these city fellows come here and think they can walk over our rocks and mountains as they would on the pavement of Fifth Avenue—and he went down perpendicularly about forty feet, striking on a mass of rocks below. Wyant hurried to him as rapidly as he could, and found him insensible when he reached him.   He was obliged to stay with him till the poor fellow recovered consciousness, which was not for over an hour, and then it was quite dark. Fortunately, by taking a short cut, he didn't have over a mile to go, and he ran all the way.   He got four men and a cot-bedstead, and on that they brought him to ' The Bear,' but it was after midnight when they got him there and sent for me."

" And yesterday morning when he passed here he was all health and vigor !   I hope he will not be lame."

" Nothing but good surgery can prevent it, and that will probably fail."

" Ah ! but, my dear, you *are* a good surgeon ; everybody says that, whatever else they may say about you.   I shall

expect you, therefore, to set that bone so that there won't
be the least lameness, not the slightest vestige of a limp.
Do you hear, sir ? Is—is—he handsome ?"

"I should say not—at least not just at this present
time. His nose is mashed nearly flat, both eyes are bunged
up, his mouth is cut and swollen, so that it looks like anything but a mouth, and—"

"Oh, don't tell me any more, please. I am so sorry !"

"At present, therefore," continued the doctor, "beauty
is not one of his strong points ; but as his facial damages are
merely superficial, a few days will make him all right in
that respect."

"I suppose he does not care to talk much ?" interrogatively.

"Really, Cynthia, my dear," exclaimed the doctor,
laughing, "considering that only a few minutes ago you
didn't want to know who he was and didn't care where he
came from, and declared that if I wanted to know where he
was going I might go and ask him—considering, I say, all
these things, it appears to me that you are now evincing
an extraordinary amount of curiosity."

"That was when I thought he was well, and had no
idea that you would have had anything to do with him, or
that I should ever lay eyes on him again. But, papa," she
continued, coming round to his end of the table and seating herself on his knee, while she put one arm around his
neck, "it is such a sad thing to be laid up as he is going to
be, and to be obliged to suffer without even the privilege of
getting up and stamping his foot."

"The luxury of swearing is still reserved to him."

"Then I suppose he does talk ?" again interrogatively.

"Now, my dear, how in the world can he talk, when
his tongue is cut nearly in two, his lips all stuck up with
sticking-plaster, and his jaws bound together by a bandage
passing over his head ?"

"But you didn't tell me he was as bad as that."

"I should have told you, but you very curtly requested me not to mention any more of his wounds."

"You said he could swear?"

"I didn't say he *did* swear. A man can swear when he can't do anything else. I have heard oaths come out of the mouth when the lips were as tightly closed as a sardine-box. Swearing is the easiest kind of talking."

"You appear to know all about it."

"None of your impudence, you minx!"

"One more question, and then I am done, and you can go down to 'The Bear,' and set his broken bone. Can he hear?"

"I believe his hearing is unimpaired, as is also his sense of touch; but his other senses—his eye-sight, from bunged-up eyes, his smell, from a mashed nose, and his taste from a bitten tongue—I should not like to vouch for. In fact, I think I may safely say that they are not of much use to him."

"Papa," said Cynthia, "is there any objection to my going to see him and reading to him occasionally? I mean after the bone is set, and when he is feeling lonely, and the time is hanging heavily on his hands."

"Being his nurse, in short. I don't know yet; I must find out what kind of a man he is first. I know very little about him so far. Besides, he may not want you. And he may be a married man, in which event I suppose he will prefer to have his wife."

"Oh, of course, but it must necessarily be several days before she can arrive, and in the mean time I may be of some service to him, and to you also. You know I am not a bad nurse."

"You are not only not a bad nurse, but you are a very good one. I will see about it. It is very kind of you, my dear, very kind. Now, if you will show a little kindness

to me by removing your not particularly feathery weight
from my knee so that I can go and see how my patient is, I
will be under obligations to you."

"Yes," she said, kissing him as she rose, "and don't
forget old Mrs. Withers. She sent here just now to say that
her 'neuraligy' is worse, and that she would like to see you
as soon as possible."

"The scheming old woman! She's heard of this accident, and wants to know all the particulars. It's simply
impossible that her 'neuraligy,' as she calls it, can be worse.
I gave her a mixture yesterday that has never yet failed to
cure her. Shall I take a rose or two to Mr. Frazier, with
your compliments and sympathy?"

"I will pluck them now, if you will wait a moment."
She left the room, and the doctor got ready for his morning
visits, which generally took him several hours, as his practice extended around the country many miles from Plato.
In a few minutes Cynthia returned with a magnificent bouquet made up of several kinds of rare roses, for which the
doctor had a mild mania.

"You haven't taken any of my Noisettes, have you?"
he said, looking closely at the flowers. "They stood the
frost last autumn, and this year I'm going to test their
hardiness with a snow-storm."

"No, I didn't touch your precious Noisettes. Good-
by," she continued, as she placed the bouquet in his hand.
"Will you be home early?"

"Yes, unless I have to go to see Judge Byers, who lives
on the other side of Pitchoff. It's a long drive. But, as he
hates to pay for medical visits, I am hopeful of escaping the
journey. He's threatened with pneumonia; but as long as
he can breathe he will not send for me."

"And after he stops breathing, you couldn't be of much
service to him, could you?"

"None of your impertinence! Well, good-by; I forgive

you." IIe left the room, and, going out into the frosty morning air, entered his buggy and drove over to "The Bear" to make his first visit for the day.

He found that Frazier had had six hours of quiet sleep, and was altogether over the immediate effects of the great shock that his system had received. IIe was still, however, very weak, and evidently, the doctor thought, as he surveyed the patient with eyes that had become experienced in the hospitals of New York and Europe, he would require careful nursing in addition to a good constitution to carry him safely through. A double fracture of the thigh is a serious matter under any circumstances, and when it is produced as the consequence of a fall of nearly forty feet, it is a still more grievous injury. Still, so far as the doctor could now see, everything was going on well.

Frazier held out his hand to the physician as the latter entered the room, but did not attempt to speak. In fact, it would have been, as the doctor had told Cynthia, almost impossible for him to utter a word, so completely closed was his mouth by plasters and bandages. IIe made signs, however, that he was hungry, and this the doctor regarded as a good symptom. Then the doctor presented the roses with a little message of kindness from his daughter. Frazier's face made an attempt to look pleased, but the effort was not very successful. IIe tried to say something, but only the word "thanks" could be distinguished. Then he signified by gestures that he wanted a pencil and paper. They were given to him, and he wrote :

"Was it your daughter I saw at the window of the stone house at the other end of the village?"

"Yes."

"And did she send me these flowers?"

"Yes, she sent them."

"God bless her! She's an angel!"

Then he wrote again :

"How long am I likely to be kept on this bed ?"

"I think you will do well if you get out of it in two months. Three would probably be nearer the mark."

Frazier gave a groan, and covered his face with his hands.

After a few moments he wrote :

"I was to have been married on the 10th of December, just three weeks from now."

"The marriage will have to be postponed," said the doctor—"unless," he added, "the lady will come here and marry you. Doubtless she would make a good nurse, and you need one badly."

Frazier thought for a little while, and then wrote :

"You will do me a great kindness if you will write to Miss Julia Drummond, care of Henry Drummond, Esq., 1125 Fifth Avenue, New York, and tell her of what has happened to me, and of the probable length of time I shall be kept here. Say that I need good nursing, and anything else of that sort that you think proper. Then I will add a postscript requesting her to come here, so as to be married according to previous arrangements on the 10th of next month. I think she will come. Yes, I am sure she will come !" He fell back on the bed quite exhausted ; and the doctor, first seeing that nothing serious had happened, left him, while he went to another part of the room to write the desired letter. When he had finished, he took it to Frazier, who read it, and then added to it in pencil the following lines :

"My Darling Julia : You see, from what my kind physician has written, that I am in a bad way, and likely to be so for a long time. It would be a great joy to me to see you. Come, dear, let our marriage take place on the 10th, and then you will be my own wife, with the right to look after your luckless George—luckless, except in the one thing of possessing your love. I know I am asking a good deal of you, and that you may have a weary month or so of it nursing a sick man ; but I am not without the hope that the idea of being of help to me will give you almost as much pleasure as the prospect of having you here gives me. Good-by, dear.

"Your own          GEORGE."

"Wyant, who is obliged to return to-night, will take this to you and give you a full account of the accident."

"There," he wrote to the doctor, "I think that will bring her."

"Now, my dear fellow," said the physician, "I must go to work, and I may have to hurt you ; but the sooner now that we get through with the matter the better."

He examined the leg, and found to his delight and as-tonishment that there was little, if any, swelling remain-ing. Then he went to work in his thoroughly scientific manner, assisted by Wyant, and, after a long, tedious, and painful procedure, announced that the bone was set, to remain undisturbed for the next two months.

"There will probably be a little lameness," said the doc-tor, "for both fractures are oblique, and it is impossible to prevent altogether the slipping of the fragments and the consequent shortening of the limb. But I hope to make this as little as possible."

"Then you think I shall be lame ?" wrote Frazier, who had borne the operation with great fortitude, though con-siderably worn out with the pain he had endured.

"Yes, I think you will be lame. Indeed, believing as I do that you should know the whole truth, I will say that you will certainly be a little lame—not much, I hope, but still a little."

Frazier appeared to be troubled ; he again covered his face with his hands and for some time remained silent, though his irregular respiration gave evidence of the struggle that was going on within him. Finally, he seemed to regain the command of himself, and asked Wyant by signs to give him back the letter he had written to his betrothed. He tore open the envelope as soon as it was in his hands, and added these words:

"The doctor says I shall certainly be lame—not much, but a little."

Then he put it into another envelope and gave it to Wyant. He tried to seem composed, but it was evident that the opinion the doctor had expressed relative to his lameness had caused him great disquietude. The physician saw the effect that had been produced, and, fearful that it might interfere with his patient's progress toward recovery, endeavored to reconcile him to the prospect before him.

"Perhaps," he said, "you don't fully understand the matter. When, in answer to your earnest inquiry, I told you the truth as it was my duty to do, I did not mean to be understood as intimating that you were going to be markedly deformed. The worst that can happen will be a little shortening; how much exactly I can not now say, but probably not over half an inch. It may be a little more— I shall try to make it less. If you were not such an athlete, I should be quite sure of less than half an inch, but your muscles are so well developed, and consequently strong, that they may, by their contraction, cause the fragments to slide over one another, and hence make the limb shorter than if they were weak and puny. Unless the shortening, however, is very great, a high-heeled and thick-soled shoe will compensate for the difference. Now, you see it is not such a bad matter, after all. But you must try to be reconciled, for if you worry over it you may start a fever, and that would interfere with the union."

"I don't care a pin's head," wrote Frazier, "so far as I am concerned. An inch more or less in the length of one

leg is a matter of very little consequence to me ; but other
considerations make it of importance. However, I shall
endeavor to bear my fate with equanimity, and hope for
the best. I have every confidence in my physician, and
that is a good deal in my favor."

"Yes, and I shall watch you closely. I'll look in again
this evening."

"Don't go till I have sent a word of thanks to Miss Grattan for the lovely roses. Would it be asking too much if I
should beg you to let her come and see me if she should be
kind enough to express a willingness to do so ? After Wyant's departure, and till Miss Drummond comes, I shall be
quite alone."

"Would you like her to come and read to you a little
every day ? "

"Would I like it ? Of course I would ! "

"Well, I'll see about it, said the doctor, with a smile.
"She'd send you something to eat, but you're not good for
much at mastication at present ; and, besides, for a day or
two I want you kept on oatmeal and milk, and, fortunately,
the *cuisine* of 'The Bear' is equal to that diet."

"Thanks ! I can never be sufficiently grateful."

After the doctor's departure, Frazier, who felt far more
comfortable since the adjustment of the fracture, but who
was greatly exhausted with the incidents of the morning,
fell into a sound sleep, from which he did not awake for
several hours. When at last he opened his eyes to the limited extent that his injuries permitted, he found Wyant
sitting by his side.

"You have had a sound sleep," said his friend, "and
you look better. The swelling about your face has greatly
decreased, and by to-morrow I think you will be able
to talk. In the mean time here is a slate that I got for
you."

Frazier took it and wrote :

"Much obliged. You are very thoughtful." Then, after a moment—

"You will see Miss Drummond to-morrow evening. Break the matter cautiously to her before you give her the letter, and make the best of it that your conscience will allow, concealing nothing, however—especially the prospect of lameness. I have special reasons for wishing that there should not be the least deception on this point. Tell her exactly what the doctor said. I think she will come."

"I am sure she will. She would not be worthy of such a noble fellow as you if she hesitated a moment. Don't smile, George," he added, with a laugh. "You disarrange the plasters; and, moreover, your success in imparting a pleasing expression to your face is not great."

They talked, or rather one talked and the other wrote, till Frazier again began to feel fatigued, and a second nap became necessary. When he awoke from this it was just in time to bid Wyant good-by, and to receive the doctor, who had called to pay his second visit.

The physician had, in the mean time, been home to his dinner, and he brought with him some delicious compound of eggs, milk, and sugar, which Cynthia had made, and which he assured his patient was endowed with the most nutritious qualities. Moreover, he said that if all went well, and especially if there were no fever, his daughter would come with him in the morning and look a little after the invalid's comfort. Mrs. Ruggles, the wife of the landlord of "The Bear," was kind and considerate, according to her light; but Cynthia he knew would be able to suggest many things that would never occur to the honest and well-meaning landlady.

"But," he continued, "it all depends on your having a good night's rest, and awaking free from fever. I can't run any risks with you. There must be no excitement, such as seeing new faces might produce. Ruggles will stay

with you to-night, and to-morrow I hope to be able to procure you a permanent nurse, though I must say that I am
at my wits' ends in that matter. Such a thing as a professional nurse is not to be found in Plato."

He took his leave, well satisfied with the condition of
his patient. "Now," he said to himself as he reached the
street, "I'll go and see how Mr. Lamar is getting along.
Poor fellow! I'm afraid he's in a bad way, and, what is especially disgusting to me, I can't diagnosticate his disease
with sufficient accuracy."

He walked rapidly up the road toward Hurricane Castle, buttoning his overcoat—for the evening air was cold—
over his massive chest, and drawing on his thick woolen
gloves. He passed Mrs. Hadden's door, when an impulse
which suddenly moved him caused him to retrace his steps
and to knock at her door. It was opened by the lady herself, who, recognizing her visitor, invited him with kindly
greeting to enter.

"I didn't come to see you, my dear," he said—the doctor called all his women-patients, of all social grades and
ages, "my dear," with the sole exception of old Mrs. Withers—"although it is always pleasant to meet you except
when you are ill. I want to have a few moments' conversation with that boy of yours. Is he in?"

"Will? Yes, I think I heard him come in a few minutes ago and go to his room. Excuse me a moment, and
I'll see."

She left the room, and the doctor, to occupy the time
till her return, picked up a book that was lying upon the
table. This proved so interesting to him that he did not,
till Mrs. Hadden addressed him, perceive that she had
returned.

"Will is at home, and will be down in a moment," she
said. "I found him busy reading. He has become a great
student, doctor, and not in a way, I am afraid, to be of

much service to him hereafter. Of course, he will have his own living to make, and I do not see how reading books on magic and sorcery and witchcraft and astrology is going to help him."

"You are right, my dear Mrs. Hadden. They are the veriest trash in existence, except to the student of human folly, and then a little goes a great way."

"He's reading a book now which purports to give directions how to raise the devil."

"I don't think Will needs any directions on that score," said the doctor, laughing heartily. "It may be attended with slight difficulty here in Plato, perhaps, where all the people are so extremely righteous—in their own estimation ; but I should be disposed to think," he added, stroking his mustache, and assuming an air of profound reflection, "that a young gentleman of Will's ability and perseverance might readily succeed in elevating his Satanic majesty to the top of a tolerably high pinnacle."

"Will is a good boy," said the mother, "but I wish he would study more wisely. He begins, too, to take some interest in writing, and has begun a story which, when done, he wishes me to send to the 'Arctic Monthly.'"

"He takes after you ; but, for Heaven's sake, don't let him send his story to the 'Arctic.' That magazine lives up to its name : it is frozen tight against all but its own little band of authors and their imitators. If Will's story has any robustness in it, they won't take it. They only want the namby-pamby stuff of Campus and Martis and Baldwick and Mudder and such like, who write good English by the square foot about nothing."

"I know Will can write good English, but whether he uses it effectively in delineating character or in portraying incidents, I do not know. But here he is. Perhaps he will show you his story."

"I should be glad to take it home with me and read it ;

but, in the mean time, I have a little business with him.
As you probably know—although you have had the good
sense, my dear, not to mention the matter to me; physicians should never be asked about their patients—a Mr.
Frazier, of Pittsburg, had the misfortune day before yesterday to break his thigh. He will be confined to bed for
probably three months, and I am in want of a nurse and
companion for him. I think Will is just the fellow for
both positions. I think the place is worth a hundred dollars a month." Then, addressing the young man, "Will
you take it?"

"Why, doctor," he answered, "I am so taken aback by
the proposition that I hardly know what to say. The first
thing that strikes me is the idea that I am not capable."

"Oh, yes, you are. You'll only have to do what I tell
you. Mr. and Mrs. Ruggles will be there to help you with
the hard work, so that your duties will chiefly consist in
making yourself agreeable, and taking a general supervision
of affairs in my absence. You know you read medicine for
a year, and I suppose you managed to get an idea or two
about the management of the sick."

"A very little, I'm afraid. Still, I am disposed to try
it, if you think I will do."

"Very well; then we may consider the matter settled,
and you can enter upon your duties to-morrow morning. You might begin to entertain him by reading your
story."

"Especially if I wanted to make him sleep. I would
rather have you read it first, and tell me what you think
of it."

"Give it to me, and I'll take it home with me. I'm on
my way now to see Mr. Lamar."

"I wish you wanted me to nurse him," said Will, "instead of Mr. Frazier."

"Why so?"

"Because he is the most interesting man I ever met. I was talking with him yesterday, and he told me of any number of remarkable events in his life."

"Well, let me have your story and lend me this book. I got interested in it while waiting for your mother to come back, and would like to read it, 'The Life and Adventures of Captain Juan de Ayolas.'"

The doctor took the story and the book, and departed on his way to Hurricane Castle.

5

# CHAPTER VII.

THE morning after Mr. Lamar's indisposition, to which reference has been made in a previous chapter, he appeared to be in much better condition, as regarded both mind and body. He came down to the breakfast-room, where Louise was awaiting him, with almost his usual punctuality, and spoke to her with a degree of cheerfulness she had not observed in him since she had arrived at Plato. Affectionate to her he always was, no matter how morbid he might be in other respects, so that there was nothing unusual in the manifestations of tenderness that he now exhibited toward her.

"You are looking much better this morning, papa dear," she said, as he kissed her cheek—"better, I think, than you have looked for several weeks past. This fresh mountain air is beginning to tell on you; Doctor Grattan says that it takes some time for it to act, especially upon those persons who, like you, have lived long in hot and unhealthy climates."

"I think I am feeling better to-day than usual," he said in a languid sort of a way, as though the matter did not interest him, "and I shall probably feel better still when I get my coffee. What I should do without my morning cup of coffee I really do not know. It sets me up for the whole day as nothing else can. I wish I knew the *rationale* of its action. I shall have to ask Doctor Grattan how it is that the infusion of a few berries can change the

thoughts from melancholy to almost gay. I think it was
Sir James Mackintosh who said that he believed a man's
mental power is in direct proportion to the quantity of
coffee he drinks ; but I think that is putting it a little too
strongly."

"I think it is," said Louise, laughing. "If it were
true, idiot-asylums would not be necessary. We should
only require coffee-houses and free coffee."

"Did you ever, my dear," he continued, after he had
taken a sip of his coffee, and satisfied himself of its excellence, "have sentences or a number of unmeaning words
get into your head and constantly recur to you, no matter
how hard you might try to forget them ?"

"I think I have, but then they do eventually disappear."

"With you, perhaps, and with most people ; but with
others they do not, but continue to haunt them with dia-
bolical tenacity, till it really often seems as though they
were being constantly whispered in the ear by the devil
himself or some of his imps. There they are, every moment
that the unhappy wretch is awake ; sometimes loud, sometimes faint, sometimes in one key, a deep *basso profundo*,
and again in a shrill *falsetto* voice, and, worse than all,
often sung to ribald tunes, that themselves are in their turn
additional causes of torment. Think of such things going
on, not for days, but for months and years—many years !"

"It must be very horrible !"

"Horrible ! it is enough to drive the poor victim to despair. I have heard of a man," he continued, his face expressing the interest he felt, "who constantly heard the
words, 'Go and kill yourself !' whispered in his ear. Wher-
ever he went, whatever he did, he heard this frightful command. He consulted physicians in all parts of the world ;
he prayed to be delivered from his torment ; he led the
life of an ascetic ; he plunged into all kinds of dissipation.

Nothing was of the slightest service : ever the words, ' Go
and kill yourself ! go and kill yourself !' were ringing in
his ears with horrible distinctness. He endured this agony
for more than five years, and then one morning he was
found dead in his room, with a pistol-bullet through his
brain. At last he had obeyed the command."

"How dreadful ! It makes me shudder to think of it.
Such a thing might happen to any one, I suppose."

"No, I think not—I am quite certain not. It only
happens," he went on, looking grave, and speaking very deliberately and slowly, " to those who are to be warned of
some impending evil, or who have committed some heinous
crime. In the latter case it is intended as a punishment,
and I believe the words are really spoken by an emissary of
the devil, who never leaves the side of the condemned, nor
ceases to utter the words he is ordered to speak."

Louise heard all this with the utmost amazement. At
first she thought her father must be indulging in a little
pleasantry ; but one look at his face was sufficient to convince her that he was terribly in earnest. But that he,
whom she had always heretofore, and with reason, regarded
as a man of the utmost good sense, and as one entirely
free from superstition, should seriously enunciate opinions
which would have done credit to a witch-hunter of the
Middle Ages, filled her with astonishment and fear. If he
really believed in the explanation he gave of a circumstance
that she was convinced admitted of a rational interpretation, then his mind was disordered, and she could understand much in his recent conduct that had hitherto been
unexplainable.

He saw that she was astounded. " You do not agree
with me, I perceive," he said. " Well, when I was your
age, I would have hooted at the man who should have
talked to me of devils and imps. Like you, I required
proofs for everything that was out of the range of common

experience. But I have grown wise with age, and I now know that there is a great deal that I can not understand, or prove by such evidence as would be taken in a court of justice, that is as true as those things that are revealed to me by my senses. There is an inner light, that perhaps all do not possess, by which the supernatural is revealed to us. *I* have this light, for I can see images and hear voices that are unperceived by you."

"You are not well, papa. You must let me send for Doctor Grattan." She came round to where he was sitting and laid her hand on his forehead. "Yes, I am sure you are not well," she continued, "for your head is quite hot. I am afraid you did not sleep well last night."

"On the contrary, I never slept better in my life, and I have not for several years felt so well as I do now. I have been fighting an enemy, or an influence, that I thought was unfriendly, but that was probably not so. I have now given up the contest. You must at times have experienced anxiety, when you thought some trouble of a serious nature was impending over you. Well, my dear child, that has been my condition for more than five years. You have felt, doubtless, after the blow had fallen, that it was not so bad as you expected, and that the certainty was far less agonizing than the doubt that formerly prevailed. Then you have accepted the inevitable, and have thenceforth been comparatively at ease. That also is my state. I am at last convinced that what I have been in doubt about, or refused to believe for the past five years, is really true. It is horrible, I admit, but I feel a degree of calmness and repose of mind, a kind of mental and bodily languor, that are rather pleasant than otherwise. I am like a man that has been fighting with a powerful adversary, and that has put forth all his strength. While the contest was going on, his mind was in a state of painful tension, his senses were strained to their utmost degree of alertness, his

muscles had stood out like hard masses of iron, his heart
had throbbed with the force of a steam-engine. At last he
is overcome, and he falls to the ground in a state of complete relaxation. He is conquered, he feels chagrined,
mortified, humbled, but at last he is at peace, and peace is
what he requires now."

Louise was terrified beyond expression. She saw, in
what her father said, nothing but the evidence of a disordered mind. She did not for a moment accept as truth a
word of what he said, but she was surprised at the entire
freedom from agitation or excitement that he exhibited,
and that was itself a cause to her of additional anxiety.
What was she to do ? To allow him to go on as he now
was, with the certainty, perhaps, of a further development
of the mental derangement with which he was affected, was
not to be thought of for an instant. She should never
cease to blame herself if she remained inactive at a time
when medical interference would more than at a subsequent period be likely to be successful. She was a woman
of decision, and one that acted promptly when she had decided. Still, she shrank from going to Doctor Grattan and
telling him that she had reasons for believing that her
father was insane. Nothing but the clearest kind of a case
would justify such a course, and it might be that the present symptoms were only the result of a sleepless night, or
of some temporary disturbance of the system that would
disappear spontaneously in a short time. Clearly, she
thought, it would be better to wait for further developments, instead of rushing off to invoke aid that might not
be required. She knew that the slightest suspicion of the
existence of insanity in a person was an opprobrium that
clings through a lifetime, not only to him, but to all his
relatives.

How to conduct herself toward her father was a matter,
however, that required immediate action. She could not

sit there in silence and let him go on with his hallucinations and delusions, for silence would be almost equivalent
to an acceptance of their reality. She was afraid to oppose
him, for she thought she had read somewhere that opposition to a lunatic's false ideas serves to fix them more
firmly in his mind. She did not think that her father was
yet a lunatic, but she was quite sure that he was on the bor-
der-line—if there is such a division between sanity and insanity—and that the greatest circumspection was necessary
in dealing with him. But he did not give her much time
for reflection. His mind was full to repletion of the new
ideas, and the expression of them was a necessity to him.

"Did I ever tell you about Alatamba ?" he inquired,
rising from the table. "Come into the library, my dear ; I
want to talk to you. It is always a pleasure to me to have
you for a listener, for you are sensible, and, what is perhaps
of greater importance, attentive. I have almost determined
to unburden my mind to you, now that I fully know the
truth, and have you help me to forget it, and to obtain
forgiveness, or that condition of absolute repose of mind
that comes from the consciousness of sincere repentance.
Come !" He took her hand as he spoke, and led the way
across the large hall to the library, a stately room, with
alcoves and oak wainscotings and antique furniture and
stained-glass windows, and that was, above all, stocked with
the rarest literary treasures that wealth, prompted by learning, taste, and experience, could procure.

"Now," he said, drawing a chair in front of the oak-
wood fire that burned on the ample hearth, " sit down
there and I will relate to you a very astonishing circumstance, that will, I think, convince you that I have this
inner light, that enables me to see things that others can
not see, and to hear sounds that others can not hear. I
have never yet mentioned Alatamba to you. I am going
to tell you something about him now.

"One night, while encamped on the Lualaba River, in Central Africa, a native chief came to tell me that he had received information that it would not be safe for my party to go forward on the following day, as a hostile band had assembled to oppose our further progress. I inquired of him how long they had been together, and he answered about an hour.

"'How far are they from here?' I asked.

"'A day's journey,' he answered.

"'How did you get this information?'

"'Alatamba told me an hour ago.'

"'Who is Alatamba?'

"'A spirit sent sometimes by God, and sometimes by the devil, to give information of coming events.'

"Then I learned that the information had been communicated to him by whisperings in his ear. He had all that day heard a voice saying to him, 'Danger at Ollalaga for the white men!' and this had been repeated, he said, a thousand times or more, and was even then ringing in his ears.

"I laughed, for I had read something about false perceptions, and was satisfied that the chief was suffering from hallucinations of hearing; but he persisted that there was no deception about the matter, for that his wife, who was endowed with what they call 'pishatook,' could see Alatamba whispering to him, first in one ear and then in the other. However, I saw only hallucinations and superstition, and I ridiculed the well-meaning chief. The next morning, in reply to my question, put in the most derisive manner, he stated that he still heard the voice repeating, 'Danger at Ollalaga for the white men!' and his wife, who was present, declared that she saw Alatamba whispering to her husband.

"Then I got angry; I called them both a couple of impostors, and drove them out of my camp. They went away, the chief repeating, 'Danger at Ollalaga for the white men!' and his wife making signs that Alatamba was flitting here and there about him, whispering in his ears.

"I resolved to go forward, and made my preparations accordingly. But now a strange thing happened to me : the idea expressed by the words, 'Danger at Ollalaga for the white men!' began to run through *my* head. At first I thought it was only the natural consequence of the words I had heard, and I tried, by thinking of something else, to dismiss the subject from my mind ; but, do what I would, there was the idea represented by the words, 'Danger at Ollalaga for the white men!'"

"But you heard no voice, papa," said Louise, who had listened with the most absorbing interest to her father's recital. "You only had the idea of the words, just as I have often had a part of a tune running through my mind sometimes for days together."

"Yes, but it was bad enough, for they came upon me with a horrible degree of fascination that was agony to me, and that I could not withstand. I tried to think of other things : I sang all sorts of songs, I talked with the rest of the party about things of interest, and of others for which I cared nothing. It was of no avail. I found that the airs I sang all fitted to those horrible words, and that I was singing them over and over again, and that everything I said seemed only the echo of what was passing in my mind.

"Still I would not yield. I did not believe that there was any reality in the idea, other than such as might be given by the morbid state of my own brain. A few days before I had had something like a sunstroke, and had suffered with dizziness and pain in my head ; and to this I attributed what I thought was the morbid working of my brain."

"And that is what it was," interrupted Louise ; "Doctor Grattan will tell you as much if you will ask him about it. Send for him, papa, and take his opinion and advice."

"My dear Louise, I am perfectly willing to hear what
Doctor Grattan has to say on the subject; but no opinion
of his could change views that are based upon my own
experience.   I have the evidence of my senses to guide
me; and by it I must be influenced, not by that of other
people."

"True, when they are in health and give you true evidence; but yours were severely disordered.   You were ill.
You were suffering at that very time, and they gave you
false evidence."

"So I thought.   As you know, I am not superstitious.
I am a man who is guided by facts, not by fancies or the-
ories.   I require things to be demonstrated before I yield
my belief, and I fought with all the force of my knowledge
and common sense against the eternal idea that was dis-
placing all others, and even the capacity for others, from
my mind.   But I could not prevail—'Danger at Ollalaga
for the white men!' was burned into my brain as with a
red-hot iron!"

For a moment he ceased speaking, as though he had
finished what he had to say, or as though he could not,
without additional pain, continue the recital.   Louise said
nothing.   She saw that argument would be useless; but she
resolved that not another day should pass without Doctor
Grattan being informed of what she was sure was her father's
ill-health.   Finally, he seemed to have nerved himself to
complete the story, for with a heavy sigh and a look of
helplessness he continued:

"The sun was pouring down upon us with all its tropical
fervor when we resumed our journey.   Ollalaga was distant
about twenty miles, and we expected to reach it before sun-
set.   It was a small village, and all our accounts had assured
us of the friendly disposition of the inhabitants.   We rode
along under the broiling sun, and I supposed it had some
influence in keeping up the everlasting idea in my mind,

for I felt nervous and irritable. My hands trembled vio-
lently on the slightest exertion, and some of the party noticed that my eyes were blood-shot. Then, as we approached
a wide, open plain that we had to cross, and in the whole
extent of which there was not a tree or a shrub, I heard a
soft, humming sound in my ears like the buzzing of a bee;
I began to fear that I was going to be ill, and I was confirmed in my notion that all the phenomena of which I
have spoken were but evidences of a diseased state of my
brain. I wanted to get to Ollalaga as soon as possible, so
that I might obtain the repose I knew I required, and I
therefore hurried forward as rapidly as I could through the
light sand of the desert, into which our horses sank over
their fetlocks at each step.

"At last the village, a straggling collection of wretched
huts on the edge of the desert, appeared in sight, and I began to think that under the shade of the palm-trees and by
a plunge into the river, on the banks of which the hamlet
was built, I might get rid of the idea that had, up to this
time, stuck so closely to me. Besides, if the logic of facts
proved that there was no danger at Ollalaga, that would be
a powerful factor in dissipating the idea.

"We approached within a few hundred yards of the village. I felt as though it would have been impossible for
me to go another mile, but I was encouraged by the fact
that everything appeared to be peaceful. We saw a few
women making baskets, and children were playing in the
water and running about engaged in their childish games.

"Up to this time I had had no impression of words being spoken to me. The whole thing was in my brain as an
idea, without the sense of hearing being implicated in the
slightest degree. But now the faint humming in my ears
seemed to be resolving itself into words—isolated and arranged without any proper sequence, but still the words
composing the sentence, the idea of which had so disturbed

me all day. Then suddenly I heard the words in their
proper order, 'Danger at Ollalaga for the white men!'
They were whispered in a soft, musical tone, not unpleasant, but with a distinctness that was wonderful; and, at
the same time, a gentle and warm breath seemed to be
blown upon my ear, and to be the medium for the sound.

"I turned involuntarily, for my first impression was
that some one of the party had ridden up to my side and
was whispering to me. There was no one there; but I
caught a glimpse of a dim, shadowy form fading rapidly
out of sight: and at that very instant a hundred savages
rose up from the sand, in which they had hidden themselves, and from every side discharged their arrows at us,
and then, rushing forward, completed the murderous work
by killing every living soul but me. I was spared—why, I
know not—and for many years I was kept in captivity.
But," he added, "I never heard the sound again, and the
idea ceased to recur to me. Alatamba had done his duty
in notifying me, and I had refused to heed his friendly
warning."

"It was simply a coincidence," said Louise. "You were
apprehensive, notwithstanding your efforts to be calm, that
there was danger. As to the chief who influenced you, of
course he knew what was contemplated. When his information was proved to have been well-founded, there was
no longer occasion for worry on your part, and the idea
disappeared spontaneously."

Mr. Lamar shook his head sadly. "You reason like a
materialist, Louise," he said; "you are a woman of little
faith."

"No—no—no!" she exclaimed, throwing her arms
around his neck, "my faith in you is supreme. There
is no one in all the world so dear to me, but I can not
view this matter as you do; I do not question a single one
of the facts, but I can not accept your explanation of them.

You were ill. The sun had disordered your brain. Dear papa, it was so! Ask Doctor Grattan. He will be here this morning to see you, as you requested last night; he will tell you what I do; or, rather, let us go to him. The morning air will do you good. Leave it all to me, and see if I do not get you rid of these fancies."

"But, my dear, I have no fancies. All that I have been telling you took place many years ago, and had gone out of my mind till recalled by more recent events."

"Do not think of them, papa dear. Come, let us go to the doctor's; perhaps a little medicine and good advice will make your mind as clear as a bell."

"My mind is as clear now as it ever was in my life. I have no fancies of any kind. I have no pain or other sensation in my head. I am to all intents and purposes in sound health, and for the first time in nearly fifteen years. You seem to think I am insane, or at least that my mind is not in a perfectly healthy condition. If you do, you never were more mistaken in your life. Of course, I have more or less remorse as the consequence of the great crimes I have committed; but I expect, through time and repentance and your society, to get rid of that ere long, and live in a state of mild and quiet happiness for all the rest of my stay on earth. In a few days I will tell you the whole story. You will need all your fortitude and all your love to support you, and it is possible you will turn from me with disgust. Of that I must take the risk."

"I do not believe you have committed any crimes," said Louise, tightening her embrace, "and, if you have, I shall not cease to love you. I know what you are now. You have always been good to me, good in everything. It is impossible that you can ever have deliberately and knowingly, and of your own free-will, been bad."

"I shall not try to convince you now," he said, with a melancholy smile. "I will tell you all, and you will then perceive for yourself. Now, I will go with you for a walk, but not to see Doctor Grattan professionally, for I do not require his services."

"I want to see Cynthia. We are practicing a duet together. Her voice goes very nicely with mine, and when we have quite learned it you shall hear it."

She said nothing more ; but she nevertheless determined that she would consult Doctor Grattan about her father's health, for she felt assured that there was ample ground for apprehension that some serious disturbance of his mind was at hand, even if it had not already made its appearance.

As they went out of the door, she stopped for a moment to sight the windows of the doctor's house, in order to ascertain which one coincided with the position occupied by the light she had seen last night. Standing where she had stood the night before, she looked over the top of the cedar-tree. The line of vision struck the large bay-window at the end of the house to the left. It was in the doctor's library.

"I have been thinking," said Mr. Lamar, after they had traversed about a half of the way to Doctor Grattan's, "that I will ask him to give me an evening this week in which I can tell him the whole story from beginning to end. I shall do this, not with the view of getting his medical opinion or advice, but in order to obtain his views relative to the enormity of my crimes, and of the course to pursue in order to lessen their effects upon the world, and to prevent the further extension of their influence."

"Doubtless you will find Doctor Grattan's friendly advice as valuable as his professional," said Louise, glad that her father was going to confer with the physician, even though merely as a friend. "He appears to be a gentleman of excellent sense."

"Yes, he takes in the essential points of a subject bet-

ter than any man I ever met, and arrives at a decision when
most persons would have done no more than to begin to get
an inkling of the matter submitted to them. His brain
works easily and well. I have often perceived, when I have
been discussing some abstruse point with him, that he has
comprehended my argument, and got ready his reply, before
I had fully put my ideas into words. What a pity that he
should be buried in this out-of-the-way village, where there
are nothing but catarrhs and lung-diseases, and an occasional accident, to engage his attention ! He ought to be
a great physician in a great city."

"He might say almost the same of you, papa," said
Louise, laughing. " But you are very much mistaken if
you think Doctor Grattan has nothing to do but to attend
to a few sick people. He has his hot-house and his daughter, and, last but not least, his book. Upon this he works
till late at night, or early in the morning."

"A medical book, I suppose ; though what he can find
in the diseases of the Platonians to write about passes my
comprehension. Spill, the carpenter, wheezes dreadfully ;
Hicks, the storekeeper, appears to have sciatica ; Tim Maddox always has a cold in his head ; and old Mrs. Withers has
a perpetual neuralgia : but I should not think these were
sufficiently interesting, from a medical stand-point, to warrant their being put into a book."

"You talk sometimes about women jumping at conclu-
sions," said Louise, who was always quick to see the weak
part of a statement, "and I heard you telling Doctor Grattan, a day or two ago, that they often make erroneous assertions for the pleasure of disproving them. Now, sir, Doctor Grattan is not writing a medical book. Consequently,
your allusions to the infirmities of the Platonians are entirely misplaced."

"I supposed a physician wouldn't care to write any
other kind of a book, even if he knew how."

"Doctor Grattan, however, does care to write some other kind of a book, and he does know how."

"Oh! then you know all about it?"

"Certainly! He has often consulted me on the subject. I feel very proud of the fact. I am describing the ball-dress of the heroine."

"A novel!"

"Yes. And why not?"

"Why not? I'm sure I don't know. Of course, he has a right to inflict a novel on the public if he chooses. Only, if he draws his characters from Plato, it will probably be rather uninteresting."

"It is not uninteresting, I can assure you. I've read a part of it—or, rather, he has read it to me. It is a remarkable book. The delineations of character in it are marvelously natural. He is a man of close observation, and—a rare qualification—he knows how to write good English."

"You seem to admire him, my dear, as much as you do his book. I am glad of it, for I have been thinking that, as I may be taken away at any moment, it would be a good thing to appoint him my executor, in which event he and you would be often brought into intimate association."

"Dear papa, how can you talk in that way? You are likely to live quite as long as Doctor Grattan. If you ever speak to me again about your dying, I'll run away."

"Alone?"

"No, indeed! I'll go off with Mr. Spill. He's very much in love with me."

"He wouldn't marry you even if his present wife were out of the way. He thinks you're the daughter of a pirate."

"The daughter of a pirate!"

"Yes. He thinks I'm a pirate-captain in disguise; or, rather, out of business for the present. He saw the skull and cross-bones that an old sailor tattooed on my arm when

I was a school-boy, and, as I did just now, he jumped at a conclusion."

"Well!" said Louise, laughing heartily, "are you a pirate-captain? You look like one, I must confess," she added, stopping to survey him from head to foot, and pretending to examine his appearance with a critical eye. "There's a certain ferocious expression in your eye, a savage curl of your mustache, a rollicking, devil-may-care, raw-head-and-bloody-bones expression on your face, conjoined with a walk-the-plank sort of a gait, that are intensely piratical, and that induce me to think that Mr. Spill is not far wrong."

"No, he is not far wrong."

"Then you are a pirate-captain?

'Up, up with my flag, let it wave o'er the sea;
I'm afloat, I'm afloat, and the rover is free!'"

She sang the words merrily, waving her handkerchief, and then, appearing to recollect that she was in the public street, suddenly stopped. Then, perceiving the grave expression on her father's face, she also became grave.

"No," he said, as though talking to himself, and as though he had not heard the refrain she had sung—"I am not a pirate-captain. I am worse than that. I shall tell the doctor and you what I am," addressing her directly, "but you must not breathe a word of it to another soul; for if it were to be known they would hang me, and I am not quite ready to die yet."

She smiled sadly. "More delusions," she thought. "It is certainly necessary for him to consult the doctor." Then to him:

"It is too cruel a subject to joke about," she said, "or I would say something that would make you laugh."

"Then say it, my dear; Cornelius Agrippa declared that it is the duty of every man to make his neighbor laugh whenever he can.    Laughter helps the digestion, quickens the circulation, purifies the brain, and rids the soul of the memory of the ills that bear heavily upon it. Surely these are desirable objects to accomplish with most people.    They are specially so with me.    Therefore, if you can make me laugh, do it by all means."

He spoke bitterly, and Louise was not sure whether he was speaking seriously or ironically.    But they were at the doctor's door, and it was not necessary for her to pursue the subject further.

But, just as they were about to enter the house, he stopped.    "Do you recollect," he said, "when the Signora Lambrochini came from Naples to see me and to ask about her son Alberto, who was one of our party?    Yes, I see you do.    Well, I told her a falsehood, or rather a number of them, and I have never ceased to reproach myself for my mendacity.    But to have told her the truth then would have been death or insanity to me.    So I lied, in order to save my life or my reason.    It was a mean piece of business meanly done.    I feel better now that I have told you of my deception.    But—you are having a sad experience of your father's character, my dear."

She made no reply.    She did not know which of the two stories was the truth and which the delusion.    But she did know that her father was incapable of willful deception. Then they went into the house.

# CHAPTER VIII.

## "MAD AS A MARCH HARE."

DOCTOR GRATTAN had been out on his first round of visits, and had got back when the Lamars, father and daughter, arrived at his house. He received his visitors in the room that was peculiarly his own. There was another, his office, that was devoted to his medical work, and that contained his medicines, instruments, and other parapher-nalia of his art, and the appointments of which were not of the most elegant description. It was here that he saw such patients as called on him, and here that he prepared the medicines that he prescribed; for in Plato there was no apothecary, and Doctor Grattan was obliged, very much to his disgust, to dispense his own prescriptions. He got over a good part of the disagreeableness, however, by giving less medicine in a year than most physicians with his practice, but with half his enlightenment, would have given in a month.

As to the other room, the one in which he stowed him-self away when his professional labors were over, or when he wished to be alone, it was different from any other room in the house; or, for the matter of that, from any other that anybody had ever seen before—essentially, radically, inherently, and from top to bottom different. In shape it was pentagonal, the only one of the kind, Doctor Grattan used to say, in the whole world. There were plenty of hexag-onal and octagonal rooms in the new-fangled cottages that

were being built, but a pentagonal one, with all the sides
and all the angles different, was unique. Originally, the
apartment had been a parallelogram, twenty feet wide by
thirty long. At one end was an immense window, taking
up nearly the whole width of the room, and on each side
there had been two other windows. It had been added to
the house by Dr. Robinson long after the completion of
the building, and was used by him as his laboratory and
library, being the one in which he had passed the greater
part of the latter years of his life. The accompanying
figure will give a correct idea of this room as originally
built by Dr. Robinson :

It will be seen that the occupant had so arranged it that
there would be no lack of light, for there were no less
than five windows, one of them very large, in the apart-

ment. At one end was his table, and here was where the greater flood of light fell ; and it came from above as he sat with his back to the large window, for the lower sections of the solid oak shutters were always kept tightly closed.

But his successor had different ideas relative to his requirements. He did not want so much light, and he did want what to his mind were certain conveniences, which, in its original state, the room did not possess. Moreover, he hated symmetry with a hatred that a Japanese decorator might have envied, whether it related to color, or form, or numbers. " The most beautiful woman I ever saw," he had one day said to Cynthia, when she was remonstrating with him on what she called the disfiguring process he was carrying out in his room, "had one eye larger than the other, and they were of different colors. The two sides of a person's face are not alike. Nature abhors symmetry as much as I do. One hand is larger and more nimble than the other. No two fingers or toes are of the same size or shape ; there is nothing symmetrical about a tree, or the two sides of a mountain, or the shores of a lake. There is only one heart and one stomach, and one liver and one spleen, and one mouth and one tongue, thank God ! Symmetry is the refuge of weak minds. This room is the most horrible-looking apartment that can be conceived of. Look at the windows, exactly opposite on the two sides and at equal distances from the ends ! Look at the door and the large window, and the fireplace centered as though placed with a micrometer ! The most perfect figure the mind of man ever imagined is an irregular pentagon, and into that I am going to convert this room."

" There must be something crooked about your brain, papa dear."

" Something crooked about my brain ? Yes, I think so. At least, I hope there is. The lower you go in the scale of creation the more symmetrical is the brain, while the higher

you go the more irregular, eccentric, and convoluted is this
godlike organ of living beings, till when you reach man it
is a mass of irregularities. No two corresponding parts of
the surface of the brain are alike. No two square inches of
any part of its exterior resemble each other in shape, arrangement, or structure. And you have only to inquire of
the first hatter you meet, when you next go to New York,
to be told that the two sides of a man's head have differed
in every individual that has ever bought a hat from him.
Look at the skulls in the anatomical museums of Europe
and America. Did you ever see one that was symmetrical ?
And if not skulls, why rooms ? Answer me that now, Miss
Cynthia Grattan ! If I had to christen you over again, I'd
call you Eurythmy."

"A medical lecture," cried Cynthia, laughing merrily.
"I think you might drop the shop when you are talking
with a woman. I'm not a medical student. As to my name,
it's good enough as it is, thank you," courtesying to him as
she spoke ; "and I don't care to change it for a barbarism
like that you mention."

"Heaven hear the girl ! A barbarism ? It's the purest
Greek—a great deal purer than Cynthia, let me tell you.
Come here, you baggage ! "

Cynthia came close to him, and he put his arm around
her waist and drew her toward him.

"What I say, my dear, about symmetry doesn't apply
to you," he said, looking fondly into her face. "You're
the loveliest of God's works for me. Now, get out and let
me alone to construct my irregular pentagon ; or, stay—
will you help me ? "

"That's the way you subdue your enemies, is it ? " said
Cynthia, with a glad smile, as she put up her face to be
kissed. "Now, I understand the devotion of old Mrs.
Withers. Yes, I'll be magnanimous ; I'll help you. What
is it you want me to do ? "

"Take hold of the other end of that chalk-line, and hold it where I tell you ; and don't let go just as I am making it snap against the floor."

For several minutes he went with her around the room, marking out with the chalk-line the places where the new partitions were to go ; and then, having completed the task to his satisfaction, he stood with Cynthia in the middle— if it could be said now to have a middle—of his newly defined room, and surveyed the proposed alterations with great glee.

The accompanying diagram will give an idea of the doctor's proposed changes :

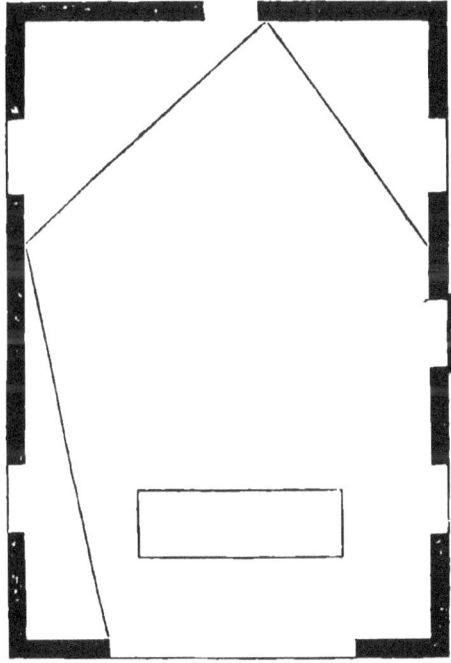

"You don't mean to say that you're going to have the room shaped like that ?" exclaimed Cynthia, looking with undisguised disgust at the lines she had helped to make.

"It's simply horrible ! It's enough to give one the delirium tremens by day and the nightmare at night." .

"I flatter myself that that is what any geometrician would call an irregular pentagon. No two of its sides are of the same length, and no two of its angles equal. It's beautiful; I'm in love with it already. Now, I'll get Spill here to-morrow, and in a day or two I'll have a room—"

"The like of which," interrupted Cynthia, "is neither in the heavens above, in the earth beneath, nor in the waters under the earth."

"Now," continued the doctor, not heeding her, "I have three good-sized closets, each one lighted by a window, in which I'll keep such books as I don't use often. Then the lines are so arranged that the heat from the fireplace is thrown into the center of the room. I'll have a table a little longer than Dr. Robinson's, and the light will come in from behind and to the right, just as I want it. Nothing could be more admirable."

Cynthia, who had been looking very critically at the lines, suddenly burst out into a laugh, while she clapped her hands with glee.

"What's the matter with the girl now !" exclaimed the doctor. "Do you mean to say that there are not five sides ?"

"Oh, no ! There are five sides," said Cynthia, almost smothered with laughter; "but, if some one doesn't hold *my* sides, I think I shall drop. Only to think that you should have made a room without any door in it ! Don't you see that you've cut off your door ? How are you going to get into this wonderful room ? "

"Cut off the door ? So I have ! " For a moment he stood and looked at the line which passed just in front of the door, while Cynthia continued to poke fun at him.

"You might have a step-ladder outside and come in through one of the windows, or you might put a hoisting-apparatus into the chimney. A pentagonal room ought to have some very extraordinary way of getting into it ; or, as it would be too symmetrical to use the same means for going in and for going out, you might enter by the chimney and depart through the window, or *vice versa.*"

While she was speaking, the doctor was walking the floor from point to point, and surveying the actual lines and the directions of many possible ones that he was forming in his mind.

" No," he said at last ; " I can't have a pentagon without shutting off the door, and a pentagon I am resolved upon. I might bring each of these lines "—standing with a foot on each of the two that came together at the right of the door—" one on one side and one on the other of this door ; but then I should have an irregular hexagon, for the door would form a side, though a small one, of my room. I'll have it as it is, and cut a door in the new partition. Then intruders will have to go through two doors instead of one to get into the room, and I shall be more secluded than with only one door. Do you hear that, you sapient young woman ? You'll find it more difficult to get in here than you have been thinking, and you'll have to exercise your talent for symmetry on some other part of the house. For, by the soul of Euclid, this room is going to be a pentagon ! "

And a pentagon it was. Spill was sent for, and the alterations were completed ; if not in the most elegant manner known to the art of architecture, certainly with due attention to strength. Then a question had arisen relative to the decoration. Cynthia had suggested a design in paper that she had seen in a book on household taste, and that could be had in New York ; but the doctor declared that he would have no paper on his walls, but that he would cover them with red canton-flannel : so red canton-flannel it was, he himself putting it on, spending several afternoons in tacking it to the walls. Then he put on

6

a frieze of the same kind of material in black, and bordered
the doors and windows with black braid, so as to conceal
the large tacks, and his walls were done.  It must be confessed that the general effect was good, even if he had, as
Cynthia suggested, put them in mourning for the degra-
dation they were compelled to submit to in being made
parts of a pentagon.

The ceiling was kalsomined in a pale green that went
well with the black and red of the walls ; and on the floor
was an old Turkey rug that had belonged to his mother,
and to her mother before her, in the early post-colonial
times, when the trade of Boston with the East was more
extensive than it is now, and much more select.

Then came the question of curtains.  The doctor insisted on his favorite material, canton-flannel in yellow ;
but on this point Cynthia made a decided stand, declaring
that, the day he put yellow curtains to the windows, that
day she would walk out of the house.

"Doubtless," the doctor had answered, with an ironi-
cal laugh, "to come back again when you have finished
your walk.  There's no such easy way as that of getting
rid of you."

"I'll get married."

"Ha, ha, ha!" laughed the doctor.  "I'm glad to
hear it.  But to whom ?  You'll find marriage not quite
so easy as walking out of the house.  To be sure," he
added, stroking his mustache, and assuming a contemplative air, "there's Will Hadden.  He was speaking to me
on the subject a few days ago.  I rather discouraged him
then, but perhaps—"

"Papa ! will you stop ?" cried Cynthia, turning as red
as a rose, and laying her hand on his shoulder.  "You
know I will never leave you.  But, O papa, don't put
yellow curtains to the windows ; yellow and red make such
a horrible contrast."

"Well, well, have it your own way ! Perhaps another shade of red would do. But if ever you threaten me again with marriage, I'll put up the yellow curtains."

Finally, a few old Delft plates, that had been in the family for nearly a hundred years, were hung on the walls. Several comfortable chairs and a lounge were brought from other parts of the house, a large table was placed at the point selected by the doctor, and last, but not by any means least, the long wall on the left of where the doctor would be seated was furnished with a low book-case, into which the works most likely to be required by the occupant were placed. This wall was over twenty feet in length, and consequently gave a good deal of book-space. Then the apartment was pronounced complete, and the doctor had taken formal possession.

All this was only a short time prior to the arrival of the Lamars. Before that time the room had remained unoccupied, and in pretty much the same condition as when old Dr. Robinson had left it.

The reason for the alteration was to be found in the change that had come over the doctor's mind. When a young man at college he had had literary aspirations, and had contemplated—notwithstanding the fact that several poets and novelists had told him that not one man of letters in a thousand makes a living by his profession—devoting himself to writing fiction.

"Don't do it," an old novelist—one who had produced about a dozen romances—had said to him. "If you want to live by your pen, write school-books, which sell by the million. Novels don't pay. You've read my last, 'The Mills of the Gods'? No? Well, get it and read it, young man, and don't only read it, but study it. It will improve your style, and teach you how to manage incident. Well, as I was going on to say, I spent six months in writing that book. I paid for the stereotype plates four hundred dol-

lars, and I have received twenty per cent of the retail price
on the copies sold—four hundred and fifty.  Now see how
the account stands :

"Six months' time in writing it......... $2,500
    Stereotype plates.....................   400
                                          ———————
        Total cost to me.............. $2,900
"Twenty per cent on four hundred and
    fifty copies, at $1.50 each, being
    thirty cents a copy .............   $135
                                          ———————
        Loss........................ $2,765.

" Twenty-seven hundred and sixty-five dollars loss on
one book, to say nothing of the others !  No, my young
friend, whatever you do, don't write novels for a living."

" But, then," Grattan had replied, " you had the honor."

" The honor ! " sneered the veteran novelist.  " Yes, I
had the honor, such as it was.  But did you ever know that
kind of honor to get a man a piece of bread and butter ?
No, sir !  It allows him to starve.  It's the worst thing he
can have, for it puffs him up with a false pride, and pre-
vents him picking a pocket or committing a highway robbery to save himself from hunger."

Grattan had laughed at all this ; and, as most young
men would have done under like circumstances, took his
own course.  He wrote several tales and novels ; but when,
after great difficulty, he succeeded in finding a publisher
who thought they might sell, he found to his disappointment that they did *not* sell, so that he had his labor for his
pains.  Yes, and something more—a knowledge of what
the public wanted, and improvement in his literary style.

For nearly twenty-five years he had done nothing in
the way of literature beyond an occasional contribution to
some medical journal ; but for the last year the desire to
write had become strong within him, and he felt that con-

fidence in himself which most men that are worth much
feel, and without which few make any great stir in the
world in any department of work, mental or physical. So
the room was altered to suit him. He was obliged, so
he said, to have certain surroundings which harmonized
with his mode of thought. Without them he could not
write.

The novel had been begun, and was well under way,
when Louise Lamar came to stay in his house till her own
was ready for her. Every night he wrote a certain definite number of pages. He found that, unless he gave himself a set task, he was apt to pass the evening in his comfortable arm-chair, smoking and indulging in reflections
more agreeable than profitable. As to thinking deeply
about his plot or his characters, when he was not at the
table with his pen in his hand, he soon discovered it to be
an impossibility. Everything had to be developed in the
act of writing.

He was not engaged with his book when Mr. Lamar and
Louise entered the room. He and Cynthia had been discussing their visit of the night before, and he had reiter-
ated the opinion he had often expressed to her—that Mr.
Lamar was threatened with serious brain-disease, if indeed
he was not already experiencing the initial symptoms. It
was natural, therefore, that he should form the idea that
the present visit had reference to the subject about which
he and his daughter had just been expressing their anxiety.
He did not have long to wait; for, as soon as the two young
ladies had left the room to go to the drawing-room to practice the duet they were learning, Mr. Lamar opened the
conversation.

"Can you give me a few minutes of your valuable
time?" he said. "I wish to talk with you about myself.
Not in regard to my health, which is now, I think, quite
good, but relative to my spiritual condition."

"I am a bad man, I am afraid," laughed the doctor, "to give advice on such a subject. Why don't you see Mr. Craig? He's a sensible man, and for a country parson a *very* sensible one."

"I prefer you, for you are a man who has seen, I think, a good deal of the world, and can, therefore, enter into my feelings better than one who has spent his life in a country village."

"I shall certainly do all in my power to aid you."

"Thanks. Have you observed that upon several occasions I have become agitated when certain subjects have been under discussion? Once, you may recollect, I let a valuable plaque fall when you made a jesting remark about the King of Congo, or some such personage."

"I remember it," said the doctor. "I supposed it was an accident."

"So it was an accident, but one produced by a cause acting upon a guilty conscience. Again," he continued, "last night you made a reference to superstitious beliefs, and again I was agitated. I determined to overcome my weakness, and I therefore asked you to look at a painting representing an escaped Siberian prisoner. I hung that picture on the wall in order that I might see it daily, and thus become, if possible, habituated to the recollections it always calls up, and last night I determined to still further harden myself by directing special attention to some of its characteristics. But I had overestimated my strength. The strain was too much for me, and I was obliged to leave you, overcome, as I was, by the dreadful thoughts that flashed through my mind."

Doctor Grattan listened in wonder.

"What," he asked himself, "can the man mean by this extraordinary exordium, which in itself is evidence of a disturbed state of mind, approaching insanity?"

There did not appear, however, to be anything for him

to say. He, therefore, looked as expectant and at the same
time as sympathizing as the circumstances seemed to require. Mr. Lamar resumed :

"As you are aware, I have suffered, ever since you have
known me, with severe pain in my head, and some other
evidences of an abnormal condition of my brain. You
must have observed at times, also, that I have been agitated and confused and absent-minded when there were
no apparent reasons for such conduct. There have been
many much more decided indications than these, of the
state of my mind, but they have occurred when I have
been alone, and sometimes in my sleep, and I have never
even alluded to them before. The chief one—the one
which has been the prime factor in inducing my morbid
condition—is what I now desire to mention to you, and at
the same time to make a confession which I confidently
anticipate will result in still further giving me peace of
mind."

"You certainly have not been well," said the doctor,
"and I am not sure that you are well now. Had·you not
better defer this explanation till you are better ? You are
now excited. Your eyes and face show it. Yes," he continued, taking Mr. Lamar's wrist in his hand, "and your
pulse shows even more disturbance than I thought. Defer
what you think you ought to say to me till you have become more quiet."

"If I do that, I shall never tell you. I am as composed
now as it is possible for me to be under the circumstances.
Of course, any allusion to the subject which for years has
tormented me produces more or less disturbance of my
mental equilibrium, and speaking of it unreservedly, as I
am about to do, will certainly agitate me. But that is unavoidable, and will take place just as surely a twelvemonth
from now as at the present time."

"Very well," said the doctor, perceiving that opposition only still further disturbed him. " Go on, and tell me all about it."

" Of course," continued Mr. Lamar, bowing his head in acknowledgment of the doctor's submission, " you have met with cases in which an idea or a set phrase has continually been present in a person's mind, notwithstanding all efforts to banish it ? "

" I have read of such cases, but I have only seen one, and in that the patient, a man, committed suicide to escape the infliction ; or, rather, in obedience to the imaginary command which at a subsequent period directed him to drown himself."

" Yes," exclaimed Mr. Lamar, excitedly, " that is a case in point. You can understand my condition, I am quite sure. But in the instance you mention there was a morbid state of the brain present that induced the constant idea and subsequent hallucinations ; whereas, in my case, there was no such origin. Now, let me explain." He then repeated the story which he had that morning told to Louise, and, continuing, said :

" Not long after that incident, when I was in the first days of my captivity, the idea, one very hot morning, occurred to me to propose to King Olluka, whose prisoner I was, that he should enter into the slave-trade, and, giving me my freedom, put me in position to carry on negotiations with the Portuguese of the Atlantic coast for the sale of such captives as he might be able to take. For a long time I resisted this idea, but it was constantly passing through my mind, and at last was never absent from it during my waking moments. It was in the form of words : ' Become a slaver ; talk to King Olluka ; you will be free ; you will be enormously rich.' All this was being made a part of my mental being just as much as my personal characteristics are parts. I could no more have prevented it than I could have flown. Try I did, by every species of mental and physical diversion at my command, but it was no use : the order to become a slaver and to talk to King Olluka was ever in my mind.

"Then, like your patient, I thought of suicide, but, unlike him, I had not the courage to attempt it. I thought of Louise, whom I had left almost alone, and I could not make up my mind to abandon all hope of ever seeing her again. Had there been only myself, I should not have hesitated an instant."

"Yes, you must have suffered greatly ; but then, doubtless, after a while you found the impression becoming less vivid, and so finally wearing out altogether."

"If it had been an impression only, such would probably have been the case, but it was not an impression that originated within, but one that came from Alatamba."

"And who or what is Alatamba ? "

"I did not mention him when I related my first experience with these recurrent ideas. He it was that told me there was danger for the white men the morning of the day that saw all the party killed but me. I saw him then for one single instant as he flitted away from my side."

"You surely," cried the doctor, rising to his feet in his excitement, "don't mean to tell me that you believe that what I call a morbidly recurrent idea and hallucinations of hearing were the results of the agency of a supernatural being ? "

"Yes, that is exactly what I intend to be understood as saying. What I know, I know, and this is a matter within my own knowledge."

"If you believe such stuff as that—you, an intelligent, educated man—I am forced to the conclusion that you are as mad as a March hare—a veritable lunatic."

"The question of my sanity," said Mr. Lamar, with dignity, "is not what I came here to discuss. On that point I require neither assurances nor doubts. My own consciousness is enough for me."

"But, my dear friend, your consciousness is not enough for me," replied the doctor. "I know that your mind is deranged. You are the victim of hallucinations and delusions, and I can not for one moment consent to accept your insane perceptions and ideas as facts."

Mr. Lamar in turn rose from his chair and began to pace the room excitedly. His face was flushed, his eyes were blood-shot, his manner was that of a man suffering acutely, and yet desirous of exhibiting as little evidence as possible of his pain. The doctor looked at him sharply, watching every gesture, every change of countenance, as though seeking for confirmation of the opinion he had expressed, or perhaps hoping to find some indication that he had judged too hastily. Hitherto he had held Mr. Lamar high in his estimation ; but now, notwithstanding the fact that he was confident that his friend was insane, he felt that he was beginning to regard him with diminished esteem. There was something weak and pitiable in a man whose whole life had taught him the folly of superstition, and whose education should have placed him above such a belief as that which he had avowed, accepting as true the silly ideas that had filled his head. Even insanity, the doctor felt, could scarcely excuse such a lamentable fall.

"As I said," resumed Mr. Lamar, after he had crossed the room several times, and had become measurably calm, "I did not come here for a medical opinion. However much I value your views upon all questions that concern my health, I am not in any need of medical advice at present. When I am, I shall be only too glad to come to you. I have now only to ask that, as a special favor, you will at this time consent to drop the consideration of my sanity conversationally. You, of course, will think what you please. You may, for all I care, regard me as the most pronounced lunatic outside the walls of an asylum. And I further request that you will hear me out. I have much yet to say. In fact, I have told you nothing of what is most on my mind."

The doctor reflected for a moment before giving an answer. He was afraid that conversation upon the subject of the delusions of his friend would tend to aggravate his excitement, and yet he knew, from experience of similar cases, that repression has often a like effect. Moreover, it seemed that Mr. Lamar only desired to state results, and with a view to his medical treatment it might be well to become acquainted with the details of his life before he came to Plato. He, therefore, signified his willingness to hear what Mr. Lamar had further to say.

"Whether," continued that gentleman, "I was the victim of delusions and hallucinations, or whether I was receiving veritable communications from a supernatural being, is a matter of little consequence now. The effect upon me was overpowering, whatever may have been the character of the influence. It was as though a continual weight was pressing on my brain, with more and more force every day. And at last I yielded. I went to the king, who had always treated me well ; I told him that I could put him in relation with coast-traders, and arrange for the selling into slavery of all his captives in war. He agreed to my propositions. I was allowed full liberty. I induced him to make war upon various peaceable tribes. I sold the men and women and children to the dealers in human flesh and blood, and subsequently I bought a ship, and became a trader on my own account. I have landed several thousand slaves in Cuba, and have thus added largely to my wealth. I knew all the time that it was a wicked, a cruel work, but I felt that I was doing the will of others, and not my own. I was powerless to resist."

# CHAPTER IX.

HE ceased, and, covering his face with his hands, bent his head in an attitude of the most abject humiliation, as though ready for any punishment that might be awarded.

"I don't believe a single word that you have said!" exclaimed the doctor, bluntly—"not one word! Of course, I don't mean to be understood as accusing you of falsehood, but I *do* mean to say that you are the victim of a horrid delusion. You a slaver! A gentle, quiet, reserved, humane, and educated man, a vile slave-dealer! It is an impossibility. Not one word of what you have said is true. Your mind is disordered—let us hope not permanently."

"I am not surprised that that is your opinion. Any physician, I suppose, would hold a like one. But that is not the question under discussion. What I want from you is advice as to the best method of repairing the injury I have done to humanity. For myself, I care nothing; but there is one who is very dear to me, dearer than all the world besides, and whom I can not bear to think of subjecting to the disgrace of being known as the daughter of a slave-trader—captain of a slaver, by law a pirate, and liable to punishment as such. What I have told you, therefore, must be, for the present, at least, a secret between us. If I could, without injury to Louise, deliver myself up to the authorities and be hanged for my crimes, I should be perfectly willing to undergo the penalty."

"I do not know what would be my feelings toward

you," said the doctor, "if I believed you to have been a slaver; but, as it is, I entertain the deepest pity for you, and shall do all in my power to make you once more a happy man. May I ask," he continued, "whether, when I first made your acquaintance, you fully believed all that you have now been telling me?"

"My dear friend," exclaimed Mr. Lamar, fixing his eyes on the doctor's face, and lowering his voice to almost a whisper, "that is another feature of my case, and one that I have not yet mentioned to you. At that time, and until up to last night, in fact, ever since my return from my absence of fourteen years, I have had the idea of confessing my crimes constantly before me. As in the other instance, I resisted. I endeavored to persuade myself that I had never been a slaver, and, strange to say, I almost succeeded. How easy it is for us to believe what we wish to believe! Had it not been for Alatamba, I should easily have brought myself to the belief that the idea of my ever having been a slaver is a delusion, just as you, my friend, think it is; but with him contests only terminate in one way. He is always victorious.

"Besides," he added, as the doctor, apparently lost in reflection, continued to gaze out of the large window, at the black, frowning mass of Pitchoff—"besides, I was visited not only by Alatamba, but by hundreds of native Africans, men, women, and children, probably the spirits of those that had died during the middle passage. Some of them were in chains, and these they shook menacingly at me—and I heard the clanking, too—as though threatening me with further trouble if I did not confess, and endeavor to repair the wrong I had done."

"In the name of God!" said the doctor, under his breath, though regardless of the presence of his friend, "what is to be done? Poor Lamar! Poor Louise! And this is only the beginning of the sorrow!"

"Oh, my dear doctor," said Mr. Lamar, with a light laugh, "don't, I pray you, give yourself any uneasiness, either in regard to me or my daughter. If I am a lunatic, I am a mild-mannered one, and not at all disposed to be violent. I shall neither injure myself nor her, nor commit any act of violence against any one else, nor destroy property. I have no recurrent ideas now ; the visitations of the slaves, with their fetters, and their angry, sometimes pleading faces, have ceased ; Alatamba has departed. I am desirous now of being a good man. Help me ! All my ill-gotten gains, amounting to over a million dollars, I wish to dispose of in some way for the benefit of the negro race in this country. It is in this that I want your aid. Will you give it to me ?"

"I will think of it," said the physician, cautiously, for he was not yet fully prepared to act in the case. "In the mean time, you must not blame me if—without revealing a word of what you have told me—I make some inquiries relative to the truth of what you have said, and in regard to your antecedents. The whole thing is so preposterous to my mind, that I can not and do not believe it. But I do believe you to be very ill, and, as you have of your own accord asked my advice, you must allow me to take such measures for qualifying me to give it as may seem to me necessary. In my inquiries I hope to have your assistance."

"All of which means," said Mr. Lamar, eying the doctor very sharply, "that you wish more time in order that you may determine whether to help me, to cut my acquaintance, or to put me into a lunatic-asylum. Am I not right ?"

"Nearly so."

"You do not believe, then, that I was the captain of a slave-ship ?"

"No, I do not."

" You admit that I am sincere in my confession—that I at heart believe it ? "

" Yes, but I can not conceive that any man in his right mind would make such a horrible accusation against himself unless it were true, and he were influenced by remorse, or perhaps repentance. Your own account of the matter convinces me that it is not true."

" Well, I will help you to ascertain the truth. About three years ago, when I was getting ready to land a cargo of slaves on the Island of Cuba, my ship was discovered by a United States cruiser. With great difficulty I succeeded in getting all the slaves ashore except half a dozen or so, who were drowned. But the next morning my vessel was surprised by the man-of-war, and I was obliged to set it on fire, and, with my crew, take to the boats. We were pursued ; shot after shot being fired at us, and eventually before we reached the shore every boat was destroyed, and every man in them either killed outright or drowned except myself. I was picked up in the surf, carried on board the man-of-war, and put in irons. I knew I should be hanged without mercy if taken to the United States ; so I bribed the sentry put over me, and one night, while the vessel lay at anchor in the harbor of Matanzas, my fetters were removed, and, dropping silently into the sea, I swam ashore. There I found friends, and shortly afterward I resumed my right name, and sailed for Leghorn. Now, all you have to do in order to ascertain the truth or falsity of this statement, is to write to the Navy Department at Washington for the particulars of the destruction of the slave-ship Alatamba, and the capture and subsequent escape of Captain Juan Lamarez—for that was the name I had assumed."

This was so circumstantial that for a moment the doctor was staggered ; but he was equal to the emergency, and again his medical knowledge came to his assistance.

"That is all very direct," he said; "but my experience, and that of other physicians, go to show that when an insane person determines to confess himself guilty of a crime he never committed, he is shrewd enough to give all the information attainable relative to the concomitant circumstances of the assumed offense. Now, I happen to know something of the case of Captain Juan Lamarez. It was fully reported in the newspapers of the day, and I read the account with interest. Besides, the commander of the American man-of-war that effected the destruction of the slaver was my cousin. Unfortunately, he is dead, but I have a letter from him somewhere among my papers minutely describing the whole affair. Perhaps," he added, "your memory of the occurrence is sufficiently vivid to permit of your giving me his name, and the name of his ship."

"Oh, yes. The vessel was the screw-steamer Canandaigua, of eight guns, and she was commanded by Commander Clyde, of the United States Navy. How remarkable that he should have been your cousin! So he is dead," continued Mr. Lamar, reflectively; "poor fellow! how did he die?"

"You had not heard that he was dead?"

"No. I have heard nothing about him since my escape. He treated me rather harshly."

"Not, if your story be true, so harshly as you treated him; for, if you are Captain Juan Lamarez, you shot him in cold blood in the streets of Matanzas, within a week after your escape."

For a moment Mr. Lamar was apparently completely stunned by this blow of the doctor's, but it was only for a moment.

"Not in cold blood," he said, in a low voice, "and not intentionally. He attempted to arrest me. I drew a pistol, which he seized, and in the struggle it went off, killing him upon the spot. I was tried by the Cuban authorities and acquitted. Do you not recollect these circumstances, doctor?"

"I believe there was a story of the kind, and that the murderer was acquitted by the Cuban court. But what could you expect in a country where all the sympathy was against the Americans and in favor of the slaver?"

"Do you believe now," rejoined Mr. Lamar, without heeding the doctor's question, "that I am an ex-slaver who formerly passed under the name of Juan Lamarez?"

"I must confess to being a little staggered," said the doctor. "Either you are the most accomplished liar that ever lived—a view which I can not accept without doing the most painful violence to my feelings—or you are, as you say, a man that has committed crimes of which he is now repentant, and for which he sincerely desires to atone, this being your view of the matter; or you are a lunatic, whose insanity is chiefly manifested by the delusional idea of a change of identity, you supposing yourself to be one and the same person with Captain Juan Lamarez. This is the theory which it still appears to me is the most probable."

"As the question can not be immediately determined, perhaps you will kindly listen to my plans for making restitution to the utmost of my ability. You will, then, I think, discover an additional reason for accepting my statements."

"I am ready to hear you," said the doctor, "but I do not promise to give you advice. The matter may be of such a character as to preclude my saying a word on the subject."

"Very well; I shall not endeavor to persuade you against your inclinations. You shall be perfectly free to speak or to remain silent. I have ascertained by thorough examination that my profits from the slave-trade have amounted in round numbers to one and a half million dollars. This sum I can no longer consent to keep, and I propose, subject, however, to your better judgment in the matter, to establish a college at some place in the South, which shall be exclusively devoted to the education of negroes of both sexes. This will be some recompense to the race I have so greatly wronged."

The doctor's face expressed the astonishment he felt. "Surely," he thought, "this is the strongest point yet adduced in favor of Mr. Lamar's sincerity. The man must feel the truth of what he says. The idea that he may, for some ultimate purpose, be lying, is altogether out of the question. Aside from the fact that no man not out of his mind would falsely accuse himself of infamous crimes is so extremely unlikely that it must be regarded at once as untenable, the willingness to give away a million and a half of dollars to establish the truth of a falsehood makes a case so utterly preposterous that that alternative must be given up also. Clearly, Mr. Lamar believes that what he has related is true. And the question still to be decided is, ' Is he sane or insane ?' "

Now, the doctor knew that the giving away of any amount of money to establish the truth of a false confession is entirely within the range of probability so far as lunatics are concerned. He had known of cases in which confessions had been made which, if true, would have caused the forfeiture of the person's life, but in which the existence of insanity was clearly shown, and the confession proved to be false. He knew that often, when some great crime has been committed, persons from all parts of the country come forward and offer to deliver themselves up to justice as the criminals, and that in their confessions they set forth with the most elaborate minuteness all the particulars of the murder or other outrage they accuse themselves of having committed. He knew, too, that, during the Middle Ages, individuals of both sexes, when accused by hysterical or malicious men and women of the most grotesquely preposterous crimes, often astonished their friends by confessing themselves guilty, and marching to the stake as witches, sorcerers, murderers, or heretics, with the utmost *sang-froid*, all the while admitting the justice of their punishment. He knew that not long ago a young girl had been, on her own confession, without the least corroborative evidence, condemned to death for the murder of her little brother, a child to whom she had always shown herself to be attached, and who was fond of her. Indeed, he had come to the conclusion that confession unsupported is almost worthless as an evidence of guilt. As yet, Mr. Lamar's confession was absolutely without support. It rested on his word alone, the word of a man subject to delusions and hallucinations, and whom he was bound to regard, by every principle of medical science applicable to his case, as a lunatic. No, he did not, could not, believe it. And this proposition to found a university for the negroes of the South, taking a million and a half of dollars from his fortune for the purpose, only made his insanity more apparent.

But he saw that Mr. Lamar was thoroughly in earnest, and that with or without his advice he would give the sum named at the earliest possible moment. The idea was strong, and it must be realized. He was framing in his own mind a reply to the proposition—one that would, while being non-committal, give him time for investigation and reflection—when his visitor resumed his remarks :

"You are surprised, I see, at the plan I have proposed, which, whatever it may be from your stand-point, is from mine a very inadequate act of justice. As though money," he continued, covering his face with his hands, "could shut out from my eyes the scenes of misery they have witnessed, or from my ears the groans, the clanking of the chains, the

pleadings for pity that have struck upon them, or banish
from my mind the recollection of all the wretchedness and
woe I have caused. No—no! nothing can ever do that,
much less a paltry sum of money.

"No!" he went on, "the most that I can hope to accomplish is to take off some of the load from my own conscience
by acts of contrition, and to do something toward amelio-
rating the condition of the race I have so grievously injured."

"I don't see that any such scheme as the one you propose will be a measure of exact justice. If you could find
the individuals that you forced into slavery, or their descendants, and could restore them to their native land with
some recompense for their sufferings, it would be well that
you should do so. But you have had nothing to do with
the negroes of our country. You did not bring their ancestors here as slaves, nor have you injured them in any way.
It would be just as logical for you to found a college for
the education of Scotchmen, because, as you say, you killed
Captain Clyde, who was of Scotch descent. And," he added,
"since you are endeavoring to straighten things out and to
ease the weight on your conscience, don't you think you
ought to do something for Captain Clyde's widow and orphan children? He only did his duty in capturing you,
and in endeavoring to rearrest you in Matanzas."

"True! but I have not forgotten them; I intend to
place them far above want. It is a matter, however, which
requires to be entered upon with caution; for, if my identity were known, I should suffer great inconvenience at
least, and perhaps I might be arrested, and have to stand
trial as a slaver."

This speech rather unsettled the doctor's convictions.
It was a rational view, rationally expressed. A lunatic, he
argued with himself, would be anxious to suffer all the pen-
alties due to his confessed crimes; but here was one who was

not disposed to place his life in danger. His remorse did
not extend that far. There was common sense in that,
whatever there might be in the rest.

"I can manage it for you," he resumed, humoring Mr.
Lamar's idea, "so that no suspicion shall attach to you.
When you are ready to make them the recipients of your
bounty, let me know."

"I certainly shall. But I have not yet fully informed
you of my plans. The renunciation of my ill-gotten gains,
and the employment of them for the benefit of the negro
race in this country, may not be strictly logical, as you say,
but it is the best thing I can do. ' I can not find the poor
creatures that I took to Cuba and delivered into slavery.
If I could, I would buy them all and send them back to
their own country. I therefore do the best I can, and I
get rid of the money and do good with it. That, however,
is not all that I propose to do. I must undergo some punishment. Retribution is due me, and I shall not seek to
avoid it. I can not, however, give myself up for the action
of the law without bringing disgrace on innocent persons,
among them my own child. If I were alone in the world,
believe me, I should go at once to New York and deliver
myself into the hands of the authorities to be hanged as a
slaver. As things are, I am forced to select my own punishment; and when you hear me, I think that you will admit that it is sufficiently severe.

"In addition to the wealth that I made by the slave-
trade, I am worth several million dollars—more, in fact,
than I can estimate with exactness, for I have made large
sums lately. This is my own to do with as I please. My
daughter has her own fortune of nearly equal amount,
which came to her from her mother, and over which I have
no control. My property consists mainly of shares in gold
and silver mines, bonds, stocks, and mortgages, easily converted into cash. My daughter's was chiefly New York

city real estate, till quite recently. Like my own, it has
been vastly increased by profitable investments. Now, I
am going to give up every cent I possess and add it to the
slave-trade gains. There will then be not far from five
millions, and with that I think a vast educational establishment can be organized, and I shall have done something toward subduing the feeling of remorse which now
fills my heart. I shall, to the utmost of my ability, have
punished myself, and this without doing injury to a living
soul."

"The money is, of course, as you say, your own, to do
with as you please," said the doctor, who had stared in
amazement at his friend while he was expressing his intention of reducing himself to poverty; "but I think your
scheme a very absurd if not impracticable one. Certainly,
I can not yet consent to aid you. If you are insane, as I
verily believe you to be, it will be my duty, as your friend
and the friend of your daughter, to do all I can to prevent
your giving away your estate. If you are sane, it would
still be a question with me how far I ought to aid in the carrying out of measures of which I do not approve. A university for people who do not need it, and who could not
make use of its advantages, except to a very limited extent,
would be an absurdity. Suppose you educate five hundred
colored youths every year, what is that number to the entire negro race of the country? You had better establish
primary schools, and give them the rudiments of a common
education. However, if you require an answer from me
now, I shall have to decline. But I am willing to hold the
matter under advisement till I can be absolutely sure of the
truth of what you have told me, and that your mental condition is not what I fear."

"That strikes me as being reasonable. I shall, therefore, in one month from to-day, come to you for your answer. Till then, we will, if you please, let the matter rest,

except in so far, of course, as it may be necessary to discuss
it in connection with the inquiries you may see fit to make.
And now shall we join the young ladies ? From the sounds
that reach my ears, I am led to believe that they have finally
mastered the duet."

"Excuse me, please," said the doctor ; "I would rather
be alone for a few minutes. The fact is, my friend," he
continued, going up to Lamar, and laying his hand on his
shoulder, "the story you have told me, and the fears it has
excited in my mind, are a little too much for me just now.
I shall try to see you before you leave ; but, in the mean
time, let me assure you that, however incredulous or harsh
I may have appeared, I have had no other thought than
that of your welfare."

"I believe you, my friend !" exclaimed Mr. Lamar,
shaking the doctor's outstretched hand. "I am quite sure
that, were I in your place, I should act in a similar manner.
The probabilities, I admit, are greatly against the truth of
my confession. At any rate, I suppose you are satisfied
that I am not willfully lying ?"

"Yes, that is perfectly clear ; but I would rather, I
think, believe in your insanity than accept your story as
true. It would be a vastly greater shock to me to know
that you had once been a slave-captain than to see you a
raving maniac."

"And to me, too. If I could accept your view of my
mental state, it would be a great relief to me. Unfortunately, I know I am sane. All I have any right to ask,"
he continued, moving toward the door, "is that you will
judge me as charitably as possible."

He was gone ; and the doctor, throwing himself into his
big chair, looked out at his beloved mountains. In succession, his eyes rested on Pitchoff, and Hurricane, and
Mount Mary, and Mount Dix, and the Giant ; but the solace
to his troubled spirit that he desired was not forthcoming.

On the contrary, each moment as it fled left him in a more perturbed condition, for each moment led to the perception of additional painful circumstances, which, whether the story he had heard were true or untrue, made the situation worse. What was to be done? What was *he* to do? If his friend were left to himself he would undoubtedly alienate his estate, and, as the doctor was convinced, through a motive that had no substantial basis for its initiation.

But this was not all. There is no limit to the delusions of a lunatic, and no way of foreknowing to what they will lead him. He believed Mr. Lamar to be insane. At present he appeared to be capable of exercising a certain amount of control over his thoughts and actions, but there was no certainty or even probability that this self-command would continue, and that he would not be forced into the perpetration of some act of violence. At any moment the spark might kindle into flame, and an accession of frenzy be induced, from which the most direful consequences might result. And if such a result should ensue, on whom would the responsibility chiefly rest, if not upon the friend and physician, who, knowing of the existence of mental disease, neglected to take such precautions as would have prevented calamity?

And yet it would be an awful thing for him to be the agent of confining in a lunatic-asylum a man who, though insane, might be perfectly harmless, and who, he admitted, might be in the full possession of his reasoning faculties, and actuated in his intentions by a very proper feeling of remorse for real crimes against humanity and the laws of his country. In that event, what right had he to interfere, even though the self-imposed plan of atonement were absurd? Clearly none. Mr. Lamar had an undoubted right to do with his own as he pleased, provided that in so doing he injured no one. Louise, apparently, had her own fortune in her own right, and therefore no suffering was

imposed upon her by her father's alienation of his own estate. "Her own fortune in her own right," he repeated.
Then he looked out again at Pitchoff, and continued gazing
fixedly at it for several minutes. At last he rose from his
chair and put on his hat and overcoat, which lay on chairs
in different parts of the room. "I have had a narrow escape from making a rascal of myself!" he said, with the
energy consequent upon the muscular exertion incident to
thrusting his arms into sleeves that were somewhat too
small. "I'll crush it all out," he added, savagely, from between his teeth, as he succeeded with a violent contortion
in getting the coat adjusted, "if I die in the attempt!"
Then, without joining the party in the other end of the
house, he went out of the door and hurried off in the direction of the village.

7

# CHAPTER X.

AFTER leaving Mrs. Hadden's, the doctor walked briskly toward Hurricane Castle, as though anxious to make his visit and be done with it. Several days had elapsed since Mr. Lamar had revealed what purported to be the great secret of his life. In the mean time George Frazier had arrived and had met with his accident, and the professional duties that had thus fallen upon the physician had absorbed a great deal of his time and attention, so that he had not thought so much of what had been told him as would otherwise have been the case.

But, for all that, it had been rarely altogether absent from his mind ; and, upon several occasions, he had sat down deliberately to think over the strange recital, and to endeavor to arrive at some definite conclusion relative to the mental state of his friend. The more he had thought of the matter, however, the more contradictory did the chief features appear to be. Evidently Lamar had suffered from illusions, hallucinations, and delusions, the three categories of symptoms which alienists regard as most indicative of the existence of insanity. But it might be that, for all this, the story was true. There was nothing at all incompatible with the hypothesis that Lamar had been insane, and at the same time a slaver, or he might have been in the slave-trade while in sound mental health, and have become insane at some subsequent period. That he was insane now the doctor had no doubt. His story might, therefore, be a mixture of truth and delusion ; but in what proportions the two ingredients were mingled, or what was truth and what was delusion, it was impossible for him to tell with accuracy. There was certainly enough of the one to establish the fact of his mental alienation. There might be enough of the other to prove him to have been at one period of his life a man whom all civilized nations regarded as an enemy of the human race, to be punished to the utmost extent of human power.

There was another matter very dear to the doctor's heart upon which the story told by Mr. Lamar bore hardly. From the first day of his acquaintance with Louise he had begun to feel an interest in her much warmer than any that mere friendship would have developed. He had felt somewhat ashamed that he should find himself experiencing a kind of emotion that he had for long supposed would never again be kindled within him. He had reflected that he was forty-five years of age, and the father of a grown-up daughter only a few years younger than the woman that he had thought of with feelings which, if reciprocated, would lead to her becoming his wife. He had done his utmost to prevent Cynthia becoming aware of the state of his heart, and in this he had been so successful that not the slightest suspicion had been aroused within her. He was not altogether sure that a second marriage would not be an act of disloyalty to one who had, ever since her birth, been first in his affections. It would seem like a reproach to her ; like an attempt on his part to better his condition, when he had all along been making her believe that nothing was needed to complete his happiness. How could there, with a wife in the house, be the same confidence between father and daughter that there had been in all the years that had passed ? Another would, then, take the first place in his heart and in his household, and Cynthia, who had stuck by

him so faithfully through her whole life, would be relegated
to a lower plane. Thinking of these things, he had fought
against the new passion with a degree of vigor that would
have been successful if the contest had been conducted
with the same intensity as had characterized it in the beginning. All the time that Louise had been an inmate of
his house he had borne himself toward her with a reserve
and a delicacy that would have commended themselves to
the most exacting sticklers for etiquette. Indeed, upon
several occasions, Cynthia had reproached him for an indifference to the presence of his friend's daughter, that she
thought was not altogether compatible with politeness, or
with his duties as a host. He had shown no disposition to
pay her any of those little attentions that he might have
given without exciting suspicion in her mind, or in Cynthia's, that there was a deeper sentiment than such as any
gentleman might properly feel for any lady. As often happens in such cases, he had gone to the other extreme, and
had been not far from causing Cynthia—who knew well
how courteous he could be when he chose—to form the
idea that for some reason or other he had taken a dislike
to Louise. This notion had worried her not a little ; for
she knew how strong were her father's prejudices, and that,
when once he had made up his mind that a certain person
was disagreeable to him, a change was almost as little to be
looked for as an alteration of the courses of the heavenly
bodies.

But, on the night that he and Cynthia paid their first
visit to Hurricane Castle, he abandoned the contest, and
had determined that he would allow his feelings to take
him whithersoever they might lead. He thought of the
matter all that day, and almost determined that he would
not accompany Cynthia on her contemplated visit. He
argued with himself that if he stood out now, when the
temptation to yield was at its greatest height, there would

be no difficulty in subduing his inclinations at any subsequent period. The prestige of victory would be with his intellect and against his emotions, and he could, he conceived, go to Hurricane Castle at any time thereafter without feeling his pulses stirred or his blood warmed at the sight of the woman that he now knew had power to quicken his heart and heat his blood.

He had allowed Cynthia to take him out of the house, ostensibly toward Hurricane Castle, but he had not intended to accompany her all the distance; and, as they walked along the path leading to the other end of the village, he thought every moment that he would turn back, and let her go the rest of the way by herself. But he had yielded, little by little, to the impulse that was gradually becoming stronger, till at last he had found himself standing at the end of the little bridge that Mr. Lamar had built over the Canemanga. Here he had made a more determined stand. It was now or never with him. If he could not win this fight, there would be no use in contesting the matter any longer. Cynthia was against him. She had even seemed to be aware that he had been thinking of this visit all day, and she had ridiculed him for the hesitation he had shown, and which she had declared in her laughing way was assumed. Then he had crossed the bridge, and from that moment he had determined that he would win Louise Lamar for his wife if he could, trusting to Cynthia's love for him, and her attachment to her friend, to cause her to view the idea of a step-mother with favor.

At the same time, he was aware that he might be reckoning without his host. He had never had the slightest reason for supposing that Louise regarded him with any feeling approaching in the slightest degree to love. She had invariably shown pleasure in his society; but he very soon perceived that this was due rather to what he knew, or what she supposed he knew, than to any personal liking for him. She was fond of natural history; she liked to talk of the habits of animals, and of their affinities one with the other, and of everything, in fact, that related to them, and she had discovered that in Doctor Grattan she had a mine of information on these and kindred subjects that she could always work with advantage. Her own knowledge was not deep, reaching only to such topics as are treated in that delightful book, "The Natural History of Selborne." But she was desirous of pursuing, for the meadows and the mountains about Plato, a course of studies similar to that that White had so charmingly carried out in the little village of which he wrote. She foresaw that without some such diversion time was likely to hang heavy on her hands in a place so isolated as was Plato, and so devoid of all social attractions. It was natural, therefore, that she should evince a predilection for an association with the only two people in the village that it was probable would prove congenial.

Besides this, Doctor Grattan's character was one of the kind that commands respect from all that are thrown into relations with its possessor. There was nothing small or mean about him; he was truthful in all things, frank, open-hearted, generous. At times, as we have seen, he was hasty; but he was quick to repair any injustice into which his heat of temper might have led him. He had fallen into the habit of disregarding many of the conventionalities of life in his intercourse with the Platonians, but he was by nature and education refined in disposition and courtly in manner, and no one could display these traits to greater advantage, when he chose to do so, than could Doctor Arthur Grattan. With Louise he was calm, neither unduly familiar nor reserved, and showing by his attention when she spoke that he was not indifferent to anything she might say. There was nothing of the schoolmaster about him in his way of giving information. He did not talk as though his knowledge were superior to that of the person to whom he was speaking, but rather as though he were simply recalling to his or her recollection a fact or an incident which everybody knew, but which the questioner had for the moment forgotten. He was not very far from being twice the age of Louise. He did not look to be forty-five; he did not act as though he were; and, so far as his feelings went, he could not perceive that they were any different from those he experienced when he was a much younger man. "If a man," as a Frenchman has said, "is only as old as he feels," Doctor Grattan could not have been over twenty-five. He was young in body, and younger still in mind. His gait had lost none of its elasticity, his arms none of their pristine strength, his body none of the powers of endurance it had possessed when he had roamed over the mountains and through the forest, when both were covered with snow, in pursuit of the deer and bears with which they had, twenty years before, abounded. His thoughts were still fresh; there was none of the cynicism that men so often exhibit when they are beginning to feel that they can no longer enjoy the pleasures of their youth; none of the querulousness of advancing years, and nothing indicating a disposition to look back at his youthful days as being those in which his happiness had reached its highest limit. With any of these traits he would never have begun to write a novel.

He, therefore, believed that, although he was more than twenty years older than Louise, he was not unfitted, on the score of age at least, for appreciating her modes of thought, or for comprehending the true methods of securing her happiness. How she might regard the matter he did not know; but he did not think that there would be any difficulty in obtaining knowledge on that point before allowing himself to become so deeply involved as to render a retreat embarrassing or painful.

Then had come Mr. Lamar's story of his life, and then he had, for the first time, been brought to the contemplation of the fact that his duty as her father's friend and physician was altogether incompatible with the idea of marriage with the daughter. And another matter, scarcely of less importance, had been forced upon his attention, and had given the finishing-blow to his matrimonial aspirations. He had thought very little of the circumstance that Louise was the heiress of great wealth, while he was a comparatively poor man. He knew, of course, that her father was rich, and he took it for granted that she would receive the bulk of his property at his death. But Mr. Lamar was likely to live as long as he himself, and the contingency of Louise coming into the possession of a large estate seemed to him sufficiently remote to do away with the idea that he was actuated by a desire to acquire any portion of it for himself. She was also much younger than he, and it was, therefore, probable that she would outlive him by many years.

But, in the course of his narrative, Mr. Lamar had incidentally mentioned the fact that his daughter had her own independent estate, large enough, too, to make her a wealthy woman in her own right. This placed a somewhat different face on the matter, and caused the doctor to think whether it was altogether a creditable proceeding for him to seek in marriage a woman whose fortune was to be estimated by millions, while his own was scarcely the year's interest of the third part of her capital.

So he resolved that the budding emotion should be crushed out before any serious damage were done. He did not anticipate that there would be a contest in this effort. His feelings had not as yet been deeply touched, and the mere determination to subdue them would, he had no doubt, be sufficient to accomplish the end in view. But it would not do, he was well aware, for him to be very much in Louise's presence till he could see and hear her with a little more cold-bloodedness than now attended his association with her. He felt that there was a magnetism in her smile, and in every word she spoke, that drew him toward her, while he remained almost unconscious of the effect that was being produced. This must cease, and the only way for him to stop it was to avoid her as much as possible, and, when forced by circumstances to be in her presence, to keep such close guard on himself that the weak spots, that he knew existed in his armor, would not be unprotected against the assaults of the enemy.

He crossed the bridge and ascended the little elevation on which Hurricane Castle stood. His visit was to Mr. Lamar, and solely of a professional character, being made in compliance with an urgent message that he had received from the patient early in the afternoon, that he would call at as near six o'clock as possible. He looked at his watch as he rang the bell, and found, to his surprise, that Mrs. Hadden and Will had kept him longer than he had intended, as it was already fifteen minutes after the hour fixed by Mr. Lamar.

The door was opened by the old butler, who had been in the Lamar family for many years, and who was, in consequence, admitted to a degree of familiarity that would not have been attempted by the other servants. He was very apt to presume upon the fact of his long service, and frequently extended his freedom of utterance to others not of the household. As to the other servants, he ruled them with a rod of iron.

"I've been on the watch for you for the last quarter of an hour," he said, as he ushered the doctor into the hall. "Mr. Lamar is getting to be very impatient, and has sent down several times to know if you had come."

Doctor Grattan looked at the old man in some astonishment. He was not accustomed to being found fault with, even by implication. He reflected, however, that it was scarcely worth his while to utter the sharp words that were on his lips; so he contented himself with a look that was, however, sufficiently expressive, and said with some asperity of manner:

"Well, I am here now, and perhaps you will have the goodness to notify Mr. Lamar," with which words he walked into the drawing-room to await the man's return. He found here ample material to engage his attention for several hours at least, even had he not been occupied with his own thoughts, which were of a sufficiently engrossing nature at that particular time to keep his mind busy. In fact, the room was almost entitled to rank as a museum, containing as it did objects of surpassing value and interest in the various departments of art, both of ancient and modern times. At another time he would have examined them with loving eyes, for he was fond of such things, but now he scarcely gave any one of them more than a passing glance. He was thinking of the man up-stairs that had sent for him, and, in spite of himself, of the woman that he had determined should henceforth be no more to him than any other of her sex that for the last twenty years had come in his way. He stood in front of a large bay-window, from which he could see several of his beloved mountains. He was beginning to lose faith in their power to give him relief from harassing emotions, for he had recently appealed to them many times in vain. He was so deeply occupied with his thoughts that he did not hear the light step on the thick rug, or know that any one was approaching him till the tones of a soft, low voice struck upon his ear, and caused him to turn around to find that Louise was coming toward him.

"I am glad you have come," she said, holding out her hand; "there is something not right with papa—something that I do not understand. He appeared to be very well all day yesterday and the day before, but this morning he came down to breakfast looking very haggard, and, upon inquiry, I found that he had sat up all night writing. He would not tell me what he had been writing about; but he muttered a few words, as though talking to himself, and I heard the word 'confession' among them, but what reference he intended by it I have no idea."

"Doubtless," said the doctor, barely touching her fingers with his, "he had a fever, and was slightly delirious. Of course, in that case he would speak wildly and incoherently."

"But he has been so before," rejoined Louise, "and then his thoughts seemed to be running on crimes of some kind or other. He has, I think, suffered some great wrong, one that has disturbed his mind to such an extent that it still weighs heavily upon him. He was absent from us on one occasion for fourteen years, and never, until a few days ago, has he spoken of anything that happened to him during that time."

"And then— ?" said the doctor, inquiringly.

"Ah! then he told me of things that I am sure could not have happened as he described them. I thought his mind was disordered, but I did not like to speak to you on the subject till I had seen something still more positive."

"Did he tell you of Alatamba, as he calls him?"

"Then he has been speaking with you, also? Yes, he told me of circumstances that I am sure could not have existed except in his imagination. But he was free from excitement, and evidently believed what he said."

"There is probably some truth in what he says, but there is with it a great deal that is, as you say, entirely baseless. He has suffered, and still suffers, from hallucinations of hearing, and occasionally of sight also. He hears unreal voices and sees unreal images. For a long time he resisted believing in the actuality of these impressions, but at last he accepted them, and now he credits them as firmly

as though they were real.   He can not, in fact, tell the difference between the false and the true.   Finally, other delusions have been developed ; but he talks so calmly about
them, and appears to be so logical in his assertions and
arguments, that I have not yet been able to determine
what is actual and what is the product of a diseased imagination."

He had scarcely looked at Louise, though, as she stood
by his side, he could at times feel her shoulder touch his
very gently as her chest rose in inspiration.   He was afraid
to turn his face toward her, for he was of a keenly sympathizing nature, and he doubted his power to restrain the
manifestation of his feelings under the influence of the expression of anxiety or grief which her words told him her
countenance bore.   To keep his professional interest entirely
separate from his personal emotion would, he was sure, be
a difficult matter, even under the most favorable circumstances.   Now it taxed his strength to the utmost.   The
easier way out of the dilemma would be to take no notice of
the effect produced upon Louise by her father's condition.
He was very much like the person who is endeavoring to
leave off a habit of using tobacco or alcohol.   It is easier
for him to stop at once, and absolutely, than to do so by
degrees.   Every cigar that he smokes, or potion that he
drinks, helps to feed the appetite and maintain the desire.
The suffering from entire abstinence is great, but the contest is a short one, and victory to the man of strong will is
sure.   As to the weak-minded, they fail under all circumstances.   Doctor Grattan was a man of iron will, and he
had in no direction manifested his power more than in the
control that he was capable of exercising over himself.   But
in this matter, and for the first time in his life, he found
that he was afraid to trust himself.   Hence he dared not
look Louise in the face, lest he should see there something
that would give strength to emotions that he intended to

crush out of his heart forever. It was a relief to him, therefore, when she asked him if he would go up to her father's
room at once.

"I will wait for you here," she continued, "for I am
anxious to know what you think of him. He does not
know you have come, for I left him asleep half an hour
ago, and I would not let him be disturbed. You will know
whether to wake him or not. He is very weak, and it appears to me that every day finds him worse than he was on
the previous day. He seems to be particularly unsettled
this afternoon. He was busy all the morning writing, and
has had Mr. Bishop, who is, I believe, a notary public, to
take the acknowledgment of his signature to some papers.
There is something wrong," she continued, in a lower voice,
as though speaking to herself—"something that I do not
understand."

Involuntarily he turned, and his eyes met hers. They
were fixed upon him with the pleading, anxious expression
that he knew he should find there, and that he had been
fearful he should not be able to resist. But he *did* withstand it. For an instant he wavered, and the words "My
dear child" were on his lips; but with a cold "I hope
there is nothing very serious," he moved away from the
window, and, leaving the room, ascended the stairs that led
to the floor above. A few steps across the hall brought him
to the door of Mr. Lamar's room. He pushed aside the
heavy *portière* that partly closed the entrance, and stood
within the chamber. All was as silent as the grave, and, in
the dim, uncertain twilight that came in with difficulty
through the closely-draped windows, it was almost impossible for him at the moment to distinguish the objects
about him. He threw aside one of the curtains, and gently
—for he thought his patient was asleep, and he did not
care to disturb him—advanced toward the bed that stood
at the farther end of the room. "Yes," he thought, "he

is asleep, and I am glad of it, for conversation with him now is what I am most anxious to avoid. No good can come of it till I have made up my mind more clearly about him." He bent over the bed and looked as intently as the faint light would allow at the recumbent form before him. Something in the attitude of the figure, or in the expression of the countenance, attracted his attention, and caused a little thrill of fear to flash through him. He placed his fingers on the pulse—very gently, as was his wont when examining a sleeping person. Suddenly he dropped the wrist and laid his face on the breast, as though to listen to the beating of the heart. "My God!" he exclaimed, rising to his full height, while a look of horror swept over his countenance—"my God, he is dead!"

For a moment he was so overwhelmed at the catastrophe that, accustomed as he was to see death in all its forms, he could not collect his thoughts sufficiently to do anything but stand and gaze helplessly at the lifeless man before him. Then he saw, almost on the very spot that his ear had touched when he had tried to discover some sign of life, a piece of paper folded like a note. He picked it up, and, carrying it to the window, perceived that it was addressed to him. To open and read it was but the work of an instant.

"I waited for you," it said, "till five minutes after six, and then I could wait no longer. Take care of Louise; I commit her to your charge.      JOHN LAMAR."

"He has killed himself!" he said in a voice hoarse with emotion. "How? Why?" He thrust the note into his pocket and returned to the bedside. Then, throwing down the coverings, he examined the body from head to foot. It was still warm, and life could not have been extinct for more than a very few minutes. But there was no sign of any wound or injury anywhere to be seen. Nor was there anything to indicate that the dead man had taken poison ; or, in fact, so far as could be discovered, that death had not ensued from some one or more of the natural causes that are classed under the designation of "visitation of God."

He was now once more master of himself ; and when that condition was predominant with Doctor Grattan, he was a man of quick resources and ready action. He therefore readjusted the bed-clothing and rang the bell, the little electric knob of which was close to his hand. In a few seconds it was answered by the old butler.

"I thought I'd come myself, sir," he began, as he entered the room. Then, seeing the doctor's grave face, he stopped, and, looking at the bed, seemed to divine what had happened, for his face became as pale as a sheet ; he trembled in every limb, and was unable to speak a word, his lips moving rapidly, but no sound issuing from them. Motioning him to approach, the doctor said to him :

"Mr. Lamar is dead. He seems to have died very suddenly. Sit here till I go and tell Miss Lamar what has happened."

The old man, still speechless, clasped his hands together and sank into the chair that the doctor pushed toward him.

"He is not good for much," said the latter to himself as he left the room, "not even able to call her maid. My God, what a trial is impending over that poor girl downstairs ! "

He stopped and leaned heavily against the wall, as though his own strength were failing him, but really overpowered with the thoughts that the awful event that had just occurred caused to spring up in his mind. How should he tell her ? How could he stand by and witness her grief, and yet restrain himself from all manifestations of sympathy ? Oh, if he could but clasp her to his heart and bid her find in his bosom a refuge from her sorrow! That, however, was still more out of the question than ever before. Between him and Louise Lamar death had placed a barrier that he could never expect to surmount—a barrier of gold, one that most lovers manage to get over easily enough, but one that he felt it would be almost criminal for him to attempt to scale. Well, it was his duty to tell her that she was fatherless, and the sooner the task were performed the better. There is nothing gained by trying to avoid the inevitable. The longer its consequences are postponed the more formidable they appear, and no one knew these facts better than Doctor Grattan.

She was still standing by the window when he entered the drawing-room, but, hearing his step, she turned toward him. He saw that she had been weeping, for her eyes were red, and they were still liquid with tears. He had thought that he would be cold in the announcement he had to make, and under the affectation of hardness conceal the emotion he felt; but one look at her was sufficient to convince him that frigidity now would be brutality. She must have seen from his face that he had bad news to communicate, for she took a step toward him with both hands outstretched, as though anxious to know the worst, and yet imploring forbearance in the telling. But, before he could reach her, she seemed to divine intuitively what had happened, for her arms dropped nervelessly, and she would have fallen had he not sprung forward and supported her.

"He is dead!" she said, scarcely above her breath, as he held her drooping form in his arms; "I saw it in your face."

"Yes, he is dead. God rest his soul!"

A low moan was the only sound that escaped her lips. He carried, rather than led, her to a sofa, upon which he gently laid her. Then he rang the bell for her maid, and, leaving her in charge of that young woman, went himself

to inform Mrs. Dobson, the housekeeper, that Hurricane
Castle was without a master.  Here he found as much self-
control as was necessary, and a mind fully capable of taking charge of the establishment in the emergency that had
come upon it.  This attended to, he went back to the
drawing-room, and in a few kind words gave Louise an account of what had happened, omitting, however, all reference to the note that he had found.  She listened in a half-
dazed sort of way, but he saw that the main force of the
shock was over, and that nothing of a serious nature, so far
as she was concerned, was likely to happen.

"I will send Cynthia to you," he said.  "She will stay
with you all night."  She held out her hand to him, without raising her face from the pillow in which it was buried.
He pressed it in both of his for a moment; and then, turning away, left the house in which Death had, at so early a
period of its existence, made his appearance.

As he opened the door, he saw a man standing on the
porch, and just about to ring the bell.  He laid his hand
on the visitor's arm.

"Don't ring, please," he said.  "Whom do you wish to
see?"

"Mr. Lamar."

"My friend, you can not see him."

"But I must see him."

"And I tell you, you can't see him."

"And I tell *you*," persisted the intruder, with some
vehemence of manner, "that I will see him, for I have a
warrant for his arrest."

"A warrant for his arrest?"

"Yes, on the charge of having been the commander of
a slave-ship."

"You are too late, my friend.  You will have to serve
your warrant in the next world, for Mr. Lamar is dead!"

# CHAPTER XI.

THE man started at these words and looked suspiciously at the doctor, as though apprehensive that a trick were being played upon him. The scrutiny seemed in a measure to satisfy him, for his features relaxed a little of their severity, and the tone in which he next spoke was softer.

"We have to be very careful," he said, "in matters like this, for attempts are often made to deceive us by pretenses that the men we are after are dead. Now, you see the crime of which Mr. Lamar is accused is a very serious one. It's a hanging matter, if he should be tried and found guilty. Of course, I can't be sure that you are not trying to fool me, while Mr. Lamar is getting off into the mountains. At the same time, I don't want to make more trouble where there is already enough. If you can prove to me that Mr. Lamar is really dead, I will go away, and that will be the end of the matter so far as I am concerned. Death, as you say, stops all arrests in this world, and I don't propose just now to go to the next world after him."

"I am the family physician," said the doctor, "and I live in this village. It is not likely that I would perpetrate a fraud of the kind you mentioned. I have just left the dead man. His death was sudden, and occurred not half an hour ago. His daughter is in there, overwhelmed with grief. If you will kindly say nothing of the object of your visit, I will take you to the bedside of the corpse. But if you disclose its purport you may kill the daughter, who knows nothing of the accusations against her father. The law, as generally administered in this country, is not unmerciful, and you don't look like a man that would willingly inflict needless pain."

"No, I am not that sort of a man; I only want to do my duty. I am the Deputy United States Marshal for the Southern District of New York. This warrant"—taking, as he spoke, a folded paper out of his coat-pocket—"was placed in my hands yesterday morning for service. Of course, I know nothing whatever about the reasons for its issue, or upon whose complaint it is based. I must make a return, and I can't do that till I know of my own knowledge that Mr. Lamar is dead. Let me see him, therefore, for one instant, and I'll take my departure for New York to-night, and no one here will be any the wiser for me."

The doctor had kept the door ajar. Telling the deputy-marshal to follow him, he re-entered the house, and the two noiselessly ascended the stairs to Mr. Lamar's room, meeting no one on the way. Keeping the lead, he approached the chamber of death, and looked in through the doorway, over which the *portière* hung. It was not necessary to enter, for a scene met his eyes that would have convinced the most skeptical officer of justice that civilization has yet produced that a dead and not a living man lay on the bed. Beckoning to his companion to approach, he drew aside the curtain so as to allow him to see what was going on within.

A lamp had been lighted, and was standing on a table by the side of the bed. Though it burned dimly, it gave light enough to show the face of the dead man in all its ghastliness. The shoulders were well elevated, and hence the eyes were looking almost directly to the front; and their dim, expressionless gaze fell full upon the officer as he peered curiously, and not without a shade of terror, into the apartment. But this was not all. At the side of the bed knelt a woman, her head bowed, her face covered by her hands, her whole attitude expressive of the most poignant grief, while her form shook with the violence of the emotion that swayed her. With a blanched face the officer drew back. "I am satisfied," he exclaimed below his breath; "I feel ashamed of myself for insisting on such proof."

"You only did your duty," said the doctor. "I do not see how you could have acted otherwise, and I thank you for the delicacy with which you have performed what I know you regard as a disagreeable task."

"I suppose that lady is his daughter?" said the officer, interrogatively.

"Yes."

They passed out of the house without encountering any one, and the two walked toward the "Bear," at which the officer was stopping. Not a word more was spoken by either as they traversed the deserted street. The doctor had more to think of than his brain, voluminous and active as it was, could satisfactorily master. He was anxious to get home, and, after sending Cynthia to pass the night at Hurricane Castle, betake himself to his pentagonal room, and give a loose rein to his thoughts and emotions. As to the deputy-marshal, notwithstanding the fact that his occupation was of a character to render him somewhat callous to scenes like that he had witnessed, he was grave to the point of taciturnity. The daughter's unrestrained grief at the bed-side of her dead father was, as being somewhat out of the run of his ordinary experience, a little too much for him. He, himself, was the father of a daughter of about, as nearly as he could judge, Louise's age; and the fact brought the matter home to him more nearly than would otherwise have been the case. So they walked on without a word till they came in front of the "Bear." Here they halted. The doctor held out his hand, which the other grasped.

"I hope you will say nothing about this matter," he

said, "while you are in the village. There are reasons that
render it quite certain to my mind that Mr. Lamar, if he
ever was a slaver, became one while insane. He certainly
was insane when he died. I shall be able to establish both
these points, and I shall make it the business of my life to
do so in a manner so thorough that no doubts can exist of
their truth. It would be a cruel wrong to his memory, and
to his innocent child, to allow false reports to be circulated
in regard to his honor before there is the opportunity for us
to contradict them. In a few days I shall be ready to meet
them, and then the sooner they are spread abroad and ex-
tinguished by facts, the better."

"As I said," replied the officer, "I am going back to
New York to-night. No one here but you has any idea of
the object of my visit. I did not even enter my name on
the hotel register as a deputy-marshal. I shall go back and
make my report to the marshal, who will make his to Judge
Conway, who issued the warrant, and that will be the end
of the matter."

"I know Judge Conway; he spent last summer here.
I shall write to him on the subject, and doubtless he will
not refuse to let me know the grounds he had for ordering
Mr. Lamar's arrest. Good-by," he continued, shaking the
officer's hand heartily. "If ever I can be of service to you,
call upon me; but you have not yet told me your name."

"Speight, Thomas Speight," answered the man. "It's
a sad affair all around, and I hope you may be able to show
that your friend wasn't guilty."

He went into the hotel, and the doctor, without going
in, as he had at first intended, to see how Mr. Frazier was
getting along, hurried on to his own home. It was a dark
night, even for Plato. The moon—if there was any—and
the stars were obscured by thick clouds brought from the
northeast by a sharp, piercing wind, betokening a snow-
storm. The mountains were indistinguishable in the gen-

eral gloom ; but, even if they had been lighted up by all the
heavenly bodies, Doctor Grattan was in no mood for regal-
ing himself with their grandeur.  As he walked along, his
head bent upon his chest, with no thought as to where he
was going, but trusting to the automatism developed by
his long acquaintance with every foot of the way, his ideas
began to crystallize into something like definite forms, and
one, more than any of the rest, stood out in painful distinctness : " What had killed Mr. Lamar ? " That was the question he asked himself a hundred times before he had arrived
at the door of " Mountain View." Not disease ; of that he
felt sure.  Not the hand of an assassin ; of that he was
equally certain. What, then, remained but suicide ? What
other interpretation could be placed upon the letter, which
the man must have written only a few minutes before his
death, and which he knew would be found by the physician
shortly afterward ? " I waited for you till five minutes
after six, and then I could wait no longer." These were
the words of the letter.  Did they mean that if he, Doctor Grattan, had been punctual in making his visit, death
would not have ensued ? If they did not mean that, what
else could they possibly mean ? Was he, then, by his tardi-
ness, responsible for his friend's death ? ' " My God ! " he
exclaimed aloud, " I could ask a thousand such questions,
not one of which I could satisfactorily answer." He looked
up as he uttered the exclamation.  He was at his own door.
His legs had brought him there of their own accord.  His
mind had been far away from them.  He opened the door
very softly and stepped gently on the hall floor as he went
toward the little sitting-room on the first floor, in which he
was sure he would find Cynthia.  The door was ajar, and
he looked in at the picture of refined comfort that was before him.  A cheerful fire of oak-logs was burning on the
hearth, in front of which was a little round table covered
with embroidery materials.  At one side sat Cynthia, plying

her needle assiduously, but every now and then stopping to
listen, as though waiting for some one whose step she expected to hear. Once a glad smile overspread her face. Of
what was she thinking? How quickly her smiles would
vanish when he told her the sad news with which his heart
was burdened, but of which he could not yet tell her the
part which concerned him most! Suddenly Cynthia
dropped the work at which she was engaged, and, letting
her hands fall to her lap, burst out into a hearty, ringing,
musical laugh. For a moment he was almost angry. It
seemed so strangely out of place to him in whose breast
were emotions very different from those that excite laughter. There was an incongruousness between the merry
peals and the gloom of his own mind that made the laughter sardonic in character, and for the moment he could not
disassociate the evidence of the mirth that was in Cynthia's
heart from the deep-seated solemnity of his own feelings.
The effect was painful to him, for it almost seemed as
though the°laughter was his own, and that he was putting
on the semblance of joy to deceive himself into the notion
that he was glad.

He remembered the instance of a woman that he had
once been called to see, and who, in one day, had had
brought to her home the dead bodies of her husband and
three children. A land-slide had occurred just above where
they had been working on the mountain, and had covered
them with earth and stones, depriving her at one fell blow
of all that she held dear in the world. But she did not
mourn or weep, or wring her hands, or sob, or faint away
in the semblance of death, as other women would have
done. She laid the dead bodies of her loved ones in a row
on the floor, and then, arraying herself in all her finery,
danced around them, singing and laughing at the top of
her voice. The neighbors came to the door, wondering at
the strange noises they heard within. She had locked it

and fastened the windows, and then, making a pile of combustible materials in the center of the room, declared that, on any attempt at forcible entrance, she would set it on fire ! Then she had continued her merry proceedings among the corpses all night. Her laugh was heard far away, till toward morning it ceased. Then the timid neighbors came back, and Doctor Grattan was sent for. He burst open the door, and there sat the woman, pointing at the corpses, and still laughing, but in a quiet, imbecile way, that was the strongest evidence of her physical and mental weakness. At the sight of the doctor and the wondering and shocked crowd of men, women, and children that stood at his back, she sprang to her feet, and, still pointing at the dead bodies, gave one unearthly peal of laughter, and dropped dead upon the floor, without, ever since her man and boys had been brought home to her, shedding a tear.

But his thoughts were not Cynthia's, and her laugh came from a glad and innocent heart, not from one overwhelmed by an appalling blow, as was the woman's. But in a moment she will change. One word from him, and then she will laugh no more for many a day. She ceased and resumed her work, but her face was still irradiated with a smile. Certainly her thoughts were pleasant ones. Suddenly she stopped again, and for a second time dropped her work and listened. The creaking of a board or some other noise had attracted her attention. She turned her face full in the direction of the door, and in an instant sprang toward her father, who stood just inside the room. Something in his look—yes, there must have been something in his look, if the face is ever an index of what is in the mind—caused her to stop midway, and to clasp her hands together.

"O papa !" she exclaimed, "what has happened ?"

"Something very dreadful, my dear. Mr. Lamar has been found dead in his bed !"

"Mr. Lamar dead?"

"Yes, he is dead, and Louise would like to have you stay with her to-night. She is suffering greatly."

"But how did it happen? Was it sudden? What did he die of? To think that he should be dead, when only last night he was in such excellent spirits, and not for a long time, as he declared, feeling better!"

"How it happened I do not know. His body was warm when I entered the room, and he had certainly not been dead longer than a few minutes. There were no marks of violence on his person, and no signs that his death had been other than a peaceful one."

"I will go at once to Louise. Poor dear! How little I can do to comfort her in her sorrow! What in the world will she do? She was so lovingly attached to her father. But what a strange death!"

"Yes, so strange that I am not sure that there ought not to be a *post-mortem* examination in order to ascertain the cause. The coroner will, of course, have to be notified. A death so sudden and unexplainable requires an inquest. I shall telegraph to him at Herodotus, where he resides. He will be here, I suppose, the first thing in the morning. Till then nothing can be done relative to the funeral. Will you ring the bell, dear, and tell Mike to hitch up the buggy? I'll drive you over to Hurricane Castle, send the telegram to the coroner, call in and see how Mr. Frazier is doing, and then come back to my den. There are many things I have to think about, and I don't care to enter on their consideration till I can do so with nothing else to distract my attention."

"Come to tea," said Cynthia, after she had given the directions relative to the buggy. "It has been waiting for you, and you must need it."

They sat down, remaining silent for several minutes.

"Did you speak with Louise afterward, papa?"

8

"Yes. It was my office to inform her that her father was dead."

"Poor Louise! How she must suffer! Of course, she was unprepared for such a sudden death?"

"I am not so sure of that. She was very sad before I went up-stairs, and, although she did not say so directly, I think she had forebodings of evil."

"What can I do for her in her trouble? She has everything she needs. There is so little that one can do for the rich."

"Ah! my dear, you can give her what will be far more acceptable to her than any material gift—your sympathy."

"That she shall have. Did you speak with her much after—after Mr. Lamar's death?"

"No, I am a bad hand at concealing my feelings. She saw from my face, just as you did, that something had happened, and then, when I told her what it was, she nearly swooned away. I left her with the housekeeper—who, by-the-by, is a strong-minded woman—and her maid. I had to return to the house, and, on going up quietly to the death-chamber, I saw her on her knees before the bed in an agony of tears and sobs."

Doctor Grattan was too much overcome to proceed. He rose from the table, and going to the window looked out, more for the purpose of hiding his tears than with the expectation of seeing anything. In a moment Cynthia was by his side and her arms were around his neck. Thus they stood, without either speaking a word, till Mike came to announce that the buggy was at the door. It did not take Cynthia long to get ready, and they were soon on their way over the dark road to Hurricane Castle. The doctor stopped at the telegraph-office, over which Mr. Bishop, who was also the postmaster, presided, and sent his message to the coroner. He found that the news of Mr. Lamar's death was already over the village, and that there were the wildest rumors, based upon the suddenness with which it had occurred, in circulation.

"You see, doctor," said the purveyor to the literary tastes of the Platonians, "I was up there all the morning, taking acknowledgments of his signatures to a dozen papers. I don't know what they were about, for he was careful to conceal their contents from me. Then he produced another that he said was his will. That required witnesses. I asked him if he had any choice in the matter, and he answered that Mr. Hicks had said that he was a filibuster, and Spill had declared that he was a pirate, and that he would like those two and me to witness his will. I went out and got them to go to the house, and we three witnessed what he declared was his last will and testament. Then he turned to Hicks and Spill and asked them point-blank why they thought that he was either a filibuster or a pirate. They were both so taken aback that they couldn't answer a word. He smiled at their confusion, and said: 'Filibustering has not been a very profitable business for any one. I certainly could not have made a fortune at it. As to piracy—have you heard anything within the last twenty years of a pirate-vessel roaming the seas? Don't you know that pirates are extinct, and have been during your and my life? Now, gentlemen, produce your proofs that I have ever been one or the other, or else confess that you have slandered me.'"

"Did he talk like that?" exclaimed the doctor.

"Like that? Yes, indeed! A more sensible man I never heard speak. The upshot of it was that both Hicks and Spill had to sign a paper in which they admitted that they had no evidence whatever to support their statements, and that they had been guilty of slander. They tried to get out of it; but he declared that, if they did not sign, he would have them indicted at the next term of court, and punished to the utmost extent of the law."

"He showed no evidence of being deranged, did he? His speech was perfectly coherent and intelligible?"

"Well, as to derangement," said Mr. Bishop, "if every person had as good sense as he showed this morning, there wouldn't be any use for lunatic-asylums. He was as clear as crystal. And, as to his speech, there wasn't a word out of place. I guess Mr. Lamar could have held his own, so far as brains go, with the best men in the country."

"Did he seem to be weak, bodily?"

"No, not specially. He was in bed, to be sure; but for the life of me I couldn't see why. I think he had been out of sorts some way or other in the night, but he did not show any signs of it when I saw him."

"When did you last see him?"

"Now, let me see," answered Mr. Bishop, casting his eyes up to the ceiling, as though it required some reflection on his part in order to make a sufficiently exact statement. "I got there," he continued, after a little time spent in contemplating the rather dingy aspect above, "at about eleven o'clock, and I stayed till half-past twelve, when I came home to dinner. Then I went there again at two, and I didn't get away till about half-past five."

"And at half-past six I found him dead. Good-night, Bishop. I shall want to talk with you again to-morrow. In the mean time, as you are a sensible man, don't speak about the matter till after the inquest, except to deny the foolish stories that are going around, that he shot himself or took poison, or killed himself in any other way."

Mr. Bishop promised discretion, and then the doctor joined Cynthia, who had remained in the buggy, and resumed his drive to Hurricane Castle.

It was the result of a hard struggle that he had with himself, when he decided not to enter the house that night; but the determination was strictly in keeping with the line of conduct he had marked out for himself. He knew that, every time he was thrown into association with Louise, he was in danger of losing his self-control. It was impossible for him not to feel tenderly toward her now. The mere idea of her suffering made his heart bleed, and, when he saw her on her knees before the bed on which her dead father lay, he could scarcely restrain himself from rushing forward and raising her in his arms. If it had not been for the presence of the deputy-marshal, he would doubtless have yielded to the impulse. So he left Cynthia at the door, after learning from the old butler that Miss Lamar was lying down in her own room, and, with an affectionate "good-night" to his daughter, drove away from the house.

He stopped at the "Bear" for a few moments, to see after Mr. Frazier, and finding that he had been comfortable all the evening, and was then sleeping soundly, would have continued on his way to his own house, but that he was interrogated first by one and then by another of the loungers in the bar-room relative to the death at Hurricane Castle. At any other time he would have treated his questioners with short courtesy; but now he felt that it was incumbent upon him to deny the foolish stories that were passing from one gossip to another.

"They say," said Mr. Hicks, who always went to the "Bear" at night to play dominoes with his cronies, "that a pistol was found under the bedclothes when they came to lay him out, and that he had shot himself in the mouth. No wonder there wasn't no wound to be found. I seen a pistol on the table when I was up there this mornin', witnessin' his will."

"Who says so?" growled the doctor.

"Oh, I don't," said Hicks, getting a little frightened, for he thought of the doctor's victory of a few days ago, and of the paper he had signed that morning; "I only tell it just as I heard it. Like enough there ain't no truth in it."

"Well, now you can tell all the fools you meet—and they probably constitute the majority of your acquaintance —that it's a lie. I examined the body from head to foot, and there wasn't even a scratch on it."

"Did you look in the ears?" inquired Mr. Spill, whose recollections of the last contest with the doctor were such as to give him a certain degree of assurance which poor Hicks could not feel.

"Did I look into the ears? Why should I have looked into the ears? Do you think that, because you took me to be a pirate, you can also take me to be a fool?"

"Oh no, not by no manner o' means—everybody in Plato knows you ain't no fool; but I guess they know too that you don't know everything. Jael, the Scripter tells us, killed Sisera by driving a nail into his head through his ear. I once killed a dog as quick as lightnin' by punching a brad-awl into his ear. There wasn't any blood, and no one never knowed what killed him. I guess a darnin'-needle drove into the brain through the ear would kill as big a man as Mr. Lamar and leave no sign neither, unless it was looked for mighty sharp."

Doctor Grattan started at this suggestion of Mr. Spill's. The idea was extremely plausible, being one that a determined lunatic could carry out with entire ease. It was a mode of perpetrating suicide that he knew had been used with success by one lunatic within his personal knowledge, and he was aware of the tendency in the minds of some of the insane to resort to unusual or *bizarre* methods of self-destruction. He looked at Spill for a moment, in astonishment at the man's perspicuity, and not without feeling a little chagrin that he, Doctor Grattan, who was presumably an expert in the ways of lunatics, should have omitted to examine Mr. Lamar's ears. Mr. Spill was not slow to perceive the impression he had produced, and started off again with an effort not only to maintain but to increase it:

"Of course, when I was up there this mornin'," he resumed, "witnessin' his will along with Mr. Hicks and
Bishop, I didn't go peerin' around the room and meddlin'
with things that didn't concern me. But when a thing's
forced on your notice, why, you've got to notice it, I guess,
whether you will or no, unless you shuts your eyes to everything. Well, I seen on the table a long needle, just the
kind sail-makers use, which, if you'll allow me, Doctor Grattan, is another proof that Mr. Lamar's been a seafarin' man.
It was about six inches long, and shaped like a spear. Right
on the table it was, within reach of his hand, whenever he
had a mind to stretch out and get it. Gentlemen! I don't
set up for a prophet, but I guess I know how to put this
and that together as well as most folks, and it's my deliberate opinion that, if Doctor Grattan had a' looked in the
right place, he'd a' found that needle a-stickin' in one of
Mr. Lamar's ears and drove into his brain."

"Well, Mr. Spill," said the doctor, in a tone in which
there was a strong admixture of contempt, though he could
not but admit to himself that there was a certain amount
of plausibility in the man's theory, "you'll have an opportunity to-morrow to air your pathological knowledge before
the coroner, and to find the needle in Mr. Lamar's brain if
there is one there."

"Mr. Lamar wasn't the man to kill himself," said Mr.
Ruggles, the landlord of the "Bear," coming from behind
his bar, where he had been sitting wiping the tumblers, with
a not over-clean napkin, when not engaged in filling them
with some of his delectable alcoholic compounds. "He
was off and on in this house for more'n a year, and a quieter
and more self-respectin' man I never seen. I guess them
kind don't kill themselves much. If there's a sail-maker's
needle in his brain, some one put it there when he was
asleep. I shouldn't wonder," he added, with a comically
malicious smile, "if Spill did it. He knows how to drive

a nail, and he seems to know just where this one was layin',
and just how it might a' been drove—"

"You shouldn't make fun out of such a serious subject," said Mr. Spill, looking as though his feelings had
been greatly injured—as they probably had been. "There's
a time for prayin' and a time for jokin', and I rather guess
this is a prayin'-time."

"I wonder what he's done with all his money?" broke
in Mr. Hicks, having recovered a little from the check the
doctor had given to his loquacity. "He had the will in a
tin box all cut and dried and ready for signin' and witnessin'. I guess there'll be a lot of it for his daughter. May be
he's founded a college in Plato."

"If he's provided in his will for your education and
reformation, Hicks," said the doctor, giving this parting
shot as he walked toward the door, "he's done a good act
for you as well as for the community in which you live."
Then he went out, and, re-entering his buggy, drove down
the street on his way home.

Suddenly an idea seemed to strike him, for he turned
off to the left and went on in that direction till he reached
a square house which stood on the edge of a little wood
nearly half a mile from the main street. It was not unlike, in general appearance, the doctor's house, except that
it had no excrescence at one side as had his, and was of
rather smaller size.

Doctor Grattan drove up to the fence which inclosed
the little lawn in front of the house, and, hitching his horse
to a post provided for that purpose, entered the inclosure,
and on arriving at the door gave a series of loud knocks
with an old-fashioned knocker fastened so high up that
even he, tall as he was, experienced a little inconvenience
in reaching it. His summons was a longer time in being
answered than was compatible with perfect domestic service, and when at last the door was opened he had lost a

good deal of the small stock of patience with which he was endowed.

" Do you suppose, you little imp," he exclaimed, addressing the small boy of African descent, who, if graded as to color after the manner adopted with cigars, would have ranked as "colorado claro," "that I have nothing to do but to stand here till it suits your sweet convenience to open the door ? What were you doing, you young rascal ? "

" Makin' the coffee. Walk in, sir ; Mr. Ellis is in the libery."

" Oh, he's in the 'libery,' is he, and drinking coffee at this time of night ! "

" Yes, sir ; he's got a headache."

" Well, I want to see him. Go on with your candle and light this hall. Why don't you keep a light burning ? "

" It's burned out, I guess. We didn't 'spect any one so late."

By this time the chocolate-colored youth had opened a door at the farther end of the passage, and a short, chubby-faced man had appeared at the opening.

"Come in, Grattan," said the rotund gentleman, in a cheery voice ; "I thought I recognized you. Glad to see you. Sit down and take a cup of coffee and a pipe. I had a headache, brought on, I suspect, by trying to understand that book on 'Esoteric Buddhism' that you lent me. You must be hard up for patients, when you have to try to get them from among your friends, by such devices as persuading them to read books calculated to unsettle their reason."

" My dear Ellis, this is no time for joking. Don't you know what has happened ? "

" Happened ? Nothing serious, I hope. How should I know, when I haven't been out of the house all day, and no one has been here but you ? "

" Mr. Lamar is dead ! "

# CHAPTER XII.

"Mr. Lamar dead!" exclaimed Mr. Ellis, starting back in astonishment with uplifted hands.

"Yes, I found him dead in his bed, at half-past six this afternoon."

"Dead in his bed!"

"Yes. Isn't that the place that people generally die in?"

"How should I know? It's your business to answer that question. But what did he die of?"

"I don't know."

"You don't know! Really, Grattan, I never before knew you to be such an ignoramus. He was your patient, and you ought to know. You call yourself a doctor?"

"No, I don't; other people call me so. The longer I live, the more I'm convinced that I'm not a doctor."

"Poor fellow! A sudden death like that always overcomes me. I expect to die suddenly myself. Look at my neck—short, thick, apoplectic. Some morning Jim will come in to wake me, and will find me dead in my bed, and then you'll come and say you don't know what I died of. Here, drink this coffee!" handing the doctor a cupful of the black beverage as he spoke; "and then light a pipe. You'll be in a better condition then for telling me all about it."

"I want your advice, Ellis," resumed Doctor Grattan,

after he had swallowed the coffee at a gulp and lighted a pipe. "I have reasons for believing that Lamar has not been in his right mind for a long time."

"Not in his right mind! Why, I've heard you say a hundred times that you thought him one of the most intelligent men you ever knew."

"So I did, so I do now ; but that doesn't preclude the idea that he was insane. A man must have a mind in order to lose it. Insanity is more common with intellectual people than with the dull-minded. It's very different from idiocy. But, if you'll not interrupt me, I'll get to the end of my story sooner."

"Go on ; I'll not stop you again."

"I am quite sure that, as many as fourteen years ago, Mr. Lamar had an attack of mental derangement. Since then he has had other seizures, and one began a week or more ago, and was in full play when he died. You will understand, therefore, that his insanity was of the periodical type, and that there were long periods of immunity, during which his mind was in as good a state of health as that of anybody else. A few days ago he came to me, and, in the course of conversation, during which I saw that there was no doubt of his insanity, he declared that he had once been in the slave-trade ; that he had long suffered remorse for his deeds, and was determined to make restitution. He intended, he said, to devote the whole of his fortune to the founding of a university for the higher education of the negro race in America."

"Certainly he was insane," said the practical lawyer. "A man who will entertain a scheme like that must be hopelessly bereft of his reason. I never heard anything more ridiculous in all my life. It's a perfect *non sequitur*. What the devil has the fact of a man having been in the slave-trade in Africa and Cuba to do with the education of the blacks in the United States ? "

"Nothing whatever, and so I told him ; but he was determined to devote the whole of his fortune, several million dollars, to this Utopian scheme."

"But was he really ever in the slave-trade ? Was not
the whole thing a delusion ?"

"That is the point that puzzles me," exclaimed the
doctor, rising, and in his excitement pacing the floor with
rapid strides. "That is the matter about which I can not
decide."

"And yet that is the very thing that you ought to be
able to determine. It seems to me the whole subject hangs
on that ; and, if you can't settle it, who the devil can ?"

"I don't know any more difficult matter to decide,
sometimes, than the question of the sanity or insanity of a
person, especially when it refers to some antecedent date in
regard to which one has only the statements of the individual concerned. It was simple enough for me to arrive
at the conclusion that Mr. Lamar was insane when he
conversed with me, and that he had at various times before
been insane. But insane people speak the truth probably
more frequently, as a whole, than those who are considered
to be in their right minds. It is perfectly possible for Mr.
Lamar to have been in the slave-trade, and to have been
insane before, during, and subsequent to the time he was so
employed. The account that he gave me of the affair was
perfectly logical and coherent, and agreed exactly in certain
points with information in my possession obtained from
an independent source. Undoubtedly, if he was ever a
slaver he was urged to become one by hallucinations of
hearing which he accepted as real voices speaking to him.
I am inclined to think that his account of the matter is
true, and that he was insane when he adopted a pursuit
which made him an outcast from the civilized world. At
the same time, as he was certainly insane when he related
the affair to me, the whole matter may be a delusion

—with which he has mixed up certain facts that have come to his knowledge. Now, do you see what a difficult point is to be determined, and how almost impossible it is to arrive at a conclusion without having other and independent evidence?"

"Yes," said Mr. Ellis, "the matter is certainly encompassed with difficulties. Did he leave a will?"

"Yes, he executed a will only an hour or so before his death, and in it I suppose has made provision for the university for the negro race."

"It will be invalid, if you can establish the fact of his insanity," said Mr. Ellis. "Not worth the paper it's written on."

"I intend to take the matter in hand," resumed the doctor; "for, if he has been a slaver, it will be necessary for his reputation to show that at the time he was not a responsible being, and if he has made a will of the kind that he threatened to make, and was insane at the time, the fact must be shown. He has left several millions."

"Splendid pickings for the lawyers!" exclaimed Mr. Ellis, rubbing his hands together and smiling, as though in anticipation of his own share.

"I suppose some of your fraternity will have to be employed; but, if I have anything to do with the matter, I shall incur no heavy legal expenses. He spoke once of making me an executor; but I can not of course accept, for to do so would be an acknowledgment of the validity of the will.

"But there is another matter," he continued, after a little pause, during which he and his friend emptied the ashes from their pipes and refilled them from a Swiss earthenware tobacco-jar that stood on the table. "As I was leaving the house, and not a half an hour after having made the discovery of Mr. Lamar's death, I met a United States deputy-marshal, armed with a warrant for the ar-

rest of the man who had just gone to answer for his deeds
to a greater power than a United States court."

"I don't know about that at all," exclaimed Mr. Ellis,
snapping up the theological allusion made by his friend,
and losing sight altogether of the other points. "Instantaneous judgment after death is a doctrine not held, so far
as I know, by any Christian sect, although the ancient
Egyptians and Greeks and Romans believed in it, as do certain heretical sects of the Brahmins. Besides—"

"My dear Ellis," explained the doctor, after he had
with many impatient writhings endured this discourse as
long as was possible, "I must say that I think such a dis-
quisition is at this time very much out of place. It is entirely unbefitting the solemnity of the occasion."

"Very well, my dear Grattan, I promise not to offend
again. But if you can have anything to contemplate more
solemn than the day of judgment, I should like to know
what it is. Go on."

"The man behaved very well. He only wanted to be
sure of his own knowledge that Lamar was dead, and then
he was ready to go back to New York without disclosing
the object of his visit. I showed him the corpse, and he
left Plato an hour ago."

"Upon whose information was the warrant issued ?"

"That the man did not know. It was issued by Judge
Conway, of the United States District Court. He is a very
prudent man, and would not have taken such a step without
full and sufficient reasons."

"Yes, he is very cautious. It looks bad, doesn't it ?"

"No, I think not. I see in the whole proceeding only
another proof of Lamar's insanity, for I am quite sure the
warrant was issued on his own confession."

"That's a strong point. If you can establish that, I
don't think you will have any trouble in proving Mr. Lamar
insane, and of setting aside any will that he may have made."

"I shall write to Judge Conway in a day or two; but I am just as sure of the correctness of my surmise as though I had the written confession before my eyes. But there is something more," he continued, "and that is the strongest piece of evidence yet brought forward to show the man's insanity. Mr. Lamar committed suicide."

"What!" exclaimed Mr. Ellis, jumping to his feet, and in his excitement overturning the table on which were the lamp and the jar of tobacco.· "Really, Grattan," he went on, as he fumbled about on the floor in the dim light of the fire, trying to pick up the scattered articles, "you are the most provoking man it has ever been my misfortune to encounter. Why didn't you tell me at first that he had killed himself, instead of keeping it for the end in that melodramatic way, and then making a sensation of it? Besides, you told me you didn't know what he died of."

"No more do I. I haven't the slightest idea yet, what he died of. I am only certain that, whatever killed him, was purposely used by himself. As to sensation, the only sensation that has been produced, you made by upsetting the table in that hysterical way."

"It's lucky I don't use that vile kerosene. If I did, you'd have burned the house down.—Here, Jim!" he continued, as he opened the door and called out at the top of his voice, "bring some candles. Go up-stairs and get the two ·from my room, and then go back for those that are in the spare bedroom. Come, hurry! Doctor Grattan has upset the table, and we are in the dark."

"Well, of all the old mendacious reprobates—"

"You did!" interrupted Mr. Ellis. "There's a legal maxim which is applicable to you: ' *Qui facit per alium facit per se.*' You made me your agent, and hence you are just as guilty as though you had done it with your own hands."

"You'd make your fortune as a sharp lawyer in New

York. Your talents are quite wasted in Plato, where we
are all simple folk, unaccustomed to such barefaced as-
sumptions as that that you have just made."

"All right—I forgive you freely. Now," as Jim entered
with candles, "that we are once more in physical light, let
your intellectual light shine."

"I am quite sure that he killed himself," resumed Doctor Grattan, "though the most careful scrutiny failed to
show any mark of violence on his body. Spill is of the opinion that he drove a sail-maker's needle into his brain through
his ear. He says there was such an instrument lying on
the table when he was in the room this afternoon. I saw
nothing of the kind when I was there. It is possible that
he employed that means. A superficial examination would
fail to detect it, and I did not look into the ears. I shall
do so, however, to-morrow."

"He might have taken poison, I suppose?"

"Yes, there are poisons that would destroy life in a very
few moments. He has lived in Africa, where they use ar-
row-poisons and ordeal-poisons, and other villainous compounds, and he may have brought some of them home with
him."

"But you haven't told me yet what makes you think
he committed suicide."

"No, but I'm going to do so now," taking, as he spoke,
the letter from his pocket which he had found pinned to
Mr. Lamar's breast. "Listen to this, and tell me what you
think of it. It seems to me to point definitely to the fact
of suicide." He read it, and then, throwing himself back
in his chair, puffed vigorously at his pipe, and awaited Mr.
Ellis's opinion.

"Read that again, won't you? Or, rather, let me read
it. I never get a good idea of a writing that requires much
thought unless I have it under my own eyes."

Doctor Grattan placed the letter in his friend's hands,

and the latter read it over very slowly and deliberately several times.

"Well, now," he said at last, "I'm prepared to answer your question, and to give it as my opinion that the letter does *not* indicate any intention to commit suicide. It does, perhaps, show that the writer felt death to be approaching. But when he says here that he waited for you till five minutes after six, you seem to suppose that he either was waiting in order that you might see him kill himself, or that he did so out of chagrin at your delay. Clearly, to my mind, he wanted to tell you something or do something in which you were concerned, and then, finding that he was dying, managed to write this note, and to place it where you could find it. The message in regard to his daughter seems to have some bearing on the point. I am quite sure that he died a natural death, and, my word for it, you will find nothing about him indicating suicide."

"By heavens!" exclaimed the doctor, "I never looked at it in that light, but of course I see the strength of your reasoning. He may not even have thought he was going to die. He may have felt sleepy, and, not wishing to be disturbed from his slumber, wrote this note. But why did he wait for me? What did he want with me? Scarcely to talk about his daughter's health. He means here professional care; he used exactly the same words a few days ago, but—"

"My dear Grattan, I think you have hit the correct view, only you seem to be a little at sea yet," interrupted Mr. Ellis. "I don't think he had any particular business with you, except probably to talk about his daughter, in regard to whom he appears to have been a little worried. He had spent the day in fatiguing work with a notary and witnesses, and he felt tired. He knew that you were expected at six o'clock. You did not come. He waited for

you till five minutes after six, and then, as you did not put
in an appearance, he yielded to his inclination to sleep,
and wrote this note, so that he should not be disturbed.
Then he went to sleep, and in his sleep he died as unexpect-
edly, doubtless, to himself as to his friends. The day was
too much for him. The fact that he had, as you say, confessed to being a slaver, and was expecting the arrest that
he desired, are facts also which, to my mind, militate
strongly against the idea of suicide. No, Grattan! the
more I think of it, the more I am convinced that he died
from disease in his sleep."

"I am strongly inclined to agree with you. However,
nothing can settle the point but a careful *post-mortem* examination. I suppose there ought to be one."

"If the coroner does his duty, and I take it for granted
that you have done yours by notifying him of the sudden
death, he will insist on one. I suppose, as he was suffering from some disease of his brain, that he was especially
liable to die in his sleep."

"Yes, I should not at any time have been much surprised at his sudden death. It was this letter that disturbed me; but I think you are right in the interpretation
you put upon it."

"I am sorry for his daughter," observed Mr. Ellis,
after a slight pause. "Although I can not claim to be
anything more than a mere acquaintance, I admire her
greatly. She seemed to be so thoroughly devoted to her
father, that I am sure she will make a good wife for some
one. Good daughters always do."

"She is very deeply affected; but I don't care to talk
about her. I saw her in the midst of her grief, when she
thought she was alone, and the sight made such an impression upon me that the thought of it makes me miserable."

"You always were a tender-hearted old fellow, in spite

of your assumed roughness. I should suppose that a man who had seen so many deaths as you have, in the effecting of which you have not been altogether non-instrumental, would have become hardened by this time to all kinds of suffering, even that of pretty young women."

"Don't make a ruffian of yourself, Ellis—at least, don't put on any extras : Nature did her part by you in that direction, and you can quite afford to let her work remain as it is. I suppose," he added, after this tirade, "there ought to be some legal representative of Miss Lamar at the inquest to-morrow ? Will you attend on her behalf ? I feel authorized to engage your services, and I wish you'd also see about the arrangements for the funeral. There's nobody but us two to whom Miss Lamar can look for assistance, and I can't do it. I'll get a request from her if you want it."

"Yes, I do want it. I am not a near enough friend to warrant any interference on my part, unless at Miss Lamar's desire. I can understand your reluctance to have anything to do with the matter. You and the family were very intimate, and of course you feel his death and his daughter's grief more than I do. You'll have enough to do to harrow your feelings in making the *post-mortem* examination. It must be a pretty severe trial to a man to have to cut up the dead body of his friend. However, when it comes to anything professional, I notice that you doctors manage to smother your feelings. It's the way you're brought up, I suppose. A Feejee-Islander, through education, contemplates with satisfaction dining on the tenderloin of his grandmother."

"Is there nothing sacred from your horrid jokes, Ellis ? " said the doctor, looking for the first time seriously annoyed at the would-be pleasantry of his friend. " It appears to me that a matter so solemn, and with which so many sad circumstances are connected, as are associated

with this death, might be allowed to escape your ribaldry.
Good-night," he continued, opening the door as he spoke,
and putting on his hat and overcoat. "I'll leave you now,
and will to-morrow inform you of the hour fixed for the
inquest."

"Don't go off angry, Grattan," said Mr. Ellis, following his friend into the hall and taking him by the hand;
"you know I don't mean anything by my 'ribaldry,' as you
very properly call it. I can't help seeing the ridiculous
side of things. For myself I don't feel Mr. Lamar's death
as much as you do, for, as I've said, I had only a slight
acquaintance with him; but I feel for you, even though I
do joke about the matter."

"All right, old fellow," answered the doctor, without
a trace of his late irritation in his voice; "I forgive you, as
I've often had occasion to do before, and as I suppose I
shall have to keep on doing till one or the other of us dies.
I know your heart is all right. Good-night! Don't stand
at the door in your bare head—you'll take cold. I can see
my way very well."

He got into his buggy and drove home as rapidly as the
darkness of the night permitted. Already a few flakes of
snow were beginning to fall, and a strong northeast wind
was blowing them right into his face. Mike was waiting
for him in the kitchen; and Milly, the cook and maid of
all household work that Cynthia did not do, had a light
supper ready for him. He looked at the old Dutch clock
that stood at the head of the stairs. It was nearly twelve.
Then he swallowed a few morsels of his supper, and hastily
betook himself to his dearly beloved pentagonal room. A
fire was smoldering on the wide hearth, and only required
two or three big hickory-logs to make it bright enough
and warm enough for all his purposes. Then he drew a
capacious arm-chair right in front of the fire, took off his
coat and boots and put on an elaborately embroidered dress-

ing-gown, and still more elaborately embroidered slippers,
both the products of Cynthia's fair hands, and finally, lighting his pipe, sat down to think.

But he found this to be no easy process. The intellect
does not work well when there is a strong emotion domi-
nating it, and there was such an emotion overshadowing
his mind, and directing his thoughts whither it would, regardless of the principles of logic or of expediency. He
was in love, deeply, hopelessly in love, and, as he saw no
way, either of extricating himself, or of conducting his
passion to a satisfactory termination, he was as miserable as
any other man of strong feelings would have been under
like circumstances. He had been fool enough to believe—
so he managed at last to think—that it would be a comparatively easy matter to subdue the love he felt for Louise
Lamar. He had never been lacking in the power to control his passions, and he *had* controlled them whenever he
had deliberately resolved to do so. He had thought that
all he had to do was to keep out of her way as much as possible, and, when unavoidably brought into association with
her, to conduct himself toward her with a degree of reserve
that would not only act chillingly on his own heart, but
would cause her to believe that he was indifferent to her.
She would probably resent this treatment, and thus a cold-
ness would spring up between them, under the influence of
which love would be crushed out so effectually that a re-
vival would be out of the question.

If Mr. Lamar had not died, this course of procedure
would probably have been effectual in accomplishing the
object he had in view. But his death had acted as a factor
of such potent disturbing power as to upset all his carefully
arranged plans, and to draw him into a vortex from which
escape seemed almost impossible. The reasoning of a man
profoundly in love is worth very little when it is antagonistic to the strong emotion which holds him in its thrall-

dom. It was in vain, therefore, that he reminded himself that he was nearly twenty years older than Louise, that he had in fact reached an age at which it is generally supposed that sentiment is on the wane, and marriage is looked at from a material rather than from a passional point of view. His heart told him, with a persistency and a fervor that he could not disregard, that, however true all this might be of other men, it was false so far as he was concerned. He knew that, though he was actually forty-five years old, he was as strong mentally and physically as he had ever been, and that his feelings were as quick and as warm as though he were twenty years younger. He had never wasted his powers in riotous living; the quiet, frugal mode of life that he had led since he had come to Plato, a mere youth in years, had not been without its legitimate influence in maintaining his vital powers at their maximum. He could endure as much hard work with his mind or body, without undue fatigue, as any man in the village, younger or older. Indeed, there was no one that could equal him in this respect. There were a few iron-gray hairs in his beard, but they had been there for fifteen years, and could not, therefore, be considered evidences of old age. As to his hair, it was as luxuriant and as uniformly black as it had ever been. There were no crow's-feet about the corners of his eyes, no hollowness of his cheeks, no defects in his splendid teeth. "Look at yourself," his Heart said to him, as he sat before the fire with his head thrown back, and his pipe emitting thick volumes of fragrant smoke—"look at yourself ; you are as good-looking as you ever were ; you are a strong, robust, healthy, well-formed man, capable of holding your own with the best of them. Why, then, should you not aspire to the hand of a woman, even if she is twenty years your junior ? When you are sixty, and she is forty, the relative difference will be still less perceptible. Besides, did she not tell you one day that her grandfather was fifty years old when he was married, and twenty-five years the senior of her grandmother? No, you can not reasonably object on the score of difference of ages." So he yielded that point, and the first victory had been gained by his Heart. As is always the case under like circumstances, the Intellect immediately went over to the enemy, and the union between emotion and reason was complete.

"But you are a poor man," Intellect said, "and she is a very rich woman. You would, therefore, be unequally matched, and the world would say that you married her for her money."

"You ought to be ashamed to allege such a reason as that," said the Heart. "Are you going to make yourself miserable, merely because she has more money than you have? You know you don't love her for her money. If she thinks you do, then drop her as soon as possible. As to what the world may say, are you, who have always heretofore acted as you thought was right, regardless of its censures, going to yield now to any supposed ill-natured feelings, that selfish, narrow-minded, and envious people may entertain? If you think you can not render her life a happy one, then, in God's name, abandon all idea of making her your wife! You would, indeed, be a scoundrel if you persisted, after arriving at that conclusion. But you don't think anything of the kind. On the contrary, you know that you love her, and that you intend to devote all your energies to the duty of cherishing and protecting her, if you should be so fortunate as to secure her love in return."

"All that is very true," rejoined the Intellect, feebly. "I think I shall have to yield that part also.

"Well! what, then, remains?" exclaimed the Heart. "The matter is settled, and as soon as she has, in a manner, recovered from the weight of the affliction that now oppresses her, you will do well to ask her to be your wife."

"There is Cynthia?"

"Cynthia! She will find her happiness in seeing you happy. Besides, do you think she is going to remain with you till she is an old maid? Not a bit of it! When she finds the right man to love, she'll marry him, regardless of you, however she may feel and whatever she may say now."

"You are a specious reasoner," he exclaimed, knocking the ashes from his pipe, as he arose from his chair, and lighted a candle, preparatory to going up-stairs to bed. "And you take advantage of the existing circumstances to advance arguments which you know I am not in a fit state to refute. I am weary with the thought of all that has happened to-day. To-morrow I shall be more than a match for you. And you talk as though it were the easiest thing in the world to gain her love; when the probability really is, that she will never be willing to sacrifice her fresh young life to one twenty years nearer the end of earth than is she. But if I had not seen her pouring out her soul in grief by the bedside of her dead father, there would have been no need for deferring a decision. *That* was a revelation of tenderness and love that overwhelmed me, and that will, I fear, keep me in subjection longer than I thought. But for *that* this unworthy passion would have faded away so gradually, but yet so surely, that I should scarcely have known a month hence that it had ever had a lodgement in my heart."

# CHAPTER XIII.

WHEN the occupants of Hurricane Castle looked out of their windows on the morning succeeding the death of its master, they saw that nearly a foot of snow had fallen during the night, and that the air was still thick with the white flakes. In addition, the northeast wind was blowing a gale, and the temperature was lower for that season of the year than had been known for several years.

Louise had passed, as was to have been expected, a restless night. She felt that vague yet overpowering sensation of unrest that occasionally torments those who suffer from some intensely depressing emotion. Do what she would, go where she would, she could not rid herself of the spirit of inquietude of which she seemed to be possessed. Cynthia's presence had been of great service to her, and in the early part of the night the two girls had sat together in Louise's boudoir, conversing a little in subdued tones, and with that involuntary mournful cadence which grief imparts to the words of those who feel it deeply. But neither was in any great humor for talking, so that ere long both relapsed into a silence that neither seemed capable of making the effort to break. Every now and then Louise's eyes would fill with tears; but she appeared to be making strenuous efforts to restrain the manifestation of her sorrow, and she indulged in no such passionate weeping as had over-

9

come her in the afternoon. Cynthia's presence acted as a support to her. Her manner was so unobtrusively sympathizing that it was more effectual in its quietness than it would have been had she shown it by lamentations and words. Then Cynthia had suggested reading, and volunteered to get a book from the library. She felt a sensation of awe as she went down the deserted staircase and through the large hall. A single lamp was burning, and cast weird shadows, made by the statues of marble and of bronze, that stood about on the tiled floor. She went to the library, holding her candle high above her head, till she reached one of the alcoves. Moving the light along the shelves, she picked out a book that she thought might excite in her friend reflections that would be more consoling to her than any expressions enunciated for the specific purpose of showing commiseration or of offering sympathy. It was "The Thoughts of the Emperor M. Aurelius Antoninus," a book which both the women knew well, almost by heart, but which Cynthia was aware could never be read without the reader finding something that tended to reconcile him or her to the ills that might be bearing heavily. She turned to retrace her steps, feeling well satisfied with the choice she had made, when she saw lying on the table a book of a different appearance from the others near it. She picked it up and turned to the title-page. "The Life and Adventures of Captain Juan de Ayolas" she read, and at the very top was the name of its former owner, but scratched over with a pen so that the writing was not legible. It was the volume that her father had borrowed from Will Hadden that afternoon, and that he had probably forgotten to take home with him. She took it with her, thinking that she would read herself to sleep with it, after she should go to her own room. Then she went back to Louise and read to her from "Marcus Aurelius" till the night was far advanced, and her friend had insisted on her going to bed.

Cynthia, therefore, went to her room, which adjoined the one in which they were sitting, carrying with her "The Life and Adventures of Captain Juan de Ayolas" for use as a somnific, should such be required. She would have thought it an act approaching sacrilege to use "Marcus Aurelius" for such a purpose.

Soon afterward Louise partly undressed, and, throwing herself across the foot of the bed, tried to compose herself to sleep. But she soon found that this was impossible : the form, the features, the words, the actions, of the man who lay dead within a few feet of her, crowded in a long procession before her mind, like so many material objects before the eyes. This was the first time that she had become personally acquainted with death. The thought to her was awful, that he, who a few hours ago was her living father, the one in all the world whom she loved most, was now an inanimate mass of skin and bones and flesh, from which the soul and the life had fled, never in this world to be united to it again.

She recalled to mind how greatly he had suffered ; how that scarcely for a day, since his return from his absence of fourteen years, he had been without pain, and yet he had borne it all without a murmur, till at last his mind had given way.

"Yes," she exclaimed, getting up from the bed and pacing the floor, "his mind could not stand the shock of all that he had suffered. The broiling sun, the deadly climate, the hardship, the exposure, the slavery, were more than he could endure. It was this that made him speak of crimes that he imagined he had committed. He guilty of crimes ! My poor, gentle, suffering father—he whose thoughts were ever for the welfare of others, and whose heart was as tender as that of a saint ! "

She opened the door of the room and looked out into the hall in which burned a single lamp that swung from the

ceiling. Her father's room was immediately opposite her
own, the door was ajar; to-morrow he would be put into
his coffin, the lid would be screwed down, and then she
should never see him again. " My God, is it possible ? "
she murmured, as she wrung her hands together, and the
tears fell in big drops from her eyes. "I can not bear it!
No, no! I can not bear it!" She sank to the floor, moan-
ing and sobbing as though her heart would break, and lay
there, heedless of the cold, heedless of everything, in the
face of the one single, agonizing thought that he was gone
from her forever.

She lay there—how long she never knew—in a state of
semi-consciousness, lost to every other idea but the one of
the great grief that had come upon her ; and this, in the
diminished state of activity in which her brain was, bore
upon her with tenfold force. She felt that she ought to
rouse herself, if only for the purpose of getting rid of the
nightmare with all its horrible fancies that had taken possession of her mind ; but, do what she would, she did not
seem to possess the power of moving hand or foot. The
restlessness from which she had suffered during the early
part of the evening had disappeared, and in its place had
come a physical inertia, a sluggishness infinitely more painful, and from which there appeared to be no means of escape. Her father! What had he done? Had he really
committed some great crime ? What was the meaning of
the incoherent words she had heard him utter in his sleep ?
Why had he been unhappy, when he had had everything at
his command that the heart of man could desire ? There
was a mystery. God grant that it was to be explained by
the fact of his insanity !

Probably she slept, for when she opened her eyes it was
broad daylight, though no one appeared to be stirring
about the house. She rose to her feet and moved instinctively toward the death-chamber, scarcely for the moment

comprehending that her father was dead, and that his corpse lay there ready for the functions of the coroner and undertaker. She opened the door and looked in ; a lamp was still burning, and the daylight was entering through the half-opened blinds. The two guardians were, after the manner of their kind, sound asleep on either side of the bed upon which the dead body reposed. Without disturbing them, she raised the cloth that concealed her father's face. The expression was scarcely changed. Had she not known that he was dead, she would have thought him asleep. She looked long and lovingly, for she knew it was the last look on earth that she should ever give him. Then she bent over and pressed her lips to his cold forehead, and, turning, left the room, with the watchers still asleep.

Yes, it was as snowy a November morning as any that Plato had ever seen. Pitchoff was invisible, as was also Mount Mary ; but the others, notably the Giant, could be dimly made out. Doctor Grattan's heart fell within him when he drew aside the heavy curtains, and saw the state of the weather, for it meant delay. He did not see how the coroner could get from Herodotus to Plato, over the mountain-roads by which he would have to come, and in which, doubtless, the snow had drifted in many places to depths that were impassable. He had fully resolved that a *post-mortem* examination of the remains of Mr. Lamar was necessary in the interests of justice as well as for those of his family. The coroner had power to order it to be made ; but he was quite sure that Louise, sensible and intelligent as she was, would readily give her consent to the procedure. Not to do so would cause her to fall many degrees in his estimation, for it would argue the possession by her of an unreasonable prejudice based on gross ignorance, which would be altogether at variance with her character, as he understood it. If the coroner did not come, then he should be obliged to break the subject to her and obtain her consent to making the examination. This would be a painful piece of work. He had resolved to avoid her as much as possible, and circumstances seemed to be conspiring to throw them together.

It was late for him when he got down-stairs to his breakfast, and the excitement and worry of the night before had told upon him in the matter not only of his sensations but of his looks. He had hitherto been in the habit of considering himself as proof against such influences ; but now he was obliged to admit that the immunity that he had experienced had resulted from the fact that he had not yet been subjected to a sufficiently powerful ordeal. The emotions most calculated to move him had not, till now, been developed. "My case," he thought, as he helped himself to an egg, more from a sense of duty than from the existence of an appetite, "is not unlike that of old Higgins, the dairyman. His wife died, and he buried her with entire equanimity. Then his daughter, to whom he was much attached, was kicked on the head by a vicious horse and also died, after lingering in insensibility for several days. But Higgins was stolid under this second affliction, and no one ever noticed that a tear or a change of countenance, or an alteration of manner, appeared when her name was mentioned. Then his son, who was a clerk in a bank in New York, stole some of the money of the institution, and was sent to Sing Sing. Higgins was impassable still. He laughed and talked about the matter, as though it were the smallest affair in the world. Everybody thought that Higgins was the personification of stolidity, and the comparison ' as hard as old Higgins' became current throughout the country. But one day butter fell four cents in the pound, and, an hour after the news was received, Higgins went out and hanged himself in his own barn. There was something, therefore, that could touch him, and I've found the thing that touches me. Perhaps I had better follow

Higgins's example. By George, were it not for Cynthia, I believe I would !"

But sleep had done this much for Doctor Grattan : it had refreshed and strengthened his brain to such an extent that he was ashamed of himself for the readiness with which he had accepted what he regarded as the flimsy arguments, based upon his love for Louise, that had arisen in his mind. He was now fully competent to decide the matter anew, and he resolved with all the determination of which he was capable that, though he could not probably prevent the existence of his passion, he could and would suffer in secret, and would never, under any circumstances, hint at its existence to the woman that was its object.

With this resolution firm in his heart, he started out on his round of duties for the day. Just as he was leaving the house, a note came from Cynthia, to the effect that Louise had passed a wretched night, and was confined to her bed in a state of complete nervous prostration. She begged that he would come to see her as soon as possible.

Instead of the buggy, Mike had brought round the sleigh, as being more suitable than the wheeled vehicle for the roads over which the doctor would be obliged to travel, in order to accomplish his day's work.

First he stopped at the "Bear." Mr. Frazier was doing as well as possible under the circumstances, though already beginning to feel lonely from the absence of his friend Wyant, and the fact that no one had come to take his place. While the physician was present, however, Will Hadden made his appearance, very much to Mr. Frazier's delight, and at once entered upon the discharge of his duties, by answering the numerous questions about the hunting, the fishing, the minerals, the plants, and a dozen other matters touching Plato, and its vicinity, which that gentleman put to him. His patient's face had improved so much that the doctor took off the bandages and gave him permission to talk as much as he pleased, so long as pain or fatigue were not produced.

"I heard of the sudden death, last evening, of one of your principal citizens," said Frazier, addressing the doctor. "He has not been here long, I believe?"

"Not as a resident, for he only moved into his house a few days ago, but he has been here superintending its construction for over a year, off and on."

"A Mr. Lamar, I think?"

"Yes, a New-Yorker, who had lived abroad a good deal."

"I met a gentleman of that name in Cuba some six years ago; but this can not be the same. The one I knew was a rather singular sort of a fellow. He lived back of Havana, in the mountains, on a plantation that he owned, and was thought by some—though he was a very learned man—to be insane."

"This Mr. Lamar lived in Cuba at one time of his life," said the doctor, at once becoming interested in Mr. Frazier's recollections.

"I shouldn't be surprised if they were the same. The one I mean had some queer notions about himself. Once I recollect he went to the American consul and wanted to be arrested as a slaver. He made the most circumstantial confession of his acts, and so far persuaded the consul of its truth that he was arrested. But just as preparations were completed for sending him to the United States for trial, it was ascertained in some way or other that there was no truth in his story."

The doctor's heart leaped for joy at this statement. He saw that here was the direction in which inquiries relative to Mr. Lamar's antecedents were to be made. It might be necessary for him to go to Cuba, in order to unravel the whole mystery; but he would not hesitate at this or any other trouble that might be necessary to show that his dead friend, the father of Louise, had not been guilty of the crimes he had confessed. He was not, however, prepared to discuss the matter further with Mr. Frazier; so, with some indifferent remark to the effect that the two might be the same individual, he prepared to take his departure.

"By-the-by, doctor," said his patient, "I hope you do not understand that, because you have obtained a companion for me, I am to be deprived of the society of Miss Grattan. If that is to be the arrangement," he continued, with a smile, "I am afraid I shall have to send Mr. Hadden off into the mountains every day to kill a bird for me."

"My daughter will probably be unable, for several days yet, to give you any portion of her society," answered the doctor, "as her friend Miss Lamar will require it all. Besides, in her present frame of mind you would not find her a very cheerful companion. I promise you, however, that I will bring her so soon as circumstances permit. In the mean time, you do not know what a treasure you have in my young friend Will Hadden. He has written a story which—why, bless my soul!" he exclaimed, "I put it into my pocket last night, intending to read it, and I forgot all about it. Here it is. He shall read it to you now, and I'll take it some other time. I had a book, too, and what I've done with it the Lord only knows! That sad affair at Hurricane Castle knocked everything else out of my mind. I must have left it there. Good-by; I'll look in on you again this evening. Don't talk too much, and, when you feel sleepy, go to sleep."

"Yes," he thought, as he drove his sleigh through the pelting snow over a road that was now covered more than a foot deep, "there is no doubt that the truth is reached, and that Mr. Lamar has been insane at times for several years. So, he was living in Cuba six years ago. That is strange, and is scarcely consistent with his story of captivity for many years in Africa; and he had made that con-

fession before ! Yes, it is all as clear to me now as that I
am on my way to examine his dead body. The whole thing
was a delusion, and he died as veritable a lunatic as there is
outside of an asylum, and as much of a one as can be found
within the walls of such an institution. I'll break that will,
at any rate, and I'll save his memory from disgrace."

When he got to Hurricane Castle, he found that a message had been received from the coroner, to the effect that
he would reach Plato by ten o'clock, and directing that the
body should not be disturbed before his arrival. Then he
inquired for Cynthia and Miss Lamar, and in a few minutes
the former entered the library, whither he had at once gone
to look for the book which he was now sure he had left
there.

"Louise is still in bed with a wretched headache," said
Cynthia, after she had kissed him and inquired after his
health. "She seems scarcely to have slept a wink all night.
She wishes to see you, not only on her own account, but to
ask you some questions about her father's death. But what
are you looking for ?"

"For a book that I left here last night."

"Was it 'The Life and Adventures of Captain Juan de
Ayolas' ?"

"Yes ; what do you know about it ?"

"I found it here last night when I came down to get
something to read to Louise ; I took it up to bed with me,
and read myself to sleep with it. It's a horrid book ! All
about slavers and the sufferings of the poor negroes, while
in the 'middle passage'—I shouldn't think it would interest you at all."

"But it does, at this particular time, interest me very
much. I read a little of it last evening at Mrs. Hadden's,
and I have a special object in wishing to read more of it. I
have a suspicion of something, my dear, that I can not mention to you now, but which relates to a matter of great

importance. Don't let me go away to-day without that book."

"Oh, you are welcome to it, especially if there is a mystery connected with it. But, now, will you come up and see Louise ?"

They ascended the broad stairs, Cynthia leading the way, and walking automatically on tiptoes, as she passed the chamber in which the dead man lay. Louise looked very haggard and very pale. She held out her hand to the doctor, which he took and then let drop almost as soon as it touched his own.

"I want to thank you," she said, "for all that you have done, and I beg you to increase the obligation by taking charge of the arrangements for my poor father's funeral. I think, had he had the opportunity to express his wish, that he would have preferred to be buried here at Plato, where he had come to spend the remainder of his days, no matter how long he might live. He loved this place, and was never tired of admiring its beauties. There is one spot on the high bank of the Canemanga, just before it enters the little wood, almost in the shadow of The Giant, where he was in the habit of going every morning to sit, and, as he has told me, to think over his past life. He had a little summerhouse built there, out of the stones that lay on the ground. Let it now be his tomb."

"Everything shall be as you wish, Miss Lamar," answered the doctor, feelingly.

"You told me once," she resumed, with a sad smile, "that you almost regarded me as your daughter."

"Yes."

"I am now more than ever in need of your sympathy and love."

"In need of my sympathy and love," he thought; "she looks upon me as an old man who can never occupy any nearer relationship to her than that of an adopted father.

If there were the slightest spark of love for me, such as I feel for her, she would have plucked her tongue out before she would have spoken those words." Then he continued aloud :

"I trust you will never have to turn in vain to me for anything that it may be in my power to do for you."

The words were spoken gravely but kindly.

"Thanks," she answered ; "you have always been kind to me. Now," she continued, "don't call me 'Miss Lamar' any more."

He bowed his head. "I will call you 'Louise.'"

"That is kind ; besides, I think you will from this time on occupy a still nearer relationship to me than that of my best friend, for I am sure, from what papa said to me only a few days before—before he died, that he has made you the sole executor of his will, and my guardian. He thought you the best man he had ever known."

Doctor Grattan rose and walked to the window to conceal his emotion. It was a way of his. He could not see much of any one of his beloved mountains, but he could look in their direction, and he did, at the same time furtively brushing away with his hand a tear or two that stood in each eye. Then he went back to the bed and stood by its side while he took Louise's hand in his, seemingly having, in the brief moments since she had spoken, resolved upon his course.

"My dear child," he said, "I can never of course be to you like the father you have lost, but, if you will allow me to treat you as I do my own daughter, I shall try to do my duty by you, whether I am your legal guardian or not. Shall it be so, my dear ?"

"Yes, I should like that very much. I shall never leave Plato ; I love you and Cynthia too much for that. Take me, then, to your heart as your daughter, as she will take me as a sister."

He stooped over and kissed her forehead, but made no other answer ; while Cynthia threw her arms around her neck, and sobbed and cried after the manner of tender-hearted women on such occasions.

Louise was the first to recover her composure. She seemed to have nerved herself to go through, without flinch-ing, the trying situations which she knew the day would bring forth. That she was suffering was easy to be seen. The edges of her eyelids were red, her face was pale, and there was an expression of sorrowful weariness on her coun-tenance that unmistakably told how keenly she felt the calamity that had fallen upon her. Doctor Grattan thought he had never seen her look lovelier than now.

"I want you to tell me," she said, turning to the doc-tor, who had resumed his seat near her, "what in your opinion caused my poor father's death. He did not seem to be ill all day. He spoke in the morning of a little weak-ness, a sort of numbness, as he explained it, in his limbs, and said that he thought he would go back to bed, in the hope that rest would dissipate it. He was well enough to read several papers and to have a notary with him attesting his signature. He also made his will, a thing that he had been going to do for some time past, but had always put off. I saw him only a few minutes before you came, and he spoke of matters that he contemplated attending to to-morrow. He said he was very sleepy, and that if you did not come soon he should have to go to sleep without seeing you. He must have died in his sleep."

"Yes, he doubtless died in his sleep ; but it is only right for me to tell you, my dear, that there is an impression in the village that he killed himself."

"Killed himself !" exclaimed Louise ; "impossible !"

"It is one which at first sight has some evidence to sus-tain it, and I must confess that for a time I thought it probable that he had done so ; but more mature reflection has, convinced me that he did nothing of the kind. A sudden death such as his, occurring in a man apparently in good health, sound in mind and body, is very apt among ignorant persons to give rise to ideas of suicide. But to me, who am aware of how your poor father suffered, the view that he died either of brain or heart disease, comes very forcibly. Yes, I am certain his death was from natural causes." He could not bring himself to the point of speaking of the letter that her father had written him ; to do so, he thought, would look like an effort on his part to force himself upon her as her guardian, and consequently into relations with her that would make it still more difficult than it was otherwise sure to be, to keep his love for her from being shown.

"It is not a matter about which there should be any doubt," she said, after a moment's thought.

"No."

"There will always be doubt in the minds of some persons unless—unless—"

"Unless a post-mortem examination is made," he said, interrupting her, and thus relieving her of the necessity for saying the words. "It ought to be made, both for the sake of his memory and your comfort."

"I do not care for myself. I know he did not commit suicide, but I do care for him and for what the world may think of him. You are right. Let it be made."

"You are a brave woman, and, what is better, an enlightened one."

"It is right, and that is enough. Now one other question. Do you think that my father's mind was deranged ?"

The doctor hesitated a moment before answering this direct question. He wished to avoid in her present condition exposing her to any additional causes of grief, but he reflected that the mere fact of her putting the question showed that she had suspicions similar in their bearing to the positive symptoms of mental alienation in Mr. Lamar that he himself had observed.

"Do not be afraid to tell me," she resumed, perceiving his hesitation. "I am able to bear anything you may say to me. To-day that is," she continued, smiling wearily. "To-morrow it may be different."

"I think he was insane—I am sure he was insane," repeating the expression, and making it more emphatic than at first, "and that fact will render invalid whatever will he may have made. That he has made a will that ought to be set aside I am quite sure."

"Yes, I think his mind was disordered, and that for many of his acts he was not responsible. But his intellect was wonderfully clear on all subjects outside of a certain range that seemed to have taken a firm hold upon him. His knowledge of individuals was astonishing. He appeared to know intuitively every person that came into his presence."

"I do not think he was competent to make a will," said the doctor, decisively.

"But, my friend, I shall never dispute it. I am his sole heiress, and the only one, as I understand the matter, who has any right to question its validity. That right I shall never exercise. Whatever he has done with his estate in his will shall be faithfully executed, so far as the matter rests with me. No, I could not go before the world and attempt to oppose my poor father's last wishes. That they are wise I am very sure, and, as for me, they shall be carried out."

The doctor was troubled. What was the use of trying to show Mr. Lamar's insanity, if the only one who could profit by the evidence he could adduce refused the advantages of the demonstration? As to the accusation that he had made against himself of having been a slaver, that could be readily disproved by a visit to Cuba and a searching inquiry into his antecedents. He was fully resolved, however, in regard to one point, and that was that he would take no part in executing the will. He knew that Mr. Lamar was insane when he made it, and that for him to accept the executorship would be an act of immorality of which he could not be guilty.

But, while he was in the midst of his reflections, the arrival of the coroner was announced, and he left the room to meet that functionary.

# CHAPTER XIV.

ON leaving Louise, the doctor repaired at once to the library in search of the coroner. He found that official in possession of the room, and supported by half a dozen or more men whom he recognized as citizens of Plato.

"I thought this an important case, doctor," said the functionary, Bangs by name ; "so, notwithstanding the bad weather, I concluded to come over. I heard in the village, as I stopped at the 'Bear' for a moment, that there are strong suspicions of suicide."

"It will be your duty to verify or disprove them," said the doctor. "For my part, though I am not sure as to the cause of death, I am quite certain that Mr. Lamar died from disease, and not by his own hand, or by that of any one else."

"Of course, I shall take your testimony first. I took the precaution to bring these gentlemen along to serve on the jury. Shall we go now and view the body ? There are some other witnesses. A man named Spill is anxious to be sworn. He declares that he has important information in his possession tending to show that Mr. Lamar committed suicide."

"Yes, he thinks that the poor man drove a sail-maker's needle into his brain through his ear. Of course, if he is right, the fact will be easily established."

"And in that case we might dispense with the post-mortem examination."

"I think not," answered the doctor, reflectively. "It is important to ascertain whether or not Mr. Lamar had a disease of his brain. His daughter wishes the examination made."

"Then I have nothing further to say."

This conversation was conducted while the two gentlemen, followed by the improvised jury, were ascending the staircase. As the party entered, one of the servants opened the shutters, and a flood of light was let into the room. The snow had now ceased to fall, and the sharp northwest wind was dissipating the clouds. A hundred snow-birds were hopping about on the white-mantled branches of the trees, twittering with delight at the assurance they had received that they had not mistaken the probabilities of the climate. On a table, in the middle of the room, lay the corpse, decently covered with a white cloth, and around it the jury, servants, and the witnesses, Messrs. Bishop, Hicks, and Spill, grouped themselves, Mr. Bangs and the doctor conversing together before one of the windows.

"I think," said the official, "that I shall take your evidence first, as you were the first to discover the fact of the dead body."

Then the jury was sworn, and the inquest began.

The doctor gave his testimony to the facts with which the reader is already acquainted, producing the letter which the deceased had written him. When asked if he could state the cause of death, he answered that for a long time Mr. Lamar had suffered from brain-disease, induced, as he had reason to believe, by a sunstroke, received in equatorial Africa some fourteen years ago; that, on the very day of the decedent's arrival in Plato, he had sent for him, Doctor Grattan, and that he had found him suffering from intense pain in his head, to paroxysms of which he had been very liable; that since then the deceased had given evidences of the existence of mental aberration doubt-

less due to disease of the brain, which itself had resulted
from the sunstroke—from all of which he, the witness,
was of the opinion that death had been produced by an
affection of the brain, the exact nature of which could only
be revealed by a post-mortem examination, though he believed that there had been the rupture of a blood-vessel
and a consequent apoplectic seizure during sleep. The
sleepiness that the patient had experienced shortly before
death was the gradually advancing stupor.

The doctor was then informed that he would probably
be called again after making the post-mortem examination.

Then Mr. Bishop and Mr. Hicks were examined. The
former testified that he had been with the deceased a good
part of the day in the capacity of a notary, and that he had
observed nothing unusual in Mr. Lamar's manner. Toward evening he had complained of being sleepy. He had
exhibited no evidences of mental derangement; on the
contrary, his mind, in the witness's opinion, had been especially active and logical. He had been perfectly aware of
what he was doing, and acted in an entirely intelligent
way.

Mr. Hicks testified to having witnessed the will, and to
his belief that the deceased was of sound mind and memory. He was in apparent good health at half-past five
o'clock. Once he had complained of being sleepy.

Mr. Lamar's valet's testimony was to the like effect.
He had noticed nothing unusual about the deceased; had
seen him last alive at about five o'clock; was then walking about the room, but lay down again, going on with the
business he had with Mr. Bishop.

"I do not think it will be necessary to call Miss Lamar," said the coroner. "The facts up to half-past five,
and subsequently up to an hour later, are very clearly established.—Now, Mr. Timothy Spill, we will hear what
you have to say."

Spill, on being sworn, kissed the book with great unction, and spoke as follows :

"I was asked by Mr. Bishop to come up here and witness Mr. Lamar's will.  When I got here it was about four o'clock in the afternoon, and he was busy with some other matters.  Seeing that I was not needed just then, I walked around the room, looking at the pictures and other things, and noticing how different it was then from what it was when I was workin' in it.  As I went from place to place I saw some things on a table right by the bed on which Mr. Lamar was layin', and among them a big needle like the sail-makers use.  When I heard that he was dead, it just struck me that he might a' drove that into his skull through his ear.  I knew that would a' killed him sudden, and I hear he died sudden.  I killed a dog mighty sudden once that way.  That's all I know, and, if I'm right in my suspicions, why, you'll find that needle in one of his ears ; and if it's there, I guess that's what killed him.  I guess the doctor won't deny that."

"Doctor Grattan," said the coroner, "please examine the head of the deceased, and tell the jury the result of your inspection."

With an incredulous smile the doctor approached the table on which the dead body lay.  Pushing aside the hair from the left ear, he looked into it carefully.  "There is nothing there," he said.  The coroner and several of the jury also examined the ear, and by shakings of their heads confirmed the report of the doctor.  Spill did not appear to be specially interested in the proceedings, though, at the doctor's words, he raised his head and spoke :

"It ain't in that ear ; if it's in either of them it's in the right ear.  A man can't easily, I guess, drive a nail into his left ear, unless he's left-handed."

Passing around to the other side of the table, the doctor gently pushed aside the long, thick hair that almost completely hid the entrance to the ear. As he did so, he started back with an astonished look on his countenance ; but in an instant, recovering himself, bent down and inserted his fingers into the ear, while all in the room crowded around him, watching his proceedings with the utmost interest.

" I guess you can't get it out with your fingers," said Spill, observing that the doctor was ineffectually tugging at something. "I thought you might need them, so I brought these pinchers along."

The doctor took the pair of pincers that Spill handed him, and, inserting them into the ear of the dead man, drew forth, after the exercise of considerable strength, a part of a spear-shaped needle, such as is used by the sewers of heavy materials like sails. A murmur of astonishment, not un-mixed with horror, ran through the assembled group. "My God ! " exclaimed the doctor, "then he did kill himself, after all. Poor Louise," he added, under his breath, "what a blow this will be to you ! "

" I told you so," said Spill, who had stood a little apart from the rest, but who now came forward, pushing his way through the crowd till he stood close to the corpse—" I told you so. I saw him eyin' that needle all the time I was in the room, and I felt certain he meant to do himself harm with it as soon as we left."

" Why didn't you give the alarm then, you bird of ill omen ! " cried the doctor. "You are morally guilty of his murder, if what you say is true. By Heaven ! I wouldn't be surprised to learn that you yourself drove the needle into his brain. You are not a bit too good for such a deed, you hypocritical villain ! I haven't forgotten your abuse of him a few days ago."

The doctor hated the man. He felt that, but for him, the fact of a suicide would never have been revealed, and hence that the sorrow and the disgrace inseparably con-nected with the deed would have been avoided. He spoke, therefore, with all the energy and anger that he usually showed under circumstances calculated to excite his ire, and, as was also commonly the case, exceeded the bounds of discretion in the language he employed.

But no sooner were the words out of his mouth, than he regretted his unseemly exhibition of temper, an exhibition which, made as it was in the presence of the dead body of his friend, was particularly out of place. He still held the pincers in his hand, and they still grasped the needle that he had drawn from the skull. Everybody looked aghast at his manner and expressions, and every eye was turned on Spill, who appeared, however, to be the most unconcerned person of all those assembled.

"It ain't Christian, doctor, for you to make such a charge as that against a man who's only tried to do his duty," he said, in a humble and injured tone of voice. "I couldn't help seein' the needle, nor seein' him lookin' at it. Perhaps, if I'd as much sense as you, I'd a' told some one about my suspicions. Perhaps I ought to a' done so anyhow, but we ain't always sure about what one ought to do at such times. As to sayin' *I* drove it in, that's a hard sayin', for you see I wasn't alone with him a minute. I'm a professin' Christian, too, though the Lord knows I ain't as good as I ought to be."

"I beg your pardon, Spill," said the doctor. "It was beastly in me to make such an accusation, for which I know there is not the slightest foundation ; but I still think that, having the suspicions you say you had, you were wrong not to mention them."

"And get myself abused and laughed at for my pains, and perhaps kicked out o' the house by some of the men-help !"

"I don't suppose," interrupted the coroner, "that Mr. Spill's suspicions resolved themselves into any definite shape. They were probably, at the time, of the vaguest

description, and have only become appreciable since the
death of the poor gentleman.—There's nothing more to be
done," looking at the doctor inquiringly, "but to render a
verdict in accordance with the facts."

"Excuse me," said the doctor, "but I do not think we
have yet got at the facts ; nor can we do so till an examination is made of the brain, and, among other points, the
exact course of the needle ascertained. It is by no means
certain yet that the needle was the cause of death. It may
not even have penetrated to the brain."

"Then proceed with the examination. I will remain
here with you, and Mr. Spill had better stay also. The
jury can, if they choose, disperse for an hour, by which
time, I presume, you will be ready to report."

Into the details of the investigation that the doctor
made it is not necessary or proper for us to go. Suffice it
to say that it was conducted in the most thorough and ex-
haustive manner, and in accordance with the most advanced
principles of cerebral anatomy, normal and abnormal. After
it was finished, the coroner called the jury together to hear
the report that the doctor had to make. It may be said that
Spill, with all his prejudices in favor of the death being due
to suicide, and the coroner, who, certainly after the finding
of the needle, shared the carpenter's theory, were entirely
convinced that the doctor's examination had led to the discovery of the truth, so far at least as the cause of death was
concerned. Omitting the technical description — though
the doctor was careful in his testimony to avoid using scientific terms where there were English words that explained
his meaning—it will suffice to say that he went on to state
that Mr. Lamar had certainly died from the rupture of a
blood-vessel of the brain, leading to the formation of a clot
of blood as big as an orange ; that this had occurred on
the left side of the brain, and was not due to the needle
found in the right ear ; that, in fact, the needle had not

penetrated the brain, but had followed the course of the
canal in one of the bones of the skull, in which the auditory
apparatus is placed ; and, further, that the needle had been
thrust into the ear and then broken off, so that only about
two inches of it remained fixed in the head, the other part
—a little more than one half—had been found on the floor
near the bedside. The clot of blood had probably been
effused slowly, and death had not been instantaneous.

When asked by the coroner if he was able to offer any
explanation to the jury in regard to the presence of the
needle in the ear, he declared that nothing positive could be
known on the subject, but that it was probable that the deceased had had the needle in his right hand when the hæmorrhage took place, and that, by a convulsive and altogether
involuntary movement of the arm, it had been driven into
the skull and broken off ; or a convulsive movement of the
head might have taken place while the needle was held in
the hand, causing the opening of the ear to be forced vio-
lently against the instrument. Exactly how it had been
done he was not able to state. It was very certain that it
had had nothing to do with the death of Mr. Lamar.

Then the coroner addressed the jury, and instructed
them that, in accordance with the facts developed by the
examination, it was their duty to render a verdict to the
effect that the deceased had died from cerebral hæmorrhage ;
and such a verdict was instantly given.

Just at that moment Mr. Ellis made his appearance.
The doctor had forgotten to notify him of the coroner's arrival ; but fortunately this functionary—as is not often the
case with country coroners—was a remarkably sensible man,
and the lawyer's services had not been required. He expressed his entire satisfaction with the verdict, which he
declared was the only one that could have been properly
rendered under the circumstances.

Three days after, the funeral took place, and, in accordance with Louise's wishes, the body of her father was deposited in the place she had selected as that which he himself would have chosen.

Nothing appeals to the rustic mind with a force approaching that which attends a funeral. A birth is nothing, a marriage excites only moderate interest, but a funeral rouses the whole neighborhood into a state of excitement, and men, women, and children stop their work and their play, and, attiring themselves in their best clothes, prepare, under the self-deception that they are honoring the dead, to enjoy the occasion. Mr. Lamar's funeral was a large one. Everybody in Plato that could go, went. They had the opportunity that might never recur of examining the house that the dead man had built, and that he had lived but a few days to enjoy. They inspected with curiosity the room in which he had died, the staircase he had ascended and descended, the chairs in which he had sat, and they would, had they been allowed, have satiated their eyes with the clothing he had worn, especially the night-gown in which he had died. Humanity, especially the female portion of it, loves morbidity.

Mr. Craig conducted the funeral services partly at the house, partly at the grave, and then, when all was over, Louise and her friends the Grattans, with the clergyman, his daughter Lucy, and Mr. Ellis, returned to the house.

Then Louise had gone up-stairs, and had in a few minutes returned, followed by the old butler with a large tin box, which he placed upon the table in the library, in which room they were assembled.

"My father was very methodical," she said, "and kept all his papers of any importance in this box. I have requested you, my friends, to be here at this time, for I propose to read his last will and testament, and then to place it in Mr. Ellis's hands, in order that it may be proved and steps taken as soon as may be for carrying out its provisions."

10

At these words the doctor made a sign to Mr. Ellis, and the two went aside to the window.

"Of course," said Doctor Grattan, "Mr. Lamar was not in a sane state of mind when he made that will. He was under the influence of delusions; the first symptoms of the climax were already present. His brain, in addition to the extravasation of blood, was in a frightfully diseased state. I think it will be my duty, though I may say nothing now, to enter my protest before the surrogate against the admission of the will to probate."

"I don't see how you can do that. No one but his daughter has any interest in his estate, and hence no one has any standing in court as opponent of the will."

"He has a sister somewhere in Europe."

"That makes no difference, as she is not a joint heir. His daughter is his sole heiress, and no one else has any right to object; but I think you had better let things go now, and, as it will be a week or two before the will can be presented to the surrogate, you will have ample opportunity for convincing her that her father was insane."

"She knows that as well as we do, but she has an exalted idea of her duty, which she understands consists in executing his wishes under all circumstances."

"Of course, his true wishes; but the wishes of an insane person are not his own. He is held in thralldom, and acts in a way that if he were sane he would never act. Still, I think it better to make no opposition now, no matter how absurd the will may be. I will take it and submit it for probate. When she is over, to some extent, the immediate effects of her grief, she may see things in a different light."

"You don't know her, Ellis, as I do," said the doctor. "She will become firmer every day of her life. If she were acting through emotion, I should believe you, but she is not. She is actuated by the highest principle of what she

believes to be right, and the whole estate will go to the nig-
gers as sure as my name is Grattan!"

They returned to the group around the table, and
Louise, unlocking the box, took from it a large envelope
that lay on the top of all the other papers. She read the
indorsement, "Last will and testament of John Lamar,"
then she opened the envelope and drew from it a paper
that, amid the most profound silence, she read aloud as
follows:

"I, John Lamar, of the village of Plato, county of
Essex, and State of New York, do, on this twentieth day
of November, eighteen hundred and sixty-eight, make, pub-
lish, and declare this to be my last will and testament:

"*Item first:* To my dearly beloved daughter, Louise
Lamar, I give, devise, and bequeath, as follows:

"The diamond and other jewelry which belonged to my
mother, and which for many years has been in the family.

"My watch and all other articles of personal wear belonging to me.

"The tract of land in the village of Plato, with the
house thereon erected, known as Hurricane Castle, with
all its contents and appurtenances, horses, carriages, and
other articles of every kind whatsoever.

"*Item second:* I give, devise, and bequeath all the
residue of my estate, real, personal, and mixed, to the best
man I ever knew, my dear friend Arthur Grattan, M. D.,
of the village of Plato, county of Essex, and State of New
York.

"*Item third:* I nominate and appoint the said Arthur
Grattan, M. D., sole executor of this my last will and
testament. No-bond or other security is to be required
of him in qualifying for the execution of this trust.

"*Item fourth:* I hereby revoke all former wills by me
made.

"In witness whereof I, John Lamar, testator, have to this my last will and testament, consisting of one sheet or piece of paper, subscribed my name and set my seal this twentieth day of November, eighteen hundred and sixty-eight.

"John Lamar." [l. s.]

"Subscribed by the testator in the presence of each of us, and in the presence of each other, and at the same time declared by him to be his last will and testament; and therefore, we, at the request of the testator, sign our names as witnesses, this twentieth day of November, eighteen hundred and sixty-eight.

"W. S. Bishop, Plato, New York.
"Joshua Hicks, Plato, New York.
"Timothy Spill, Plato, New York."

While the paragraph relating to the disposition of the estate to Doctor Grattan was being read, the utmost astonishment was depicted not only on the face of the recipient of Mr. Lamar's bounty, but upon that of every one present, not even excepting Louise. She, however, continued to read on without a change of her voice ; and, when she had concluded, very deliberately folded the paper, placed it in the envelope, and handed it to Mr. Ellis.

"Please take the necessary steps with all possible dispatch to have this will admitted to probate," she said. Then, going over to the doctor—who was writhing uneasily on his chair, and whose countenance bore an expression of a concentrated determination to do something with all his might and main—she held out her hand to him.

"I am sure I need not tell you," she said, in a voice that all in the room could hear, "how gratified I am at learning of my father's determination relative to his large estate. He has done with it the one thing in all the world that could please me most, and it does please me."

"You are very kind," said the doctor, rising at her approach and taking her outstretched hand, which he continued to hold while he was speaking, "and I am overwhelmed with the good intentions of your father toward me, but I can never accept the provisions of this will; I know that it is not a valid instrument, and it is only honest for me to declare that I shall oppose its being admitted to probate."

"I was afraid you would take that stand," observed Louise.

"I am compelled by every consideration of decency, and morality, and professional honor, to take it," he exclaimed, warmly. "I should despise myself if I did otherwise. No! I am not so low as that. I shall never regard that paper as a valid will—never, so help me God!"

He spoke in a low tone, so that his words were undistinguishable to all present, except Mr. Ellis and Cynthia, the latter of whom rose and approached her father.

"For the sake of your daughter you will change your mind," said Louise. "You have no right, I think, to injure her, as you would by declining to accept my father's will."

"But I am with papa," exclaimed Cynthia. "Dear Louise! he can not accept. It is impossible. I know how he feels, and I feel with him and like him. The estate is yours, and neither of us will ever touch a penny of it."

"Grattan," said Mr. Ellis, "it strikes me that you are very foolish in this matter. Even if you have doubts about the validity of the will, the fact that the next of kin and the sole inheritor of the estate approves her father's action, ought to set your mind at rest. Here are, as I understand, five or six millions of dollars left absolutely to you for the very good and sufficient reasons set forth in the will. If the estate had been devoted to founding an absurd nigger university, I would have been with you, for that would,

under the circumstances, have been an irrational disposition
of the property. But—"

"There is no use in urging me to change my determination," interrupted the doctor. "It is quite irrevoc-
able. No earthly consideration can move me a hair's
breadth."

During this discussion Mr. Craig, and Lucy, his daughter, had been sitting somewhat apart, both feeling uncomfortable with the thought that they were present at a conversation that was not intended for them to hear; and, as
the doctor finished his emphatic declaration of his intention, they both rose to go; but Louise interrupted the
movement.

"We are all friends here," she said, "and this matter
is certain to be talked of, not only here in Plato, but over
the whole county. It is essential that the truth shall be
known by as many as possible, and thus that erroneous
statements shall not pass current. I beg, therefore, that
you will not go, for there are other papers here that I wish
to read, and that may, perhaps, not be without some effect
on our friend." Whereupon Mr. Craig and Lucy resumed
their seats, and Louise, taking a letter from the box, spoke
again :

"This letter is, I see, addressed to me ; and, with your
permission, I will read it, especially as I perceive it is ex-
planatory of the objects that my father had in mind.

"' My dear child,'" she read, "'you will understand that
it is not from lack of affection for you that I have devised
the bulk of my estate to my friend Doctor Arthur Grattan,
to whom I commend you as the best friend you are ever
likely to have. Your own fortune is so large, and your
appreciation of great wealth so small, that I am not doing
you a wrong or inflicting upon you a slight, in making this
disposition of my property. As you know, we have often
talked the matter over, and you have always said that you

preferred that I should do exactly as I pleased in making
my will, and especially that I should not give any part of
my estate to you. I have, as you will see, disregarded your
wishes to the extent of leaving you the Hurricane Castle
property.

" ' I had contemplated making quite a different disposition of my estate ; but in a recent conversation with Doctor Grattan he convinced me that my intentions were not
wise, and, in thinking the matter over, I concluded to give
it to him, satisfied as I was that he would make a wise and
liberal use of it for the benefit of mankind. I have, however, placed no restrictions on him. He can do with it in
whole or in part exactly as he pleases. My own ideas would,
perhaps, be best coincided with if he should determine to
use two thirds of it for some benevolent or educational purpose, and retain the remainder for his own use. However,
all is left to him.

" ' And again, I think I have perceived that—' " Here
Louise stopped, and with a flushed face and some degree of
confusion of manner, folded the paper and placed it within
the envelope.

" The rest is, I see, of a private and personal character," she said, in a low tone. Then she sat down, still showing that she was embarrassed, and busied herself in looking
through the other papers in the box.

" The remainder are all deeds, mortgages, bonds, and
certificates of stock," she said at last, though still exhibiting a lack of her usual equanimity, "and the reading of
them would not be of interest. Perhaps Mr. Ellis will
kindly take charge of them."

" I think this letter places the matter in an entirely
different light," said that gentleman, returning the papers
to the box, with the exception of the letter which Louise
still held in her hand. " Grattan, you surely can not hold
out longer."

"I am more than ever positive that I shall never change," he answered. "The letter distinctly states that the alteration was made in consequence of my representations. I don't see how you can for a moment suppose that I would accept an estate of several millions of dollars under such circumstances. But, come, let us drop the subject.— My dear child," he continued, turning to Louise, "Cynthia and I wish you to come to us for a few days at least. Will you do so?"

Cynthia had already broached the matter to her, and she had determined to accede to the wishes of the doctor and his daughter. She felt the need of society such as they could give her, and she desired also to escape for a time from the house of death. Besides, she was not without the hope that she might yet succeed in causing the doctor to give up his intention of opposing the probate of the will. She therefore accepted the invitation, and that night saw her again an inmate of Mountain View.

# CHAPTER XV.

SEVERAL days elapsed without the occurrence of any notable event in the lives of our friends in Plato. Louise had made no further attempt to convert Doctor Grattan from his opinions relative to his duty in the matter of her father's will. She had settled down into a placid sort of an existence, and had not once visited Hurricane Castle. But there was nothing morbid about her mental processes. She was not one of those persons who, desiring to avoid all recollections of the loved ones they may have lost, shut up the rooms in which they have lived, and hide away the books and other things they loved. She intended to go back to Hurricane Castle, to let the light and the sunshine into every part of it, and to keep before her everything that could remind her of her dead father.

There was no bitterness in her heart in regard to any act of his life. To her he had always been good and kind, and, so far as she knew, good and kind to everybody. She pitied him. She knew how much he had suffered, and at times she felt that he had escaped still greater suffering by the catastrophe that had occurred. After she had been at Mountain View a few days, Doctor Grattan had, at her request, informed her of all the details of the coroner's inquest, and of the results of his own examination. He told her that the revelations of the scalpel had placed the fact of her father's insanity beyond the possibility of a doubt,

and that it was only strange that there had not been still
more decided evidences of mental derangement than those
that he had exhibited.

"If you had seen as much of my father as I did," said
Louise, "you would have perceived the very evidences of
which you speak. He was gradually getting into a habit
of exaggeration that was altogether at variance with his
real character."

"I observed at times something of the kind, but nothing very decided. He appeared still to have power to restrain himself in a measure when talking to me. But the
symptom you mention—the tendency to exaggeration, to
boast of his greatness, his importance, his immense wealth
—is that to which I refer, and the existence of which is
exactly in accordance with the diseased state of his brain."

The conversation had taken place in the doctor's pentagonal room, into which he had invited Louise and Cynthia, to hear the description of the personal appearance of
the hero in the novel he was writing. Cynthia had been
called off on some household matter, and the doctor had
been left alone with his guest. It was then that he had
told her of the inquest, and of what he had himself discovered.

After his last remark, Louise sat in silence for some
time, while the doctor impatiently turned over the leaves
of his manuscript, waiting for Cynthia's return, in order
that he might read to both the word-portrait of the chief
character of his book. Louise to his eyes had never looked
lovelier, except perhaps when he had seen her on the morning after her father's death. Hers was a face that was
sanctified and illuminated by sorrow, and that yet, at the
same time, never looked lugubrious. It gave the idea to
the observer that it belonged to a woman that could feel
and that could also think. The combination is a rare one.

But the doctor, though he had occasionally taken a furtive glance at the woman he loved—an act for which he inwardly cursed his weakness—kept his eyes for the most part fastened on his manuscript, making believe to be intensely interested in its perusal. He was embarrassed at finding himself alone with Louise. During the few days that she had been a member of his household, he had succeeded in avoiding all such occasions as the present; but this had been forced upon him in a way that he could not control. He had, it is true, arisen from his chair when Cynthia left the room, intending to make some excuse for following her, but a moment's reflection sufficed to bring him to the consciousness that such an act would be one that Louise would not fail to understand, and would also be a piece of gratuitous impoliteness of which he could not afford to be guilty; so he had sat down again, and begun to pore over his book as though there were nothing on earth half so interesting as the pages he had covered with his thoughts.

Louise likewise, for a reason that will be made apparent hereafter, did not feel entirely at her ease after Cynthia's departure left her and her host alone together; but, as is usual with women, she had tact, while the doctor was almost entirely devoid of this valuable quality. She knew that sitting together in silence was not conducive to ease. On the contrary, every moment that passed without something being said increased the feeling of restraint that she experienced, and, she could not doubt, added to that under which her companion labored. She perceived that his occupation was assumed for the occasion. She had seen him glance at her, and she was quite sure that, although his attention was absorbed in the manuscript he held before his face, he did not comprehend a word that passed before his eyes, but that his thoughts were fixed upon her, probably busy with the idea as to how he could get out of the room without infringing the rules of good-

breeding. Perhaps it was as suitable a time as would likely
be afforded her for making a final attempt to change his
determination relative to the course he meant to take in
regard to her father's will. Monday of the following week
was the day fixed upon for presenting it for probate, and
on that day, she, the doctor, and Mr. Ellis, would be
obliged to go to Elizabethtown, the county-seat, in order
to appear before the surrogate. She knew that in his present frame of mind the doctor would protest against the
validity of the will, in which case a trial would have to
take place, and evidence for and against her father's sanity and testamentary capacity brought forward. Yes, she
would make a final attempt to cause him to see the matter
in what she regarded as its true light.

"My father was insane on some subjects," she said,
raising her eyes from the contemplation of the Persian rug
that covered the center of the floor, and looking at the
doctor, "but upon others he was singularly clear and
exact. His appreciation of individuals never left him.
Hence the high estimation in which he held you. It is
not strange, therefore, that he should devise the bulk of
his estate to you."

"Pardon me," said the doctor, rousing himself, "but
it appears to me—and will also, I think, to all persons who,
unlike you, are able to see me as I really am—that the provisions of his will that refer to me are the most conclusive
evidence of his mental derangement that has yet been advanced. They are what I shall chiefly rely upon Monday
next in the testimony that I shall give before the surrogate. He spoke of me as the best man he had ever known.
There is the tendency to exaggeration which is so characteristic a feature of the form of insanity from which he
suffered. That one expression ought to be sufficient to upset the will."

"You did not know my father as I did," remarked

Louise, her face flushing a little with the interest that the discussion aroused. "He was full of warm feelings that he seemed to be constantly endeavoring to conceal, but which yet at times would show themselves. I know how highly he esteemed you, and not only that, for I know that he regarded you as the one person among his acquaintances who had never hesitated to tell him the truth, even when it might have been unpleasant for him to hear it. When he wrote that you were the best man he had ever known, he believed it as firmly as Napoleon Bonaparte believed what he wrote in his will, that Baron Larrey, his chief surgeon, was the most honest man he had ever known."

"Yes; but Napoleon Bonaparte had known Larrey for a great many years; he had trusted him in many things, and had never found him faithless; he had had abundant opportunity for observing his integrity in all his relations with others. Now, your father knew me for only a short time, and, I may say, scarcely intimately at any time. Of my antecedents he knew absolutely nothing. It was, therefore, a totally unwarranted opinion that he expressed when he said that I was the best man he had ever known."

"Then you adhere to your determination in spite of all I can say. You will bring forward all the evidence you can obtain relative to my father's mental derangement, and this you will do merely to satisfy your own sense of pride. I do not think it will be kind. It will grieve me very much."

Doctor Grattan looked troubled at this speech. He rose from his chair, and, going to the big window at the end of the room, looked out at the Giant, white with snow from top to base. He felt that she was unjust, and he wondered whether or not she really understood his position, a position which, in his opinion, was one that absolutely forbade his acceptance of the estate that had been willed to him. He stood for several minutes thinking of what he should do in the way of further discussing the matter with her. His back was turned to her, and he began to feel that it would be a difficult matter for him to face her and let her see the change which he knew had come over his countenance. If Cynthia would only return, and thus save him the necessity of a reply to her assertions, which were almost of the nature of accusations, he would be thankful. It was cowardly of him, he felt, to wish to escape the ordeal that sooner or later must be met, and perhaps, after all, it were better to meet it now. Yes, he would tell her all—all that her father had confessed relative to his life as a slaver; of his remorse; of the attempt that had been made to arrest him, and which was only unsuccessful for the reason that he had gone beyond the jurisdiction of any earthly court. Then she would see that there were other reasons than those that concerned him for showing to the world that her father had not been a responsible being.

But a moment's further reflection was sufficient to convince him that such a course would be still more cowardly than an entire evasion of a reply, for it would be an attempt to justify himself by causing her pain, and that, too, at a time when she was ill able to bear any increase of suffering. No, the whole matter of the confession and of the attempt made to arrest him, must be kept from her, at least till he had obtained the most irrefragable proof that there was no real foundation for either; and, in the mean time, he would go on and do his duty as he understood it, even though she should misjudge him.

As to Louise, no sooner had she spoken and noticed the effect that her words had produced upon the doctor, than she began to experience the remorse that all well-constituted persons—especially women—feel when they know that they have wounded the sensibilities of a friend. She perceived that she had been unjust, and that her language had been of such a character as to make him believe that

her idea of his contemplated course was, that he was actuated by lower motives than those he had alleged ; that,
in fact, he had assumed a virtue that he did not possess.
She rose and approached him, but so gently that he did
not know that she was near him till he felt her hand
touch his arm ; then he turned, and their eyes met.

"I was wrong," she said, still letting her hand rest
upon his arm, " cruelly wrong, after all your goodness to
me and to my father. After all that I know of your truth
and honor, to say what I said was an outrage for which I
ask your pardon. Forgive me ; I suppose it is impossible
for women to see such things as men see them. Some one
has said that we are devoid of all chivalrous feeling. I believe we are."

"Yes, you were cruel," he assented, looking very grave
and sad ; "but perhaps, after all, the fault is mine for not
having clearly placed before you my idea of my duty to
you and to myself. Now, give me five minutes, or even
less, and, if at the end of that time you still think that I
can honorably accept your father's bequest, I shall act in
accordance with your wishes."

"But first," she said, taking his hand and raising it to
her lips, " you must say that you forgive me."

"I do forgive you, my dear child," looking fondly at
her, "and," he added, not seeking to extenuate her trans-
gression, "I was sure you would see for yourself that you
had been unjust. Now, listen to me, for this is the last
time that I shall make an attempt to justify myself in
your or anybody else's eyes.

"In the first place, I know that your father was insane.
That fact would, of itself, be sufficient to prevent me, as
an honest and honorable man, from accepting his bequest.

"In the second place, he informed me that he intended
to make a disposition of his property that I told him was
absurd. In consequence of my representations, he changes

his determination and leaves his estate to me. No honorable man could consent to be placed in the position in which acceptance of his bounty would place him. I pretend to be an honorable man.

"These two reasons are imperative. Were I to disregard them, I should forfeit the very highest source of happiness that I possess—my self-respect. It is with me greater than everything else in all the world. I could be made to suffer continual bodily torments, and yet wish to live ; I could be deserted by all mankind, and the love of existence would still remain. I could even see my dear child perish before my eyes, and still the desire for life would be in me. But, were I to lose my self-respect, as I should with the consciousness that I had committed a dishonorable act, I should put a pistol to my head and blow my brains out ! Now do you understand ?"

He spoke the last words brusquely, almost fiercely. His face was flushed, his eyes sparkled—glared, in fact—and his whole form trembled with the emotion that actuated him. Louise was frightened. She had never seen him moved like this, and yet she felt her whole heart go out to him—to this man who, for the sake of an idea, refused millions of dollars, which the law would give him if he would only keep silent and let things take their own course.

"I understand," she said, at last ; "and again I ask your forgiveness ; I shall never renew the subject. You shall do what you think is right."

"Do you think it is right that I, knowing what I do, feeling as I do, should take this money ?"

"I consulted my own wishes rather than my sense of right," she said, with downcast eyes.

"Louise, be frank with me—unreservedly frank. Do you think I ought to take this money ?"

"No," she answered, raising her eyes to his.

"Thanks ! Now I am happier than at any time since

your poor father died." He took her hand, held it for a moment, and then turned as though to depart, but, as he did so, Cynthia entered the room. She started as she saw her father and Louise engaged in what was evidently an earnest conversation. But ere she could retreat, the conference was broken, so she came smilingly forward.

"Papa, dear," she said, "are you going to see Mr. Frazier now?"

"Yes, and if you don't go with me I believe the man will jump up and come here. Something has upset the fellow. What, I can't conceive. He is doing splendidly, and may not be a bit lame; but for all that he is awfully low-spirited."

"And all on account of not seeing me?"

"I didn't say that, Miss Vanity. A letter he received, so Will Hadden tells me, preceded the melancholy. Some business trouble, I suppose. Pig-iron has gone down while he's overloaded with it, or has gone up when he hasn't any. That is the sort of thing that upsets these people. Business—business—business! They're never satisfied. What does it profit a man, I'd like to know, if he makes a million dollars a year, and gets softening of the brain? Somebody else enjoys his money, and he gets his board and clothes —pretty bad, too, both of them—in a lunatic-asylum, with the chance of having his ribs broken by a murderous attendant!"

"Have you quite finished, papa?" said Cynthia, demurely, as the doctor stopped to take breath—"because, if you haven't, Louise and I will sit down while you give us the rest of the lecture."

"Did you ever see a man so browbeaten by a petty tyrant?" exclaimed the doctor, addressing Louise, upon whose face a smile was beginning to appear. "I declare I scarcely dare say my soul's my own, or even open my mouth to say anything."

"What have you got to do with souls, anyhow?" said Cynthia, linking her hands around his arm. "A man that believes in Buddhism and Nirvana, and I don't know what other incomprehensible things, has nothing to do with souls. Come, kiss me, and tell me whether or not I'm to go with you to see that poor man who is dying for the sight of me."

"Of course, you're to go; didn't I tell you so long ago?"

"No; you said that if I didn't go he would come here, and I wasn't sure that that was not what you wanted. It would suit me quite as well, sir, quite as well," making a mock courtesy to him as she spoke. "But, no," she continued, "Louise is going for a walk, and it wouldn't be proper for me to have him here. So I'll go with you."

"Beautiful ideas of propriety, upon my word!" exclaimed the doctor, with a laugh. "You can go to see a young man, but he mustn't come to see you—or rather two young men."

"Two young men?"

"Yes, of course. There is Will Hadden, his companion and nurse."

"Oh, I had forgotten that. I don't think I'll go."

"I can send Will Hadden out of the way, and bring in Mrs. Ruggles, who doubtless will be perfectly willing to chaperone you during your visit. But Louise?"

"I am going to take a walk," she said. "I think I shall stroll over to Hurricane Castle, if only to see that all is going on well."

"You are not getting ready to leave us?"

"No, not if you will keep me awhile longer yet. I don't think I could bear to stay there yet awhile."

"A year, two years, all your life, if you will!" cried Cynthia.

"Louise knows we shall never tire of her," said the doctor.

" Yes," she answered, "I know that. You are very kind ; so kind that—that—"

She stopped, overcome by her emotion, and, turning away, left the room, Cynthia following her.

It was only a few minutes before the latter returned, fully equipped for her drive.

" Louise is not strong yet," she said. " A very little upsets her ; she will go out after awhile, and the walk will do her good."

When they arrived at the " Bear," the doctor left Cynthia in the sitting-room with Mrs. Ruggles, while he went up-stairs to perform his surgical duties to his patient. He found him getting along admirably ; his face had almost resumed its natural appearance, and he saw now, what he had not seen before, that George Frazier was a remarkably handsome man. Will Hadden was sitting by the bedside with a manuscript in his hand, from which he had evidently been reading ; but, on the doctor's entrance, he laid it aside and prepared to assist him in the work which the patient required to have done for him every morning.

"I am sorry to interrupt you, Will," said the doctor, "but doubtless the story, which I perceive is your own, will keep a few hours.—How are you to-day, Mr. Frazier ? "

"I did not sleep well last night, and I think I had a little fever."

" Yes, and you have still—not only a little, but a good deal. What have you eaten ? "

" Oh, nothing of any consequence. The fact is, I've had bad news—"

" Nothing serious, I hope ? "

" That's according to the way in which it is regarded. To me it seems very serious. I suppose, if I had looked at it indifferently, I wouldn't have had a sleepless night and a fever    I think I ought to tell you," he continued, as Will Hadden left the room to get some hot water. " You are my physician and, I trust, my friend. You may be able to help me in both capacities if I make a clean breast of it."

"You alone can judge properly on those points. I certainly shall help you, both as physician and friend, to the utmost of my power."

"You recollect," resumed Frazier, "that, the morning after I broke my thigh, I was very particular to get your opinion relative to the probability of my future lameness. You said you thought I should certainly be a little lame. I was engaged to be married to a lady who I thought loved me; but as I had often heard her declare, in a laughing sort of a way, that she would never marry a man that was lame or in any way deformed, I added a postscript to a letter I had written her to the effect that you had said I would have one leg a little shorter than the other. In this letter I had begged her to come to me and to be married on the day that had been fixed for our wedding."

"And she refuses!" exclaimed the doctor.

"She not only refuses, but she declares that our engagement is at an end. She expresses a great deal of sorrow for me and for herself, but says that she is so constituted that the very sight of a lame or malformed person makes her faint, and that marriage with such a one would be an impossibility."

"I think you are well rid of her. You are to be congratulated on having broken your leg before rather than after marriage."

"I was very fond of her, and she seemed to be fond of me. I suppose she has an unconquerable prejudice against lame people. In that case she is scarcely to blame."

"It is not necessary to consider whether she is to blame or not. She is evidently not the sort of a woman to be your wife, or the wife of any other man that is not gifted with a charmed life, or does not live shut up in a fire-and-burglar-proof safe. But is the affair off absolutely?"

"Yes, she has sent back all my letters and the engagement-ring."

"It would be a good punishment for her if you should not be lame, after all."

"But is that possible?"

"Yes, quite so. There was no shortening yesterday when I measured the limbs. If you continue to go on as well as you have since the accident, I should not be surprised to find you well without any appreciable shortening. In that case you could resume relations with your lady-love."

"That would be impossible, I think."

"Then, for Heaven's sake, my young friend, don't be feeling as though the end of the world had come because you have ended an engagement to an unnatural woman! I say unnatural, for, whether she is foolish or possessed of an idiosyncrasy that she can not control, she is unnatural, or rather abnormal. Never marry a woman with an idiosyncrasy. There's no telling what may come of it."

"I suppose that by idiosyncrasy you mean peculiarity?"

"Well, yes, a pathological peculiarity, a deranged instinct, a something that women in general don't have, and that renders her a nuisance to herself and others. Now you must cheer up. Depressing emotions interfere with the process of bony union. If you want to make perfectly sure of not being lame, you must be jolly."

"But I can't be jolly. How can I, when I am constantly thinking of my disappointment? She is so lovely, so intelligent!"

"And so idiosyncratic that she won't marry you because she thinks you are going to be lame?"

"Yes."

"Get her out of your mind. Put some one else in her place."

The doctor had no sooner spoken the words, than the

thought struck him that Cynthia was down-stairs, waiting
to be introduced to the patient. He was horrified at the
turn matters had taken, for he saw that under the circumstances it would be out of the question for him to allow
his daughter to visit this young man, who had lost one love,
and whom he had just advised to get another. No, the
idea of Cynthia coming in under this changed state of
affairs was entirely out of the question. It was a narrow
escape, and he shuddered as he reflected upon the possibilities that had been so near. Visits from his daughter to
this young man would be certain to be misinterpreted, and
he and she would both lay themselves open to the charge
that they had manœuvred to catch a matrimonial prize.
He was not that kind of a man, and Cynthia was not that
kind of a woman.

Just as he was in the midst of his reflections, Will Hadden entered with the hot water.

"Miss Cynthia," he said, "wants to know whether she
will have time to go over to Hurricane Castle for a moment
with Miss Lamar."

"Yes," answered the doctor, eagerly. "Go down, Will,
please, and tell her I'll join her there in a few minutes."

"Is Miss Grattan down-stairs?" inquired Frazier, and
then, without waiting for an answer—"Didn't you promise that she should come and read to me for a little while
every day?"

"I believe I did," replied the doctor with some embarrassment of manner, "but then circumstances alter cases.
In the first place, you've got Will Hadden to read to you;
and, in the next, you're not a married man, or, what is next
thing to it, an engaged one."

"Then you won't allow her to come?"

"I'm afraid I shall have to come to that determination."

"It's very hard. At any rate, there can be no objection

to her coming here to see me this morning while you are present. I am sick and a stranger ; let her come, if only to ask me how I am. The sight of a kind and good woman, such as she is, will be of more service to me than all your pills and potions."

" Well, I suppose I might allow that much," said the doctor, reflectively. Then to Will Hadden, " Tell her to come up for a moment, before she goes to Hurricane Castle."

Will, who had listened with interest to this conversation, and who was rejoiced at the turn it had taken, went off on his errand, a little chagrined that Cynthia was, after all, to visit Mr. Frazier, even for a few minutes, and in her father's presence. He knew that his own case was hopeless, but he had not yet reached that stage of decline in the intensity of his feeling that would permit him to view with indifference the attentions of another man ; and that attention would come if she visited him and read to him, he felt morally certain. He was aware, too, that with many men the period when they are just off with an old love is the very one at which they are most apt to be on with a new, and, though he knew nothing certain in regard to Mr. Frazier's love-affairs, he had strong reason for believing that the mental depression that he had exhibited during the past few days was the result of some kind of a disarrangement in their course. Will was a very honorable and straightforward young fellow. He would have scorned to pry into other people's business, but he had brought a letter to Frazier, the direction of which was in a woman's handwriting, and that was post-marked New York. He knew that Miss Drummond, the lady Frazier expected to marry, lived in New York, for Frazier had told him so, and had even informed him of the date on which the wedding was to take place. Since the receipt of the letter, nothing had been said about the marriage, and nothing about the

advent of the young lady herself to take the charge of the
nursing arrangements for her maimed lover.  He was quite
certain, therefore, that Frazier had met with an obstruction to his matrimonial plans.  And he was sure that the
present was a dangerous time for Cynthia to make the acquaintance of the young man.  Nevertheless, he delivered
his message, and Cynthia, following him, was ushered into
Mr. Frazier's room.

# CHAPTER XVI.

THE appearance of Cynthia Grattan in his room was
an event that was calculated to stir Mr. George Frazier's
pulses to no inconsiderable extent, even if Miss Julia
Drummond had not—to use his friend Digby Wyant's
phrase in a letter he had that morning received—"gone
back on him." In the first place, she was looking remarkably pretty. The jaunty little hat that she wore, with its
single eagle's feather rakishly (nautical word) set on one side,
the trim jacket that fitted her graceful figure to perfection,
the dainty dark-brown gloves that incased her little hands,
all added to the effect which her face and her general *en-
semble* produced. As she stood in a half-hesitating way
just inside the door, waiting a moment for her father—who
was bending over his patient and did not at once see her—
to introduce her, Frazier thought he had never seen a vision of more perfect loveliness. "By Heaven," he thought,
"she looks as though she had just dropped down from the
skies, or come up from a fairy grotto!"

"I'm sorry you are so ill," she said, advancing toward
the sick man and holding out her hand to him; "but
papa tells me every day how you are getting along, and
doubtless now in a few weeks you will be all right
again."

She spoke with a smile on her face and a cheeriness in
her voice that went straight to Frazier's heart.

11

He took her hand, retaining it a second, while he thanked her for the flowers and the little delicacies that she had repeatedly sent him. "I was hoping that you would come and read to me and tell me of what is going on in the outside world," he continued ; "but the autocrat, who governs you and me, has put a veto on that arrangement. Perhaps you can come in and override him, just as a two-thirds vote in Congress upsets a presidential veto."

"Oh, you don't know him yet," exclaimed Cynthia, who with her ready tact had discovered at once that something had occurred to change the plan that had been agreed upon. "I'd as soon think of trying to upset the Giant. Perhaps you don't know what the Giant is. It's not a man, but the high mountain that shuts off the rays of the sun for an hour or more after they ought to shine on us in the morning."

"Is he as bad as that ? Then I'm afraid the case is really hopeless. I ran against one of your mountains and broke my leg. If I run against him, I shall break my head."

"So long as it isn't your heart, you needn't mind it much," said Cynthia, archly.

"Which means, I suppose, that my head isn't worth much. Well, I agree with you. If I had broken it instead of my leg, it might have been better for me in the long run."

He spoke with a little bitterness in his tone that was not lost on Cynthia, and that at once awoke all the sympathy of her warm and generous disposition.

"You have suffered very much," she said, softly. "Papa has told me how bravely you have borne the pain and the confinement. It must be a horrible thing for a man in full health and strength to be struck down as you were, and condemned to absolute inaction for several months."

" Yes, it is very horrible. Day after day to lie here, cut off from all association with one's fellow - creatures, is a condition calculated to bring the blues if anything can."

" But you wouldn't be much better off if you could walk all over Plato. You have the two best men in the village to associate with—my father and Will Hadden."

" Yes, they're very good, but—"

" But you get tired of seeing so much of them and of them only. Think of me, shut up in the house with the biggest and most ferocious of the two ! "

" I have thought of you. Ever since you sent me those first roses I have been wondering what you looked like, and wishing that you would come to see me."

" And now you know what I look like, and I have come to see you."

" But you are going away again in a few minutes. The Great Mogul said so before you came up. I think I've been treated very badly."

" I'll lend you some books. Do you read much when you're at home ? "

" Not so much as I ought, for I'm very busy at my works. I have to look after nearly a thousand workmen. But I could not do without books."

" And now the thousand workmen have to look after themselves ? "

" Yes, and very badly they are doing it too, I'm afraid. I saw by a paper that I got yesterday that they are contemplating a strike."

" And if they strike, the works will stop ? "

" Certainly."

" That must make you very anxious."

" No ; on the contrary, I don't care anything about it, except for the suffering that will ensue to the poor women and children."

Cynthia thought for a moment before pursuing the subject further. She was agreeably impressed with Mr. George Frazier, and pleasant people were not so plentiful in Plato that she was not willing to avail herself of the opportunity now offered her of improving an acquaintanceship that promised well. At the same time she was aware that, for some reason or other, it was not thought by her father desirable that she should see much of his patient. She was very obedient to his slightest wish, the moment she perceived that he was in earnest; and something in his look, his manner—something—told her that he was in earnest now. Upon the whole, she thought she had better go; so she arose from the chair upon which she was sitting near the head of the bed.

"Don't go yet," said Frazier, imploringly; "I have not told you what books I like; in fact, I've scarcely had a chance to say a word to you."

"My friend Miss Lamar is waiting for me down-stairs. But, as to books, tell me what you like. I judge of people very much by the books they read."

"In that case I shall have to be careful. Let me see," turning his eyes up to the ceiling as though in deep thought. "Upon the whole, I'll let you choose for me. Send me whatever you think will best suit a man with a double fracture of his thigh.—And, doctor, you'll bring Miss Grattan with you to-morrow, won't you?"

"No, I think not quite so soon as that. Perhaps in a day or two. It will not be necessary for me to see you every day now. You are getting along so nicely that you can dispense with the frequent visits that have heretofore been requisite."

"That I will not submit to. I insist on your coming every day. If you don't put in an appearance here every morning, I'll pull off the whole apparatus, and sue you for malpractice."

" Well, well, we'll see about it.—Come, Cynthia ; Miss Lamar will think you have forgotten her."

" Yes, papa.—Good-by, Mr. Frazier. I'll send you a book that I think you'll like.—Good-morning, Will. Is that the famous story you have rolled up there ? "

" He was reading it to me when your father came," said Frazier. " It interested me greatly. Hadden has power, and will make his mark some day."

" That he is sure to do.—You will lend it to me, won't you, Will, when you have finished reading it to Mr. Frazier ? "

" Yes, if you would like to read it."

" Of course I would like to read it. Literary Platonians are not so plenty as blackberries, that we can afford to neglect them ; so bring it to me as soon as you have harassed Mr. Frazier's soul sufficiently with its pathos or expanded his heart enough with its wit."

She was gone, and Frazier felt for a moment as though he had awakened from a delicious dream to the dull realities of life. He closed his eyes, as if by so doing he could bring back the delightful image ; and thus he lay in silence, while Will Hadden stood by his side with the manuscript in his hand ready to go on with the story. He too had his thoughts, but they were such as showed him, still more strongly than had any others he had yet entertained, the hopelessness of his love for Cynthia. There had been no unkindness in her manner toward him ; no evidence that she was offended at the attempts he had made to gain her heart. She had treated him exactly as though she had never heard of his passion, and with a friendly indifference, even familiarity, that he knew she would never have assumed if there had been any special feeling for him in her heart. Nothing she could have said or done could have so thoroughly demolished the castles in the air that he had occasionally, notwithstanding the rebuffs she had given him when he had ventured to speak of his love, delighted to build, as the good-natured indifference she had exhibited toward him.

As to Frazier, he continued to lie with his eyes shut for several minutes, his face wearing a troubled expression that Will Hadden did not fail to notice. Will was a very human young man as well as a very good one, as young men go ; but it was scarcely to be expected that he would view with indifference the possibilities of the acquaintanceship of Cynthia Grattan and Mr. George Frazier. He had no difficulty in perceiving that each was pleased with the other. He was quite sure that his employer was lying there with his eyes shut, in order that, by closing them to all external objects, he might reflect more coherently and concretely on the visit he had just received. In fact, Will was beginning to experience the first twinges of that most stinging of all the passions—jealousy.

He wondered how long Mr. Frazier was going to keep him standing there with his manuscript in his hand. He arranged the bedclothes, hoping that the act would disturb the man and make him open his eyes. This not succeeding, he poked the fire, and let the tongs fall with a sharp clatter on the hearth. Still the man lay there with his eyes shut, and without moving an arm or twitching a muscle of his face ; his legs he could not move, for they were bandaged together and fastened to cords, which, with weights and pulleys, kept one of them continually on the stretch. Finally, he said :

"Are you asleep, Mr. Frazier ? "

Frazier opened his eyes and looked about him in a dazed sort of a way. Then he smiled.

"Really, Hadden," he said, " that is the most difficult question to answer that was ever put to me. I think I must have been hypnotized. I was completely abstracted. Have you been here all the time since Miss Grattan went away ? "

" Yes. I suppose you won't care to hear the rest of the story now ? "

" Oh, but I do ! Where were we ? Let me see ! Hugh Loftus had just discovered that his employer was in love with the girl. Poor devil ! I'm afraid things are going badly with him. Girls, unless they are much more high-toned than the majority, don't take up with the man when they can get the master. You know Miss Grattan very well, don't you ? "

" Yes, we were children together," answered Hadden, a little uneasily.

" She seems to like you now very much."

" Oh, yes ! we have always been friends."

" Has she always lived here ? "

" Ever since she was an infant ; but I think she was born in New York."

" She's very pretty."

" She is not only pretty, but she's good. I never saw her out of temper."

" Yes, she's jolly ; but if she's never been out of temper, it's because she's never had anything to ruffle her much. She's got spirit enough, I'll bet, if you do or say anything to rouse it, or I'm no judge of women. Now go on with the story, please—I'm interested in the fate of Mr. Hugh Loftus."

Louise and Cynthia, after leaving the " Bear," walked over to Hurricane Castle ; while the doctor, getting into his sleigh—into which the two girls declined to enter, prefer-ring, as they said, to walk—went on his rounds among his patients. It was not a very busy day with him, so that he was through early, and enabled to return home and resume work on his novel, in which he was becoming every day more and more interested.

But he found, on sitting down to his work at the big table in the focus of the pentagonal room, that his mind was not in the state most favorable for literary composition of the kind he affected. He could have run off strings of the insipid stuff which has recently, because it is grammatical and rhetorical, been lauded to the skies by a narrow coterie, as segments of the long-looked-for "American novel." He could have said a great deal about nothing, as can most men that have received a good education, but he did not regard this as the true purpose of fiction. He thought the imagination is the first mental faculty to be brought into play in the construction of the novel, and he believed that no one who has not seen a great deal of life in all its phases is competent to evolve characterization out of his inner consciousness. He therefore skimmed over, with an indifference amounting almost to contempt, the many pages devoid of incident and filled with descriptions of uninteresting and lack-luster men and women, or with delineations of others such as no human being had ever encountered. He knew that the authors of these colorless compositions prided themselves on the skill that they had exhibited. Yes, they showed skill. He was ready to admit that, but it was the sort of skill that the painstaking and altogether unprofitable drudge displays that makes Westminster Abbeys and Warwick Castles out of cork. His productions are pretty to look at for a moment or two, but no one cares ·to put one of them among his artistic treasures or even to glance at it a second time. To-day his imagination failed him altogether—he was not in the mood ; and he might as well have tried to lift three hundred pounds' weight with muscles that could only raise two hundred and fifty, as to attempt to compose satisfactorily, with a mind unequal to the work.

But there was something he could do, and that had to be done now, and that was to look up the account of the killing of Captain Clyde in the streets of Matanzas, and all the other circumstances connected with the capture of the

slaver Alatamba. He knew that he had preserved the letter that his cousin, the commander of the Canandaigua,
had written him, and that the newspapers of the day, containing accounts of the shooting of that officer and of the
trial of the assassin, had also been carefully put away. He
was not, however, very methodical in keeping such things,
and it was some time, therefore, before he found them. At
last, however, he discovered them, and sitting down before
the fire began their perusal.

First, there was the letter from his cousin, Commander
Clyde, describing the pursuit and capture of the slave-ship
Alatamba, commanded by that notorious person, Captain
Juan Lamarez, who, the letter went on to state, had at last
a prospect of meeting with his just deserts. Then there
was a postscript dated two days subsequently, to the effect
that Lamarez had escaped and was supposed to be hiding,
more or less protected by the Cuban authorities in Matanzas.

So far, the account tallied very closely with that given
by Mr. Lamar in the confession he had made to the doctor.

Then came a series of newspaper articles, consisting of
telegrams and letters from Cuba, giving accounts of the
killing of Captain Clyde by Juan Lamarez, the slaver-captain, and of the arrest, trial, and acquittal of that individual, on the ground that he had acted in self-defense—Captain Clyde having had no right to attempt his arrest on
Cuban soil.

In another paper was the report of the action of the
United States Government in the premises. A demand
had been made on the Spanish authorities for the rendition
of Captain Juan Lamarez, to be tried on the charge of
piracy. To this, polite answer had been given that the
man had left Cuba, and was hence no longer under the
jurisdiction of Spain. This seemed to be the end of the
matter.

On the day following Mr. Lamar's death, the doctor had written to Judge Conway relative to the warrant issued by that magistrate, and which the deputy United States marshal had ineffectually endeavored to serve. To this, he had that morning received an answer that had fully confirmed the suspicions he had formed, to the effect that action had been taken upon a very circumstantial confession made by Mr. Lamar, and which, as the judge declared, left him no alternative but to proceed in the manner already known to the reader. The judge went on to state that the inquiry that had been instituted left no doubt upon his mind that the statements made by the self-accused man were substantially correct, so far as all the details of Juan Lamarez's life were concerned. "Of course," he wrote, "if Mr. Lamar was insane, grave doubt must exist in regard to the truth of his story ; but if, on the contrary, he was of sound mind, I do not see how we can escape the conviction that he and Juan Lamarez are one and the same person, and therefore that he was guilty, as he himself has alleged. The ends of justice do not require that publicity shall be given to the matter, and therefore all the papers in the case shall remain, for the present, at least, among the archives of the district attorney's office."

The subject, therefore, was narrowed down to one chief point for investigation, and that was the question of the identity of John Lamar with Juan Lamarez, and Dr. Grattan did not see how that was to be settled otherwise than by a visit to Cuba, in which island Mr. Lamar had certainly resided prior to his return to Italy, after his absence of fourteen years. Yes, there was no escape from it—to Cuba he must go, and that as soon as possible after the submission of the will to probate.

Upon reflection, he had concluded that it would be better for him to allow the probate to go by default. It would be easy enough to reopen it when he returned from

Cuba with indubitable evidence that the dead man had been the victim of delusion relative to his life, and that he and Captain Juan Lamarez were two separate and distinct persons. It would be easy, he felt assured, to obtain this evidence. There must be many persons in Matanzas and other parts of Cuba, who were well acquainted with the slaver-captain, and who could therefore describe his personal appearance, as well as give salient details of his history, that would serve to show conclusively that the opinion he held was correct. He would go armed with photographs, specimens of the handwriting, and other means of identification. It was not beyond possibility that Juan Lamarez himself was still alive, and that he might be found and induced to furnish evidence that would be irrefragable in character. "It is my duty," he said, "to do all in my power to clear that poor child of the stigma of being the daughter of a slaver. It will be impossible to keep the matter quiet for all time. Little by little it will leak out. All the officials will not probably be as kind and considerate as is Judge Conway, and then she will be crushed by a blow to which the death of her father will seem as nothing. I must go to Cuba, and that at once."

He turned to his table, at one end of which were his writing-materials, and began to write a letter to a physician in a neighboring village, asking him to look after his practice for three or four weeks, during which, as he said, he expected to be absent in the South. As he folded the letter, his eyes fell upon the book that he had borrowed from Will Hadden, and of which he had already read a few pages—"The Life and Adventures of Captain Juan de Ayolas." He directed his letter, and placed it in the receptacle, to which Mike made several visits a day for the purpose of getting the contents and mailing them, and then, still not feeling like going to work on his novel, he picked up the book and settled himself to the occupation of reading it till Louise and Cynthia should return in time for dinner. He had still half an hour at his disposal, and in that time he thought he could make himself master of the chief points in the career of the somewhat remarkable individual to the history of whose life the book was devoted. He had, while at Mrs. Hadden's, on the evening of Mr. Lamar's death, read a few pages relating to the boyhood of Captain de Ayolas, and had been interested in the account of the escapades of the young man, and of several adventures in which he had displayed the most wonderful courage and powers of endurance. He had not read far on the present occasion before his interest became aroused to a still more extraordinary degree. Occasionally he would utter some emphatic exclamation, and again stop, and, dropping the book on the table, throw himself back in his chair, and, with closed eyes, appear to be thinking deeply on what he had been reading. Finally, he closed the volume, and, rising, went to the big bay-window at the end of the room and looked out at his mountains. But only for a moment. He was too much excited to remain quiet even at such a solacing occupation as that of regarding the peaks and ridges, which were white with snow, and glistening in the noonday sun. So he turned, and impatiently strided over the floor as a lion or a tiger treads the narrow cage in which it is confined. Suddenly he darted through the two doors which connected his room with the rest of the house, and, going to the kitchen, at the other end of the building, called out to the cook and maid-of-all-work, "Tell Miss Cynthia that I shall not be home to dinner," and was in the act of putting on his hat and fur coat, when the front door opened, and Mr. Ellis stood in the entrance. "Hallo, Ellis!" exclaimed the doctor, "you're the very man I wanted to see; I was going round to your house. I've got to the bottom of this thing at last. Come in ; I was going to ask you to give me my dinner while we talked it over. Now you shall dine with me, and then we will go into my room and give the after-noon to it."

"Then we are both of a mind, for I have important information to give you. I've been going over Mr. Lamar's papers, and I find a good deal about which I want your ad-vice."

"Come in—don't let us waste time here ; I can get through what I have to say before dinner, as Cynthia and Miss Lamar have not yet returned."

The doctor led the way to his pentagonal room, and, after he had got Mr. Ellis into a chair—he was himself too much excited to sit down—he opened his batteries.

Taking "The Life and Adventures of Captain Juan de Ayolas" from the breast-pocket of his coat, he said :

"Do you see that book ? Well, that book is the auto-biography of Mr. Lamar ; or, to be exactly correct, as I understand the matter, it is the source whence he obtained the material for the account of himself that he gave me."

"How do you know that ?"

"How do I know it ? That's a sensible question. I know it because I recollect the whole of what he told me of himself, and I have just read that book, and I find the account there given by Captain Juan de Ayolas of his own life and adventures is the same even to the most minute particulars."

"That is very extraordinary. But how do you know that Captain Juan de Ayolas and Mr. John Lamar are not one and the same person ?"

"By certain features which I think point conclusively to the fact that Mr. Lamar has read this book, and that it made so deep an impression upon him that he gradually got to think that it described his own life. He, in fact, considered himself to be Juan de Ayolas."

"But you told me, I think, that his other name was Juan Lamarez."

"Yes, I did, and that was the identical name assumed by Juan de Ayolas when he went into the slave-trade."

"It's very remarkable."

"No, it isn't so very wonderful. Mr. Lamar undoubtedly had a diseased brain. He read this book, and, as I have just said, he adopted the name, life, adventures, everything, so far as he could, of the hero. He in his own estimation became Juan de Ayolas and Juan Lamarez."

"I don't think you make it clear that he really is not Juan de Ayolas. He might have written this book himself."

"I don't think it is possible; but listen to me a moment while I give you the points. Captain de Ayolas," he continued, turning over the leaves of the book as he spoke, "was born in Seville forty-five years ago; John Lamar was born in New York nearly fifty years ago. Juan de Ayolas was brought up as a sailor, and was engaged in the trade between Cadiz and the west coast of Africa; John Lamar was a student at Oxford, and never knew anything about the sea more than could have been obtained by crossing the Atlantic as a passenger. Juan de Ayolas is shown by this book to have been thoroughly a sailor; I know of my own knowledge that John Lamar did not even know the names of a ship's sails or parts of her rigging. Juan de Ayolas went into the slave-trade twenty years ago, and continued in it till captured, nearly five years since, by the United States cruiser Can'andaigua; John Lamar, according to his own account, became a slaver about ten years ago. And, finally, Juan de Ayolas, under the name of Juan Lamarez, was alive in Cuba three years since, when this book was published, and is probably living there now, while John Lamar lies in the ground under the shadow of the Giant."

" Those are strong points of difference, I admit. They seem to show very clearly that the individuals are not the same."

" Yes. Now, here is where he got the idea of having been a slaver and other incidents of the fictitious life that he related to me. Juan de Ayolas was taken captive by an African chief soon after having had a sunstroke and having had hallucinations of hearing, warning him of the covert attack that was going to be made upon him and his party. These hallucinations were supposed, by the natives to whom he mentioned them, to be given by a supernatural being called by them Alatamba. They consisted of words or ideas, and assumed the form of the expression, ' Danger at Ollalaga for the white men !' They were disregarded, and all were killed except Juan de Ayolas. After having been kept in slavery for several years, he again had hallucinations of hearing, this time telling him to become a slaver. He resisted for some time, but finally yielded, and he and the chief went into a partnership, the chief capturing the natives and Juan de Ayolas conducting the trading. Now, all this is almost exactly, even to the names, the same as the story told me by Mr. Lamar. That the two have a common source is absolutely beyond doubt."

" There can be no question of that."

" Then," continued the doctor, " he resolved to become a dealer on his own account. There was a vessel lying in port at Calanda, owned by an American citizen by name John Lamarez. He bought this craft. John Lamarez was soon after drowned in the harbor, and Juan de Ayolas assumed the name and the nationality of the dead man and former owner. He called his vessel Alatamba. For five or six years he was successful, landing several cargoes of slaves each year on the Cuban coast, till at last his ship was destroyed and he captured by the American cruiser

Canandaigua, commanded by my relative, Philip Clyde. Shortly after, Ayolas, or Lamarez, as he then called himself, escaped by bribing the sentries, and shot and killed Captain Clyde in the streets of Matanzas. For this he was tried and acquitted by the Cuban authorities, the plea of self-defense being sustained before the court. A requisition for him was made by the American Government, on the ground that he was a citizen of the United States, it being supposed that he was the Captain John Lamarez who had sailed from New Orleans in command of the clipper-ship Osceola, the name of which, it was known, had been changed to Alatamba; but his rendition was not granted: first, on the ground that he had disappeared and could not be found; but, as though this were not sufficient, the reply went on to state that in any event the demand for the delivery would be refused, for that Juan Lamarez, *alias* Juan de Ayolas, was a Spanish subject. Now, isn't that a straight story ?"

"Perfectly so; all you have to do now, to make it absolutely conclusive, is to find out where John Lamar spent the fourteen years of his absence. When you do that, all will be done. By-the-by," continued Mr. Ellis, "where did you get that book ?"

"I got it from Will Hadden. Where he obtained it I do not know, but I suspect it was brought here by Mr. Lamar. As you see, the name of the owner has been carefully obliterated."

"There will be no trouble in ascertaining all the facts in the case. But what further do you propose doing ?"

"I am going to Cuba next week. It is positively known that Mr. Lamar arrived at Leghorn in an Italian vessel that sailed from Matanzas. I am going to take up his life at that point and carry it back till I know all the facts of his career during his absence of fourteen years. I shall not be satisfied till I have made myself master of the whole matter, even if I have to go to the east coast of Africa and cross the continent."

"You are a wonderful man when you once get a notion into your head. Now, listen to what I have to say."

"After dinner. Here are the ladies. We will come in here when we have dined, and over our pipes you shall disclose your knowledge."

# CHAPTER XVII.

AFTER dinner, and before joining Mr. Ellis, whom he had sent into the pentagonal room to begin his pipe, Doctor Grattan remained in the dining-room, and taking "The Life and Adventures of Captain Juan de Ayolas" from his pocket, handed it to Louise, asking her whether or not she knew anything of it.

"Oh, yes," she said ; "how strange that a copy of it should have found its way to Plato ! My poor father translated it from the Spanish. I think he had some knowledge of the author, who was a very bad man, but something of a literary character. My father had read his 'life' several times in the original, and then undertook to translate it into English. He began the work while on his way from Matanzas to Leghorn, but did not finish it for several months after his return. He was a good Spanish scholar —all the Lamars have made it a point to become proficient in that language ; but Captain de Ayolas was a poet, and papa found some difficulty in rendering his poems into English verse. He bothered over the thing more than it was worth, sitting up often till three or four o'clock in the morning, endeavoring to make satisfactory English out of the Spanish poetry. I have always thought that that had a good deal to do with the pain in his head, and the subsequent mental symptoms."

"You are quite sure that your father was not the author?" "Oh, yes! Why, I have a copy of the Spanish edition at Hurricane Castle, and I have repeatedly seen him working away at the Spanish rhymes. The whole book is very deeply impressed upon me, for I often tried to help him. I know it page for page. Look," she continued, "on page 284; you will there find a sonnet that I helped papa to put into English rhyme. Perhaps you will not think much of the version, but I shall never forget how we toiled over it all through the night, until sunrise. Papa had the characteristic of application to work, that he had set himself to do, so strongly developed, that I have often wondered at his power. After that night, he had a terrific headache of several days' duration."

Doctor Grattan turned to the page mentioned, and there found the sonnet to which Louise referred. Here, then, he perceived was all the evidence that was required to show that Mr. Lamar and Captain Juan de Ayolas were different persons. And now he saw how his dead friend had been led to merge his identity with that of the slaver-captain. Intense and long-continued mental concentration in one direction had at last brought him to the delusion of imagining that the incidents described in the autobiography had occurred to himself. It was only another instance to be added to the long list of those of similar character, with which the treatises on insanity abound.

He could scarcely conceal the joy that Louise's revelations gave him, but he was not yet ready to explain everything to her. There could not be too much evidence on a point of such great importance as was the one in which his whole heart and soul were interested. The proof must be so overwhelming as to satisfy everybody, and should be independent of any supplied by members of the dead man's family. It would probably still be necessary for him to go to Cuba.

"I see," he continued, after he and Louise had verified other parts of the volume with the data stored in her memory, "that the book was published in London, two years ago. Have you any information in regard to the transaction?"

"Yes. As you perceive, it bears the imprint of Stokes & Templeton. I went with papa to the publishing-house of these gentlemen, when he took them the manuscript. Doubtless there is somewhere among his papers a letter that they wrote him accepting the work, and congratulating him on the admirable manner in which the translation had been made."

"That will be of great value," he thought to himself. "That is the sort of collateral evidence I require." Then to Louise, interrogatively:

"Your father wrote under an assumed name?"

"Yes, but one the identity of which with his own is easily discovered. The name that he adopted was *Ramal.* It is formed, as you see, by spelling Lamar backward."

"There can be no doubt that the translator of this work was your father. My dear child," he continued, "an infinite load has been taken from my mind—not one that prevented me seeing the truth, but one that consisted in the knowledge of the difficulty that would be experienced in proving that truth to others. Now there is no doubt. Your father's memory will be unstained."

"My father's memory unstained! I don't understand."

"No, but very soon you will. Do not ask me now for an explanation. In a few days you shall know all. In the mean time be sure that there is no cause for anxiety."

Leaving her somewhat mystified, but full of confidence in his assurances, he joined his friend Mr. Ellis, who had already filled all the angles of the pentagonal room with smoke, and who was still puffing away vigorously at his pipe.

"I think I may be able to escape the journey to Cuba," he said, as he entered the room. "There will be plenty of collateral evidence, in addition to the positive statement of his daughter, that Mr. Lamar was not Juan de Ayolas. Now see," he continued, holding up the book. "He translated this from the Spanish, using his own name, spelled backward, as a *nom de plume*, R-a-m-a-l—Lamar. Miss Lamar is cognizant of all the facts connected with his literary labor, and the publication ; there is one letter at least from the publishers to him, accepting the book, and perhaps there are others in regard to it. He devoted himself to the work with a constancy and a persistency and an intensity that in the end, laboring as he was with a brain that had already suffered from a sunstroke, led to the dethronement of his reason. He had thought so much of Juan de Ayolas, had lived with him in imagination, night and day had concentrated his emotions, his intellect, upon this man, to such an extent, that at last he began to imagine that he himself was Juan de Ayolas. This delusion was doubtless formed with the greater ease, from the fact that Juan de Ayolas had taken the name of Juan Lamarez when he went into the slave business on his own account, a name very similar to that of John Lamar. It's all as plain now as a thing can be : that sunstroke in Africa was the starting-point of the whole matter, and then the mental concentration upon one subject did the rest. It's a lamentable case, but it's much better than discovering that he had been a slave-trader."

"Of course it is ; but when, do you think, did he begin to form the idea of change of identity ? He certainly could not have entertained it when he came here, for, if he had, it seems to me that he would have acted more nearly in accordance than he did with the character of the rather undesirable person that he thought himself to be."

"No, nor do I think that he ever reached the point of constant acceptance of the delusion. It came upon him at

times only, and then he believed it; but then there were
periods in which he doubted, and others, again, in which it
had no lodgment in his mind. At first it appeared as a
fear that he was Juan de Ayolas, and then it was that his
mind was in a state of terror at the idea of what would
happen to him should his fears be confirmed. Doubtless
there were hallucinations of hearing, telling him that he
was the slaver-captain, and these helped in the most terrible manner to impress the idea upon his mind. Finally,
he accepted it, and then being altogether a different kind
of a man from Juan de Ayolas, who doubtless never in all
his life experienced a shade of regret for any of his acts, he
became filled with remorse, and conceived the notion of
giving up his property for the education of the blacks in
the United States, and of delivering himself to the authorities for trial as a slaver. I think all these fears and delusions were of quite recent origin. I never saw any sign of
them previous to his moving into his new house. Probably, however, he experienced them at times, and doubtless
he fought against them with all his power, but finally they
overcame him."

"They did not exist when he made his will—that is
certain," said Mr. Ellis, with decision. "For, if they had,
he would have carried out the intention that he expressed
to you of leaving his estate for the foundation of a university for negroes."

The doctor looked at his friend for a moment. "It's
no use, Ellis," he said, at length; "sane or insane, I'm not
going to accept that will as a valid one. But, of course,
he was insane all the time. Insane people change their
minds, and it is not essential that any delusion they may
hold should be constantly thrust forward. No; the property shall go to the daughter, to whom it rightfully belongs."

"Well, well! I've no intention of reviving the subject.

But the man that in this age of the world refuses a fortune
of several millions of dollars in order to be consistent is an
anomaly not often met with. Did you ever see such a person, Grattan, before you looked in the glass when you
went to bed the night of the day Mr. Lamar's will was
read ?

"I saw one on that night, and I hope to see him for a
great many days and nights yet to come. But you had
something to say to me that brought you over here, hadn't
you ?"

"Yes ; but it has almost gone out of my mind under
the more engrossing subject that you had to talk about;
and then, with the persistence of your determination to
have nothing to do with the will, either as executor or lega-
tee, there is not much to be gained by further discussion.
However, perhaps it will be as well for you to listen. There
never was a decision, not even of the highest appellate
court, that was absolutely irreversible, and even Doctor
Grattan may change."

"Not in this matter ; but go on. What have you got
to say ?"

"I've been going over the papers in that tin box,"
said Mr. Ellis, "and, to judge from them, I should think
that Mr. Lamar was a very rich man, and that even those
who placed his wealth at the highest figure I have heard
mentioned have understated the amount. I find, for instance, that he owned *all* the first-mortgage bonds of the Tal-
lapoosa and Jonesville Railroad, amounting to over a million dollars ; *all* the stock of the Sandy Hill and Blue River
Railroad, amounting to more than two million dollars ; and
*all* the stock and *all* the bonds of the Salamanca Improvement Company. He also owns gold and silver mines in
California, Nevada, Colorado, Idaho, and Dakota, besides
several coal-mines and petroleum-wells in Pennsylvania.
Of course, it is difficult to estimate the extent of this

wealth, but, from certain data I find among the papers, I am disposed to place the yearly income at over a million."

"I am glad to hear it. She will make good use of it."

"So far as I can ascertain, there is no real estate except the property here in Plato, and that, by the terms of the will, goes to Miss Lamar."

"It will all go to her. I shall refuse to accept a dollar or a share of stock or a bond."

"She can not acquire a title, if the will is admitted to probate, except through you, and she may, and probably will, refuse to take your gifts. The act of proving the will vests all this property in you, and, unless you take care of it, or do something with it, a good deal will go to ruin. Property has to be watched like children and servants."

"You mean to say, therefore, that I can escape from this load only by establishing the fact of Mr. Lamar's testamentary incapacity?"

"Precisely."

"Then I shall have to take that step. His insanity will have to be shown some time or other, and it might as well be done now as at any other time."

"But you are an executor under the will, and you may remember in the letter that was addressed to you, and that you found, he requested you to exercise a watchful care over his daughter. I think he alluded to the matter, also, in the statement that she read when the will was opened."

"I know all that; but Miss Lamar is of age, is endowed with excellent sense, and is perfectly competent to look after her own affairs without interference from me. If any trouble should come, it would be time enough for me to interpose my aid or advice."

"The surrogate has appointed Monday next for the presentation of the will. I shall move that it be admitted to probate. A few days ago you were disposed to allow the will to be proved without opposition, and you thought that when you had collected your evidence you would move to have the probate reopened."

"I have changed my mind. I shall go before the surrogate and oppose the validity of the will; I shall state some of my reasons for believing Mr. Lamar to have been insane, and shall ask for a continuance till I return from Cuba, to which, after all, I shall probably have to go. These new developments are constantly making me change my mind. I never was so unstable in my determinations as I am now."

"That is because your intellect and your emotions are at war with each other. Now, my friend, I am an old bachelor, and supposed to know nothing whatever of the ways of lovers, but I am not so ignorant as I look. I've been watching you, and you're in love with Miss Lamar. Stop, now," as Doctor Grattan rose from his chair with an angry expression on his face, "don't fly into a rage with me, or peril the safety of your immortal soul by lying about it. It's true, and you know it."

"Ellis," said the doctor, in a voice that was tremulous with passion, "how dare you speak to me of such a subject? If it were not that you are my guest, I should forget our friendship of twenty years and should kick you out of my house!"

"My dear fellow, don't talk in such a ridiculous way. Don't you see that every word you speak only makes it more evident that I have told you the truth? I could tell you something else, too, that perhaps you don't know, but you receive my amicable intentions with such savage ferocity that I shall let you find it out for yourself. I'm not as blind as a mole or as deaf as an adder. I can see as far through a millstone as any of my neighbors, and, as for ears, little pitchers never had larger ones."

"Nor asses either!" exclaimed the doctor, somewhat more good-humoredly.

12

" ' Nor asses either,' if the comparison does you any good. Now, I am your friend, and I want to help you out of your difficulties, and I have discovered a plan that will, if carried out, end the whole matter in a way satisfactory to all parties. It can be stated in three words—marry Miss Lamar."

" Impossible ! "

" No, it is not impossible, except through your obstinacy and folly. If you marry her, you will settle all the difficulty of the money, for it will be kept in the family."

" I tell you it is impossible ! I am at least twenty years older than she, and she is rich and I am poor."

" As to the twenty years' difference, if she doesn't make any objection on that score, it need not concern you ; and, as to the money, if you'd be less morbidly scrupulous and accept this will, you'd have as much money as she has."

" And got by robbing her of what would have been willed to her but for her father's insanity. Is all sense of honor gone out of the world," he exclaimed, indignantly, " that you and others can see nothing unworthy of a gentleman in the acceptance of the estate of a lunatic by a man that knows he was a lunatic ? Good God ! " he continued, raising his hands, " I do not understand it. And you," turning to Mr. Ellis, " whom I have hitherto regarded as a severe man in such matters, one more liable to err on the side of rectitude and purity than on that of moral turpitude, can sit there calmly after what I have told you and advise me to take the bonds, stocks, and other stuff that you have discovered. It is astonishing, absolutely incomprehensible ! "

During this speech Mr. Ellis had risen to his feet, walked over with great coolness to the end of the mantelpiece, had filled his pipe from the jar of tobacco that stood there, and, lighting it, had sat down again and had begun to smoke, with as much deliberation as though he were alone in his own library. For a few moments he continued to puff away at his pipe, taking no notice of his friend, but apparently concentrating his whole attention on the process of the vaporization of tobacco that he was conducting. Then, without the change of a muscle of his face, he said, in the most commonplace tone, " How is Mr. Frazier getting on ? "

" Damn Mr. Frazier ! "

" What an inconsistent old man you are, Grattan ! If that is your feeling toward the poor fellow, you might have contributed to your pleasure by making his leg crooked, instead of which you have done your best, as I understand the matter, to make it straight and restore it to its full length. Well," he continued, getting up again and, after laying his pipe on the table, going toward the door, " I'll bid you good-afternoon. Drop in this evening after you've had a chance to get cool."

He closed the door after him, the doctor taking no notice either of him or his remarks, and was about making his way out of the house, when he was intercepted by Louise Lamar, who had apparently been on the watch for him.

" I would like to speak a few words with you, Mr. Ellis," she said ; "shall we go into the drawing-room ?"

He bowed his assent, and followed her into the room.

" I am very much worried about the state of affairs connected with my father's will," she said. " Doctor Grattan positively refuses to accept the estate devised to him, or to recognize the will as a valid one, and, after full reflection over the matter, I am obliged to come to the conclusion that he is right, although by so doing it may seem to some that I am actuated by a desire to advance my own interests."

" No one could think that, for every one would know that Doctor Grattan had refused to be benefited by the will."

"Don't you think he is right?"

"Yes, he is right."

"I am glad to hear you say that. I think he is the most honorable man that ever lived."

"Yes, he is unpurchasable."

"My father thought him the best man he had ever known; he is the best.*I* have ever known."

"He is certainly a unique specimen of humanity. He is refusing anywhere from seven to ten millions of dollars."

"At least that. For more than a year before his death my father invested nearly all his estate in stocks and bonds, which his sound financial judgment showed him to be advantageous purchases. They have probably more than trebled in value since he purchased them. He was confident that they would make him the richest man in America, if not in the world. He invested my fortune similarly, and I suppose it has also become largely augmented."

"Your father seems to have been a very competent business man. His papers are all in admirable order, and he evidently gave a great deal of attention to the subject of his investments, for I find many reports, schedules, and other papers bearing on the matter."

"Yes, it was almost constantly in his thoughts. He converted all his New York and other real estate into cash, and reinvested in property that gave quicker and larger returns. At his suggestion, I disposed of the larger part of the real estate that came to me from my mother, and invested it in silver-mines near Zacatecas and San Luis Potosi, in Mexico. The returns have been over one hundred per cent per annum, and papa reinvested the income in other mines as fast as it was received. But, about the will: I shall have to go to Elizabethtown, I suppose, when it comes up for probate."

"Yes, for Doctor Grattan has just told me that he has

changed his mind, and that he will oppose the admission of the will to probate. It is unfortunate that there should be a necessity for you and him to be on different sides in the matter."

"We shall not be on different sides. If my evidence is requisite, I shall testify that my father was insane. It will be the truth—he *was* insane."

"The witnesses will of course depose to his sanity, but with your evidence and that of Doctor Grattan, to the effect that your father was not of sound mind, the will can not stand."

"I hope to be spared the necessity of going on the witness-stand, but I shall not shrink from the duty, repugnant though it may be, if the truth can only be made apparent through me. Doctor Grattan is right."

"There will be no contest before the court for some time yet," said Mr. Ellis. "Doctor Grattan will, through his counsel, state his objections to the will, and will ask for time to get the evidence he requires. Probably several months will elapse before the case comes up for trial. It will be safer, however, for you to be present next Monday."

"There is another matter," said Louise, "in which I must ask your assistance. The refusal of Doctor Grattan to act as executor, and the fact that he has said nothing to me relative to the request contained in the letter that I read to you after the funeral, the request from my father," she continued, hesitatingly, "that he would interest himself in me, leaves me without the advice that my business affairs require. I know very little of such matters; I should be glad if you would accept the management of my property. If you will kindly do this, on such terms as are customary, and that I leave to you to determine, you will confer a great favor upon me."

"But, my dear young lady," exclaimed Mr. Ellis, "surely Doctor Grattan is the proper person to act as your guardian or agent. If you feel a hesitancy about consulting him on the subject, I will bring it to his notice."

"No, I would rather you should say nothing to him about it, except that, if you grant my request, you may inform him of the fact. There are many reasons why I prefer you. I am of age, and can appoint my own agent. As to a guardian, I do not require one. You are a lawyer, and that of itself is sufficient warrant for my preference. I desire to place my affairs in your hands, and with your permission will in a few days give you all the papers that relate to my property."

Mr. Ellis reflected for several minutes before giving a final answer. The proposition was one that was agreeable to him : it was in the line of his profession, and would prove a legitimate source of a considerable augmentation of his income. There was no reason why he should not accept it, unless it were that his friend Grattan might view such action as one of disrespect or unkindness to him. He felt morally certain that, so far from objecting, the doctor would be glad enough not only to get rid of the *quasi* obligation that rested upon him, but at seeing Miss Lamar's interests placed in safe hands. Still, it would be no more than decent to obtain these assurances from his own lips, so he answered : "I feel highly honored by your proposal, but, before deciding to accept it, I must confer with our friend, in order to ascertain how far he feels himself obliged by the charge laid upon him by your father to look after your pecuniary interests. If I know him, I am quite sure that he hates all business involving money, and that he will be glad to have the responsibility lifted from his shoulders. The letter that your poor father wrote to him, almost with his last breath, was—"

"Letter," interrupted Louise, "I did not know there was such a letter. Doctor Grattan has never mentioned it to me."

Mr. Ellis at once perceived that he had taken it for granted that the doctor had made Miss Lamar acquainted with the fact of the letter found pinned to her father's night-gown, when, in fact, he had, for reasons of his own, kept the matter a secret from her. He had therefore unwittingly made a revelation that was likely to lead to trouble, and one that it was impossible to neutralize by any attempt at mystification. There was nothing, therefore, for him to do, but to treat the affair as though it were of no consequence, and as one that the doctor would explain at some future time.

"I suppose," he said, though he had not yet recovered from his confusion, "that the fear of reviving sad recollections has prevented the doctor alluding to the circumstance. He will, doubtless, in a short time, tell you of it."

"Then I shall ask you nothing more about it," said Louise, not wishing to appear inquisitive, though she thought it strange that the contents of such a letter, its very existence even, had been concealed from her. "Doctor Grattan will, as you say, inform me of all that I ought to know. But, relative to the proposition I have made you, I am quite sure you need have no feelings of delicacy on his account ; he will only be too glad to have the matter out of his hands." She spoke these words with a little bitterness of tone, that was not unnoticed by Mr. Ellis, nor altogether a matter of surprise to him.

# CHAPTER XVIII.

NOTHING further was said between Doctor Grattan and Louise in regard to her father's will, and, on the Monday following the conversations detailed in the immediately foregoing chapter, the doctor, Louise, Mr. Ellis, and the three subscribing witnesses, repaired to Elizabethtown, the county-seat, and the lawyer submitted the document to probate. He had, in the mean time, obtained the doctor's full concurrence to the proposition Louise had made him of taking charge of her property, and acting generally in the capacity of her attorney and agent.

In laying the paper before the surrogate, Mr. Ellis announced that he appeared for the daughter of the deceased, one of the legatees under the will, and that, as he understood the matter, the objections to its probate that would be offered were dictated in the highest spirit of unselfishness, and with a view of promoting the ends of justice. All that was desired by his client—and he had no doubt his friend, who, for the purposes of this case, must be regarded as the other side, was actuated by a similar motive —was, that the truth might be definitely established. The interests at stake were large, very large, and it was an unusual circumstance, to which he would ask his honor's attention, to see two persons coming before him moved only by a desire for the establishment of the truth, and with no regard for what the world would consider their personal advantage.

He then produced the will, and, while stating that he presumed there would be no contest in regard to the proper execution of the instrument, deemed it advisable as a measure of regularity to call the attesting witnesses. Messrs. Bishop, Spill, and Hicks were then successively sworn, and deposed that they had witnessed Mr. Lamar's signature to the instrument now in court, and which the decedent had told them was his last will and testament; that they had done this at his request, and that they had signed the same, and that the signatures exhibited were written by them. They further deposed that at the time Mr. Lamar appeared to be of sound mind and memory, and entirely aware of the nature of the act he was performing.

Then Doctor Grattan's counsel, a young lawyer named Larcom, who had shown some ability in a recent will-case of importance that had been tried before the present surrogate, arose, and, after reciprocating the kind expressions of the proponent of the will, proceeded to state in outline the reasons why his client could not see his way clear to the acceptance of the estate that had been devised to him. He concluded by asking that the case be set down by his honor for that day two months.

Then Mr. Ellis, in a few words, united in the request of his learned brother, and the surrogate adjourned the issue to the day agreed upon by the contesting parties. As, however, Doctor Grattan refused to act as executor, and as, indeed, he could not till the will had been duly proved, the surrogate, with the consent of both sides, appointed Mr. Ellis to take charge of the estate of the deceased till such time as an authoritative decision on the validity of the will should be rendered. He required him, however, to give bonds in the sum of five hundred thousand dollars, and, though Doctor Grattan and Louise united in the request that this formality might be dispensed with, the surrogate was inexorable. To obtain the full amount required, it was necessary for Mr. Ellis to see some wealthy friends engaged in the iron business in the northern part of the county, so that Doctor Grattan and Louise found themselves obliged to return to Plato alone.

The vehicle was a large sleigh, capable of holding four persons, and the horses were of the tough Hambletonian breed so common in that part of the country, and remarkable for their strength and endurance. The doctor took his place on the front seat as the driver, while Louise occupied the rest of the sleigh, both being well protected from the cold weather by furs and wraps of the various kinds that experience has shown are most capable of affording comfort. It was at about two o'clock in the afternoon that he drove through the long, main street of Elizabethtown on his way back to Plato. The distance was not over ten miles, and, on a good road, with the horses he was driving, it could easily have been made in an hour ; but the way led over Cobble Hill, and had not been traveled enough since the late fall of snow to make it a pleasant one to drive over. Still, making all possible allowance for the badness of the road, the doctor had no doubt of his ability to reach Plato by four o'clock. The first part of the way led over level ground, and he improved the fact by making the horses go at a brisk pace. Neither he nor Louise felt disposed to talk, both being occupied with thoughts of the recent action before the surrogate, and of the circumstances that might grow out of it. She had been lately thinking a good deal about the doctor. She could not fail to admire him for the honesty and unselfishness he was displaying in the matter of her father's will ; but, although his conduct toward her was always kind, she thought she perceived that there was an underlying feeling which, if not amounting to dislike, was not very far removed from that emotion. There

was consideration for her ; his words were always gracious,
he anticipated every wish that it was in his power to gratify,
but he appeared to be actuated by pity, and not by the affection which she desired to excite in his heart. The fact, too,
that he had said nothing to her in regard to the commen-
dation of her to his care, which her father had made in the
letter that she had read just after the will had been opened,
was a damper to her which she was not able to overcome.
She knew nothing but what Mr. Ellis had accidentally let
out about the letter from her father to Doctor Grattan, and
which the latter had found lying on the dead man's breast.
Had she known that the request, " Take care of Louise ; I
commit her to your charge," was contained in that note,
and that, in fact, it appeared to be the chief object that her
father had had in view in writing it, she would have wondered still more at the indisposition manifested by the doctor to assume any duties connected with her or her property.

She had got through the ordeal of the surrogate's
court as well as could have been expected. She had not
been called upon to testify, and the remarks made by Mr.
Larcom, Doctor Grattan's counsel, had been so couched as
to spare her feelings as much as possible. She saw that the
doctor was animated by a stern sense of duty, and she did
not perceive that there was mingled with it any incentive
based upon a personal regard for her. She began to think
that his heart was hard, especially toward her, and she wondered what she had ever done to incur his indifference, almost his neglect, except in those matters wherein his sense
of duty caused him to assume, for the time being, an appearance of friendship.

But, with all this, she was conscious of a growing regard for him that caused her, when she thought of it, to
be surprised at herself. He had always, since she had
known him, commanded her respect. She had always
liked him, but it appeared to her that now a very different

feeling from either respect or liking was gradually being developed within her, and for which she could not satisfactorily account. She found herself thinking of him often when there was no obvious reason why she should do so ; and her thoughts did not so much relate to the practical kindness that he manifested toward her as to the personal characteristics that she discovered him to possess, and which she was under the impression the world at large did not ascribe to him. Her estimate was, she thought, a different one from that formed of him by the Platonians generally. She had set to work to study his disposition and character, and she was quite sure that she had discovered traits in him that not even Cynthia, with all her advantages derived from years of constant association, had recognized.

It was on the occasion of his first visit to Hurricane Castle that she became fully conscious of the fact that her interest in him was deepening to a degree that a month before she would have thought to be impossible. It was on that night, as the reader knows, that Doctor Grattan had crossed what might be regarded as his Rubicon. He had hesitated at the little bridge that Mr. Lamar had built over the Cancmanga, but had, with only a slight delay, taken the step that he then regarded as decisive, and that was the initial measure toward winning Louise Lamar for his wife.

Of course, she had known nothing of the struggle that had gone on in his mind, and of the result that had been reached, but doubtless his way toward her that evening had been different from any that he had previously adopted, and that had not been without its influence in causing her own heart to awaken to a consciousness of what it was doing. At any rate, she began on that night to regard him differently. She would not have called the feeling "love" had she stopped to inquire of herself what was the character of the emotion that had taken possession of her heart, but her answer would have been dictated by ignorance of the way in which love makes its first assaults on its victims. Louise all through the period of her life in Italy had seen a good deal of the "best" and which is, at the same time, the most uninteresting society. Young Italian, Austrian, French, and English noblemen and gentry, as well as a superior sprinkling of the American "upper class," as it is now beginning to be called, had frequented her aunt's house; but not one of all the succession of visitors had excited the slightest ripple of an emotion—so that, up to the time of her arrival at Plato, her heart had been absolutely untouched.

Then she had spent a couple of months in the same house with Doctor Grattan—in his house—and there had been thrown into association with a man who she at once saw was very different from any whose acquaintance she had yet made.

There was something in him that she had never met with before, and that was deep-seated, tender, emotional power, that could, she was sure, only be evoked by some strong influence that he would find himself incapable of resisting, try though he should with all his might and main. He seemed to be one whose roughness was on the surface, and which was, therefore, readily displayed upon slight exciting causes, while it required a stronger emotional disturbance to reveal the gentleness that lay hidden down in the depths, below the reach of the every-day emotions of life.

While an inmate of his house there had been long afternoon walks in the woods and on the mountains, during which she had learned new phases of his character. He was a devout lover of Nature in all her forms and moods. She had already gone through a somewhat similar experience with her father in Italy; but he had looked at the objects around him with a somewhat somber spirit, while

Doctor Grattan found a source of pleasure in every plant or bird or insect that he studied. Even the very stones taught him their lessons of gladness.

Cynthia had for a long time felt the influence that her father exercised upon all into whose companionship he was thrown, and Louise soon began to perceive that in Doctor Grattan there was a man who, if he chose to exert his power, would be able to lead her mind whithersoever he might desire.

It was not so much what he said or did as it was the way in which he said or did it. He was one of those rare persons who disdain to follow blindly the lead of any one. He had more confidence in himself than he had in others; his ways were his own, and he did not stop to think whether they would be liked or disliked. He meant to please himself, and if, in so doing, he displeased others, he did not care. But he pleased himself most by pleasing those he loved. He liked several persons, among them Mr. Ellis, Mr. Craig, and Mr. Lamar, but he loved only one, his daughter Cynthia, and his sole object in life appeared to be to make her happy.

Had Doctor Grattan been a man of bad impulses, mean, narrow-minded, and regardless of the proprieties of life, such a disposition as that which he possessed would have rendered him a very disagreeable person, and would have kept him in hot water all his life. But as he was the very reverse of all these, he was a man whom all intelligent and educated persons respected and liked.

Louise began by respecting and liking him, but ere long she thought she perceived that at times he put himself very much out of the way to do what he thought would please her. For instance, she had one day become interested in some remarks he made to her and Cynthia in regard to the tourmaline, that wonderful gem which she had never seen, and of which she had scarcely ever heard. He had descanted eloquently of its beauty, of the superstitions in regard to it that had been entertained at various periods of the world's history, of its remarkable mineralogical characters, and of its astonishing electrical and optical properties. The doctor had some wonderful specimens of this gem that he had gathered during a visit he had made several years previously to Mount Mica in Maine. There was one that Louise especially admired. It was over three inches in length ; and she thought she had never seen anything so beautiful in the way of precious stones as this one, with its dark, emerald-green hue at one end, shading off to a paler green, then to white, and terminating in a ruby-red of surpassing brilliancy. Then the doctor had heated it, and had exhibited its strange electrical properties, and by moving it in different directions its play of colors, from a light crimson to a violet, a green, and a brown hue ; and finally he had shown her how, when held in one way, the light passed through it, while, when placed in another position, not a ray was transmitted, and the crystal, even when held up to the full blaze of the sun, was as opaque as a piece of coal.

Louise had never seen anything that excited in her more astonishment than this gem, almost unknown and unappreciated by the world at large, and probably destined to remain so till some royal or other woman that fashion follows shall affect it. She was fascinated, awed at the contemplation of its mysterious qualities, and she did not wonder that even at this age of the world there were to be found otherwise intelligent people who ascribed to it supernatural powers.

The doctor was delighted with her appreciation of his treasures and of himself, and had insisted on her acceptance of the finest of his crystals, the one that was more than three inches in length, and that had such a bewildering play of colors. At first she had of course declined, but he had become so importunate, and she saw that she would really please him by taking the gift, that she had yielded. Then she had sent it to New York to be suitably mounted, and had worn it as a brooch, in preference to any other of her numerous breastpins.

A few days thereafter, when Louise had been reading all she could lay her hands on about the tourmaline, the conversation turned on the mineral, and she asked whether it was not found in the mountains near Plato.

"I am not sure," answered the doctor; "I have often thought that there might be deposits of it on Cobble Hill. There are large masses of feldspar there, and it is in such localities that the tourmaline is found."

Louise reflected for a moment. She would like to visit this place on Cobble Hill where the feldspar existed and search there for the tourmaline ; but the doctor was a busy man even when not engaged with his professional duties. He was writing his novel, and this was the joy of his life next to Cynthia, and to it he devoted all the time he could snatch from his labors with his patients. Louise knew all this, and she was diffident about asking him to go with her in search of the gem that had so taken her fancy. It was no unusual thing for the doctor to go with Cynthia and her for an hour's walk on the nearest of the mountains, Hurricane, but Cobble Hill would require nearly a whole day to do it justice in the attempt to find the tourmaline, and she knew that the doctor could not take the requisite time without the sacrifice of work that she was sure he liked better than he would that of roaming with her in what was likely to prove a fruitless search. She was dismissing the subject from her mind, when he said :

"Would you like to go to Cobble Hill and look for the tourmaline ?"

"Yes, but—"

"Then we will go to-morrow if it should be a fair day.

Cynthia, my dear, of course you will go too, and you will get ready a lunch for us."

Cynthia raised her eyes in astonishment. She could scarcely believe her ears. Her father take a whole day to scramble over the mountains with a young woman that he had known scarcely a month ! They had often had visitors from New York, men and women, but never had her father made any one of them so liberal an offer as that she had just heard. Some of the ladies had been fair to look upon, and at least two of them, one a widow of style and beauty, had made unmistakable attempts on his heart, but to no avail. He had treated one and all with politeness, but he had never once proposed to give a whole day to studying nature with them in the mountains of Essex County. With her, Cynthia, it had been different, as the reader already knows, but his tramps with her had been conducted without the presence of a third party. Now this comparative stranger was the invited guest, and she, Cynthia, was asked to go along probably for propriety's sake, and to look after the lunch ! It was very surprising.

She made a pleasant answer, however, of course, and the next day they had gone on the excursion. On the north side of Cobble Hill, not far from where the road to Elizabethtown passed, was a steep ledge of rock composed of granite in the main, but also of quartz and feldspar in varying proportions passing through it in veins. At the base of this ledge was a mass of decomposed feldspar, and it was here that the doctor thought it to be just possible that the tourmaline might be found.

They had started off on foot immediately after the doctor had seen the three or four patients that required his care, and by noon had walked the six miles necessary to bring them to the ledge of rock on Cobble Hill. Then they had taken lunch, and the doctor with the pick-axe, and the two girls with light hoes, had gone to work in search of the tourmaline, not very hopeful of success, but still satisfied that, come what might, they were enjoying themselves. Suddenly the doctor's pick tore away a big piece of quartz imbedded in the rotten feldspar, and disclosed to view a small cave, or rather hole, the bottom of which was covered with sand. Bearing in mind a like discovery that had been made at Mount Mica, more than forty years ago, he called Louise to him and bade her explore with her hoe the loose sand that lay on the floor of the cavity. She had not made half a dozen digs before she revealed to her own and the delighted doctor's eyes a dozen or more splendid tourmalines of all degrees of radiance, shining in their variegated hues of purple, blue, red, green, yellow, and without a flaw in their crystalline texture. The two girls were wild with joy, and the doctor was almost as much excited. With his pick he had opened other cavities in the rock, and the hoes of the ardent workers had brought to light more than a hundred of the most splendid tourmalines the doctor had ever seen. One of them was more than three inches long, over an inch in diameter, and perfect at both ends, being a magnificent crystal of emerald-green and ruby-red at the ends and of topaz-yellow in the middle, such as the doctor had never seen or even imagined. Then they had gone home, taking their gems with them, and delighted with the extraordinary success that had attended the excursion.

Louise felt that the doctor had done a great deal to please her, and he was eager to declare that, but for her suggestion, the tourmalines of Cobble Hill would probably have remained hidden till the end of time. She thanked him more than once in those sweet accents that seemed to come as naturally from her pretty lips as clear water from a mountain spring. She had detected him looking at her with admiring eyes, and she felt happy that she had been able to gain his favor. But the next day he was more than

usually distant. He answered her questions in monosylla-
bles, and scarcely took any notice of the beautiful tourmalines she had discovered among the great number she had
brought home. Then she had been hurt, a tear or two had
started to her eyes, and she began to think that either he
was an incomprehensible and fickle man, or that she was
not the kind of a woman that he could like for longer than
a day at a time.

Matters went on in this way during the whole time that
she was an inmate of his house. Sometimes he was genial,
almost affectionate in his treatment of her, and again distant and reserved ; as a rule, however, the latter line of
conduct predominated, and was sometimes so well marked
that Cynthia was quite sure that Louise was no favorite
with her father.

Then had come the visit to Hurricane Castle. That
night she had sat in the large hall, thinking of what he had
said and of the graciousness of his bearing toward her.
She had gone to the door to look out on the night, and
had wondered whether or not it was the light in his room,
that she had seen far off in the distance. Yes, she was
quite sure that night that he liked her very much, and she
knew, better than she had ever known before, that she
liked him.

But her father's death had changed him greatly. He
was now uniformly kind—studiously, frigidly kind. He
had never once alluded to the last request that her father
had made of any one, though doubtless, she thought, he was
complying with it in his own way. There was a distance
between them, however, that it seemed to be impossible
for her to lessen, and yet there was something in it all
that told her he was acting a part that was not natural to
him. She saw that he was unhappy, and she was sure that
in some way or other she was associated with his unhappi-
ness. She knew there was yet a mystery connected with

her father's life, perhaps even with his death, and she knew that Doctor Grattan was engaged in the effort to unravel it.

"Oh," she thought, with a thrill of joy in her heart, "it must be partly for my sake that he wishes to clear my father's memory of any real or fancied reproach that may rest upon it!"

There was no bad feeling between them in regard to her father's will. Of that she felt sure. If he would only soften toward her, she thought, as she sat in the sleigh as it glided swiftly over the snow-covered road, what difference would it make who had the money?

It was the first time that the conception of the real nature of her feeling for Doctor Grattan had occurred to her. She knew that she liked him, but never before had it ever flashed through her mind that she loved him well enough to wish to be his wife. At first she was startled at the suggestion that had, as it were, come up unbidden from the depths of her heart. Then a feeling of gladness appeared to spread in a moment throughout her whole being.

"I love him," she thought. "He is good and wise and strong. He is a masterful man, and I love him for that. How grand he looked when my poor father's will was read, and he stood up and declared that never would he accept one dollar of the estate devised to him! He is right, and it is better to be right than to inherit millions! Yes, he is grand and noble; but," she continued, as a sudden pallor overspread her face, and she felt a sinking sensation at her heart, due to the new line of thought that in its turn was excited within her, "his nobility and grandness are not for me. He does not care for me as I care for him. I can never be his wife, and yet, at one time, he almost loved me, I am sure. Even my father," she went on, thinking, as she spoke, of the letter she had read at the time the will was opened, and the reading of which she had stopped

when she came to a part that was intended only for her—
"even my father saw that, and died in the hope that some
day I would be his wife."

All this time the doctor had not said a word. Already
they had passed beyond the limits of the village of Elizabethtown, and were turning around the north side of Cobble Hill. They were not far from the place where they
had found the tourmalines, and in a few minutes they
would pass it, covered as it now was with several feet of
snow. Surely, the associations connected with the place
would loosen his tongue! But, no; his attention was apparently altogether concentrated on the horses he was driving, and on the clouds overhead, from which a few snow-
flakes were beginning to fall. They had yet more than six
miles to drive, and over a part of the road on which it would
be impossible to go at a faster pace than a walk. For all
he seemed to know or care, there was no one in the sleigh
but himself.

# CHAPTER XIX.

THE road was less distinctly marked than was that part near to the village of Elizabethtown, and the snow, that was now falling heavily, served still further to cover up the tracks that the first vehicles that had traversed it had made. The ledge of rock where the tourmalines had been found was passed, and the doctor had given no sign that he recognized it. Once or twice he had looked back, as though to see that Louise was still in the sleigh, and, apparently satisfied that she was not only present, but was' as comfortable as was possible under the circumstances, had turned again to his horses.

Shortly after turning round the northern side of Cobble Hill, the road made a *détour* to the left, in order to avoid a deep gully, over which a bridge, though contemplated for several years, had not yet—owing to the parsimony of the tax-payers—been constructed, and entered a deep ravine, bounded on either side by steep, almost perpendicular, walls of rock.

This part of the road was only about half a mile in length ; but, in the greater part of its extent, it was barely wide enough to admit of the passage of a single vehicle. At certain points, within sight of each other, the rock had been cut away, so as to allow two wagons to pass ; but even these were not sufficiently ample to afford turning-space for anything of the character of a vehicle that might once have entered this chasm. Originally, it had been only a crevice, through which the water from the surface trickled, and which, in the course of ages, had enlarged it to something like its present dimensions. In warm weather there was a small stream flowing through the bottom of the ravine; but in winter this was frozen solid, and the snow, thawing on the mountain-side, ran down the rocky walls, and then, freezing again, added continually to the thickness of the ice, till in places it was at times almost impassable.

In the morning the doctor had driven through this part of the road with some difficulty, but the air was then clear, the surface was well-defined, and it was comparatively easy for him to avoid the excessive jolting that passing over the icy hummocks produced, no matter how carefully he drove. Now, however, he entered the ravine with some degree of apprehension. The snow had covered up the landmarks, and treacherously smoothed over the inequalities of the surface, so that they were no longer to be distinguished. In addition, the air was full of flakes, the wind was beginning to rise, and it swept through the narrow gorge, driving the snow into his eyes, and stinging his skin as the fine icy particles struck against his face. Every now and then the sleigh would come down with a jar as it glided over some unusually prominent lump of ice, that nearly threw him from his seat, and that caused him to look back apprehensively to see that Louise was safe.

He had gone about half-way through the narrow defile, and was already congratulating himself on the prospect of getting safely to the end with no greater mishaps than some tolerably hard knocks, when suddenly the horses came to a dead stop. The doctor tried to peer through the thick atmosphere, but everything around him wore the same dull, leaden hue, and it was impossible for him to see that any obstacle impeded the advance of the team. He urged them forward, and even went so far as to apply the whip to their

flanks—a means of excitation not often required, for they
were spirited animals ; but they refused to budge an inch.
Then he got out, still holding the reins in his hands, and,
walking a few paces beyond the horses' heads, saw that a
mass of ice, three or four times larger than his sleigh and
horses, had become dislodged from some point above, and,
falling, had entirely closed up the road.

In a moment all the possibilities of the situation burst
upon him. To go forward with the sleigh was out of the
question, though it might be practicable to climb over the
obstruction, and to proceed to Plato on foot. To turn and
go back to Elizabethtown was the only alternative worthy
of consideration to that of remaining all night in the ravine, or the almost equally severe one of walking to Plato,
a distance of some three miles. To Elizabethtown was at
least seven miles, and it would be quite dark before they
could arrive there. Besides, the road on the plain, just
after leaving Cobble Hill, was indistinct when they passed
over it an hour ago, and was now probably entirely obscured
by the snow that had fallen. It would be nightfall before
they could get through that part of the journey, and the
risk of losing the way, and of being therefore probably compelled to pass the night in a farm-house, if not in wandering about the open country, was certainly great.

Louise had said nothing when the horses came to a full
stop, and the doctor, after trying in vain to urge them forward, got off the sleigh to discover the cause of their refusal to advance. She was piqued at his long silence. She
thought he was beginning to show a degree of unkindness
that he had never before exhibited. That he should pass
over an hour alone with her and never address to her a
word, argued, she thought, a state of indifference that was
inexcusable. And yet, if he would but speak kindly to
her, were it only a word, how ready she would be to forgive him !

He staid in front for several minutes, and she was sure that something important had occurred. Then he came back to the sleigh. She saw that his face wore a troubled expression, and her heart beat a little more quickly as the idea arose in her mind that it was on her account that he was anxious. She raised the thick veil that covered her face as he approached, but she did not ask a question.

"An accident has happened," he said, as he stood by the side of the sleigh. "We have had a narrow escape. I heard a noise not more than five minutes ago, but I did not know what caused it. Now I find that a mass of ice of several tons' weight has fallen from one of the walls of the ravine, and has completely blocked up the road."

He spoke with a tone of anxiety that she had never observed in him before, and she noticed that the corners of his mouth twitched nervously, as though he were endeavoring to prevent his muscles of expression betraying the existence of any deep emotion. When he had spoken he turned away his face, and appeared to be busy doing something with the reins that he still held in his hands.

"Is there no possibility of getting around it?" she said, bending toward him, though, as his face was turned away from her, he did not see the movement.

"Not the least," he answered, still fumbling with the reins. "It chokes up the full width of the road."

"What are we to do?"

She spoke without a tremor in her voice or the slightest agitation of manner, though she knew that the situation was a perilous one, and every moment becoming more so.

He turned toward her now, having evidently obtained complete command of himself.

"You are a brave woman, and a sensible one," he said. "Get out of the sleigh, and come and see how completely we are prevented going on our way."

13

He held out his hands to her, and, with the support thus given, she stepped on the edge of the sleigh, and leaped lightly to the ground.

"We are about three miles from Plato," he said, as they stood in front of the mass of ice and snow that lay like a thick wall across the ravine, closing it as effectually as though it had been put there for that special purpose. "I think I can manage to get you over it if you are a good climber, and then, in an hour, we shall be at home."

"But the horses?" she said, inquiringly.

"They will stand, and I can protect them from the cold and snow till Mike can get here."

"Can we not turn and get out by the way that we entered?" she inquired, looking somewhat apprehensively at the obstruction, which rose to a height of at least ten feet before her.

"Yes, I think so. There may be some difficulty in turning the sleigh, for this is about the narrowest part of the road, but, by unhitching the horses, I think I can manage it. Would you prefer to return? We shall have to pass the night either at Elizabethtown or at some farmer's house, for it will be too late to go on through the darkness and the snow to Plato. It is at least fifteen miles by the other road."

"I will do whatever you say." She spoke with firmness and decision, as though she felt perfectly safe in relying on his judgment and courage, and held out her hand to him in token of her trust.

He took it, held it for a moment in his own, and then, with just the slightest possible pressure, let it go.

"I will do my best," he said; "more than that I can not do, and that may not be enough."

"I will risk it with you."

"Thanks! You are a brave girl. Now come back to the sleigh and sit there, wrapped up as warmly as possible, while I climb to the top of this icy wall and see how things look on the other side."

He led her back to the sleigh, helped her in, and then with woolen rugs and fur robes completely protected her from the snow and the cold. He was as tender as a woman now.

"Our decision must be made quickly," he said, as he finished the tucking-in process, and saw the look of thanks that she gave him, "for every minute adds to the difficulty. It is snowing now faster than ever, and in an hour it will be dark."

Then he took a hatchet from somewhere under the front seat of the sleigh, and Louise heard him cutting the ice with it, making as she surmised foot-holds, so that he could climb to the top and take a survey of the road beyond. In a few minutes he returned.

"We can not get through," he said, "even on foot. There have been several slides like this, and before we surmounted them it would be quite dark. Now keep your seat, my dear child"—her heart leaped at the words: she knew he meant them now—"and I will get the sleigh turned without disturbing you. Are you cold?"

"Oh, no! You have wrapped me up so nicely that I am as warm as though I were sitting in front of the big fire in the pentagonal room."

He looked at her for a moment, and a smile appeared on his countenance, but he said nothing, and at once began to unhitch the horses. One by one he led them around to the other end of the sleigh, there being just enough room for them to pass singly between the vehicle and the rocky wall of the ravine. Turning the sleigh was a more difficult piece of work. Louise begged that she might be allowed to get out, not only in order to lighten it, but that she might help him manually; but to this he would not listen. "You would get your feet cold, perhaps wet. The snow is now

six inches deep at least. I can get it around without much
trouble. It is not the weight of the sleigh, so much as it is
the narrowness of this defile."

He pushed and pulled, and turned the vehicle first in
one direction and then in another ; but the tongue was in
the way, and as it was not one of the kind that can be readily detached, and as it was, he found, impossible to turn the
sleigh without removing this part, he took his hatchet and
with a few stout blows cut it loose. He then turned the
sleigh without further trouble.

To lash the tongue into its place and to hitch up the
horses took but a few minutes, and then, resuming his place
as driver, he hurried as rapidly as possible out of the ravine,
trusting yet to reach Elizabethtown before it got quite dark.

But he had not gone more than a few hundred yards,
when again the horses came to a stop, and again he got out
to see what the matter was. Another mass of ice had fallen ;
but this was much smaller than the other, occupying only
about three feet of the width of the road, and being only a
couple of feet in height. This he knew he could surmount ;
so, giving the reins to Louise, he took the hatchet, and after
several minutes' hard work succeeded in breaking the ice
up into such small fragments that the sleigh could be pulled
through and over them.

But all this had consumed valuable time, and when the
sleigh emerged from the ravine it was so late that the in-
cipient darkness and the snow-laden atmosphere conjoined
prevented his seeing beyond the horses' heads. There was
nothing, therefore, to do, but to trust to the superior vision and sagacity of the animals. They had repeatedly
traveled the road, and could doubtless, he thought, find
their way back to Elizabethtown, unless some fresh and altogether improbable obstacle should come in the way. He
therefore let the reins lie loose, and left the matter entirely
to them.

But, since the obstruction had been encountered in the ravine, a great loosening of his tongue had taken place. He talked of everything that he thought would interest Louise, and every two or three minutes inquired if she were warm, or tired, or hungry, and, receiving satisfactory answers to these interrogatories, would launch off at once into some anecdote that was calculated to amuse her, or told her of some event in the early history of the country that he imagined might take her mind from the contemplation of the possible dangers that beset them.

Thus they went on for more than half an hour after leaving the defile, and still no sign of any human habitation was perceptible. Several times the doctor had got out of the sleigh, and had carefully examined the ground in order to ascertain whether or not they were still on the road, and each time he had returned satisfied that the horses had not deviated from the beaten track. It was now quite dark, and according to his calculations they ought to be on the outskirts of Elizabethtown ; but not the slightest evidence of the existence of such a place or of any other, where human beings resided, could he discover. Then he had stopped, and again giving the reins to Louise, had started off to one side of the road to see if he could find any land-mark that would tell him exactly where he was ; but then discovering nothing, and starting to return to the sleigh, had wandered about for several minutes without being able to find it. He shuddered, when at last he stumbled across the vehicle, at the possible consequences to his companion had he missed it.

"We are on the road," he said, when he joined her, but not telling her of the difficulty he had experienced in finding his way back ; "I do not see, however, why we are not by this time at the end of it. Are you cold, dear ?"

He did not appear to notice that he had made use of a term of endearment, and before she could answer he went on :

"You are covered with snow, and the sleigh is quite full. You must be cold."

"No," she answered, "not very. My feet are a little cold, but otherwise I am quite comfortable."

He stooped down and with his hands cleared away a spot a yard or more in diameter.

"Come," he said, holding out his hands for her assistance, "get out and stand here while I brush the snow from you and empty the sleigh. No wonder your feet are cold, with that freezing load on them! I ought to have thought of it before."

"You think so much for me!" she said, as she obeyed him. It was inexpressibly sweet to her, this loving interest he exhibited. The tender word he had applied to her, so different in its meaning from the paternal phrase, "My dear child," the only affectionate expression he had ever before used to her, had caused her a thrill of joy. "He loves me," she thought. "What is it to me whether we are lost or not? He loves me! yes, I am sure he loves me!"

She stood on the clear spot that he had made for her while he emptied the sleigh of the great quantity of snow that it contained, and brushed off the white covering from her hat and seal-skin jacket.

"Now," he said, as he prepared to help her back into the vehicle, "you will be more comfortable." Then a sudden idea seemed to occur to him, for he stopped just as she was about putting her foot on the rail preparatory to resuming her seat. "Will you sit in front with me?" he continued. "Perhaps it will not be so lonely as back here all by yourself."

She scarcely knew what to do or what reply to make to him. She did not know whether he wanted her by his side or not; whether he had asked her out of pity, or because he would like to have her close to him.

"Would you like me to sit with you?" she inquired, hesitatingly.

"Yes."

In an instant her foot was taken from the rail, and he was helping her to her place on the front seat.

"Now," he said, as he took his place, and she nestled closer to him, as though at last she had come to regard him as her sole support, "we will try again. There is no use endeavoring to guide the horses; to do so would be certain to mislead them, for I have not the slightest idea where we are."

He took his watch from his pocket, and, lighting a match, ascertained that it was after six o'clock.

"We have certainly missed our way," he continued. "If we had not, we should have been at Elizabethtown long ago. Yes," as they passed a big tree, and narrowly escaping contact with it, "there is no such place as this on the right road. There is not a tree between the gully and Elizabethtown."

He spoke the words with a tone in which apprehension and sorrow were mingled, and as though he keenly felt the responsibility that rested upon him.

"I am not afraid," she said, instinctively drawing nearer to him, "so long as I am with you."

"You are a brave woman. You—ah! there is another tree, and another—many; and rocks, too!" he exclaimed, as they passed close to a big bowlder that overtopped the sleigh. "We are on the mountain!" He reined up the horses, and, getting out of the sleigh, walked over the snow-covered ground in several directions—never, however, going more than a few yards away; and, stooping down and examining the stones that lay around him, endeavored to ascertain by their character the place in which he was. Then he struck a light with a match and scrutinized them still more closely, extending his observations to the trees that were on every side.

"We are on Wood Mountain," he said, as he joined Louise ; "I know by the rocks and the trees. The former are
all granite, and the latter all hickory. There is no other
place near Elizabethtown in which such a formation and
growth exist. We have passed Elizabethtown, and are probably on the road that skirts the western slope of Wood
Mountain, and that leads to Lewis. That place is about five
miles from here, and the road is a bad one even in good
weather. It would be dangerous to attempt it on such a
night as this."

"I will do whatever you say. I know you will act for
the best. If we perish, it will be because human power is
weaker than the elements."

"God bless you, dear ! You more than double my courage. There is no cause for fear," he continued, after a
moment's reflection, "but you may suffer. Fortunately,
however, we are well provided with wraps, and I think I
shall be able to make you comparatively comfortable. We
shall have to stay here all night. A few paces to the right
is a large rock, and on each side of it another almost as
big. A blanket stretched across will make a good roof, another will close the front, and then, with the snow cleared
away, a couple of buffalo-robes on the ground, and a rousing fire near your feet, you will get along, I think, till
morning."

"And you ?"

"Oh, I shall do very well. I'll turn the sleigh on its
side, and that will cover my head, and then my feet will be
at the other side of the fire. When one's feet are warm the
rest of the body does not suffer. Now, keep your seat till
I make a fire. That is the first thing to do."

There were plenty of dead logs and twigs around him,
and he had soon scraped away the snow from a large space
of ground in front of the rocky inclosure he had discovered, and kindled a fire. Then he helped Louise to alight,

and, taking the seats from the sleigh, placed them close to
the fire. For some time she had been cold; not that the
temperature was very low, but probably because she was
hungry. The fire, however, soon quickened her circulation. She *was* hungry, for, expecting to get home in time
for a late dinner, she had eaten nothing since breakfast.
But she could stand that discomfort. Yes, even ten times
more, for was she not with him, and did he not love her?
What were hunger and thirst and cold and exposure, when
set off against the consciousness that he loved her? She
followed him with her eyes as he went about in the lurid
light of the fire, gathering fuel. How strong, how self-re-
liant, how uncomplaining, how brave, he was! "And he
loves me," she whispered to herself; "I know it! Oh,
yes, I know it now! He is doing all this for my comfort,
and nothing for himself!"

She was sitting on one of the sleigh-seats, her little feet
resting on a big stone that he had placed for them close to
the fire. By the light of the flames, that rose high in the
air, she could see a considerable distance around her. She
saw that she was on the side of a steep hill, and in the
midst of a thick forest. The snow-flakes were still falling
heavily, but she was in a measure protected by the. boughs
of a large tree, under which she sat. Not a sound did she
hear except the crackling of the sparks that shot up from
the fire, and the crashing of the brush as the doctor rolled
the heavy logs he had collected into a pile near where she
sat. There was much food for thought in the circumstances that the day had brought forth, and in those that
now existed, and, under other conditions, Louise would
have given her mind a loose rein. But now of what could
she think save of the one overpowering event that had burst
upon her with a suddenness that had almost stunned her
with its glory? Over and over again the words returned
to her mind, till she could almost hear them murmured

into her ear—"He loves me." There was a world of thought for her in that little phrase. She had grown up to the full comprehension of its meaning, and she drank in all the delicious sweetness that the idea conveyed, till she was fairly intoxicated with a sense of the perfect rest to her soul that she had at last obtained.

He finished his work of gathering fuel, and came and sat down on the other seat. She tried to thank him ; but the words refused to come at her bidding, and she could only hold out her hand to him, while tear after tear ran down her cheeks.

" Poor child !" he said, as her little palm rested in one of his, and he covered it with the other, "you are tired and hungry. What an idiot I am !" he continued, as he hastily rose and went to the sleigh, and fumbled in a locker that was in the front part of the vehicle. "I have allowed you to suffer from hunger, and here all the time was a nice sandwich, that was specially meant for you." He came back in an instant, unwrapping a parcel that he held in his hands. " Forgive me," he said, as he held it out to her. " I was so intent on making you warm that I forgot this better source of heat and strength than all the wood on the mountain. Eat this while I look after the horses and get your room ready for you."

" No," she answered ; "you have done all the work ; you need it more than I do."

" No ; I am not hungry. Country doctors are accustomed to go without their suppers."

He smiled, still holding the sandwich in his outstretched hand.

" I could not eat it," she said, "if I were dying of hunger, which I am not. Every mouthful of it would stick in my throat and choke me."

" Take it."

" I can not."

She looked up at his face, and saw the look of determination that it bore.

"If you insist, I will take it," she continued, "and throw it into the fire."

"Louise!"

"Yes."

"Do you wish to grieve me very much?"

"No."

"Then you will take this sandwich and eat it forthwith. If you do not, you will be ill before morning. Give me your hand."

She held out her hand, and he placed his fingers on her wrist.

"Your pulse is very frequent and weak," he said, in a low tone. "You can not deceive me—you are suffering from hunger. You have eaten nothing since the early breakfast you took before leaving Plato."

"I can not eat it. It is impossible. Do you wish to make all the sacrifices? Will you leave none for me? Are you to give up everything for me?—always, always?"

"I will leave no sacrifice for you to make. I will give up everything for you. God desert me, if I ever change!"

She covered her face with her hands, while her bosom rose and fell with the excess of emotion that only partly vented itself in tears and sobs.

Doctor Grattan stood for a moment, apparently hesitating what next to do. He knew now that she loved him; but this thought, so far from giving him joy, made him, for the time, more miserable than he was when he had the hopelessness of his own love only to contemplate. There would be two to suffer instead of one. But he now began to feel a sense of his own weakness more than he had ever experienced it before, and little by little he felt that the strong resolutions he had formed were, in the presence of

this weeping woman, who loved him, and whom he loved,
melting away like an iceberg in the Gulf Stream. But
above all was the consciousness that, if she did not take the
nourishment he had provided for her, she would almost
certainly be ill, and that was a contingency not to be allowed to occur, if there was any power in him to prevent
it. And he knew, also, that he was a different man from
the Arthur Grattan who, six hours ago, had driven out of
Elizabethtown. Then he was a very Stoic ; now he was—
well, at any rate, his stoicism had gone. He had acted his
part well while he acted. Now he had thrown off the act-
or's trappings, and his true nature was once more in the
ascendant.

"Louise," he said.

No answer.

"Louise," he continued, in kind tones, but with a firmness in the accents that had many a time before brought
unruly persons to do the things he had commanded, "I
have spoken to you as a friend, as one who loves you very
dearly, but my entreaties to you to do your duty have been
unavailing. Now I am speaking as a physician, who knows
what will be the consequences of your refusal to do as I request. I am responsible for you in two very different relations. Your father, in the last words he ever wrote, committed you to my care. And I am your physician. It is
true I have never spoken to you before of your father's last
request to me. I have been afraid—yes, afraid, to assume
a position toward you that would necessarily bring me into
close association with you, for I discovered that I loved
you, and love from me, a poor man, one past the meridian
of life, an obscure country physician, for a woman that,
from her wealth and beauty and intelligence, could have
her choice from among those better suited to her, was an
anomaly, a crime, that I knew should never be allowed,
and one that my pride would not permit me to perpetrate.

I, therefore, endeavored to crush out the feeling, and with success, I think, till to-night."

As he spoke the last words, Louise dropped her hands from before her face, and stood up before him; but she staggered, as though from weakness, and would have fallen had he not supported her, and gently made her sit down again.

"Go on," she said; "I shall not try to stand again till I am stronger."

"There is little more to say in that connection," he resumed. "It is useless for me to contend against a power that is stronger than my reason. You have made it absolutely impossible. I have, under the impulse of the moment, spoken words to you to-night that you have not rebuked, but that you would have rebuked had they been displeasing to you. And now I tell you, without impulse, but with a calmness that I hope is based upon my knowledge of right and wrong, that I love you.

"Stop," he continued, seeing that she was about to speak; "I have not done yet, and you are too weak to spend your breath in words. You knew that I loved you when I asked you to eat this sandwich, and you refused, thinking, poor child, that by so doing I would take the food out of your mouth as you thought I would take your fortune. Well, if I were racked to death with all the pains that man or devil could inflict, I would not eat one mouthful of this sandwich! I begged you to take it, and you would not; now I order you as your physician, and I tell you solemnly that, if you do not obey my command, you will be very ill, and that perhaps you will die. Your vital powers are weakened by the exposure and hunger you have suffered, and you must eat this, and you shall, if I have strength enough to make you. Take it!"

Again he held the sandwich toward her. She stretched out her hand without a word, and, taking the slice of bread and meat, began to eat it.

He turned away, and, going to where the horses were
still standing, unhitched them and covering them with
their blankets fastened them securely to two saplings. Then
he proceeded to arrange the recess in which Louise was to
sleep. He had built the fire immediately at the opening,
so that the earth and the walls were much drier than when
he had cleared them of snow. To roof it over with a
blanket, to hang another in front so that it served as a curtain, and then to spread a couple of buffalo-robes on the
earth, took very little time. At intervals he looked at
Louise, and saw with satisfaction that she was diligently
engaged in eating the sandwich that he had almost with
physical force compelled her to take. When she had swallowed the last morsel, he took from his pocket a flask, and
taking the cup from the bottom poured into it about a
tablespoonful of the contents. Then he mixed a little
snow with it, and going to where Louise was seated held
the cup toward her.

"It was not well," he said, "to give you a stimulant
till you had put some solid food into your stomach. Here
is a little brandy and a good deal of snow-water. Drink it,
and then go to bed."

There was something so ludicrous about the situation
that Louise, who had a keen sense of the humorous, could
not refrain from a little merry laugh. She took the cup.

"You are still my physician, I suppose," she said, looking up at him and smiling; "well, I will admit that since
I have eaten the sandwich I feel a good deal stronger."
She drank the brandy-and-water, making a wry face as she
took the little silver tumbler from her lips.

"You will take some yourself, won't you?" she said,
as she handed him the cup.

"No; I never drink brandy on an empty stomach."

"Now I am sorry that I ate the sandwich."

"And I am glad; but, indeed," he added, seeing that

she was worried, "I am not in the least hungry. I am much obliged to you for eating that bread and meat, even though you preferred to do it as my patient rather than for my sake."

"You did not ask me to eat it for your sake. There is nothing I would not do for you."

"Nothing?"

"Nothing. If, as you have just said, you love me, what is it that I would not do for you? You must know that."

"Yes, I know it, for I know you. Sit down here, and let us talk it all over."

She allowed him to lead her to the sleigh-seat by the fire and to place himself by her side. Still holding her hand in both of his, he spoke.

# CHAPTER XX.

"My darling," he said, "I am going to unburden my heart to you. I do not know that you can help me. The matter seems to me to be one that is beyond the reach of help, but I am losing confidence in my ability to see things as they should be seen. Perhaps you may be able to open my eyes to conditions and circumstances that now escape them, and cause me to see with a less perverted vision. In any event, I come to you now to speak unreservedly, and with some little hope in my heart that you will try to help me.

"I do not know when I began to love you. You stole into my affections so gradually that, when I came to examine into the matter, I found that you were there, and that you were not to be dislodged without pain. Nevertheless, I honestly made the attempt, for I thought that, in the first place, there was very little hope that you would ever love me ; and, in the second, that, even if that obstacle were within the range of possible removal, I—being at least twenty years older than you, set in my ways, and some of them not perhaps pleasant ways—was not the man calculated to secure you the utmost possible happiness."

"You might safely have left those points to me," said Louise, softly ; "your ways have always been pleasant to me. My father thought you the best man he had ever known. I knew you to be everything that is good and true. Twenty years' difference in ages ! What is that, that you should have allowed it to peril your happiness and mine ?"

He caressed her hand while she was speaking, and then raised it till it just touched his lips.

"You are right," he resumed, "and I came to a like conclusion, for you remember the first visit Cynthia and I paid to you at Hurricane Castle ? Then it was that I determined to win you for my wife if I could."

"And the same spirit that moved you, actuated me, for it was then that I knew that my heart was yours."

"Dear heart !" he exclaimed, passionately. Then rising to his feet, as though afraid to trust himself further, he strode up and down in front of the fire, through the snow that covered the earth, though it had for some time ceased to fall, and the stars were shining brightly overhead.

"I made up my mind," he continued, "to win you if I could, and in a few days I should have spoken to you and your father ; but then came the information from him that you were rich in your own right, the possessor of millions, while I owned scarcely enough, outside of my moderate professional income, to keep me and my daughter in reasonable comfort. Your wealth was a barrier that I could not surmount, and it still stands between you and me a wall of adamant that bids fair, so far as I can see, to keep us apart forever."

"No ! no ! a thousand times no !" cried Louise, springing up and throwing her arms around his neck, while he pressed her to his breast and held her there as though she were a part of himself. "This, then, is the dragon you have been fighting," she continued in passionate accents, every word of which went to his heart with a force that made it swell with a joy greater than any he had ever known. "This has made you moody and sad and almost unkind. O Arthur ! my love, my love, do you think so meanly of me, so meanly of yourself, as to let a thing like that come between you and me, a man and a woman with senses to feel, with hearts to love ? God knows I would give it to the poorest beggar that lives, rather than let it plunge us both into life-long misery !"

It was inexpressibly sweet to him, this coupling of her life with his. He caressed her fair head, and, taking her face between his hands, looked into her eyes long and lovingly. Nothing could have touched him more deeply than the willingness that she exhibited to thrust aside the one bar that he regarded as an insuperable obstacle to their marriage. He felt that she was more generous than he. She was ready to sacrifice her wealth for him, while he found it difficult to immolate a prejudice for her, and yet he loved her with all his heart and soul. He would have given his life for her without a pang other than that due to the fact that death would be separation from one that was dearer to him than all the world besides. But it was hard, very hard, for him to stand out against her magnanimity and devotion. He almost yielded. The words, "Do what you please with your wealth, keep it or give to the beggars, so that you give me yourself," were on his lips, but his pride was stubborn almost beyond belief.

"My dear child," he said, "when a woman is willing to make a sacrifice for the man she loves, the sacrifice is as good as made. I know you would, without a regret, scatter your wealth to the four winds of heaven were I selfish enough to make the demand. You love me, and that with you overshadows every other consideration. But I am a cold, hard man of the world, and forced to look at these things in a different light from that in which you regard them. I do not know which would grieve me most—to see you the wife of a poor man, and that man me, or me the husband of a rich woman, and that woman you ; and yet, if you knew what pain it gives me to say these words, you would pity me even more than you love me."

He bent his head and kissed her forehead. Then, turning away, he walked off into the darkness of the forest, leaving her standing alone, with her face buried in her hands, her whole form trembling with emotion, and her heart chilled with the thought that she had lost him forever.

But with it all was a little feeling of indignation as she recalled the fact that he had virtually refused to accept her for the reason that she was burdened with a load that, at the same time, he was not willing to allow her to throw off. She felt that she had more than met him half-way; she was conscious of the palpable truth that she had, as the saying goes, "thrown herself at him," and this, too, without avail. There was no bitterness in the thought. She knew he loved her; she knew that his hesitation proceeded from the impossibility he experienced of doing what from his stand-point would be a meanness. She felt that he was wrong, that he was almost narrow-minded in his sense of honor; but she could not, nevertheless, fail to respect him for his adherence to his honest convictions, mistaken though she knew them to be.

What was she to do? She saw that a contest was going on in his heart, and that it would probably, unless some unforeseen event occurred, terminate against her. She was sure that such an ending would make him as miserable as it would her; but she was helpless to do more than she had already done. All she could do was to wait patiently, trusting that his love for her would, in time, brush away the barriers that stood between her and her happiness.

But she could not stand there all night with her hands covering her face. She was about to turn and go to the apartment he had prepared for her, when she heard the crunching of the snow, as though of some one walking over it, and then she felt a pair of arms around her, and her head drawn to a breast upon which it had already rested. A sense of calm delight swept through her. She had conquered just as she had almost begun to despair. She yielded to the intoxication of the moment, and turning her face to his, their lips met in a kiss, the ecstasy of which would never fade from her memory.

"Good-night," he said; "you are tired, and we must be off early in the morning. Go to your den. God bless you, my darling!" Again he strode away abruptly, and she heard him speaking kindly to the horses, some twenty paces distant. Then she went into what was almost as comfortable as a room in a house, so careful had he been in its arrangement. She lay down, and tried to compose herself to sleep; but, though she closed her eyes, she could not shut out the mental images that coursed, in uninterrupted succession, through her brain, and therefore she did not sleep. For more than an hour she lay, scarcely stirring a limb, and feeling a sense of peaceful happiness beyond all that she had ever felt before. Perhaps the perfect repose was almost as beneficial to her as sleep would have been. Then she heard, or thought she heard, a distant growling, like what might have come from a wild beast. She knew there were panthers and bears and wolves in the mountains about Plato, and for a moment she felt alarmed. She rose quietly to her knees, and pushed back the blanket that hung like a *portière* before the opening of her "den." He was there, sitting before the fire, on guard, while she rested and slept: his head was raised in the attitude of attention; doubtless he, too, had heard the roaring, and was on the alert against any danger to her. She knelt for some moments, watching him. Evidently he meant to sit there all night, without sleeping a wink. She took her watch from her pocket, and, by the light of the fire, saw that it was eleven o'clock. Then she lay down again and slept, how long she did not know, but when she awoke all was as still as death. Again she pushed aside the curtain and looked out. The fire was burning brightly, and before it sat Doctor Grattan, watching the flames as they flickered in the night air. He had wrapped a blanket around his shoulders, but looked otherwise as though he had not moved from the post that he occupied as sentinel. "Was ever such love as his?" she thought. "God make me worthy of it!"

When she next awoke it was broad daylight. She arose, feeling a little feverish; but, washing her face and hands in the snow, cooled and refreshed her. The doctor was busy hitching the horses into the sleigh. He did not see her, and she, anxious to do something, folded up the blankets, rugs, and robes that had served as roof, curtain, bed, and covering for her through the night. He finished his work, and, looking round, saw what she had done. He came toward her with a smile upon his face, and though, as she knew, he had never once closed his eyes all night, nor eaten a mouthful since the morning of the previous day, showing no signs of fatigue. He held out his hand to her, and, drawing her to him, kissed her lips. "You are fitting yourself," he said, "for being a poor man's wife. But you should have left that work for me. You are not strong. But you look refreshed," he continued, fixing his eyes upon her face, as though studying every feature of her countenance. "Did you sleep well?"

"Better than you did," she answered. "I looked out twice in the night, and each time saw you sitting before the fire, wide awake."

"I could not have slept even on a bed of roses. I had a treasure to guard more precious to me than my life. Did you hear any unusual noise in the night?"

"Yes; I heard something like the growling of a wild beast."

"It was a panther, a cowardly one, like all the rest of his kind. He came down close to our camp—so close that

I saw his eyes glaring in the darkness ; but the fire and a brand that I threw at him made him scamper off as though a thousand fiends were after him."

"You must be very tired."

"No ; I am used to sitting up all night, and going without my supper. Besides, I had enough pleasant thoughts to keep me awake."

She gave him a loving look, and then went on with the work of folding the wraps.

"Are we going direct to Plato ?" she inquired, after a silence of several minutes, during which he had replaced the seats in the sleigh, and otherwise got ready to resume their journey.

"No, for the direct road is closed, and the road around the other side of Cobble Hill is too far for the horses, half starved as they are. We can not be more than two or three miles from Elizabethtown, and I propose to go there, get breakfast and a fresh team, and then proceed on our way home. Does that plan suit you ?"

"You know better than I do," she answered, smiling. "Whatever suits you suits me. I must confess, I should like my breakfast and some water as soon as I can get them."

"You shall have both in half an hour, I hope. Now, dear, get in !"

Before obeying him, she looked around her, as though endeavoring to fix the locality in her memory past all chance of being forgotten. He smiled, as he mentally interpreted her object.

"We shall neither of us forget this place," he said ; "some of these days we'll revisit it. It has witnessed the crisis of our lives."

She sat down on the front seat by his side, and in a few minutes they had emerged from the wood. The morning was clear, and not by any means cold for that season of the year. About ten inches of snow had fallen, but, by a little careful observation, he was enabled to trace the lines made by the sleigh on the previous night. Moreover, the country was so familiar to him, he having for more than twenty years traveled it night and day, that when he had the opportunity of noticing the many landmarks around him, there was no possibility of his missing his way. He found, so soon as he had reached the open country, that the horses had left the main road leading from Plato to Elizabethtown, and had wandered into that going from the latter place to Lewis. Instead, however, of continuing on the road to Lewis, they had taken a charcoal-burner's road that led off to the right, and had consequently gone a considerable distance up Wood Mountain. To his great delight, and equally to that of Louise, he discovered that they were not over a mile distant from Elizabethtown. This place they soon reached, and had an excellent breakfast at the principal tavern in the place, besides making themselves reasonably comfortable as regarded their toilets. Another team was procured without difficulty, and they were just about starting for Plato by the road leading around the east side of Cobble Hill, and which was nearly twice as long as the more direct road, when a man in a sleigh drove up to the door, and in a state of great excitement inquired for the landlord. On the arrival of that functionary, he proceeded to say that he had left Elizabethtown that morning early for the purpose of going to Plato, and that soon after entering the ravine in Cobble Hill he had discovered that the road was entirely blocked up by a large mass of ice and snow that had fallen just as a horse and sleigh with two men were passing under it. The horse was standing in the road uninjured, the ice having struck close behind him, entirely covering up the sleigh and the men. He had with great difficulty, he said, helped them out of the mass that had crushed them, but had found that they were both dead.

"I'm something of a stranger here," he went on, "and I don't know the men, but I think I saw them in court yesterday about that matter of Mr. Lamar's will."

"They must be Mr. Hicks and Mr. Spill," said the landlord.—"They left here about two hours after you did, doctor. It was snowing very hard then. I guess one of them slides such as stopped you took place and mashed them."

"I'll go back with you," said the doctor. "They may not be dead, and may require assistance."

"No, you needn't," rejoined the man, "they'll be here in less than half an hour; but I guess you'll find them dead enough to bury. I stopped at old man Thompson's and got him to send a sled for them. They'll be along directly."

"At any rate, I'll go and meet them," said the doctor. "There may be a spark of life in them, that possibly may be revived.—My dear child," he continued, turning to Louise and speaking in a whisper, "stay here till I return. I shall probably be absent only a few minutes."

"I would rather go with you," she answered. "I may possibly be of some service, and, as I am to be a country physician's wife, I can not go too soon into training. Let me go."

"Come, then," he answered, smiling, "and receive your first lesson; there is no time to lose. In a matter of this kind, every moment counts."

She got into the sleigh, and he, following, drove rapidly over the road they had traversed the previous afternoon. They had not gone over half a mile when, on the outskirts of the village, they met the sled with its load. The driver at once recognized the doctor, and quickened his horses' pace, calling out, "Hurry up, doctor! one of 'em's alive sure, and may be the other one too." In a few seconds the doctor had jumped from his sleigh and was examining the two men.

As had been inferred, they were Hicks and Spill. The doctor bent over them, and at once announced that they were both alive. They had not, he said, been suffocated, but had both been struck on the head by the ice and were suffering from concussion of the brain.

"There is nothing to be done but to keep them quiet," he said. "The symptoms are all favorable, and in an hour or so they will probably be conscious.—Send for Dr. Brown," he continued, addressing the driver of the sled, "as soon as you get to Elizabethtown. He knows how to take care of such cases.—Now," he went on, getting into the sleigh and addressing Louise, "we shall be in Plato in an hour and a half, unless some new misfortune overtakes us. You have missed an opportunity of showing your aptitude as a nurse, but doubtless you are not sorry for that."

"No, but I am unhappy at thinking how worried Cynthia will be about us. I have thought of her all the morning."

"I telegraphed her," he replied, "as soon as we reached Elizabethtown, giving her a pretty full account of the situation. Her uneasiness is over long before this."

"You think of everybody but yourself," she said.

He smiled. "I am thinking a good deal of myself now," he answered, "and I am thinking what a narrow escape from destruction we had yesterday afternoon. As well as I could make out from the driver of that sled, Spill and Hicks went on through the defile till they were stopped by the same mass that kept us from going through, and, while they were deliberating what to do, a second piece fell and struck them. It could not have happened later than an hour after we left the place."

They continued to converse as the sleigh, drawn by a pair of fast horses, glided through the snow. It was not necessary to return to Elizabethtown, as the road to Plato that went round the east side of Cobble Hill branched off from the more direct road just at the edge of the town. They had nearly reached Plato—already the tall wooden spire of the only church in the village could be seen glistening in the sunlight, as the rays fell upon its planished tin-covered surface—when Louise, after having been silent for a few minutes, laid her hand on Doctor Grattan's arm.

" Arthur," she said.

" Well, dear."

" You'll not be angry with me if I say something ? "

" No, I never expect to be angry with you as long as I live."

" Don't be too sure of that; but you won't be angry with me this time ? "

" No, I promise you that, no matter what you say, I'll keep my temper."

" Then don't you think that it would be better to withdraw your opposition to—to papa's will ? You would then be richer than I; whereas, if you succeed in upsetting the will, I shall be still more undesirable than I am now."

She was looking at him with a smile on her countenance, the sweetness of which melted his heart. He had at the first words frowned a little, and was preparing a short answer to the effect that the subject had already been sufficiently discussed and must be regarded as constituting what the lawyers call " *res adjudicata*," when he caught sight of her lovely face, with its inquiring and happy expression. The severity that was just beginning to form itself into words vanished like a flash. He put his disengaged arm around her and drew her toward him, but made no reply. She was too wise to pursue the subject further at that time, and he continued to keep his arm around her till they saw a sleigh approaching them from the direction of Plato, and then a regard for the proprieties compelled him to remove it.

The sleigh proved to be one containing Mrs. Spill and

Mrs. Hicks, who had been telegraphed for, and who were on their way to administer to the comfort of their respective husbands. Of course, there was a halt of several minutes' duration, during which the doctor gave the ladies his assurance that all would go well with the injured Platonians.

"I am glad," said Louise, after the journey had been resumed, "that you have so keen a sense of the power of public opinion. You will all the more readily agree to the plan I shall have to carry out."

"Plan? What plan?"

"I shall have to go back to Hurricane Castle at once."

"Go back to Hurricane Castle! I don't suppose you will ever live there again."

"Oh, yes, I shall go back to-day. It would not be proper for me to remain under your roof, now that I am going to be your wife. It would be contrary to all the rules of etiquette in such cases made and provided."

"But I don't care for the rules of etiquette."

"Ah, but I do! Men do not require to be so closely bound by them as women."

"Who is there here in Plato whose opinion you care for?"

"Not one whose good opinion I value, and that I would be sorry to lose, except Cynthia and Mr. Ellis and Mr. Craig, and Lucy and Mrs. Hadden and Will—as you all call him —and they would never say an unkind word against me, no matter what they might think. But all the rest of the town would, and I expect to have enough to do in the way of exerting such powers of endurance as I may possess."

"My dear Louise, what do you mean?"

"Don't you suppose, dear," she said, as a slight blush suffused her cheeks, "that malicious and ill-natured people will talk over the fact that we have been alone together so long? Of course, it was unavoidable; but they won't care for that, and perhaps will not even believe it. There are many persons in every community, good enough in their way, ordinarily regarded as charitable, who would minister with kindness to your material needs should they find you in distress, and yet who would not hesitate to say that about you that, if true, would be dishonorable to you. Doubtless there are many such in Plato."

"Perhaps there are," said the doctor, grimly; "but, if any one of them opens a mouth to say a word against you, it were better for that person that a millstone were hanged about his or her neck, and that he or she should be cast into the uttermost depths of the sea."

"They would most likely be women, and you could do nothing to stop them."

"On the contrary, they would probably be for the most part men, and I should choke them ere they had a chance to repeat the slander."

Louise laughed. "It is better," she said, "to let such people alone. Now," she continued, taking the hand next to her in both of hers, and stroking it with her daintily gloved fingers, "have you quite made up your mind to my going back this afternoon to Hurricane Castle?"

"I suppose I shall have to submit," he muttered, with something like a growl.

"Of course you will, and there is another thing you will have to do to please me, and that will make it easier for you to come and see me."

"What is that?"

"You must let Cynthia come and stay with me."

He thought for a moment before answering. "Yes," he said, at last, "I suppose that will have to be."

"Thanks. Does Cynthia know that—that—?"

"That I love you?" he interrupted. "No, she thinks I hate you. She has often reproved me for being unkind to you."

"Will she be pleased that I am going to be your wife?"

"Yes, of that I am sure. She knows that in loving you I shall not love her less, and she will be pleased with anything that I think is for my happiness. She loves you very dearly."

"Yes, I know, but not more than I love her. She is a charming girl. The fact that I am going to be your wife may make a difference, however, in her feeling toward me. It would grieve me very much if I thought such would be the case."

"You need not fear; she is all sweetness and gentleness."

"Then we shall be very happy together." She had taken off the thick seal-skin glove that he wore, and she raised his hand to her lips.

Then he looked up and down the road, and, seeing no one in sight, bent over and kissed her.

"There is nothing commonplace about you, Arthur," she said, after another little pause.

"What put that idea into your head just at this particular moment?"

"I was thinking about that sandwich that you made me eat."

"What about it?"

"A commonplace man would have divided it, taking half for himself."

"What a student of character you are!" he exclaimed, with a laugh. "A brute would have said nothing about it, I suppose, and would have eaten it all himself."

"Yes."

After a few moments—

"Louise."

"Yes, dear."

"Your poor father's last thoughts were of you and me. I can show you this now without feeling that I am forcing myself upon you."

He took from his pocket-book as he spoke the note that he had found pinned to her father's night-gown and placed it in her hand.

She read it with emotion. "Yes," she said ; "he had evidently set his heart on our marriage, for, in the letter that he left for me and that I began to read the afternoon that his will was opened, he requested me to marry you if you asked me to do so. He must have seen that we loved each other."

"Ah ! that was why you stopped so suddenly."

"Yes, that was the reason. May I keep this ? I would like to keep it with the other."

"Yes, you may keep it."

"I wonder if he knows now that his wish is going to be fulfilled ? If he does, it will add to his happiness."

But to these words, spoken musingly, as though addressed to herself, the doctor made no reply. What, in fact, could he have said ?

They were now at the very edge of the village, and in less than five minutes would be at Mountain View. Louise was evidently again deep in thought. They had already met several persons that the doctor knew ; but he had merely nodded to them, and they had passed on without seeking to have a word with him. Clearly nothing was generally known yet in Plato of his adventures, for no true Platonian would have exhibited such a degree of indifference to anything so calculated to excite his curiosity as were the incidents of the past twenty-four hours that had occurred in the life of one of the most prominent citizens of the village. They had passed through the main street, and were about turning off by the road that led to the doctor's house, when Louise again spoke.

"Arthur," she said.

"Well, Louise."

"Are you tired of my questions ? "

"No, dear ; ask as many as you like."

"There is only one more—that is, only one more now."

"Well ?"

"It is about the sandwich."

"What ! more about the sandwich ? " he said, laughing.

"Yes, I want to know what you would have done to me if I had persisted in my refusal to eat it ?"

"Done to you !" he said, trying to assume a stern expression, though she was looking archly into his face, and could see the smile that he could not conceal. "Some one has said that a man should never lay hands on a woman except in kindness. Well, in very kindness, I think I should have taken you by the shoulders and have given you a good shaking."

She laughed happily. "I am more than ever glad that I ate it," she said. "But here we are, and here is Cynthia coming out of the door to meet us. Will you tell her, dear Arthur ? I am so afraid she may not love me. Tell her to be kind to me."

"My darling, I am all the world to Cynthia, and the woman I love will stand first among women in her heart. I shall tell her all before she sleeps to-night."

# CHAPTER XXI.

"OH, you horrid man!" said Cynthia, throwing her arms around her father's neck and weeping and laughing by turns, while she lavished an infinitude of kisses on him. "Where have you been? How did it happen? What have you been doing? All last night I sat up and cried, waiting for you to come, and then I thought something terrible had happened. Tell me all about it; are you hurt?"

Then she went to Louise and plied her with similar questions and deluged her with similar kisses, till at last her powers in both directions being apparently exhausted, she permitted them to come into the hall, while they, being at last allowed to breathe freely, by turns gave her an account of the affair, without, of course, touching at that time on the most important part—the love-passages.

"I knew something serious had happened," said Cynthia, when she had obtained a tolerably complete idea of all the tellable parts of the adventure, "for, if you had been within reach of the telegraph, you would have sent me word at once. I was just going to the office to telegraph for information about you, when your message arrived. Poor dear," she continued, turning to Louise, "how you must have suffered! As for papa, he's used to going supperless to bed and to sitting up all night. It isn't often, however, that he gets them together. Mr. Ellis and Mr.

Craig and Lucy are in the drawing-room, and Will Hadden has been here twice from Mr. Frazier's."

"What about Mr. Frazier?"

"Nothing special," she answered, with a little laugh. "He's lonesome."

"Ah! I understand. It was you he wanted, and not me. The rascal! I'll teach him to send after my daughter in my absence."

"Oh, you old ogre! But you needn't bother yourself," making him a courtesy and tossing her head in assumed disdain. "Your daughter isn't going to 'demane herself by kapin' company with the loikes o' he.' That's the way I heard Delia Maguire, who cleans house and does the laundry work for us, putting it to the cook yesterday. It's an effective speech, don't you think so?"

"Get out, you baggage! Mr. Frazier is too good for you. Now take Louise up to her room and let her lie down for an hour or so, and, when she awakes, give her a cup of strong coffee and a piece of toast and an egg."

"Why, oh why, this sudden interest in Louise?" inquired Cynthia, still laughing.—"Come, dear," she continued—"come, I don't want my head knocked off, and if you are delayed another instant I see by the way he fixes me with his glittering eye, as the ancient mariner did the boisterous young man, that my 'cephalic extremity,' as his books call it, will not be worth its weight in gold any longer than he can snap it off.—By-the-by, I forgot to say that old Mrs. Withers sent here last night, and again this morning. She's got the 'neuraligy' in her 'forward.'"

"The neuralgia in her forehead! She knows just as well what to do for it as I do." He turned to go into the drawing-room, while the two girls, Cynthia at a scamper and Louise more sedately, went up-stairs.

On entering the room in which his friends were assembled, the warm congratulations he received showed how

highly he was appreciated by those who knew him well.
Lucy Craig came forward and kissed him. He had officiated
at her birth, and had ever since been her friend and physician. She was not a pretty girl, but, like many other
young women not remarkable for beauty, she was good.
Dr. Grattan used to say that she had more patience than
any woman he had ever known. She kept the village school
for boys and girls, and hence had every opportunity afforded
her for the development of the godlike virtue of forbearance. "Indeed," he had exclaimed upon one occasion,
when some especially aggravating case of imposition upon
her had come to his knowledge, "if I were the principal of
that school I'd have been hanged for murder a dozen times
before now. I mean I'd have killed a dozen of the little
brats long ago. Johnny Scannell hit you in the face with
a spit-ball, did he? The next time Johnny gets the colic
I'll bring that spit-ball to his memory by means of a mustard-plaster over the pit of his stomach, the horrid little
ruffian! I wish all the boys in Plato had one pit of the
stomach, and I stood by with one big mustard-plaster to
cover it with. Don't cry, my dear; I'll not forget Johnny."
And he didn't.

Mr. Ellis and Mr. Craig both shook hands with him.
The former had returned from Elizabethtown by the road
running to the east of Cobble Hill, having some law business in New Russia, where he had staid all night. He
had only arrived an hour or so before the doctor and
Louise, and had come up to the house to talk over the
matter of the will, and of the administratorship to which
he had been appointed by the surrogate. Mr. Craig and
Lucy had come to make inquiries, Cynthia having early the
night before apprised them of the fact of the non-arrival
of her father and Louise. He had telegraphed to Elizabethtown for information of the missing ones, but, from
some cause or other, the message had not got through.

"I should think," said the clergyman, after they had heard Doctor Grattan's outline account of his adventures, "that you would—bearing in mind your narrow escape—see some things in a somewhat different light from that in which you have hitherto viewed them. For instance—"

"Now, Craig," exclaimed Mr. Ellis, interrupting the speaker rather brusquely, "what in the world does Grattan care about a future state now? He's got enough to think of without you bothering him about the state of his soul. I hardly suppose you mean to go so far as to say that if he'd been sound on theology from your point of view, the ice wouldn't have fallen and blocked up the road."

"Now, Ellis, stop," said the doctor. "I won't have Craig interfered with. I get a great deal more good out of his conversations than I do from yours."

"Oh, very well! just as you please," remarked Mr. Ellis, in a tone that he intended should, as well as his words, convey the idea that the matter was one of the utmost indifference to him. "Your soul's your own, and what becomes of it hereafter isn't, I take it, a matter of supreme importance to any one but yourself."

"That is true, and therefore the less you say about it the better.—Lucy, my dear, how is the school getting on?"

"Oh, splendidly. Sally Springer has the chicken-pox, and all the others are afraid they'll get it too. They treat me, therefore, with the greatest respect."

"Ha! ha! Then they haven't forgotten Johnny Scannell and his mustard-plaster. Let them understand, my dear, that mustard-plasters are just as good for chicken-pox as they are for colic.—Don't you think, Craig," turning to that gentleman, "that Lucy has had about enough of that school?"

"Yes, quite enough. I wanted her to give it up last year, but she thought she would keep it for another session. It is occupation for her, and the salary is something too."

"A beggarly twenty dollars a month! The school board ought to be ashamed to give a lady a pittance like that!—By-the-by, Ellis, did you get your bond settled to your satisfaction?"

"Yes," answered that gentleman. "I didn't have to go far on the road to Au Sable Forks. I met Mr. Tolland just as I was leaving the tavern. He very willingly went my security, and promised to get Somers and Judd to join him, and the matter was arranged in an hour."

Then the three visitors rose to depart, the doctor going with them as far as the "Bear," for he felt some anxiety in regard to his patient, Mr. George Frazier. He found, however, that all was going on well with the young man, except that he was beginning to fret under the confinement to which he was necessarily subjected.

"I sent up to request Miss Grattan to come and talk with me; but she replied with an excuse, and a book that she requested me to read as a special favor to her. How she got hold of it I don't know, for it belongs to me."

"Belongs to you! How did my daughter get a book belonging to you?"

"That is just what I don't know. I brought it here and left it in the bar-room. Some one found it, and, as you see, has scratched my name so that it is no longer recognizable."

The doctor took the book into his hands, but the moment that he did so started with astonishment.

"Why, this is the 'Life and Adventures of Captain Juan de Ayolas'!" he exclaimed. "It is the very copy I've been reading, and I got it from Will Hadden. Where is Will?"

"He'll be back in a few minutes. His mother sent for him a little while ago."

"May I ask where you got the book?"

Frazier hesitated for a moment. "I suppose," he said

at last, "that I might as well tell you all I know of Mr. Lamar, for it was from him that I got the book. The man I knew, and the one who died here the other day, must be the same, though I was not aware that he had come here to live. About two years ago the gentleman of that name whom I knew in Cuba came to Pittsburg, and while there consulted me in regard to certain petroleum-wells that he thought of purchasing. I made some inquiries, and, as the result, advised him to have nothing to do with them, as they were in the hands of a lot of sharpers. Nevertheless, he did buy them, and was rather indignant at me for having spoken slightingly of gentlemen—as he called them— who were his friends. A few days afterward he called and apologized for his intemperate language, and brought me that book, which, as he informed me, he had translated from the Spanish. Although I did not personally know Captain Juan de Ayolas, I knew of him and had seen him once or twice in the streets of Havana and Matanzas. I took the book, of course, as a peace-offering. Although I was interested in the hero, I never had an opportunity of reading it, or it escaped my mind, till I came on this trip to Plato, and then I took it out of the book-case resolved to read it while traveling. I have not, however, read a page of it. I carried it in my hand all the way from New York here, and looked out of the car-windows and talked. I recollect having it when I came to this house."

"That is all very interesting, but how do you know that this is the copy you had?"

"I recollect his writing my name in it, and I can make out to read it, even though it is scratched over so effectually. Besides, while he was talking to me, he took a pen and marked certain letters in the book, which, as he said, spelled his name, John Lamar. It was a way, he further informed me, that the Italians had of indicating the owner-ship of a book. J is the tenth letter of the alphabet. Now look on page ten, and you will find a J with a line drawn under it."

"Yes," said the doctor, after doing as Frazier had requested, "the first *J* on the page is marked."

"Very well," continued Frazier. "O is the fifteenth letter. Examine page fifteen, and you will find that he has marked the first *o* in like manner."

"Yes," said the doctor, "the first *o* is marked with a line."

"Well, you will find all the other letters of the name indicated in a similar manner, so that John Lamar is spelled out by letters of the book."

In a few moments the doctor had satisfied himself that Frazier's information was correct.

"The identification is complete," he said; "the book is yours, and you got it from Lamar, beyond a doubt. I am glad of it."

"It's of no consequence. I'm a little curious, however, to know how it got into Will Hadden's hands, and who scratched my name out with such an evident intention of making it unrecognizable."

"That I can not tell you. You may be very sure that Will Hadden came by it honestly, and that he did not erase the name."

"Oh, I take that for granted."

"I wish you would read this book," said the doctor; "read it carefully, and then tell me what idea, if any, occurs to your mind. I can not say more now without making suggestions, whereas I want you to read it without information or bias."

"No, I'll be hanged if I do!" exclaimed Frazier, with a degree of irritation that was more assumed than real. "How would you like to lie here all day and read a book that you didn't care anything about? You promised that you would allow Miss Grattan to come and see me occasionally, and you have brought her once, and she staid five minutes."

The doctor laughed. "I suppose you do feel the restraint and the loneliness," he said ; "but, here, take the book, and read it to-day. You can do it in a few hours, and to-morrow, when I come, I'll bring my daughter with me, and you shall tell us what you think of the book."

"And you'll let her stay awhile and talk with me ? "

"I don't know about that ; but perhaps I will if you can get Mrs. Ruggles to do her knitting here, and Cynthia cares to stay."

"I suppose she does pretty much as she pleases. If I had a daughter like that she should have everything she wanted, and do everything she liked."

"And a pretty daughter you'd have in a few years," replied the doctor, laughing. "So far as the taint of original sin goes I suppose there's no exemption for women. They *do*, however, appear to have it in a different way, and they possess certain compensating qualities that take off the edge of the curse."

"I never saw a thoroughly bad woman in my life," said Frazier, warmly.

"Young man," exclaimed the doctor, with a look that was half pity and half contempt, "when you've seen a little more of the world, you'll probably know more about women. They're better than we are, though. But here's Hadden," as the young man entered the room.—"Will, where did you get that book that you lent me ? "

"'The Life and Adventures of Captain Juan de Ayolas' ? " answered Will, interrogatively. "I bought it from Mr. Hicks."

"Bought it from Hicks ! And was the name scratched over like this when you got it ? "

"Yes ; I spent half an evening trying to make out the

name of the former owner, but I couldn't distinguish a single letter."

"Take it now and see if you can do any better," said Frazier. "Perhaps it will help you when I tell you that the book is mine, and that the name is George Frazier."

"Yes," replied Will, after he had scrutinized the name for a little while. "I can make out the G and the F very well."

"So you got it from Hicks," said the doctor, musingly. "I almost thought as much."

"But I should like to know where Hicks got it," remarked Frazier; "and why he should have erased my name."

"He is not in a condition to tell you at present," replied the doctor. Then he related the facts of the accident that had put Messrs. Hicks and Spill in a condition to know very little of anything. He had not intended to say much about his own adventures, but this story caused him to touch upon them to some extent, to the great amusement—as he told of them in a humorous vein—of his two listeners.

"Hicks," he said to himself, as he got into his sleigh to go farther on his rounds, "will go to prison some day if he doesn't die of the concussion of the brain he got yesterday. This is the third or fourth thing that I know of his having stolen. He's a bad fellow—worse than Spill!"

.    .    .    .    .    .    .    .

Cynthia ran nimbly up the hall-stairs, Louise following at a slower pace. She began to feel the mental and physical weakness that attends close upon excitement of mind and body, and yet she felt that calm intellectual happiness that comes when there has been time for reflection, and when there is the consciousness that all has gone and is going on well—not so intense, perhaps, as the joy that springs from satisfied emotions, but more persistent, and, in the long run, more comfortable. She had no sooner entered her room, whither Cynthia had preceded her, than the latter threw her arms around her, exclaiming :

"I was awfully frightened about you last night. I thought something terrible had happened. The night was so dark, and the snow so blinding, that I feared you had lost your way, and had fallen into Cobble Hill Gully. Two years ago a team of horses with a sleigh and four men went down into it, in a snow-storm, and men and horses were killed."

"There would have been danger of it if we had passed there later in the evening when it was dark. Your father was very kind, dear ; I can never forget his watchful care of me last night. Sit down here till I tell you all about it."

Cynthia, nothing loath to hear the story, would not do so, however, till she had gone down-stairs and brought Louise a cup of tea and a couple of slices of bread and butter. Then she devoted herself to listening. It is needless to say that Louise's "all" did not embrace the most important of the incidents.

"And now, dear," continued Louise, as she finished her recital, "I am going home to-day."

"This is your home. Fit up Hurricane Castle as a summer resort, rent it to a New York hotel-keeper, and stay with us."

"I am afraid, dear, that that would scarcely do. Cynthia, my darling, do you love me very dearly ?" She was standing by the window at the time. It was just as the doctor and his friends were going down the walk leading to the road, and she was watching them, or rather him, as he walked through the snow with as erect a form and as active a gait as though he were only twenty-five, instead of that and twenty years more. She turned as she spoke the words, to meet Cynthia's mirthful, happy face beaming upon her.

"Do I love you !" said the girl, taking her friend's face between her little hands and imprinting kiss after kiss upon the lips that were pursed up by the pressure. "I could not love a sister any better, and now you tell me you are going away!"

"But only to my own home, and that is not so far off. But, if you will grant a request I am going to make of you, we shall not be separated, after all. Come and stay with me a while."

"But papa! I can not leave him; he depends so much on me. He wouldn't know anything about making himself comfortable, if I didn't see to matters."

"You could pass a good deal of your time here," said Louise, "and—and—your papa could be at Hurricane Castle whenever he liked. I shall be very lonely there without you."

"Then why do you go? I don't see the necessity for it. You must stay; I'll get papa to make you, and he'll do it, just as he made you eat the sandwich last night. Oh, he's a terrible fellow for making people do what he wants!"

"But you will come with me, if your papa does not object, for I really must go?"

"Yes, dear, if papa doesn't make you stay, and is willing, I'll give you the light of my countenance for a few days. He's gone to see Mr. Frazier."

"The gentleman at the 'Bear,' with the broken leg? Is he getting better?"

"Oh, yes! He had the impudence to send up here for me yesterday, just after you had gone to Elizabethtown. As if I were going to see him without papa!"

"Is he nice?"

"Well, my dear, you can't tell much about a man when he's in bed with a broken leg, at least I can't; but I should say that, as men go, he's a pretty fair specimen."

"Handsome?"

"Scarcely," said Cynthia, musingly. "But, really, I don't know. At present he's very pale, one of his eyes is

still black, he has a plaster across one cheek, and there's
another over his forehead.    No," more decidedly, " I should
say that, at this particular period of his existence, he is not
what would be called handsome."

After a few moments' pause—

" Louise."

" Yes, dear."

" Can you keep a secret ? "

" I think so."

" It's an awful one, and you must promise never to
breathe a word of it to a living soul."

" I promise," said Louise, smiling.

" Then listen," rejoined Cynthia, putting on an air of
great mystery and stepping on tiptoe till she came close
enough to Louise to whisper in her ear.    " He's been
jilted ! "    Then she started back, and stood watching with
wide-opened eyes the effect of her communication.

" It isn't possible ! " exclaimed Louise, humoring Cynthia's assumption of the importance of her information and
raising her hands in affected astonishment.

" It is !    I had it direct from Mrs. Ruggles.    His sweet-
heart in New York has shown herself to be a ' whited sep-
ulchre.'    She's turned him off neck and heels—sent him to
Jericho ; and what for, do you think ? "

" Poor fellow !    I can't imagine."

" Poor fellow ?    I don't think he cares a bit.    But can't
you guess why ? "

" No, I haven't the slightest ghost of an idea on the
subject."

" Well, I know, and it's the funniest thing in the world.
She vowed, it seems, that she would never marry a lame
man, and, when he wrote her that he should be lame, she
sent him off."

" What a horrid woman ! "

" Yes, but the best of the joke is, that he is not going

to be a bit lame. Papa says he'll walk as well as he ever did."

"Then it will all come right again, if—"

"Come right again!" exclaimed Cynthia, in real earnest this time. "Do you suppose Mr. Frazier is such a weak-minded idiot as to—as to—as to resume relations that have been so propitiously interrupted?" finishing her remark with the highest-flown language she could, at the time, imagine.

"Pardon my ignorance, but you know I am not acquainted with the young man."

"Clearly not, or you wouldn't suppose that he could be such an imbecile. Mr. George Frazier is not that sort of a man."

"You seem, my dear, to have studied his character very thoroughly," said Louise, laughing, "considering that you have only seen him once."

"But papa has told me a good deal about him, and Mrs. Ruggles declares that 'he's just the sweetest-tempered young gentleman as ever put up at the "Bear," eatin' his victuals as is sot before him, and never sayin' nothin' to nobody'!"

"What an interesting person! You ought to set your cap for him."

"Me! I marry? I wouldn't marry the best man that lives. I'm going to stay with papa. He and I agreed long ago that we'd never marry."

"But your papa is comparatively a young man yet."

"He was forty-five the 25th of last October. There was a widow up here last summer that laid siege to him, a 'Mrs. Clotilde Barkerville, née Howard,' she called herself. Poor papa couldn't put his foot out of the door before the widow was after him. She seemed to be lying in wait for him, and she pounced on him and tried to carry him off on excursions and croquet-parties and picnics and things of that kind. I never knew what Roman firmness papa possessed till the widow 'Clotilde Barkerville, née Howard' taught me. My dear, it was sublime."

" You wouldn't have liked her, then, for a step-mother ?"

" Liked her ! I should have hated her ! No," she added, more seriously, after a moment's reflection, " I should have tried to love her if papa had loved her. It would have been wicked and unkind for me to oppose papa or to do anything to make him unhappy—he who has always been so good to me. Yes, if papa had loved her, I should have loved her ; but she wasn't nice, and papa knew that, and so he fought shy of her."

The words "Should you love me if your papa loved me ?" were on Louise's lips, but upon consideration she thought it better to leave the revelation, as had been agreed upon, to the doctor. But she was in an affectionate mood that morning ; she was greatly attached to Cynthia ; she knew that Cynthia was fond of her, and she could scarcely refrain from opening her heart to the doctor's daughter and pleading her own cause under circumstances that she thought would lead to a favorable verdict. But she *did* restrain herself from saying anything on the subject, though she was quite certain that, had Cynthia been in the least degree suspicious, she would have noticed that there was something under the surface that was not allowed to come to the top.

The fact that Cynthia did not apparently have the slightest idea that her father and her friend were contemplating matrimony together, was calculated to act somewhat as a damper on Louise. It showed, she imagined, that Cynthia regarded such a contingency as so far out of the range of probability as not to be thought of for a moment as a cause of apprehension. What, therefore, was her surprise when Cynthia, who was at the time looking out of the window, turned to her and said :

"Papa is just coming up the walk. Sometimes I think he would be happier if he were married to a good woman ; such as you, dear," she continued, putting one arm around Louise's waist. "Oh, wouldn't it be nice if you and papa should fall in love with each other ? But I suppose it's not to be thought of. You'd think him too old, and he'd think you too rich."

"You wouldn't love me so much as you do now were I your papa's wife ?" The words were spoken with a slight interrogative inflection, which, however, did not escape Cynthia.

"I would," she said with emphasis, "and a great deal more too." Then, turning her face toward that of Louise, she saw the look in her eyes that told the story more eloquently than words could have done. "And it's true," she continued. "Oh, my darling, my darling, how glad I am !"

"Yes, dear, it is true," said Louise, returning Cynthia's caresses. "I'm almost as much pleased now as when your dear papa told me he loved me."

"That's why you're going away, and that's why I'm to stay with you. Oh, you deep young woman ! And papa can come and see *me !* Much he'll care about me now !"

"Don't think that, my darling, or you'll make me very unhappy. Your papa is one of those men that do not change readily. You are all in all to him, and it will be my duty to keep you so. O Cynthia ! you have made me so happy ! It was the only thing I feared. I was afraid that you might look upon me as an interloper, that you might think it cruel of me to come apparently between you and your father, and take the love that is yours. I'll never do that, dear. He will love you now, if possible, more than ever, and I shall help to keep you always in his heart as his darling, his well-beloved daughter, the friend who, in all her life, has never faltered in her affection or duty."

"Come!" exclaimed Cynthia; "he's down-stairs in his pentagonal room, thinking of what he'll say to me to-night. Let us go down, and ease his mind."

She drew Louise after her, and the two entered the pentagonal room hand in hand. The doctor was sitting at the table, with his back to the big window, and his face turned toward the door. He was busily engaged in trying to frame a reasonably plausible excuse for killing off one of the characters in his novel, that was beginning to cause him some anxiety, when he heard the door opened and shut, and, raising his eyes, saw the two girls coming toward him.

"Papa, dear," said Cynthia, with an arch smile on her face, and still holding Louise by the hand, "allow me to present to you the future Mrs. Arthur Grattan." Then, with a profound courtesy, she transferred Louise's hand to her father's, and, raising both of her own, said, "Bless you, my children!"

"Now," she continued, with an affectation of offended dignity, "having done my duty in that station of life to which it has pleased God to call me, I must say that, of all the underhanded pieces of work that it has ever been my bad fortune to encounter, *that* is the worst. I wonder you aren't ashamed of yourselves to have had such goings on 'unbeknownst' to the mistress of the house." Then, suddenly throwing herself into her father's arms, she burst into a passion of tears.

"What is it, dear?" said the doctor, soothingly, while Louise stood by, looking anxiously at the weeping girl, as though endeavoring to determine the incentive to that precise form of emotional disturbance. "You're not sorry that Louise is to stand in the relation of a mother to you? You—"

"It's because I'm glad, darling," she answered, interrupting him, and smiling through her tears, while she stroked his face with her hands. "It's right that you should marry, and where could you find a fitter wife than Louise will be ?  Think of her, and then of 'Mrs. Clotilde Barkerville, *née* Howard' ! "

" I intended to tell you all about it this evening, dear, and to ask you to keep on loving Louise.  I knew you would be kind to her.  I told her she had nothing to fear from you."

" No, she has nothing to fear from me.  Your wife will, next to you, be my beloved."

" Then," he said, smiling, " since you have given your consent, we may regard the affair as settled."

# CHAPTER XXII.

THE next day, before beginning his visits to his patients, Doctor Grattan proceeded to Hurricane Castle. He had had a message from Cynthia early in the morning to the effect that she and Louise were quite well, and another from Louise inviting him to breakfast. He had never yet, although often invited, taken a meal at Hurricane Castle, and he experienced some curiosity as to what would be his emotions when he found himself the guest of the woman he loved.

He began to feel that his affection for her was deepening with every moment of his life. Love is worse than the veriest cannibal that ever lived, for it feeds on itself, and grows by the assimilation of its own products. With him, his passion had assumed a form that it had not possessed previously to the episode in the forest of Wood Mountain. There was an object now that he had not dared to think of in connection with himself and Louise, and he therefore, in that respect, experienced a degree of mental rest and self-satisfaction that he had not before felt since she had come to Plato.

And yet, he was not altogether comfortable. With the few hours that had elapsed since he had made it evident to Louise that he loved her, and since she had, as she admitted to herself, almost "thrown herself at him," there had been a return, to some extent, of his scruples relative to

15

marrying a woman so wealthy as was she. He admitted that, as things now stood, there would be nothing dishonorable in such an act as there would be were he to accept the estate willed to him by Mr. Lamar. It would simply be going in the face of an opinion that he had held for many years, and that he had never been tired of expressing, to the effect that a very poor man should never marry a very rich woman, and mainly for the reason that by such a marriage he placed himself in a position of subordination that was contrary to the best interests of society, and at variance with the eternal decrees of Nature. As for fortune-hunters through marriage, he held them in utter contempt and hatred, and, though he was aware that he was not one of that class, he had, by his denunciations, drawn so much attention to his views on the subject, that he was quite sure that his marriage with the wealthy heiress, Louise Lamar, would be considered, by the world that knew him, as an inconsistency, to say the least, not very creditable to him.

Another circumstance added greatly to the embarrassment that he experienced. Do what he would, it seemed that he could not rid himself of the incubus of Mr. Lamar's wealth. He had done what he could to prevent the estate coming to him directly, and now the upsetting of the will and his marriage with the decedent's daughter, would put this estate almost, if not quite, as much within his control, as though he had allowed the will to stand without protest. Envious and ill-natured people, of whom there are always plenty, when a person has been unusually successful or fortunate, would not hesitate to think or to say that his exhibition of self-denial and heroic firmness and honor had been a sham, and that he had obtained by indirect means what he had not the boldness to take directly.

These reflections, and others, born of the occasion, had occurred to him as he had sat in his pentagonal room be-

fore the big wood-fire, smoking his pipe, after the departure
of Louise and Cynthia had left him alone. They had not
resulted in producing any change in his desire to marry
Louise, but they had succeeded in making him feel a few
self-reproaches, a species of moral punishment, particularly
disagreeable to him. He had Louise, and he had no intention of giving her up, but if she could by any happy
combination of circumstances, get rid of the load that he
had to take with her, he would be delighted beyond measure. He now bitterly reproached himself for not having
allowed Mr. Lamar to institute his university for the education of the negro race in America, and he began to entertain serious ideas as to whether it would not after all be
better for the estate of the dead man to be appropriated to
that object, whether the will should or should not be sustained.

Then he thought of his contemplated visit to Cuba in
the effort to clear Mr. Lamar's memory of the taint that
now rested upon it, of having been the captain of a slave-
ship. He was now more than ever determined that the
suspicion should be entirely removed from the minds of all
honorable men, and especially from those of the United
States Government officials. He did not want to go to
Cuba if the journey could, without the sacrifice of the objects he had in view, be avoided, and he was not without
the hope that through his patient, Mr. Frazier, it might
be possible to obtain all such needful evidence of Mr.
Lamar's non-identity with Juan de Ayolas, *alias* Juan
Lamarez, as to render the trip unnecessary.

But again and again would come up in his mind the
matter of the money, and it was all the more persistent,
like all mental ghosts, in that he had no way of laying it.
His power of exorcism did not extend that far. He had
quieted many similar visitants before, but this was one that
would not down, and that he clearly foresaw was destined

to cause him many an uneasy moment. There was but one
way, so far as he could perceive, of getting rid of the
thought, and that was for Louise to do as she had said she
was ready to do, give the money away, all of it, her own
and her father's, when the latter should come to her.
Then they would stand on equal ground, so far as material
wealth was concerned.

But a little reflection sufficed to show him that the
remedy would be worse than the disease. Not only would
it be selfish and cruel of him to demand such a sacrifice
from the woman that loved him, but it would be certain
to subject him to criticism much more severe and well-
deserved, too, as he well knew, than any he would receive
for marrying a rich woman. It was more than he had a
right to ask ; and though he was quite sure that, on the
slightest hint to that effect from him to Louise, she would
part with her fortune in some way or other, it was not
within the boundaries of human nature that she should not
in her heart of hearts condemn him ; and then, in after-
years, when the first warm flush of their love had gone to
be succeeded by that calmer passion, to last, he hoped, till
their lives' end, would it be possible that she should not
feel a little bitterness at the recollection of what she had
renounced for him, and would not he very certainly be
visited by self-accusations and reproaches as hard to bear
as those that might result from the consciousness that he
had married a rich woman ? Altogether, the subject was
a troublesome one, but it was one that had to be met, and
decided, too, ere long.

He did not falter in the least in his determination to
marry Louise. His heart and his intellect were on this
point in perfect accord. He had not yet said anything to
her in regard to the time of the wedding. Probably, on
account of the death of her father, she would desire a delay
of several months. As for him, the sooner it was over the

better, and he intended the next morning to urge an early
day. Then there would be no longer any opportunity for
the discussions in his mind that he saw were going to be
of daily, hourly occurrence.

He visited Hurricane Castle now as the accepted lover
of its mistress. He had not as yet announced the new relation to any one, but he intended to inform his friends,
Mr. Craig and Mr. Ellis, at the earliest practicable moment,
and to give them authority to circulate the intelligence
throughout the village. It would spread fast enough.

Just as he was driving over the bridge that crossed the
Canemanga, at the foot of the hill on which Hurricane Castle stood, he saw Cynthia coming down the road to meet
him, and in a few moments she had joined him, and climbed
into the sleigh.

"Where is Louise?" he said, as soon as the first greeting was over.

"I have not seen Louise this morning. We sat up late
last night, talking. It was very trying to her to have to
come back here so soon, but of course she had to do it."

"I suppose so, my dear; but I think the state of society
that requires such an act under such circumstances is very
lamentable."

"She would infinitely have preferred to be with you.
Papa, dear, I believe she positively adores you."

The doctor made no answer to this assertion, but the
muscles of his face twitched a little—a sign with him that
he was endeavoring to control the manifestation of his emotions—and then they reached the porch. A groom came
forward to take the horses, and Cynthia and her father
entered the house.

It was the first time that Doctor Grattan had been inside the doors since Mr. Lamar's will was read. Nothing
had apparently been disturbed, and he could scarcely for a
moment bring himself to the recollection that the master

had gone never to return. He had scarcely taken off his overcoat, when he saw Louise descending the staircase. She was paler than usual, but in his eyes more than ever beautiful, dressed as she was in deep mourning, without a speck of white in its composition. He gave a glance around the wide hall. Cynthia had discreetly disappeared, and there were no prying eyes to act as checks to the morning salutations of the lovers.

"I meant to have gone down the road with Cynthia to meet you," she said, "but we sat up late, and then I disobeyed you yesterday, in not taking a nap after our return. You see," she added, with a smile, "I am beginning early. But really I did not know how tired I was till I got to bed last night."

"Fatigue sits well on you," he observed, looking at her with admiring eyes. "You have never looked lovelier."

"Is that so?" she said, while a pleased expression appeared on her face. "I always want to look well to you. But then I am not tired now. If you had seen me last night, when I went up these stairs, scarcely able to walk erect, and with red eyes, half closed from weariness and want of sleep, you would have spoken very differently. But come to breakfast. It ought to be on the table. We shall find Cynthia waiting for us. Dear Arthur!" she continued, as he gave her his arm and they crossed the hall to the breakfast-room, "I wish I could make you fully understand how happy your presence here makes me."

"I think I understand," he answered. "I have only to look at your dear face to see it all."

"Now, my young friends!" exclaimed Cynthia, coming forward from the breakfast-room, "if you think this sort of thing is going to be allowed as a permanent institution, you are very much mistaken. I shouldn't wonder if it would prove to be the greatest error of your lives. Here are the coffee, the muffins, the eggs, the chops, cold. Cold,

I say ; and I, Cynthia Grattan, waiting for my breakfast! I shall stop it, if I have to marry Mr. Ellis, and set up for myself. Perhaps you may not have noticed it, but he's been very attentive to me lately, and I might go farther and fare worse."

" That you might," said her father, laughing, as Louise took the head of the table and proceeded to dispense the coffee from the pretty little silver urn before her—" that you might ! If you can manage to inveigle Ellis into marrying you, you have my consent."

" On second thought, I don't think I could make up my mind to take him."

" Why not ? "

" Well, in the first place, he doesn't believe in the lake of fire and brimstone. I regard that belief as a *sine qua non*—isn't that what you call it ?—in my husband."

" What has that to do with a husband, I should like to know ? You'll be putting absurd notions into Louise's head, for I don't believe in it either."

" Oh, no ! every woman for herself. But *my* husband has got to believe in a real lake of fire and brimstone, devils, pitchforks, melted lead, and all. If he didn't, how could I frighten him into doing what I wanted ? Answer me that, most noble parent ! "

" There is Mr. Spill," said Louise, laughing. " I think he possesses more of your essential qualifications for matrimony than any other man in Plato."

" Thank you, mamma ! " replied Cynthia, with a low inclination of her head and an expression of such good-humored sauciness that neither the doctor nor Louise could refrain from laughing. " It's very kind of you to take such a deep and I may add such an early interest in me, but, unfortunately for your good intentions, Mr. Spill already has the legal allowance of wives, and I have no desire to have him punished for bigamy. Besides, I am not quite sure that he is at this time in the possession of a sufficient amount of consciousness to be able to appreciate my many excellences. But I am obliged to you all the same, dear—all the same."

"There is Mr. George Frazier," said her father. "I think you might get him without the slightest effort. He made me promise to bring you with me to-day, when I make my visit."

"Good people," exclaimed Cynthia, coloring a little this time, but still admirably preserving her bantering spirit, "pray don't trouble yourselves about my matrimonial prospects. I think I have arrived at years of discretion, and may safely be trusted to look out for myself without interference or suggestions. As to Mr. George Frazier, if I'm to be trotted out for his delectation and inspection, I'll stay at home this morning. If he wants to see me, he'll have to come here."

"You're perfectly safe, my dear, in making that assertion. It will be a full month yet before he will be able to come here, and then he may prefer to go to Pittsburg."

"No, he won't! So soon as you take off those horrid splints, he'll limp up here as fast as his legs can carry him."

"By-the-by, Louise," said the doctor, changing the subject as an idea occurred to him, "have you any photographs of your father? If so, I wish you would let me have them for a day or two."

"There are three, I think," she answered—"one of them full-length. They are in an album in the library. You can either take them out or take the book."

She did not ask what he wanted them for, though doubtless she felt a pardonable degree of curiosity in the matter. So thought the doctor, at least; and he debated with himself whether it would not be better, now that his relations to Louise were of so intimate a character, to enlighten her in regard to her father's statements to him, and of his own purposes in connection therewith. He reflected, also, that her good sense might be of great service to him in the inquiry he was about to institute, and that she might also be able to supply important evidence relative to her father's mental condition. It would be an act, too, going to show the confidence that he reposed in her, and might serve likewise to strengthen his position relative to her father's will. Yes, he would tell her all.

"My dear Louise," he said, "while Cynthia is getting ready to go with me to see Mr. Frazier, I should be glad if you would give me a few minutes' conversation in the library. You spoke once of having a copy of the book your father translated, 'The Life and Adventures of Captain Juan de Ayolas.' I should like to see it, and then you can give me the photographs."

"Then you had better go at once," exclaimed Cynthia, rising from the table; "for I shall be ready in less than half an hour."

Louise led the way to the library, and in a few minutes succeeded in finding the copy of the book, and in placing it in the doctor's hands.

He opened it, and at once started, while a look of pleasure overspread his countenance.

"This," he said, "is indeed important, for it contains a photograph of Captain Juan de Ayolas with his signature to it. I suppose it was presented by him to your father."

"Yes, I have heard papa say that it was an excellent likeness. And here," she continued, as she handed him a large book, "are the photographs of which I spoke. They also are good likenesses." Her eyes filled with tears as she looked at them, and she walked away to another part of the room, leaving the book in the doctor's hands.

"My dear Louise," he said, after he had examined the photographs and compared them, and when he judged that her emotion had in a measure subsided, "I think the

time has come for me to tell you all I know of your father's
life, or at least what he told me was his life.  Of course,
you have known that there was something concealed from
you, and you may have thought it strange that there should
have been any such reservation ; but I thought it better to
wait for a more suitable time for giving you my knowledge
than that immediately after your poor father's death.  Sit
here, my dear child," making room for her on the sofa,
"and I will tell you all."

"I knew there was something," she said, as she took
the place by his side, "but I knew you would tell me when
you thought the right time had come."

Then, as succinctly as possible, but with the omission
of no essential detail, the doctor told her of her father's
confession ; of his reasons for thinking it based on hallucinations and delusions ; of the attempt that had been made
to arrest him ; and of the reasons he, the doctor, had for
supposing that her father had taken the story of Captain
Juan de Ayolas and fitted it to his own life.

Louise listened with rapt attention, never interrupting
him except once or twice to utter an exclamation of surprise at the coincidences that existed between the history
as given by the doctor, and facts that had occurred within
her own knowledge.

When he had concluded, she raised his hand to her lips.

"You are teaching me something new every day in
regard to your goodness," she said.  "You have made it
one of the chief objects of your life to set my poor father
right, and to clear his memory in advance of the aspersions
that sooner or later would have been cast upon it.  For
this I can never thank you enough ; but O Arthur, my
love ! you know at least how deeply you are set in my heart.
Now I understand you better than I ever did before.  Now
I see how impossible it would be for you, with your knowledge of my father's condition, and situated as you are, as

his physician, his adviser, to take the money he gave you in his will. He thought you the best man he had ever known. You are all that in my eyes, and more than that, you—"

"Stop, dear," he said, as he kissed her, thus enforcing his command by a material occlusion of her pretty mouth ; "you will develop that latent vanity that is in every man's breast, and quite make me think that I really am something superior to the ordinary run of mankind. But," he continued, "I am not done yet. This Mr. Frazier knew both Captain Juan de Ayolas and your father in Cuba. The copy of 'The Life and Adventures' that I showed you belongs to him, and was given to him by your father. He had never read the book up to yesterday afternoon, but he promised me that he would do so by this morning. He knows that your father, before he left Cuba, had begun to conceive the idea of his identity with the slaver-captain, and is acquainted with many details of his delusion. His evidence therefore will probably, when conjoined with mine, be sufficient to satisfy the United States authorities that your father's confession was the offspring of a disordered mind, and an official statement to that effect will be given. That is all we desire. Doubtless, too, it can be strengthened by evidence from Cuba that Mr. Frazier will be able to suggest. These photographs will be of great value. No two persons could be more unlike than Captain de Ayolas and your father, both in face and figure. The former is a short, thick-set man, with coarse, prominent features, and coal-black eyes and hair ; whereas your father was tall and slender, with delicate features and light hair and eyes. Your father looked like a gentleman, while Captain de Ayolas is apparently an ideal ruffian. The strangest thing about the whole matter is, that a man with tastes as refined and correct as those your father had, should have seen anything to admire in the career of

Captain Juan de Ayolas, who must in appearance and manners have been an offense to all well-bred people."

" I am quite sure papa never admired that man," said Louise. " He seemed to have been infatuated with him, to have been brought under a spell, as it were, by some traits, notably his courage. He never sympathized with him in his occupation ; on the contrary, he loathed it. Years ago his ancestors in Charleston liberated their slaves, not apparently that they thought the people would be any better off, but solely because they thought they themselves would be doing what was right. How clear now the last few months of his life seem to me ! His visions of chains and manacles and groans, his strange conduct when Africa was mentioned, or even the most distant reference made to captives of any kind, his vague statements to me of crimes he alleged he had committed, are all explained. The delusion was on him then, and he was full of apprehension that he would be discovered. Do you remember that night— the first night you came here ? The night when, as you say, you felt your love for me growing so strong that you could no longer resist ; the night," she continued, softly, " when I first knew to a certainty that I loved you ? It was that night that he left us and went to his room, overcome by the picture of the escaped Siberian convict. As I told you, dear, I heard him in his sleep muttering of fetters and chains, and evidently the victim of some horrid dream. Oh, yes !" she went on, clasping her hands together, "it is all as clear to me now as the sun in a cloudless sky."

" May I come in ? " said Cynthia, knocking gently on the door, and then, after a discreet interval, opening it a little way.

" Yes," answered Louise ; "come in, dear. You might as well have been here all the time. I will tell you all to-night. Now I shall only say that your papa has been giv-

ing me additional evidence of his thoughtfulness and kindness."

"Oh, you'll find lots of things to make you think well
of him the longer you know him. I wish, dear, you could
cause him to be a little more kindly disposed toward old
Mrs. Withers. She's just sent here to say that she's got a
'vertigue,' and wishes him to call immediately."

"Well, come along," said the doctor, rising. "Are
you ready to go? I'll leave you with Mr. Frazier, if you
care to stay, and Mrs. Ruggles will promise to sit with you.
I'll be back for you in half an hour."

"I've only my hat to put on, and then I shall be ready.
Louise, dear," she continued, addressing her future step-
mother, "I wish to warn you in the most solemn manner
against old Mrs. Withers. She's the biggest old schemer
there is in all Essex County. She's determined to marry
papa, and, if you allow him to visit her alone, she'll get
him yet. He fights well, I admit, but little by little I can
see that she is making an impression on him. Not long
ago she sent word for him to call, as she had a 'spine in
her back.' He went, after abusing her in very violent language—so violent, in fact, that it is scarcely proper for me
to repeat it—and when he came home he said that, for a
woman of her years, old Mrs. Withers had very plump
shoulders. Now, what do you think of that?"

"I declare, Cynthia," said the doctor, looking a little
annoyed at the sallies of his exuberant daughter, "you are
incorrigible."

"Forgive me, dear," she said, putting up her mouth to
be kissed; "I didn't mean to say that when I began, but it
came out before I knew what I was saying. One thing
leads to another, and somehow or other I feel in such splendid spirits to-day that my joy gets the better of my discretion. Now say that you forgive me, and I'll never
plague you about old Mrs. Withers again."

"Come along, then ; I forgive you.—Good-by, Louise," he continued ; "I shall come over this evening and tell you what Mr. Frazier says. I hope he will be able to save me that journey to Cuba."

"Will that be necessary in any event ? I do not want to lose you just as I have fairly caught you," she said, with a sad smile.

"I can't help thinking that Frazier will settle the matter definitely in our favor."

"Oh, you won't lose him," exclaimed Cynthia, as she got into the sleigh. "When he's once caught, he seems fairly to revel in having the hook in his mouth. Now, there's old Mrs. With— O papa, I almost forgot," she continued, putting her little hand over her mouth, and pretending to be very much frightened.—"Good-by, Louise, dear. When you will see me again is 'one of those things that no fellow can find out.' It depends altogether upon how long Mr. Frazier and I make ourselves mutually agreeable.—Drive on, papa ; Mrs. Withers will be sure to pop out of my mouth if you stay here any longer."

The doctor felt more than usually loving toward his daughter. He had, before she became acquainted with his matrimonial intentions, been naturally somewhat apprehensive in regard to the stand-point from which she would view them. He had endeavored to assure himself that she would receive the intelligence of his proposed marriage with the kindness and respect that she had always shown toward him and his acts, but he was obliged to admit that there was some ground for fearing that she might feel a little chagrin at being deposed from the first place in his heart for another, who, however worthy, and however much beloved, was, a few months ago, unknown to either of them. Cynthia's fit of weeping the day before had come as the climax of her excitement. At first he did not know how to regard it. It looked to him as though her immediately previous behavior had been forced, and that this was an involuntary bursting forth of her real feelings.

But the words uttered as soon as she could recover sufficient composure to speak sufficed to reassure him, and to cause him to think that the *quasi*-hysterical attack was only the culmination of a state of feeling that could not find adequate expression in speech or manner. He knew that all good and feminine women are more or less hysterical. It is only the so-called ' strong-minded ' ones that are not, and hence the extreme emotional disturbance manifested by his daughter had endeared her to him, and had made him feel grateful to her for relieving his mind of a source of considerable anxiety. He loved her very dearly, not one whit the less since he had begun to love Louise, and now he felt his whole heart go out to her, and he longed for an opportunity for showing her how fully he appreciated her kindness to him, and to the woman who, ere long, would stand to her in the relation of a mother.

For a few minutes he drove along in silence. He was thinking whether or not he was doing just right in allowing his daughter to visit Frazier, even though he were an invalid, and then the thought of her goodness to him came up again first in his mind.

" My dear," he said, " I am overpowered with a sense of your kindness to Louise and me. A good many girls would have felt bad at having a step-mother brought into the house ; but you love me so dearly and your affection for Louise seems to be so true and strong, that you are enabled to gratify me very much. I thank you for that, my darling, and I will never forget it."

Cynthia was overcome for the moment. She laid her hand on her father's knee, and a few quiet tears came into her eyes.

" Louise is very good, papa," she said at last. " If there had been a single bad trait in her, I think I should have found it out, and then perhaps I should not have been altogether happy at the idea of your marriage. Because she is going to be my step-mother will never make her any the less my friend. She will always treat me as one very dear to her, for she loves me, papa ; of that I am sure. But you, O papa ! how could I have said a word to mar your happiness, even if I had felt like saying it ? I have long thought you ought to marry, but I have been a little afraid that you might choose some one I should have to try hard to like. But Louise I already love. There is no effort required, and I shall not love her the less, but more, if possible, because she is your wife. Only, papa, dear, let me always be the same to you, always free to come to you without reserve, always free to treat you as—as—a big brother as well as a father."

"There shall be no change in that, my darling, so help me God !" exclaimed the doctor, emphatically. "Louise will not come between you and me. God bless you !—Good-morning, Will !" he continued, as young Hadden came out of his mother's house and took off his hat in salutation. "How are you, and how is your mother ?"

"Both well, doctor, thank you.—Good-morning, Cynthia. You are out early this morning."

"I am staying with Miss Lamar at the Castle, and I'm going now with papa to read a little to Mr. Frazier."

"He can see very well ; he doesn't want any one to read to him."

"Yes, he does ; he wants me, and I am going to oblige him," said Cynthia, a little nettled at the way in which Will had taken her remark. "Sick people get tired, and besides they often have fancies that it is pleasant to be able to gratify."

Will said nothing more, and in a few minutes they arrived at the "Bear." Entering the inn, the doctor inquired for Mrs. Ruggles, and, leaving Cynthia with that lady, went at once up-stairs to his patient.

# CHAPTER XXIII.

"I HAVE been very impatiently waiting for you, doctor," said Mr. Frazier, as the physician entered the room. "That book has been a revelation to me from the beginning to the end, and I've read every page of it. Of course, I know that Mr. Lamar was not Captain Juan de Ayolas, but any person who had been an hour in the company of your friend would have found out on reading that book that he had obtained the details of his life from that romance. Incident after incident is the same."

"Yes; he appears to have merged his identity completely in that of the slaver-captain. Did you ever see the two men together?"

"I don't think I ever saw them together," answered Frazier, reflectively; "but I have seen them on the same day and in such situations as to make it impossible that they should be one and the same person. For instance, one morning at about ten o'clock I left Captain de Ayolas, or Juan Lamarez, as he then called himself, at a *café* in Havana, and I went at once on board of a steamer lying out in the harbor, where I met Mr. Lamar. It was impossible that Captain Lamarez could have got there before me. Indeed, he could not have got there at all."

"Were the two men very different in appearance?"

"Very. In fact, there was not a single point of resemblance. Mr. Lamar was tall and thin, Captain Lamarez

short and stout.  Mr. Lamar had light hair and blue eyes,
Captain Lamarez black hair and black eyes.  There is
scarcely a man now living in Matanzas or Havana, that was
there when the two men were there, that does not know the
difference."

"Now, my friend," said the doctor, "there is a point
to be cleared up, and that is the identity of the Mr. Lamar
whom you knew, with the one who died here a couple of
weeks ago.  There is already enough evidence to settle the
matter in my mind, but no amount of testimony to the fact
can be too much.  I have here thirty photographs of different men.  I want you to take them and tell me if any
one of them is the portrait of Mr. Lamar."

Frazier took the photographs that the doctor had selected, some from his own collection and others from the
album at Hurricane Castle, and looked through them.  He
had not inspected more than half a dozen, when he threw
one down on the bed.

"That is Mr. Lamar!" he exclaimed.  "The likeness
could not be better.  It is exact ; and there's another and
another.  Why, hallo !" he continued, as he examined
another of the photographs, "if here isn't Captain de Ayolas, *alias* Lamarez !  Where in the world did you get that ?
Now look at these, and tell me if any one in his senses could
mistake one for the other."

"That," answered the doctor, "was inserted into the
copy of 'The Life and Adventures of Captain Juan de Ayolas' that belonged to Mr. Lamar.  As you say, there is no
resemblance between the two men.  Now, my friend, you
can render his daughter and me a service.  Draw up in
writing the statement of the circumstances relative to Captain Lamarez and Mr. Lamar that you have just made to
me, and call attention to your knowledge of the fact that
they were two very different persons.  I will send a notary
to you to take your affidavit to it.  Then I shall attach to

it the photographs as exhibits. I shall then make my own statement and shall swear to it, and Miss Lamar will do likewise. I shall then send them all to Judge Conway, and I shall request of him an authoritative declaration that the warrant issued for Mr. Lamar's arrest was based upon a misapprehension of the facts of the case, and that there is no doubt of his entire innocence of the charge he made against himself of having been a slaver. It will not, then, be necessary for me to go to Cuba or even to get additional evidence from there. The facts as they are are ample for his complete vindication. As to the life of Mr. Lamar during his fourteen years of exile, let that remain unknown to us. Neither I nor his daughter will ever seek to explore it. It may have been unhappy, but it was not criminal."

"You may rely upon me to do all in my power. I shall be ready for the notary by to-morrow morning. I think the matter can be so placed before the authorities that not the slightest doubt will remain relative to the state of Mr. Lamar's mind."

"I shall ask that his confession be returned to me. They have no business with such a paper in their archives, when it is shown to have been the offspring of a disordered mind."

Then the doctor examined his patient's leg, and found that, as usual, everything was going on well.

"There will be no shortening," he said, "and consequently no lameness. In a month from to-day I shall let you get up."

"Another month in this bed !" exclaimed Frazier ; "I don't think I can stand it."

"Oh, yes, you can ! You have only to recollect, when you are especially minded to get up and dance a hornpipe, that if you do so, or even put your foot out of the bed, before I tell you, you will be lame all the rest of your life !"

"But you do nothing to help me to make existence

tolerable. You sent me Will Hadden, it is true, and he's good enough in his way, but I have thoroughly exhausted his capacity for entertaining me. In another week I shall hate him. You promised to let Miss Grattan come and sit with me a little while every morning, and you have allowed her to come once. It would have been better if you had kept her away altogether than to have permitted me to see her once, and then never to be trusted to lay eyes on her again."

" My dear fellow, when your leg is well, you shall come to see her and me as often as you like."

" But I want to see her now. O doctor, if you only knew how sweet it is to me to look at a face like hers, to hear a voice like hers, I am sure you would in very pity bring her here ! "

The doctor was on the point of saying, " That's the very reason I don't care about your seeing so much of her," but a little reflection served to show him that a speech of this kind would be likely to suggest the very thing he wished to guard against. He saw plainly that it would take little to make Frazier over head and ears in love with Cynthia. He had no objection to the development of such a passion in the young man at the proper time, but he was decidedly adverse to doing anything to promote its inception in that gentleman's present state of helplessness. Moreover, he had, as yet, very little knowledge of Frazier's character or antecedents. A sick man is very often at his best before his physician ; at any rate, he knew very well that a man with a broken thigh is not in a normal condition, either of body or mind, and he had no intention of accepting Frazier or any other man as a husband for his daughter till he had possessed himself of all possible knowledge of the aspirant's character and position, and had found that both were what they should be. If, when Mr. Frazier had recovered his health, he should be disposed to fall in love with Cynthia, and Cynthia should be similarly affected toward him ; if, after full inquiry, it should appear that the young man was worthy to be the husband of his treasure, and if there should be no impediment to the marriage, he would interpose no objections.  On the contrary, he should countenance the proceeding to the full extent of his influence and power, for his predilections were all in favor of Frazier, who he perceived was a gentleman, with a gentleman's instincts and habits.

While, therefore, he was not inclined to be harsh, he was fully determined to be wary, and to allow no great degree of intimacy to spring up between the two, till such time at least as Frazier should be more capable than he was at present of forming an unbiased opinion.

"Mr. Frazier," he said at last, "my daughter is very young, and you, as a man of the world, must know that visits from young ladies to young gentlemen strangers, even when the latter are confined to bed with broken legs, should be of rare occurrence, and, even when permitted at all, should only be allowed under peculiar circumstances, and with all proper restrictions.  I can enter fully into your feelings, and I am not anxious to be severe.  My daughter is down-stairs now.  I brought her here to sit with you a little while this morning.  I am willing that she should come, say twice a week, to stay for an hour each time, and never to be an instant here without the presence of another respectable woman, Mrs. Ruggles, for instance, or her friend Miss Lamar ; and," he continued, with the utmost gravity and impressiveness, "I rely on your honor as a gentleman not to take advantage of this favor, for it is a favor, to say or do anything that a gentleman ought not to say or do."

"I will treat her as I would an angel."

"No, that will not do," said the doctor, dryly ; "I have no knowledge of how angels should be treated, my acquaintance with them being extremely limited, but I know something of ladies and gentlemen, and I expect you to behave toward her as a gentleman should behave to a lady —I think you know what that conduct should be."

"My dear friend," exclaimed Frazier with feeling, "you can trust me; that is enough for me to say, is it not?"

"Yes, that is enough." He left the room, and in a few minutes returned, accompanied by Cynthia and Mrs. Ruggles.

"It is very kind of you to come, Miss Grattan," said Frazier, as he shook hands with Cynthia; "I have just been threatening your father with getting up and letting the broken leg do what it pleases. I am getting thoroughly tired out with the confinement."

"Ah, but your broken leg wouldn't do anything at all if you were to get up. I suppose it would bend under your weight, and then you'd be like 'Old Bear-that-eats-hickory-nuts-in-the-mountains.'"

"And who or what, in the name of all that is orthographical, is 'Old Bear-that-eats-hickory-nuts-in-the-mountains'?"

"He is an Indian chief," said Cynthia, smiling, "who broke his leg somehow and who would insist upon walking on it. Papa set it for him; but there was an Indian 'bone-setter' who said he knew more about it than papa, and he took off all the splints and pow-wowed over it, and then told 'Old Bear-that-eats-hickory-nuts-in-the-mountains' to run a hundred yards on it. 'Old Bear-that-eats-hickory-nuts-in-the-mountains' did as he was ordered by the medicine-man, and the consequence was that his leg is now very much the shape of a capital letter V. You wouldn't like that, would you?"

Frazier laughed over this story more than he had laughed since he broke his leg. It was evident that his good spirits were in a fair way to be restored. Saying that he would call for Cynthia in an hour, the doctor proceeded on his visits to his other patients. Just at the door he met Will Hadden, who had evidently been walking up and down the passage, uncertain whether or not he should be superfluous were he to enter Mr. Frazier's apartment.

"Go in, Will; Mrs. Ruggles and Cynthia are there," said the doctor—"'the more the merrier'."

"I don't think they want me," replied the young man, in lugubrious tones. "Mr. Frazier's getting tired of me ; he prefers Miss Grattan."

The doctor looked at him in astonishment and indignation till Will's eyes fairly broke down under the gaze, and sought the floor.

"You ought to be ashamed of yourself," said the elder gentleman, "to make such a speech as that. You know very well that Cynthia is a friend of yours. If she can't love you well enough to be your wife it is because she can't, and you ought to be more of a man than to be hanging around the door and uttering ill-natured words. She's told you half a dozen times, to my knowledge, that she won't marry you. What's the use, therefore, of your urging the matter, and getting melancholy when you see her, and making rude speeches because she comes with me to see a man who is helpless on his back, and who needs pleasant people about him ? If you were a friend of hers, you would be the last one to say anything offensive about her."

"I didn't mean to say anything offensive about her— I'd cut my tongue out before I'd do it ; but it's very hard for me, who have known her all my life, to be thrust aside, and a mere stranger favored with visits ; and it's worse still to see him looking forward to her coming, and to hear him talking about her every minute of the day."

"Such things can't be helped, Will," said the doctor, kindly. "If he's in love with her, and she should get to loving him, and there is nothing wrong about him, they'll marry, I suppose. Why shouldn't they ? She won't marry you in any event, and you can't expect that she is going to keep her heart closed to every other man merely because she won't let you in !"

"It's very hard, though, for me, who love her better than I do my life, to have to see another man preferred. It isn't in human nature not to feel bad about it."

"I suppose it is hard ; but you've got to learn to bear such things. I don't know that Cynthia likes Mr. Frazier more than she would any other gentleman circumstanced as he is, and under her father's professional care, but if she does you'll be unpleasantly situated, feeling as you do. I think it might be better for you to stay away on the days that she comes. By-the-by, why don't you fall in love with Lucy Craig ?"

"Lucy Craig ? She's not to be mentioned in the same breath with Cynthia."

"Of course she's not," said the doctor, proudly ; "but Cynthia is out of the question. I know that you have not the slightest chance in that quarter. If you were the only man in the world, she wouldn't have you," he continued, thinking it the better plan to show the young man how utterly hopeless was his passion. "You're not suited to her, either. You're a good fellow, and she likes you, but as to loving you, Will, my dear fellow, it's entirely out of the question. Just as impossible as her marrying her own brother, if she had one."

"I think I'll go away," said Will, in a rather mournful voice ; "I'm quite sure I can't stand it. A man must be pretty blind if he can't see how things are going, and my sight is quickened by the position in which I am placed. He likes her, and she likes him, and they like to be together. Didn't I see the light in her eyes when you came down-stairs for her just now to take her up to his room ? And then to expect me to stand by and see it all without

feeling bad about it, is asking more than I can do. I'll
go away. I suppose I might as well tell you that I've made
my arrangements for going. I shall start for New York
to-morrow, and see if I can't get some literary work to do.
I have got about a thousand dollars that my father left me,
and I can live on that for two or three years, till I get
started."

" I think it is the best thing you can do ; but don't act
hastily. I'll do what I can to help you. I can give you
some good letters of introduction, that will probably aid
you in getting work. You've got talent, and when you are
out of Plato you'll forget all about this affair in a little
while. Take to-day to think it over, and come to me to-
morrow." With which words the doctor took his departure ; but, instead of going farther on his rounds, he went
home, and, entering his pentagonal room, sat down at his
big table and wrote the following letter :

"MY DEAR BUXTON : I have not forgotten the joke
you played off on Baron Liebig when we were students together at Leipsic ; but the remembrance, I am honest
enough to say, would not have induced me to write to you.
This letter is due to quite another cause.

" One of your townsmen, a Mr. George Frazier, was unlucky enough to fall from a high rock on one of our mountains, and to break his thigh. He is doing very well. If
you were here, I would call you in consultation, knowing
how much better a surgeon you are than is your humble
servant and friend, who took more to philosophy than to
the more practical parts of his profession.

" It is somewhat probable, however, that Mr. Frazier
will lose his heart—if he has not already lost it—to my
daughter ; and I am naturally anxious to know something
about the social standing, habits, etc., of the young man
before I allow matters to go any further. Please, therefore,

16

put yourself in my place, and imagine the sort of information you would need. Send me that knowledge at your earliest convenience.

"I suppose you are busy; I hear of you occasionally in the medical journals. Can't you get away next summer and make me a visit? I will take you into the Adirondacks and give you any amount of splendid hunting and fishing.

" Yours sincerely, ARTHUR GRATTAN."

Then he addressed this letter to William Henry Buxton, Esq., M. D., Pittsburg, Pennsylvania; and re-entering his sleigh, which he had left standing at the door, hurried off to the post-office.

"The mail goes in ten minutes," he said, "and it is evident that there is no time to be lost." Having posted his letter, he went off to see old Mrs. Withers, whose last complaint was a "vertigue," and sundry adults and babies of both sexes, suffering from various of the ills that flesh is heir to. It was an hour and a half since his departure from the "Bear" before he got back for Cynthia, and he had not half completed his professional work for the day. He didn't go up-stairs; but sending Mrs. Ruggles for her, waited on the porch for her coming. She did not keep him waiting; but, accompanied by the buxom landlady, soon made her appearance. He noticed the look of gladness in her eyes of which Will Hadden had spoken, and the exuberant spirits that cropped out with every word she uttered.

"O papa," she said, after she had taken her seat in the sleigh, "I think Mr. Frazier is the most entertaining man I ever met, and so witty! He told story after story, each one funnier than the other, till I thought I should die of laughter. Ask him, when you see him, to tell you about the Rev. Nicholas Coalscuttle. I believe he made up every one of them. They were too ridiculous to be true."

"Humph!" muttered the doctor, "this morning he was

tired of life, now he seems to have taken a new lease of it.
And did you tell him any funny stories ? I thought he was
the one that required amusement, not you."

" Oh, but, papa dear, he's one of those men that are best
amused by seeing others amused ! "

" Oh, that's it, is it ? "

" Yes, that's it ; and, when he saw how I laughed, he
laughed more than I did."

And what did poor Mrs. Ruggles do all the time that
you and Mr. Frazier were laughing so heartily ? "

" I don't think she understood a single one of the jokes,
but she laughed all the same, just because we laughed."

" I see, Mr. Frazier told a funny story and you laughed,
and your laughing made him laugh, and his laughing made
Mrs. Ruggles laugh ; and I suppose Mrs. Ruggles's laughing made you laugh again, so that there was laughing in a
circle, so to say—"

" Papa, dear, you are laughing at me ! "

" And all your laughing makes me laugh," continued
the doctor. " Well, my dear, I am glad you enjoyed your
visit. Doubtless Mr. Frazier will be very much improved.
There's nothing like a cheerful mind to facilitate the union
of broken bones. Now, my dear child, seriously, is Mr.
Frazier gentlemanly with women ? "

" Oh, yes, papa, always."

" I am glad he passes your ordeal, my dear, for you are
strict in such matters ; but I don't want you to visit him
again for five days. After that, I hope to be able to allow
you to go every day if he wishes you, and you wish to go."

" Yes, papa, he did not ask me to come again. He said
you would determine when I should come."

" That looks very much as though he were a gentleman.
But here we are at the Castle. I shall not go in now," as
he helped her out, " but tell Louise I'll come over after
tea."

He drove off to finish his work. Matters were going well with him. Frazier's recollection of Mr. Lamar, and of Captain de Ayolas, were amply sufficient to establish the fact of the non-identity of the two men, and of the insane character of his friend's confession. Louise's father's reputation would therefore be unscathed.

Frazier was evidently in love with Cynthia, and Cynthia with him—Frazier very much in love, Cynthia a little. He had no doubt that the information he should receive from his medical friend in Pittsburg would be entirely satisfactory, and then there would be nothing to stand in the way of his dear child's happiness.

Louise was getting deeper and deeper into his heart. He wondered now how he had been able to maintain so long the impassivity that had characterized his bearing toward her till the night they had passed together on Wood Mountain ; and yet with it all he was not comfortable. The money that belonged to Louise—and that made her one of the richest women in America—still rankled in his heart. It was the only thing that disturbed him, and it did disturb him very much. If for a moment in her presence that morning he had forgotten it, it returned with tenfold violence while he was driving over the country roads or talking to his patients. It gave him an absent air when old Mrs. Withers explained to him that the " vertigue " in her head kept her from moving about, and that she had nearly, through it, fallen head-foremost into the fire, just as she was putting the coffee on to boil. This last statement had roused him, for he had said, with a degree of ill-nature, that the old lady remembered to the last day of her life, " Madam, you should not put coffee on to boil. The woman that puts coffee on to boil ought to fall into the fire ! "

Before Louise had left his house the night before, in a conversation on the subject, it was agreed that it would be

better to announce their engagement at once ; and, in accordance with this understanding, the doctor had that
morning told Mrs. Hadden and Mr. Craig, and was on
his way to Mr. Ellis's house to break the glad tidings to
that gentleman, when he overtook him as he was on his
way home, and, while the lawyer walked, the doctor drove
slowly by his side, keeping up a running conversation on
various subjects of an indifferent character, but neither
venturing on topics that were prominent in his mind.
For these matters they preferred more complete seclusion
and absence from disturbing factors than was afforded by a
country road. They entered the house together and proceeded to Mr. Ellis's library. Mr. Ellis lit a pipe and mixed
himself a glass of whisky-and-water. The doctor never
smoked nor drank any alcoholic beverage before dinner, but
he had, while a student in Paris, acquired a liking for *eau-
sucrée*. He always asserted that there was more art in
mixing this innocuous drink, than in compounding the
most elaborate vinous or spirituous concoctions known to a
San Francisco bar-keeper. The temperature of the water,
the kind and quantity of sugar, the extent of the stirring
process, were all points that required due consideration,
and that necessitated a delicacy of management of which
the bar-keeper aforesaid had no conception.

" Ellis," said the doctor, opening the conversation, while
he dropped two little cubes of beet-sugar into a carefully
measured quantity of water, the temperature of which he
had ascertained by repeated tastings—" I'm going to be
married."

" I thought it would come to that," said Mr. Ellis,
dryly.

" Yes, I'm going to marry Miss Lamar."

" You've reconciled yourself to the fortune, then, have
you ? "

" No, I have not, but I see no way of escaping it. Now,

Ellis, I want you to do me a favor. I want you to suppose for a moment that, instead of being my best friend, you are my worst enemy, but an honest one. How would my course appear to you then ? "

" I think, Grattan," he answered, after a little reflection, " that you are putting a very ungracious piece of work on me. It is almost impossible for me to imagine myself your enemy, or to rid myself of certain ideas relative to your scrupulous sense of honor, that a long acquaintanceship with you has caused me to form. My prepossessions are all in your favor. As your enemy, they would be against you."

" Yes, I know that, but you have nevertheless not hesitated, when you have thought occasion existed, to speak your mind freely enough, and to point out any faults you thought I possessed or indiscretions you imagined I had committed. I want you to do so now."

" Well, Grattan, since you insist upon it, I suppose I must do my duty by you, disagreeable as is the task. If I didn't know you as well as I do, I should be very apt to form the opinion that your repugnance to Miss Lamar's wealth is assumed, and that your conduct in regard to the will is an attempt to get a reputation for unselfishness that you do not possess. For, you see, if you upset the will, the property goes to the daughter ; and if you marry the daughter, you'll get it all, any way."

" And you would think that, even as one of the general public—neither friend nor enemy ? "

" I am afraid I should," answered Mr. Ellis, sipping his whisky-and-water. " You see, Grattan, the world is so damned uncharitable, and I'm only about an average specimen of humanity. No one, I think, in the village of Plato, except the Craigs, the Haddens, Miss Lamar, your daughter, and myself, will attribute your renunciation of Mr. Lamar's fortune to its proper motives. And now that you are going to marry the daughter, that aggravating expression, 'I told you so,' will be on the lips of all the scoffers."

"That is just what I supposed," said the doctor, in a melancholy tone of voice.

"But what, in the devil's name, do you care for the opinions of the world at large?" exclaimed Mr. Ellis, rising in his excitement, though not oblivious of the tumbler of whisky-and-water that he held in his hand. "If you please yourself and Miss Lamar first, and your friends in the next place, you can afford to let the rest of mankind view you with all the uncharitableness that human nature can extract out of your conduct. After a while they will settle down into acquiescence. Except," he added, after a little pause, "the members of your own profession, who may be inimical to you. You doctors have among you some of the most generous and some of the meanest of men. The latter never forgive a successful brother till after his death. Then, like a lot of narrow-minded jackasses, when he is fairly out of the way, they rush in to be the first to head subscription-lists for building a monument to him, or setting up his statue somewhere, and this for the man who, during his lifetime, they had denounced as a fraud and a quack. Disregard them, one and all, absolutely. Do what you think is right. Please yourself and those you love, and let the rest go to the infernal region, if there is any such place."

"What you say is true, I know. It commends itself to my best judgment. But, unfortunately, I am so constituted that I can not shake off the ideas that oppress me."

"You don't mean to break off the engagement?"

"No; that I can not do, even if I wished, which I do not; but, nevertheless, I am far from being as happy as, but for this money affair, I should be. It is an incubus that I can not shake off."

Mr. Ellis made no reply to this speech. He smoked his

pipe and sipped his whisky-and-water, and looked wise ; but, whatever was the nature of his reflections, he did not seem inclined to speak of them to his friend.

"I'm going to New York this afternoon," he said, at last. "There are some matters connected with the administratorship of Mr. Lamar's estate that require immediate attention, and I shall not be back for several days. In the mean time, there is a little matter that you may think requires your attention. Hicks and Spill got back this morning. They are none the worse for their accident ; but Hicks has been giving a version of the series of misadventures that befell you and Miss Lamar that has all his mean characteristics in it, and that is calculated, if uncontradicted, to do both you and her injury. I think you had better stop him."

Before this speech was fairly out of his mouth, the doctor, without a word, had left the house, and was driving rapidly in the direction of Mr. Hicks's store.

# CHAPTER XXIV

It did not take the doctor long to arrive at Mr. Hicks's store. He drove as rapidly as his fast trotters could go, and those who saw him as he traveled along the main street of Plato thought that some very ill person required his services at the earliest possible moment. Nevertheless, rapidly though he went, he had time to allow his indignation to cool a little. His first idea had been to go to Hicks, ascertain exactly what he had said, and then to horsewhip him within an inch of his life. That is what he would have done a week ago if Hicks had circulated reports injurious either to Louise or Cynthia. But, under the influence of the love that he felt for Louise, his nature was becoming less impetuous, and his manner less hard. He was conscious of a greater disposition to reflect than had previously characterized him, and then, when he had reflected, to resort to less extreme measures than he would have adopted before she softened and refined him. And the chief point that was made apparent to him by the consideration that he gave to the subject, was that the more he agitated the matter the more talk there would be. A public castigation of Hicks would inevitably create a scandal, during which Louise's name and his would be bandied about the county in a way that would be extremely repulsive to both of them. No, whatever he should do to Hicks must be done quietly, but so effectually as to cause him to see the absolute necessity, if he valued his well-being, of keeping his mouth free from the utterance of slanderous words.

He was glad to find that Hicks was alone, and he saw at once that he had sustained no serious injury from the accident that had befallen him. The man came forward with outstretched hand ; but the doctor appeared not to see the friendly gesture. He was in no mood for civilities.

" Hicks," he said, with as much calmness as he could command, " I have just heard from Mr. Ellis that you have made some impertinent observations relative to Miss Lamar. I intended to ask you what you said, but, upon second thought, I have come to the conclusion that I don't care to know. It is sufficient that it was impertinent and slanderous."

As soon as the doctor began to speak, Hicks turned as pale as a sheet. Before he had said a dozen words he was trembling like an aspen-leaf.

"I am not well," he said, at last. " You know I was badly hurt a couple of days ago."

" I don't care how badly you were hurt. You were well enough this morning to slander a lady, and I came here to punish you. If you were on your death-bed, I should still give you a lesson in decency that you would not forget during the time you might have to live. As it is, you will recollect what I say and do to you to-day if you live a thousand years."

" I didn't intend any harm ; I was only joking."

" There are some things that can not be joked about, and one of them is a lady's name. I came here to horse-whip you so long as I might be able to stand over you ; but I have changed my mind about that. You may recollect that several weeks ago I came into your store when you were slandering Mr. Lamar. I said a word to you then that made you turn almost as pale as you are now. It was only a single word, but that word was 'thief'."

"I'm not a thief!" exclaimed Hicks, in desperation. "I'll make you prove that, Doctor Grattan ! Who's the slanderer now, I'd like to know ?"

"You won't have any further trouble to make me prove it," rejoined the doctor. "I intend to prove it, not only to the satisfaction of everybody in Plato, but to that of a grand jury as well. I have the proofs of six distinct acts of theft committed by you, one of them being a burglary for which, when you get your deserts, you will receive any-where from ten to twenty years in the State's prison. You broke into old Mrs. Withers's house less than a week ago. She recognized you, and I have her statement in my pocket. Up to that time you had only pilfered. Mr. Frazier's book, for instance, that you sold to Will Hadden, after erasing the owner's name, and Mr. Lamar's pocket-book, that he left on your counter one morning, and—"

"I didn't steal any of them things. I found 'em, and was goin' to give them back to the owners. And whoever told that lie about me breaking into Mrs. Withers's house will have to pay for it. I'll take the law of him as sure as my name's Hicks !"

"You'll get all the law you want, you rascal, without exerting yourself ! Mrs. Withers lay awake watching you while you ransacked her room. She saw your face as you took her watch from the table on which it lay, and Tim Maddox saw you enter the house and come out. I've had a conversation with both of them this morning, and they are ready to go before Squire Williamson and make their affidavits. In fact, Tim has already gone."

Hicks glanced round the room furtively, and then, sud-denly springing on the doctor, seized him by the throat, and tried to throttle him. But he had reckoned without his host, for Doctor Grattan shook his antagonist off with scarcely an effort, and, picking him up in his arms, as though he were a baby, carried him to a chair, and, forc-

ing him into it, deliberately proceeded to tie him fast with
a cord that he found near at hand.

"Hicks," he said, when he had completed this operation to his satisfaction, "I should have had you arrested
before this, but for the fact that I really thought you were
a kleptomaniac, and therefore not morally or legally responsible for your thefts.  But this recent robbery of Mrs.
Withers is altogether out of the range of a kleptomaniac's
acts.  The old lady, out of regard for your wife, has kept
the matter a secret till this morning ; then she told me."

"Doctor," said Hicks, in a feeble voice, "let me go.
I'll leave town within a week, and I'll sign a statement that
I lied in what I said about you and Miss Lamar.  Besides,
what I said was only in fun.  I didn't suppose anybody
would believe it.  I only said—"

"Don't tell me, you blackguard !  If you do, I may still
pound you to a jelly.  As to letting you go, I have not the
slightest intention of doing anything of the kind.  I don't
want your statement.  You'll soon be in such a position
that statements from you, for or against a person, will be
of no importance.  Besides, you know me well enough to
understand that I never compound felonies.  You'll go to
Clinton prison as sure as my name's Grattan."

The man ceased to implore his captor for a mercy that
he felt perfectly sure would not be granted.  Apparently
he abandoned himself to his fate, for he let his head fall
upon his breast, and looked doggedly at the floor, as though
waiting for the constable to make his appearance, and take
him into custody.  The doctor had taken the precaution to
close and lock the front door, and he, too, evidently expected the advent of the officer of the law.  Indeed, it
could not now be many minutes before Gough, the constable, would be rapping at the door, with a warrant for
Hicks's arrest.

But Hicks was thinking of a plan for obtaining his release that he had a faint hope might prove effectual. He had abandoned all idea of getting mercy from the doctor. He thought, however, in his extremity, that an appeal to his curiosity might be more effectual.

" I know something about Mr. Lamar's death that ain't known to another soul," he said, looking anxiously at the doctor, with a little hope expressed in his face. " If you'll take me in your sleigh down to your house, I'll tell you all about it, if you'll let me go as soon as I get through. I can get away from Gough easy enough. I'll tell you all, and it'll be worth your while to know, I guess."

" I have suspected you, Hicks," said the doctor, " of knowing more about that poor man's death than the rest of us. But what you've got to say on the subject must be said to the authorities. I'm going to watch you till the constable comes, and then I'll turn you over to him. Mr. Lamar died from cerebral hæmorrhage. You didn't kill him, but I am inclined to think that you drove that needle into his skull. Perhaps you started out to kill him, but Nature took the act out of your hands. You can keep your knowledge to yourself, and settle that account with your Creator. Now you are going to the State's prison for burglary."

" Then I'll tell all I know about Mr. Lamar's being a slaver-captain. I've got some of his papers, and they prove it, and I've got lots of letters addressed to him as Captain Juan Lamarez. I'll damage what reputation he left behind him, and I'll disgrace that daughter of his, that you spent the night with on Wood Mountain, still more than you've disgraced her."

" Nothing that you can say will disgrace anybody. Besides, I know more about Captain Lamarez and Mr. Lamar than you are ever likely to know. The book that you stole from Mr. Frazier, and sold to Will Hadden, is the life of Captain Lamarez, translated from the Spanish, with notes and additions, by Mr. Lamar. There are many more of Captain Lamarez's papers at Hurricane Castle, that were placed in Mr. Lamar's hands for use in the work upon which he was engaged, and that escaped your notice. Perhaps you stole other things from them besides the papers. I'll inquire into that, and you'll probably get ten or twelve years additional in the penitentiary. But here is Gough," as a loud knock was heard, "so that my duty as your guard is over."

He opened the door, and admitted a tall, gaunt-looking individual, carrying a folded document in his hand. He looked around the store, and, espying Hicks seated in the chair to which the doctor had tied him, approached that individual.

"I'm sorry, Mr. Hicks," he said, "to have to arrest you, but here's my warrant, all in proper form. I'll go with you up-stairs, and you can have as much time as may be necessary to get things in order before going with me to Elizabethtown. Mrs. Hicks, I suppose, will look after things for you, or I guess there wouldn't be any great objection to her going with you. The jail's a comfortable one."

"Mrs. Hicks isn't here to look after things for me, or any one else," said Hicks, sullenly. "She went home to her father, in Plattsburg, yesterday, and she's gone to stay, I guess."

"Yes," said the doctor; "I heard this morning that, in consequence of your ill-treatment, and of her knowledge of your conduct, she had left you. She has saved you up to this time, for, if it had not been for her, I'd have had you punished a year ago, when you stole my pocket-book."

"I didn't steal your pocket-book."

"You did! I left it accidentally on your counter. You found it there, and you knew it was mine, for it had my cards in it, and some valuable papers, besides fifty dollars."

"I tell you I didn't take it. I never saw your pocket-book."

"Don't lie about it any more, Hicks. The next morning your wife brought it to me, knowing that the papers were valuable. You had taken the money out of it, however. She begged hard for you, and I yielded to her entreaties, and let you off."

Hicks, seeing that further denial was useless, relapsed into silence, and the constable, loosening his bonds, took him into that part of the house that served as his residence, in order that he might make preparations for a long absence. As the officer of the law passed by the doctor, he whispered :

"There's a good deal more against him than what you know of. They say he was the leader of the masked party that gagged old man Scudamore, and robbed him, about a year ago, of his coupon-bonds. One of them's been traced to Hicks."

Again the doctor entered his sleigh. He had finished his work for the morning, and it was near his time for dinner ; but, although things had apparently resulted to his satisfaction, he was not altogether happy. Now, that his anger at Hicks's slanderous remarks was in a measure appeased, he began to feel uncomfortable at the thought of the part he had taken in that person's discomfiture and arrest.

"I ought to have let him alone," he said, as he drove along the road on his way home. "It was unworthy of me to stand there, when I had him in my power, and taunt him with his crimes and his helplessness. It was undignified, too. There's a good deal to do to me yet before my nature will be brought down to the proper degree of fineness. Poor devil, I feel almost sorry for him ! Not a friend in the world ! Even his wife has deserted him ! Still, I'm glad he's going to get his deserts. It will take a good deal of super-refining work to be done on me before I shall regret that the law has got him in its clutches. To think that the scoundrel should have dared to say a word ! Well, he's nipped in the bud ! It's astonishing how despicably vile some men can be."

He drove up to his door as he uttered this last sentiment, and, pulling a stout cord that hung from one of the posts that supported the roof of the porch, and that was attached at the other end to a bell in the stable, waited for Mike to come and take his horses.

"Has any one been here, Mike ?" he inquired, when the man made his appearance.

"Yes, sorr. Mr. Ellis was here. He only stopped to say that he was on his way to New York, and that for all he knew he mightn't be back again for a wake or more."

"Any one else ?"

"Yes, sorr. Miss Cynthia's in the house now. And did ye hear about Mr. Hicks, sorr ? They say he's the man that robbed farmer Scudamore a year ago, and there's a warrant out against him for robbing Mrs. Withers."

"Yes, I heard all about Hicks. He's gone to jail by this time."

"I don't know, sorr, what we're all coming to. It's mighty bad, sorr."

"Yes, it's a bad state of affairs when a man, apparently so respectable as Hicks, can turn out to be such a thorough rascal."

"It's part your own fault, sorr."

"Partly my fault ! What do you mean ?"

"Sure, an' if you'd a done your duty when he took your pocket-book, he wouldn't a been able to gag and rob farmer Scudamore, or get into Mrs. Withers's house."

"How did you know he stole my pocket-book ?" exclaimed the doctor, in astonishment.

"How did I know it, sorr ? Well, sorr, I couldn't help

knowing of it, for I heard ye tell Miss Cynthia one day when I was driving ye."

" And have you kept this information to yourself, Mike ?"

" Yes, sorr ; devil a person knows it in all Plato from me, sorr."

" Mike, you're an honest and a discreet man. Here," he continued, putting his hand into his pocket, and taking out a twenty-dollar gold-piece that had been given him by a patient that morning for his professional services for nearly a month, "take this as an evidence of my appreciation of your wisdom."

" Thank ye, sorr," said Mike, grinning from ear to ear. " I never saw an Irishman that wouldn't take money when he could get it honestly ; though your honor knows I don't want this to make me do my duty by your honor. God bless you, your honor !"

The doctor entered the house, and proceeded direct to his pentagonal room, without even going to hunt up Cynthia, who was somewhere about. He was more and more disquieted. Mike's reminder had caused him to see his conduct in another and altogether different light from that in which he had just before been viewing it. Then he had reproached himself for his harshness ; now he was obliged to condemn himself for leniency. If he had had Hicks arrested when he committed the theft of his pocket-book, not only would the crimes mentioned by Mike have been uncommitted, but others of which Mike knew nothing would have been in the same category, and the slanderous words against Louise and himself would not have been spoken. He began to see that he was becoming morbidly sensitive. A year ago such matters would not have disturbed his equanimity. He would have done what he thought was his duty, and the consequences would have been left to take care of themselves. They would not have troubled him in the slightest degree. He recollected having had a discussion with his friend Ellis on this point. The doctor had given a hypodermic injection of morphia to a poor woman suffering the acutest agony from neuralgia of the face. There was nothing else known to science that was likely to afford her a moment's relief. In fact, everything that hypothesis or experience suggested had been tried in vain. Then he inserted a small quantity of morphia under the skin of the sufferer, and in a few minutes she was asleep, for the first time in several days, and when she awoke she was free from pain. But, in less than a week, it was back again, and again the morphia subdued it. Then she found that she could use the drug with a little syringe, that she sent to New York for, as well as could the doctor, and she availed herself of her knowledge to such an extent that the morphia-habit became established, and she craved the pain-subduing agent, not only because it freed her from suffering, but on account of its own inherent, pleasurable effects. One day she took too much, and, before relief could be afforded, she was dead. For this Mr. Ellis had reproached the doctor, and the latter had opened his batteries on his friend with all his power of argument and invective.

"You are talking, as you often do, about things of which you know nothing," he said. "Opium and its preparations have saved tens of thousands of lives where they have destroyed one, and they have given peace and comfort to millions of the human race, who, but for them, would have suffered the tortures of the damned, and perhaps have been driven to suicide. The idea of holding the physician, who prescribes morphia in good faith for a proper purpose, and with warnings against indulgence, responsible for any abuse that the patient may make of the remedy, is not only absurd, but it is atrocious. I should no more think of reproaching myself for such misconduct, than I should blame myself for the shipwreck of a vessel upon which was a patient for whom I had advised a sea-voyage."

" I call that very specious reasoning," rejoined Mr. Ellis. " It's full of fallacious statements. Suppose you had advised a person to stick his hand into the fire for the cure of an ulcer, and he did so, and burned his hand, wouldn't you be responsible for that burn ? That's the way to put it. You don't necessarily injure a person by sending him on a sea-voyage, but you do necessarily injure him when you prescribe opium for him."

" Ellis!" exclaimed the doctor, " whenever you attempt to go beyond the law in your discussions, you exhibit yourself as an ignoramus. The moderate and proper use of opium for the relief or cure of disease does no injury to the system. On the contrary, it does good. It is the excess that is bad—the using of it for itself, and not in the treatment of disease. For such abuse I am not responsible. If your views prevailed, a boy would never be allowed to play cards at home with his mother and sisters, lest he might become a gambler, or to drink a glass of wine at his father's table, for fear of his getting to be a drunkard. I heard a man once denounce the teaching of writing because some men become forgers. People are born with appetites that are meant to be kept in subjection. If they allow them to govern their minds and bodies, they themselves are responsible, and no one else."

As is usual in such cases, neither party was convinced, but Mr. Ellis had been silenced by the superior knowledge of his antagonist, and his appropriateness of illustration.

The doctor thought of this discussion as he sat in his big chair in the pentagonal room, and he was annoyed at the idea that his emotions now should be so very different from what they had been on the occasion of the death of Mrs. Hodgin from an overdose of morphia.

" It is all that money," he said to himself. " It has

demoralized me completely. I am not myself. I am trying to regard with composure the act of marrying an enormously rich woman, and I can't do it. It is a contradic-
tion of my whole life. It is a violation of principles I have
held ever since I was capable of thinking for myself, and it
will inevitably make me more and more unhappy every day
of my life. No man, with a nature as sensitive as is mine,
can violate his sense of right without being made miserable. And yet," he continued, " I am ashamed of myself
for being so constituted as not to be able to accept the great
gift of Louise's love with all the joy that it ought to excite
in my heart. It shows that I have a smallness of soul that
I did not think I possessed. However, we never know ourselves till occasions arise that bring out qualities that have
lain dormant, and some persons pass through life in such
oyster-like torpidity of mind and body that they never get the
opportunity for finding out what manner of people they are."

He was standing in front of the big window, looking
out at the bleak landscape before him. All was white with
the snow that had recently fallen, except Pitchoff Mountain, which stood right in front of him, and the leafless oaks
and chestnuts and maples, of which, together with the
dark-green pines and hemlocks, gave it a mottled white-
and-black appearance.

"It does not help me now," he said, in a despairing
tone of voice. " Time was when, no matter how disturbed
my mind might be, a look at that mountain, whether in
winter or summer, never failed to quicken my mental processes, and to make me see matters in a satisfying, if not
an absolutely true, light. But now I might gaze at it till
my eyes grew dim, and the spirit of unrest would not be
crushed out of me. Oh, you inert mass ! " he continued,
"how can I expect you to aid me when she whom I love,
and whose heart is in my keeping, as hers is in mine, is
powerless to enlighten my soul ? "

But, even as he spoke, he felt a thrill as though a gentle undulation had passed through his nerves. The mountain seemed to grow before his eyes, and finally to fill the whole landscape. His ideas appeared to be less vivid, and then to fade out altogether.

"I have not got over the fatigue of the night before last," he said, as he roused himself a little, and walked, almost staggered, to his big chair before the fire. He dropped into it, and in an instant was sound asleep.

How long he slept he never knew exactly, for he had not looked at the antique clock on the mantel-piece before losing himself, but probably he was in a state of obliviousness for half an hour. He was aroused by some one pulling at his mustache, and, opening his eyes, saw Cynthia standing before him and just about to try the effect of tickling his ear with a piece of paper that she had twisted for the occasion.

"I never saw any one sleep so soundly in all my life," she said, laughing. "If this had not succeeded, I should have held a bottle of hartshorn under your nose, as I heard you say you did once to old Mrs. With—I mean the lady that lives just to the right of the church. Dinner is ready, and I propose to honor you with my presence."

"I don't know what came over me," said the doctor, rising and stretching himself. "I was standing in front of the window, when all at once I felt myself overpowered with sleep, and I had barely time to reach this chair before I was incapable of resisting the influence."

"You were tired, dear," said Cynthia, now all sympathy and kindness. "I'm so sorry I awakened you. Go to sleep again, and you shall have your dinner nice and hot when you have finished your nap."

"No, I do not feel at all sleepy now. It's a common enough circumstance, but it never happened to me before. But why are you going to dine with me? Is Louise alone?"

"Louise could not bear the idea of your being all by yourself at dinner; so she asked me to give you my company, which, of course, I was only too glad to do. You shall take me over this evening, as she expects you to tea."

"It was very kind of you both. What has she been doing this morning?"

"Oh, lots of things—writing, especially. She had Mr. Ellis with her for an hour before he left for New York, and he went off with several bundles of papers."

"She was fortunate in getting Ellis to look after her business matters. She has a clear head on her shoulders, but a woman with so much property as she has requires an agent."

Then, while they were at dinner, he, greatly to her astonishment, told her of the difficulties into which Mr. Hicks had got himself, and of the probable consequences to the freedom of that individual that would result therefrom. And then she had her piece of news.

"Will Hadden has gone," she said.

"Gone! Why, I saw him this morning."

"Yes, but he left for New York with Mr. Ellis. He came up to the Castle to see Louise and me, and would have come to bid you good-by, but he knew you were not at home. He left his address with me, and a request that you would send him the letters you promised."

"But I can not account for the suddenness of his departure."

"You had a conversation with him this morning, had you not, papa?"

"Yes."

"And you advised him to go?"

"Yes, I told him I thought he would be happier out of Plato just at this time than in it."

"So he told me, papa," she continued, with a blush and with downcast eyes. "Will is a good boy, and I like him very much."

" Yes, and I'm almost sorry you could not have done more than only like him."

" That was impossible."

" So I suppose."

" Yes, it was quite impossible."

" Then we will say no more about it."

" Thank you, papa."

That evening Cynthia went back to Hurricane Castle, the doctor going with her. He had gone to his bedroom after dinner, and from a little iron safe, that stood in a closet, had taken a diamond ring, that a family tradition said had been given by Queen Mary of England to a Grattan for gallant conduct at the battle of the Boyne, he having at the great risk of his own life saved that of William the king. Ever since that time the ring had been worn by some one of the women of the family as a marriage-engagement ring when there had been any women to wear it. When he placed it on Louise's finger he felt that the tie between them was as indissolubly fixed as though the ceremony of the law or the church had been performed.

But the strangest experience of his life was the fact that since his apostrophe to Pitchoff Mountain, and the curious and overpowering sleep that had come upon him, his views in regard to Louise's wealth and its relations to himself had undergone a radical change. Whether the mountain really had in some mysterious way affected him, or whether the change had been wrought by some subtile alteration taking place in his brain at the time he felt the languor and drowsiness and during his profound sleep, he was never fully able to determine. As a philosopher, inclined to take a practical view of the affairs of life, he was a firm disbeliever in all kinds of so-called occult influences, and therefore he inclined to the opinion that a modification in the structure of the brain had ensued, and that, as that organ was different, so the product of the organ, thought, was also differ-

ent. He knew that a person is rarely the same after as
before an attack of congestion of the brain, or even a severe
blow on the head. He had known cases in which the subjects had been kind and generous, and had subsequently,
from an apparently slight alteration in the quantity of
blood in the brain, become brutal and selfish. He had had
a case under his own charge in which a blow on the skull
from a brickbat had changed a pious and honest man into
a ruffian and thief ; and he had also heard of an instance in
which as great a blackguard and drunkard as New York
had ever produced had become fanatically religious and an
advocate of the total prohibition of the sale of alcohol,
after falling out of a third-story window and breaking his
skull while in a state of beastly intoxication. He thought
of all these cases, and he was strongly inclined to the belief
that his abstinence from food and sleep, together with the
excitement attendant on recent matters of great moment,
had produced a sudden anæmia of his brain, from which
sleep was the first consequence, and a change in his mental
peculiarities the next.

But he had been tired and hungry and sleepy before
this, and no such softening and refining influence had been
produced upon him. He had often looked at Pitchoff
Mountain, and had never experienced more than a slight
calming effect, such as a pipe of tobacco might have produced, and which Cynthia had always declared *was* caused
by the sedation of the fragrant weed. There must have
been something else, and what could it be, if not the love
that had taken him captive ? *Amor omnia vincit.*

# CHAPTER XXV.

## "OH, YES, I LOVE YOU!"

A WEEK had elapsed. Hicks was in the Essex County jail at Elizabethtown, and the grand jury had found a true bill against him for burglary.

The doctor had sent off the affidavits in the case of Mr. Lamar made by Mr. Frazier, Louise, and himself, together with a copy of the translation of "The Life and Adventures of Captain Juan de Ayolas" and certain important papers, all going to show the non-identity of Mr. Lamar with Captain Lamarez. Judge Conway had replied very promptly, to the effect that he had carefully read all the evidence and exhibits submitted, and that the conclusion was absolutely unavoidable that the two men were separate and distinct persons, and that Mr. Lamar was the subject of a delusion, and was hence of unsound mind. He returned the "confession," and expressed his regret that he had acted at all in the matter, though he thought there was some excuse for the course he had taken. All this had been very gratifying to Louise and the doctor, who now began to see the beginning of the end of their troubles.

Will Hadden had been heard from. He had started a periodical publication called "The Meteor," and wrote to say that his prospects were excellent. The characteristic feature of the magazine, which was a monthly, was short stories, of which Will proposed to write the greater number himself. He begged that the doctor would consider the

17

proposition he made to print the novel which he knew his friend was engaged in writing.

Mr. Ellis had not yet returned to Plato, nor had a word been heard from him since his departure. It was known, however, indirectly, that he had found it necessary to extend his journey to Philadelphia, Baltimore, and to points much farther south, on business connected with the estates of the late Mr. Lamar and his daughter Louise.

The doctor had heard from his medical friend in Pittsburg, who, after the expressions of friendship and of delight at hearing from his fellow-student of many years ago, went on to say that Mr. George Frazier was a gentleman against whom no slanderous remark had ever been uttered, so far as he knew ; that he was personally acquainted with him, had, in fact, known him since he was a boy, and was, therefore, familiar with his whole career. He, the medical friend, had no hesitation in saying that no one in the city of Pittsburg stood higher in the estimation of honorable men than did George Frazier, and that if he, the medical friend, had a daughter, he would think that her life-lines had fallen in pleasant places were she to be married to as estimable a man. He was sorry his young friend had met with so serious an accident ; but, if it should prove to be the means of uniting him for life to a woman worthy of him, no one would be more rejoiced than the man who was writing that letter. He then stated that Mr. Frazier was engaged in the very prosperous business of making steel and steel-castings of various kinds, and was reputed to be very wealthy.

During the delay, Frazier had said nothing about Cynthia's coming to see him. He seemed to know intuitively that the doctor was making inquiries, and that his proper course was to wait till they were answered. But, on the fifth day, the doctor had broached the subject by stating what he had done, and telling him the general purport of the answer he had received—and then Frazier had spoken. He told the whole story of his love for Miss Drummond, and of the heartless manner in which she had acted toward him. He did not blame her; he admitted that the unconquerable repugnance that she had for malformed persons was constitutional, and a matter altogether beyond her control, but it was nevertheless real, and the existence of which showed her to possess a form of mental organization altogether incompatible with his idea of that which a wife should have. The discovery of her peculiarity had, he said, entirely effaced from his heart the love he had once felt for her. It had gone immediately, not without regret, he admitted, for he had loved her dearly so long as he had thought her a woman with a heart, but certainly without any bitterness or gnawing grief. She was gone clean out of his life.

And Cynthia had come in while the door was still ajar. He loved her, of course, more than he had ever loved before, and he wanted her father's permission to plead his suit with her in his own way, and he wanted the opportunities for gaining her love—opportunities that could only be given him by her being allowed to visit him untrammeled by the presence of Mrs. Ruggles, or of any one else.

"Surely," he said, "now that you know who I am, and that I avow that my object is to make her my wife, you can allow her and me more freedom than you have heretofore seen fit to grant us. It is I that take the initiative. I ask her to come. God knows that, if I could, I would go to her!"

"That is all very true," the doctor had answered, "and she may, if she chooses, come and talk with you, and read to you, but there must be no love-making till you are well enough to carry out that part of the programme elsewhere than in your own apartment. Get to know each other as well as you can. In a few weeks now you will be able to

be up and walking about, and then you will have ample
opportunity to talk of love if she chooses to hear you.
There's no necessity for any hurry in the matter."

"I have no objection to that," rejoined Frazier ; "only
let her come. She is gentle and kind, but I have no idea
that she cares any more for me or differently than she
would for any other poor devil situated as I am. Let her
come, and I promise you, on my honor as a gentleman,
neither by word nor deed will I betray the existence of any
stronger feeling than friendship."

"I have not much faith in such promises made under
such circumstances," said the doctor, laughing. "The
emotion will probably crop out in ways and at times that
you little suspect. Still, I rely on you to act in good faith
to the utmost of your ability.—By-the-by, I have not told
you that I am going to be married."

"You !"

"Yes, I. Is there anything surprising in the fact ?"

"Not at all. I only wonder that you have not married
long ago. I congratulate you with all my heart," holding
out his hand, which the doctor grasped warmly. "May I
ask who is the lady ?"

"You are very kind, and I thank you for your good
wishes. The lady is Miss Lamar."

"Of course ; I might have known that."

"Why of course ?"

"Mainly, my dear doctor, for the reason that there is
no one else in Plato that you could marry."

"That's true ; nor anywhere else on the face of the
earth."

"You ought to feel your heart grow warmer toward
me."

"Something in the nature of 'a fellow-feeling,' I suppose ?"

"Yes, that's what I mean."

" You've had the benefit of that. Haven't I given you my consent to getting Cynthia if you can ? "

" Yes ; you've been very good to me. I ought to be satisfied, and I am satisfied. I'll be the happiest man in the world when Cynthia tells me she'll be my wife."

" You'll have every reason to be. She's everything that's good. But I'm not going to stay here praising my own daughter. You'll find her out for yourself. Good-by. I think I can trust you, and that, should you succeed in winning her, you will make her happy."

Another affair of importance had been settled. Before Mr. Ellis's departure for New York he had, as the reader knows, spent some time with Louise at Hurricane Castle. Chief among the matters that she had brought to his attention was a plan she had formed for disposing of her father's estate, if, as seemed now very certain, it should descend to her as the sole heir-at-law. Up to that time she had, with her bright perception, noticed that the doctor was unhappy on the subject of this estate. He had told her as much, and she saw that with all his efforts he was not able to overcome his feelings in the matter. She had, therefore, proposed to Mr. Ellis that the entire property left by her father should be devoted to the establishment of a free library in the city of Charleston, from which place his ancestors had come, and that this should be not only an institution at which books should be collected and read, but that there should also be a department of art open to all that should resort to it for purposes of instruction or amusement. Mr. Ellis had warmly commended her idea as being one that led to a happy solution of the difficulty into which the estate had plunged his two friends, and engaged that, during his stay in New York, he would obtain such information in regard to the details of the organization of such an establishment as might be necessary to Louise's further enlightenment. After his departure she had men-

tioned the subject to the doctor, and he also had given the
project his warmest approval. He had, it is true, and as he
told Louise, got over his repugnance to her wealth, and he
had likewise in a measure become reconciled to that which
she would acquire in consequence of the upsetting of her
father's will ; but this proposition of hers made him feel
much more comfortable than he had felt before, not only
because the money was disposed of, but because it showed
that she appreciated his position, and was prepared to do
all in her power to make it more tolerable.

She had asked him whether it would not be possible for
him to withdraw his objections to the probate of the will,
and for him to make the disposition of the estate that she
had suggested ; but it required no long argument from him
to convince her that this was impossible. In order to save
the reputation of her father, it had been necessary to show
that he had acted under the influence of a delusion, and
that he was of unsound mind. The confession that he had
sent to Judge Conway was true, it was a deliberate falsehood, or it was the offspring of an insane mind. They
knew it was not true, or a willful falsehood, but that it was
based upon delusions produced by a disordered mind. It
would not do, reasoned the doctor, for them now to go before the surrogate with a different story from that which
they had told to Judge Conway. Consistency was necessary, and consistency was truth.

Louise had at once perceived the force of his reasoning,
and had acquiesced.

The middle of January came. The wedding had been
fixed for a day early in the following March. It was to be
very quiet. The doctor and his bride would spend a week
in New York, and then would return to Plato and probably
live in Hurricane Castle, though this point was not positively settled.

Mr. Ellis had returned from his journey. He had been

busy for several days making out statements and schedules, and was evidently getting ready his report for submission to Louise.

The will-question had come up before the surrogate ; and, with the evidence before him, there was nothing for that official to do but to declare that the paper submitted was not the last will and testament of John Lamar. There was no other will ; so that Louise, as sole heir-at-law, succeeded to her father's estate.

Hicks had been tried and convicted of burglary in the first degree, and had been sentenced to ten years' confinement at hard labor in the Clinton prison. He had made no disclosures relative to the driving of the sail-maker's needle into Mr. Lamar's ear, nor were any questions asked him on the subject, though it was strongly suspected by the doctor and others that he had made the attempt at murder in order to rob and to get possession of the statement he had signed, and that Spill, though he never said so, knew more of the matter than he cared to reveal. The statement never was found. That both the men had signed such a paper Mr. Bishop was positive, though Spill strenuously denied the fact.

Frazier had gone on improving every day, and at last the doctor had settled upon a time for his making an effort to stand on his legs and to take a few steps around the room. The extension-apparatus was to be taken off ; but, as measures of precaution, he was to use crutches for several days, and then a cane, or two if necessary, and light splints bound to the thigh with plaster-of-Paris bandages were to be worn for several days to come.

Cynthia had visited him almost daily—sometimes with Louise and sometimes with Mrs. Ruggles present, and occasionally alone. Frazier had religiously stuck to his promise, and not a word had been said that the most scrupulous duenna could have interpreted into an expression of love or even of admiration. Indeed, he had said nothing at all indicative of the state of his feelings except such words as "I'm so glad you've come!" or "Don't go just yet!" or "I've been waiting this hour or more for you!" or "Now I shall not know what to do with myself till you come again to-morrow!" and such like, accompanied by facial expressions so exactly corresponding in their import to the language used, that Cynthia would have been a fool had she not been able to discover that Frazier was madly in love with her.

So, when the 20th of January came, the doctor went up to Frazier's, accompanied by a young man named Bliven, who had taken Will Hadden's place as nurse, though he made no attempt, nor was it intended that he should, to fill that of a companion.

"Now," said the physician, as he entered the chamber in which Frazier had lain awake from an early hour in the morning anxiously expecting him—"now we'll free you from these bonds," saying which he proceeded with Bliven's assistance to remove the weights from the cords that passed over the pulleys on the foot-board of the bedstead, and then to take off the rest of the apparatus.

"It isn't shrunk as much as is usual in such cases," he said, as he proceeded to examine with his skillful fingers the seat of the fracture; "and it's as hard as a rock," he continued, a smile of pleasure overshadowing his face. "Now, wait till I measure it." Taking a tape-measure from his pocket, he carefully ascertained the exact length of the limb and then that of the opposite member. Then he went over the process again, Frazier watching the proceedings with a great degree of anxiety depicted on his features.

"There's a difference of exactly the sixteenth of an inch," he said, rising to his feet. "Not so much as the thickness of the cover of that book you have in your hand. It will be absolutely inappreciable."

Tears started into Frazier's eyes. He held out his hand to the doctor, but for a moment was unable to speak. "You have done your duty to me, and you have done it skillfully," he said, at last. "I can never repay you for your kindness and care, and the knowledge you have brought to bear, but let me at least make an attempt to discharge my pecuniary obligation." With these words he took from under the pillow a piece of paper and handed it to the doctor.

"What's this?" exclaimed the physician, without waiting to open and read it, but at the same time fumbling with it. Then, having succeeded in becoming acquainted with its purport, he held it out toward Frazier.

"I can't take this," he said, while his eyes moistened, and his voice trembled a little. "I acknowledge the right of every patient to show his gratitude to his physician to the utmost extent of his pecuniary ability, but our relations are somewhat peculiar, and they don't admit of this kind of a manifestation."

"Then," exclaimed Frazier, with a mortified expression of face, and a tone in which there were both sorrow and indignation, "because I am in love with your daughter, and hope to make her my wife, I am to be debarred from showing my regard and thankfulness to her father?"

"That's about it, I think."

"It's very hard. You have no right to impose such an obligation upon me, and then to wrap yourself in your cloak of pride and say you will accept nothing from me."

"You will discharge all legal and social obligation to me when you pay me my fees. I am a high-priced doctor for this part of the country. I shall send you a memorandum of your indebtedness this afternoon, and you will find that you owe me five hundred dollars. That is a large amount according to the standard here, for there isn't a medical man north of New York that would have charged you half that sum. But when you hand me a check for five thousand dollars, you would, were I to accept it, place me under an obligation to you that I can not, with my sense of what is proper, consent to incur. My friend, you must take this back."

"You are a very sensitive man, more so than any other I ever met."

"Perhaps I am, but I think a little reflection on your part will convince you that I am right. I am free to say that were you not, as you told me yesterday, on the point of proposing yourself as a husband to my daughter, I would take your check with pleasure, and look upon the act as an honorable one to both of us."

"Then, should Cynthia reject me, you will take my offering?"

"Yes," rejoined the doctor, laughing; "if she refuses you, I will console you by taking your money, and thus putting you under additional obligations to the family. But, seriously, my dear fellow, I appreciate your feelings toward me just as deeply as though I put your check into my pocket. Now, get up, and let me see how you can support yourself on your underpinning."

"I suppose I shall have to submit," said Frazier, ruefully, "but you are certainly the most extraordinary man about money I ever saw. There," he continued, as with Bliven's assistance he threw his legs out of the bed and stood erect upon his feet, "how does that do? It feels splendid to be once more on my legs, weak and numb as they are."

"You're as straight as a die," said the doctor, surveying him with admiring eyes. "Now, take these crutches," handing them to him as he spoke, "and step out very carefully. You see your knees are stiff yet, as are all your joints, but they'll soon limber up. That's it!" as Frazier took two or three steps. "Now, keep on around the room

two or three times, and then get Bliven to bend your knees
and ankles, and rub your legs well. You may walk again
in an hour or two, and in the mean time you can dress yourself and come down-stairs to the parlor. Doubtless Cynthia
will be along in an hour or so. She knows this is your
trial-day, and she's anxious to congratulate you."

Cynthia came soon afterward, and congratulated him to
his heart's content. He was able to stand erect, and even
to lean in a careless manner against the mantel-piece. He
even went so far as to punch the fire, only supporting himself with a cane. He was certainly a handsome fellow, tall,
well made, and doubtless of robust frame when in good
health. Now he was a little pale, but his brown hair set
off his broad forehead to advantage, and his hazel eyes had
lost none of their luster or expression. Yes, he was handsome, and so thought Cynthia as she looked at him admiringly while he essayed various little movements of agility
or strength in the effort to test the solidity of his broken
leg.

"So your visits to me are over?" he said, a little regret-
fully.

"Yes, this is the last time I shall come to see you here.
You are now able to return all my visits, day for day; but
to do so you will be obliged to remain in Plato more than
a month."

"The first time I go out I shall call to see you and your
father, to thank you for all your kindness to me. I can
never forget either of you—never!"

"I am glad if I have in any way been able to lighten
the weariness of your life since your accident; and I know
papa is over-rejoiced at the excellent cure he has made of
you."

"Your father is the most remarkable man I have ever
encountered—one of the noblest and the best."

"I am glad to hear you say that," she said, in a low

tone, but with great feeling; "he is almost divine sometimes."

"Yes, he is almost divine when extraordinary events
occur. He appears then to rise far above the plane of humanity. He is magnificent, phenomenal."

For a few moments there was silence, both being apparently busy with thoughts that they were not ready to
express. At last he spoke :

"Shall you be at home this evening ?"

"Yes ; but it is too soon yet for you to venture
out."

"But I *shall* venture out, and, unless you positively
forbid me, I shall call at your house."

"Both papa and I will be glad to see you ; but I am
sure you are going out too soon."

"I'll risk it. I must see you this night in your own
house."

"Then, as I am to see you again so soon, I'll proceed
on my visit to Mrs. Hadden. Good-by."

She was gone ; and Frazier, feeling a little fatigued
with his exertion, and wishing to save himself for the evening, lay down on a sofa. At last his long silence was to be
broken. At last he could, without violating his promise,
speak to Cynthia of the love that for the last month and
more he had tried honestly to keep from her knowledge.
The struggle with himself had been a severe one, and at
times he had felt that it was more than human nature could
endure without yielding to the power of the emotion that
took precedence of every other mental faculty. Occasionally he had thought that it would have been better if Cynthia's visits were stopped—stopped, at least, unless the doctor would release him from his promise. But, just as he
had about reached this conclusion, the desire to see her
again had become overpowering ; and thus matters had gone
on, every day seeing him more and more unable to extri-

cate himself from the net in which he was entangled, even
had he desired to do so.

It was dark when the sleigh that he had ordered was
driven around to the door of the "Bear." Assisted by Bliven,
he had managed to get in without much trouble, and then
the attendant, seating himself by the side of the driver, the
order was given, and they were whirling along the street
toward the doctor's residence.

It was not without some misgiving that Frazier entered
the drawing-room, to wait while the servant announced his
arrival to Cynthia. He had inquired for both her and her
father, but was informed that, while Miss Grattan was at
home, the doctor had been called out to a patient living
some three miles from Plato, and would not be back till
about eight o'clock. He looked at his watch, and found
that he had an hour and a half for the conversation he proposed to have with Cynthia. Little enough, but yet sufficient for the principal matters he had to submit to her.
He had thought many times of this moment. He had
looked forward to it with alternate hope and fear, for he
could never, for any considerable length of time, determine
whether Cynthia loved him or not. She had always been
kind, sometimes even affectionate; but her kindness and
affection came so naturally, and with such complete freedom from embarrassment, that he had almost brought himself to the point of believing that they proceeded from pity
and friendship, such, perhaps, as a girl with her sweetness
and gentleness might feel for a brother injured as he had
been. But his hour had come, and when he was requested
by old Milly to follow her to the doctor's study, for that
Miss Cynthia would see him there, he trembled a little, as
even the bravest men will tremble, not with fear exactly,
but with anxiety and uncertainty.

"I thought you would be more comfortable here, Mr.
Frazier," said Cynthia, as she came forward to meet him

with outstretched hands, and a glad smile of welcome on her face. "Papa has a splendid chair here, in which you can sit with great ease. He will be here by eight o'clock, and he asked me to request you not to go till he returned. I need not say how glad I am to see you."

"You see I am as good as my word," he said as he took her hand, and held it in his while he spoke. "No, I can not sit down, or do anything, till I have unburdened my heart of the load it has carried all these days since I have known you. Cynthia, you have been the one sole joy of my life. You are the angel whose ministrations have been sweeter to me than would have been the kindly offices of all the members of the hosts of heaven. And now I come to tell you that I love you. I promised your father that I would say nothing of this till I could say it in your own house. I have tried to keep faith with him, both directly and indirectly, but at times I have thought that you must know what was in my heart, for when you were with me the whole world seemed full of the love I felt."

He ceased speaking, and her hand still remained clasped in his. Indeed, she had made no effort to withdraw it, but she did not answer him in words. She seemed to be critically examining his scarf-pin, if one could judge of her thoughts by the direction of her eyes.

"Cynthia."

Still no answer.

Then he drew her toward him with the hand that still held hers, and, placing his other hand on her head, by a little dexterous turn, that was entirely unresisted, brought the right side of her face in contact with his broad chest at a point a little below and to the left of the before-mentioned scarf-pin.

"Now I know that you love me."

"Oh, yes, I love you!"

Very softly were the words spoken, for her lips must

have been partly in contact with the scarf, the pin of which she had so steadfastly regarded, and hence her voice was somewhat muffled.

"With all your heart?"

"Yes."

"Then look up at me; let me see it in your eyes."

She turned her face toward him, and he looked at her as though he were trying to gaze into the very depths of her soul.

"Yes," he said at last, "you do with all your heart. My darling!"

Then he bent his head and kissed her lips and eyes many times, and would doubtless have continued so doing had she not quietly released herself from his embrace.

"Come," she said, "you must sit down now, for you are not yet strong. And just see how you've rumpled my hair! And I arranged it with extra care this evening, expressly for you!"

"Let me fix it for you."

She came closer to him, and he smoothed with his hands the little curls on her forehead that had become slightly disarranged by the performances of the last few minutes. Then he sat down, and she drew her arm-chair up close to him—so close that he could keep one arm around her waist, and she could stroke his hair with one of her little hands.

"You belong to me now," he said, with the sense of possession.

"Yes, I am yours now."

"When will you marry me?"

"Oh, that I don't know exactly—some time next summer, I suppose."

"Next summer! I've got to go to Pittsburg next week, and I'm not going without you."

She laughed merrily. "Do you think a girl can get

ready to be married in a week?" she said, while she pulled his beard and played with the thick growth of hair on his temples.

"Yes, of course I do. I never could understand what all this getting ready to be married means."

"Well, my dear George"—it was the first time she had ever addressed him by his Christian name, but the words came out as glibly as though she had been saying them all her life—"you will now have an opportunity of acquiring an experience that has hitherto been a sealed book to you. Then you will feel that you did not come to Plato in vain."

"I'll appeal to your father."

"In what cause?"

They started, for it was the doctor's voice.

"I am back sooner than I expected," he said. "I coughed as I came into the room, but you did not appear to hear me. Well, what matter does it make? You are happy, both of you; that I can see.—Come here, my darling," to Cynthia. "You are happy, are you not?" as he drew her to his breast.

"Yes, papa, very happy."

"Thank God for that, dear!—And you, Frazier! Give me your hand. You are an honorable fellow, and I feel that, in giving you my daughter, I am sure of securing her happiness and mine. I have never seen the man, before I saw and knew you, that I would have been willing should have her as his wife. She is a good girl."

"O papa, dear!" interrupted Cynthia, throwing her arms around his neck.

"Yes," he continued, as he caressed the head that lay on his breast, "she's a good girl in the best and truest sense of the word. I've never known her to do a mean or a dishonorable act," raising his head and looking around the room, as though addressing an assemblage of people, "and that's a good deal for a father to be able to say of any child.

A good daughter makes a good wife. Take her," he went on, gently forcing her toward Frazier, who stood close to them, and who opened his arms to receive the charge transferred to him. "She's worthy of you, and I believe you are worthy of her. I'll come back in a few minutes," going toward the door as he spoke, "and you'll let me stay with you awhile to night, for I've many things to talk over with you both.—You don't smoke ?" to Frazier. "Well, I suppose your city of Pittsburg has smoked enough for you. I'll light my pipe when I return, if you've no objections. I'm always in a better humor when I have a pipe than when I haven't, but it will not be needed to-night, for I'm almost as happy over this matter as you are, and then, you know, I have my own— Well, I'll be back in half an hour or so."

# CHAPTER XXVI.

## " YES, I WILL DO IT ! "

ALTHOUGH Mr. Ellis had returned, Louise had not seen him. He had sent her word that he was preparing his report, and that as soon as it was completed he would call and submit it to her. Doctor Grattan had spent parts of several evenings with him, and he had smoked a half-dozen pipes in the pentagonal room ; but, though he descanted freely of his adventures during his absence from Plato, and told numerous funny stories, or stories that were meant to be funny, he never alluded directly to the main object that had caused him to travel through the West and South, or to the results that had been obtained by his journeyings.

Louise had perfected her scheme for getting rid of the money that was now (by the refusal of the surrogate to admit her father's will to probate) hers. The doctor was apparently not altogether satisfied with the turn affairs had taken. He was never tired of commending her for the generosity and magnanimity of her conduct. It was the best evidence he could have, he said, that her love was built on firm foundations, and yet the fact that she was making this great sacrifice for him made him uncomfortable. He bade her to understand that he had not exacted it. He told her, as he had told her before, that, when a woman expresses a willingness to make a sacrifice for a man, she has shown her devotion, and that only a brute would exact its fulfillment. The weight of obligation was even greater than it would have been had she kept the money, but he was at any rate relieved from the load that would have pressed upon his soul had he been obliged to share in the wealth she had derived from her father's estate. He said very little on the subject, and Louise could only infer the nature of his thoughts from an occasional word that he let fall inadvertently or from some not very specific allusion made to the subject and which indicated to her what was passing in his mind. But there had been nothing to cause her any great degree of unconcern, except that uneasiness that came from the suspicion that he was not entirely happy. She had, as he said, made the best possible disposition of the estate. He told her this a dozen times a day, and this fact showed her that the subject was almost constantly in his mind. To her he was ever loving and tender. Cynthia had returned home, but he never passed a day without spending a portion of it at Hurricane Castle. The weather was too cold for long walks, but they often went sleighing together, and one afternoon they had taken an early start and had gone over the road that had been the seat of their misadventures and of the beginning of their happiness, even to the place on Wood Mountain, at which they had passed the night, and at which the secret of their two lives had been told.

All Plato had professed to be very much astonished at the knowledge that the doctor was going to marry again. Even Mrs. Hadden thought it a wonderful occurrence, and was not quite sure, as she ventured to tell him, that it was, all things considered, a wise undertaking. She was very certain that it would interfere with his usefulness to the community; and the doctor had replied that he didn't care a sixpence whether it did or did not, that the Platonians cared nothing for him beyond the consideration of what they could get out of him, that they had had nearly twen-

ty-five years of his life to suit themselves, and that the rest
of it, please God ! he meant to pass to suit himself.

Then Mrs. Hadden had asked him whether or not he
thought he had made the best possible choice of a wife.
"Not," she added, "that there is anything about Miss Lamar to which the most scrupulous could object. She is
very beautiful and good and accomplished, and what would
be considered in most men's eyes a superlative qualification,
rich."

The doctor had winced a little at the mention of this
last advantage, but he had said nothing ; and Mrs. Hadden,
after watching the effect of her blow, and perceiving that it
had wounded him slightly, went on : "But she is too
young, my friend, for you. When she is forty, in her
prime "—Mrs. Hadden was just forty—" you will be sixty,
and a man at sixty is generally considered old. Now, to
my mind, husband and wife should grow old together."

"I don't agree with you," rejoined the doctor with
some degree of fervor. " I shall feel no older at sixty than
I do now, unless by some cataclysm it should be my fate to
be thrown into association with a nagging woman. Louise
Lamar is one of those women whose influence over their
husbands is to keep them young. No, I am not too old
for her. There is but one argument you can use, and that
is one that I have employed against myself a thousand
times. I am unworthy of her. Tell me that, and I will
admit it at once ; but, as she thinks differently, I am going
to marry her all the same."

Mrs. Hadden had not been without hope that at some
time or other the doctor would ask her to be Mrs. Grattan.
It had appeared to her that she was just the woman most
calculated to make him happy, and to be of assistance to
him in the furtherance of his professional labors. She was
a very good sort of a woman in her way, but she was altogether on a lower plane than that on which the doctor

moved, and he would just as soon have thought of going to Timbuctoo for a wife as to have taken her or any other woman in Plato to his bosom. It is at all times difficult for a woman to act otherwise than as she feels ; hence her remarks antagonistic to the marriage of her friend were to be viewed with many grains of allowance. She saw that her chances were gone forever ; but she nevertheless did not any the more become reconciled to her loss. That he should have given his heart to a comparative stranger to him and his ways, a woman too young, she thought, to enter into his ideas or even to be a suitable companion for him, while she, who had known him half her lifetime, and had looked for him as a probable husband almost throughout the whole period of her widowhood, should be doomed to continued isolation, was not only mortifying to her, but it almost passed the limits of her comprehension. But at heart she was a good woman. There was no element of malice in her composition ; she was really friendly both to the doctor and to Louise, and she had no doubt that by a strong effort, such as she honestly intended to make, she would succeed in overcoming the very natural chagrin that she experienced when the doctor told her of his matrimonial intentions.

It was the evening after that on which George Frazier and Cynthia Grattan had concluded that their happiness consisted in their passing through life together as husband and wife. Louise had just finished her dinner, which she had eaten alone. The doctor had been obliged to go to Elizabethtown to see a patient, and Cynthia had remained at home to entertain George Frazier, who was expected to tea. Louise had made no change in her establishment since the death of her father. She had never in all her life known what it was to want money. It had always been at hand for any purpose for which she required it, and her father had at his death a balance of nearly ten thousand dollars in the Essex County National Bank at Elizabeth-town, and she had even more than that to her credit in the same institution. There had been no need, therefore, to practice economy for the want of ready money. As to her fortune, her father had always looked after that for her, and the management of it was now in Mr. Ellis's hands.

The surrogate, in denying probate to the paper sub-mitted as the last will and testament of John Lamar, had appointed Louise administratrix of the estate. This was eminently right, for the whole property reverted to her as the sole heir-at-law. Mr. Ellis was getting ready to trans-fer the nominal control to her, though she had requested that he would still as her agent retain the practical man-agement till the arrangements for the establishment of the library and art institute in Charleston could be perfected. Already measures had been taken to obtain from the State of South Carolina an act of incorporation for "The Grat-tan and Lamar Institute," that being the name that she had finally resolved upon, though the doctor had begged that, as the idea in its conception and execution was all her own, and as all the money came from her, his name might be omitted ; but to this she would not listen.

"Don't deny me the pleasure, Arthur," she said, "of having my name go down to posterity with yours. Besides, if you had allowed matters to go their way, the money would have been yours, to do with as you pleased. It is only through your disinterested and honorable course that the institute is a possibility."

So he had yielded, to please her, and had even consented to act as one of the incorporators and trustees. Indeed, he had already begun to feel that there was an outlet here for all his surplus energy, and that the institute would be a source of great pleasure to him and his wife. Nevertheless, he was sensible that she had made a sacrifice to please him, and, while he honored and loved her for her self-denial and affection, he writhed a little under the load saddled upon him—a load, too, that he knew he had himself, by his refusal to accept the estate devised to him, and his repugnance to receive it indirectly through Louise, been the chief agent in imposing.

It was in vain that he told himself, and as Louise's conduct also told him, that she did not consider that she had sacrificed anything. The fact existed, and it could not be ignored. She had alienated all her father's estate, without stopping to ascertain its amount, and she had done this as the only means in her power of relieving him from his own reproaches or those of others of having obtained the estate, notwithstanding his open renunciation of all claim to a single penny of it. And yet he knew in his heart that, but for his feeling on the subject, the idea of " The Grattan and Lamar Institute " would never have entered into her mind.

She had finished dining, and was sitting in the library alone. She was thinking of the new life upon which, as Arthur Grattan's wife, she was soon to enter. The contemplation was a common one with her, and it was one that gave her almost unalloyed pleasure. That he loved her for herself she knew very well. His whole course in relation to her own and her father's wealth showed this to her in a way clearer to her mind than could any other line of conduct that he might have adopted. It was she he wanted, not her wealth. Nothing that could have happened to her in the whole range of earthly occurrences could have given her more pleasure than the consciousness of this fact. If he could only be made to understand that in giving up this wealth she was doing nothing that she regarded as a sacrifice, nothing for which he could justly now or hereafter reproach himself for having exacted of her, then her happiness would be complete.

She was quite sure that at times he believed this as firmly as she did herself, but she could not fail to perceive that his reflections continually brought him back to the same point from which he had started. Ah, well! when she became his wife, and lived with him day and night, her influence would be more constant. It would be strange indeed, she thought, if she could not banish every shadow of regret from his mind.

She was deep in meditations such as these when a servant entered the room, bearing a large tin box, and announced Mr. Ellis. Before the words were fairly out of his mouth, that gentleman walked into the apartment.

"I would have sent you notice of my intended visit, Miss Lamar," he said, after Louise had welcomed him, and he had taken a chair in front of the table on which the box had been placed, "but the fact is, I did not know till a few minutes ago that I should be able to come. I finished late this afternoon the task of going over your late father's papers and making a synopsis of their contents. I have here a complete report on the condition of the estate left by him as well as one on your own property. I have also prepared abstracts of both, so that you will have no difficulty at any time in getting at the exact truth in regard to any item."

"I am very much obliged to you," she answered; "I know how great has been your labor, and with what persistency you have devoted yourself to it. I will not trouble you now to read the report. It is doubtless so clear that I shall have no difficulty in mastering its contents. If you will kindly inform me of the valuation of the estate left by my poor father, I shall be obliged to you. Doctor Grattan and I were talking this morning about the purchase of a collection of paintings to be sold next month by the Prince von Schlaffenstein, and which will probably bring a million dollars. But we came to the conclusion that unless the estate amounted in value to at least five million, it would not be safe to pay that sum. The collection is a noted one, and it would be a splendid nucleus for the art-gallery of 'The

Grattan and Lamar Institute.' The first object, however, is a library. We can only at present take our surplus funds for pictures."

Mr. Ellis looked embarrassed. He coughed a little, and then fumbled a little with the mass of papers he had taken from the box, and then got up, and, without there being the least necessity therefor, poked the fire. Then, after taking a few strides across the floor, he sat down again, apparently having by these means restored his mind to a state of equanimity.

"Miss Lamar," he said, "the details of the general statement I am about to make are here on the table. You can go over them at your leisure; but, to cut a long story short with very few words, I have to tell you that, beyond the money in the bank at Elizabethtown, and this property in Plato, there is absolutely nothing left of your father's estate."

"Nothing left of my father's estate!" exclaimed Louise.

"Nothing! Perhaps 'absolutely' is a little too strong a word to use, as eventually one or two of the concerns in which your father invested his money may pay something, but the rest is gone. Not a single one of the other securities will ever be resuscitated, and many of them are fraudulent, and were so at the time your father bought them. He seems to have been the easy dupe of every sharper with whom he came in contact, and to have had most extravagant ideas of his wealth, and recklessness in investing it."

"But," said Louise, without evincing any more mental disturbance than would have resulted from the discomposure of any other of her plans, "he often told me of the large dividends he was receiving from the stocks and other securities he had purchased."

"Yes; but either these assertions were based on delusions, or the scoundrels deceived him, by paying him money as profits which they knew he would reinvest with them.
18

If we had only known this in time, the contest in regard to
the will might have been avoided."

"No, I think not. That was necessary for other objects."

"Your father, about two years ago," continued Mr.
Ellis, "began to sell the real estate and good stocks and
bonds that he possessed, and to invest the money received
therefrom in the most absurd schemes. Many of them I
find were of his own devising, and he associated with him
certain persons whose whole lives had been passed in the
perpetration of frauds. Into these schemes they did not
put a single dollar, but they boldly took his money and
divided it among themselves. Some of these affairs were
of so preposterous a character that it seems almost incomprehensible how an educated man like your father should
have been led into them. One, for instance, was 'The
Lake Mahopac Improvement Company,' the object of
which was, as stated in the prospectus—a copy of which
is among these papers—to convey sea-water from Long Isl-
and Sound through pipes to the lake, and thus to convert
it into a salt-water lake upon which large hotels, bath-
houses, etc., were to be built. Mountain scenery and air
would be conjoined with sea-bathing, and people would
flock to the place winter and summer in pursuit of health
and pleasure. The capital stock of this swindling company
was stated to be ten million dollars, of which the only
amount ever paid in was the five hundred thousand they
got from your father. There were others fully as ridiculous as this—"

"And all is gone?"

"All, except, as I said before, the money in the Essex
County National Bank, at Elizabethtown, and Hurricane
Castle with its contents and the land on which it stands.
Your father reserved the sum of two hundred and fifty
thousand dollars, bought this tract of land and built the

house. When he got through, there were left some ten or fifteen thousand dollars, which sum is secure. I suppose the pictures, books, and other things in the house are worth fifty thousand dollars. These with this property go to you in any event."

"No, they do not go to me. The will by which I was to inherit them was set aside, so that they only descend to me as the heir-at-law. I suppose they will be required to pay the debts."

"Fortunately, there are no debts, and I think that in two or three years' time the mining interests in Mexico will prove of value. Some persons that I have consulted professed to believe that they would eventually be worth more than the whole estate ever was; but this is, I think, doubtful. It is very certain that now they would not sell for five hundred dollars, and that all the rest of the securities taken together are not worth the paper that describes them."

"Then," said Louise, "I shall have to establish 'The Grattan and Lamar Institute' out of my private fortune."

Mr. Ellis moved uneasily on his chair, but he had taken the first step in telling disagreeable news, and the rest was easier. Louise noticed his manner, and was in a measure prepared for what he had further to announce.

"What I have next to tell you, my dear Miss Lamar," he said, "is very bad. You have no fortune beyond the money to your credit in the bank and this property of Hurricane Castle. All that you got from your mother is gone, gone with your father's. He, animated doubtless by the best motives, and acting, as he thought, for your benefit, as he had a right to do, invested your money in the same concerns in which he placed his own. It is all gone, every cent of it."

For a moment Louise felt a little sinking sensation at

the heart, and a slight feeling of dizziness came over her,
but it was only momentary.  She closed her eyes, as though
for the purpose of shutting out all extraneous images, and
for perhaps a minute remained without saying a word.  Mr.
Ellis watched her attentively.  He knew that the shock of
such information as that which he had communicated to
her would be severe to most people.  But he saw that she
was bearing it heroically, and that she was not going to be
overcome in any alarming manner.

"Then I am afraid," she said, without a tremor of her
voice, "that we shall have to count 'The Grattan and Lamar Institute' among those things that die ere they are
fairly begun.  I am sorry the money is all gone.  It would
be absurd for me to say that I feel no regret ; but the loss
is not going to break my heart.  There are worse things
than that which might have happened, and this will have
its compensations.  Yes," she added, thoughtfully, after a
moment's hesitation, "full compensations."

"You bear your misfortunes nobly, Miss Lamar," said
Mr. Ellis, looking at her with admiration depicted on his
countenance.

"Why should I repine over what is lost beyond my
control ?  What I have to do is first to thank you for the
labor you have given to the matter, and for the kindness
with which you have discharged an unpleasant duty."  She
held out her hand to him.  "This I do most heartily," she
continued.  "In the next place, I shall have to reduce my
scale of expenditures, so as to bring them within my present means.  This may be a little disagreeable at first, but
doubtless I shall be able to do it without much inconvenience, certainly without suffering."

They conversed a little longer about some of the details
of the losses that had occurred, and in regard to arrangements that the altered condition of affairs required should
be made, and then Mr. Ellis took his leave, stating, in an-

swer to her question, that he thought he could easily find a purchaser for Hurricane Castle.

After he had gone, Louise sat for several minutes reflecting upon the situation. Then a smile passed over her face, and she arose, and, going to the door, looked out in the direction of Mountain View. It was about eight o'clock ; the moon and the stars were shining brightly, lighting up the snow-clad summits of all the mountain-peaks, and casting their giant shadows into the valley below. The air was cold and sharp, but dry and crisp. There was a light in the drawing-room of the doctor's house. Cynthia and George Frazier were there, happy in each other's society. At the other end all was dark. But, even as she looked, a light flashed from the window that she now knew by long experience opened from the doctor's pentagonal room. He had just returned, doubtless, and was sitting down to work on his novel, the last chapter of which, he had told her that afternoon, he expected to finish to-night. She watched the light, calling to mind as she did so how, a few weeks ago, she had wondered whether or not it came from his room. Then she was just beginning to feel the first gentle promptings of a love that now filled her whole being. Then she liked him—now he was all the world to her. The day for her wedding was fast approaching, and then she would be all his, and he all hers. Two weddings, for it had been settled that George and Cynthia should be married at the same time.

Thoughts like these flitted through her brain as she stood on the porch in the cold, crisp night-air, looking at the light that flashed from his window.

" Yes," she said at last, " I will do it ! Why should he have one minute's discomfort when I can prevent it ? "

She re-entered the house, and, leaving the light burning, reappeared at the door, having in the mean time put on a long seal-skin jacket, and thrown something soft and

fleecy, but evidently warm, over her head. There was the
barest suspicion of a smile on her face as she thought of
what she was about to do. She remembered how, upon
the other occasion, she had contemplated going to him,
but then on a far different errand from that which actuated
her now. She looked at the light a moment, and then,
closing the door behind her, put her little foot upon the
hard, frozen snow, and began the descent of the hill by the
path that led to the road. It was a full mile to the doctor's house ; but she walked fast, and it did not take her
many minutes to reach the base of the slight elevation upon
which Mountain View was built. She stopped a moment
before ascending the hill, as though to determine the exact
course she should pursue. Then she resumed her quick,
light step, and in less time almost than it takes to write
these words, she stood in front of the big window that filled
nearly the whole of one end of the pentagonal room, and
was looking in through the small, diamond-shaped panes
of which the window was composed. Yes, he was there,
sitting at one end of the long table, not ten feet from where
she stood. He was not writing, though his manuscript was
before him. He had apparently just thrown down his pen,
and had taken into his hand a photograph that stood on a
little easel on the table, so that he could always see it
when he wanted to do so. He was holding the photograph
under the lamp, so that the full light fell upon it.

" It is mine," she said to herself softly, while a bright
smile of pleasure passed over her face. " He is thinking
of me."

She got down from the hummock of snow upon which
she had stood while looking into the window, and went
toward the door. She knew it was not locked, and that
dead-latches were a thing unknown in Plato. She therefore had no trouble in getting in without disturbing the
rest of the house. She was well acquainted with the way

to the pentagonal room, and she reached the door without
meeting any of the inmates. The drawing-room door was
half open, and, as she passed by, she gave a glance inside.
Cynthia and George Frazier were there. He was reading
to her from a book of poetry, and with an accent and tone
that told his listener that the words expressed his own feelings as well as they did those of the love-sick swain by
whom they were supposed to have been spoken.

She opened the outside door of the room, and then very
gently the inside one—for the reader will kindly call to
mind the fact that there were two doors—and stood in his
presence. He had replaced the photograph, and was sitting
with his elbows resting on the table and his face buried in
his hands. Very quietly she crossed the intervening space,
and then she stood by his side without his having heard her
approach. She had intended to reveal herself by kissing
him, but there was nothing of his face left to kiss, for it
was all concealed by his hands. She therefore laid one
hand—the one from which she had removed the glove—on
his head.

"You little witch!" he said, thinking doubtless that
it was Cynthia, who often played her pranks with him in
this way, "how cold your hand is!"

"Yes, dear," she murmured so very softly that the
words barely reached his ears, "but my heart is warm."

He started to his feet.

"Louise!" he exclaimed, and in an instant she was
folded in his arms.

"Yes, dear," she said, while her tears began to flow as
she sobbed upon his breast with the joy that came from the
consciousness that now the one little shadow was gone from
their life-path—"it is I. I could not help coming to tell
—to tell you—that I am at last poor Louise Lamar, who
comes to you with nothing save her love, but in that richer
if possible than ever before."

"What do you mean, my darling? I do not understand you. You are nervous. Something has disturbed you. Kiss me, dear, and then sit here and tell me all about it."

"It is soon told, Arthur," she said, after she had kissed him not only once but several times, though she still continued to stand with his arms supporting her. "The money is all gone, papa's and mine. I am almost as poor as a church-mouse. Poor papa lost it all, Mr. Ellis has just been telling me; and he says there is nothing left but Hurricane Castle, and 'The Grattan and Lamar Institute' is already a thing of the past."

He smiled as he drew her closer to him. "I told you I would make all the sacrifices," he said, as he stroked her hair with his hand, "but I could not at once sacrifice my prejudices. I fought them hard, dear, and in time with your aid I should have conquered them. Now, however, I am saved the trouble of making any further effort. Come, sit here, while I read you the last paragraph of the last chapter of my novel. See how beautifully I have brought the hero and heroine out of all their troubles!"

He read a few lines from the manuscript on the table.

"Nothing could be more touching," she said; "and you have expressed yourself so eloquently that it brings tears into my eyes. After we are married, you shall read me the whole story before you send it to the publisher. You have such a correct idea of women that I am sure every woman in the land will want to read your book, and see the man that wrote it. I shall be prouder of you than ever then. Have you selected a name for it?"

"Yes, I am going to call it 'The Doctor's Novel.'"

"Have you put Cynthia and me in it?"

"Ah! That you will find out when I read it to you. Cynthia is very happy now. She's in the drawing-room with her young man."

"Yes, I saw them as I passed the door. He was reading poetry to her. It was delicious to watch her face as he read from Bailey's ' Festus' the lines beginning—

" ' Ask not of me, love, what is love.'

But do you know you'll have to take me home ? I left the lights burning, and the servants will think I have run away. Are you glad I came ? I knew you would be glad to hear that all the money is gone, and so I committed the indiscretion of paying you a secret visit. Yes, I see you are glad," she went on after a little pause, during which her questions were answered, but not in words—" glad to see me, and glad that the money is gone. But are you not sorry for one thing, dear ? ' The Grattan and Lamar Institute ' will never be established."

" Yes, it will. I am a Grattan and you are a Lamar. We'll have our own institute here in Plato, and we'll be the members, you and I."

And his words came true. The Grattan and Lamar institute was established in due season, and from time to time additional members were added to it, till in the course of years it numbered many, all worthy of its founders.

.

THE END.

# WORKS OF FICTION.

**THE MONEY-MAKERS:** A Social Parable. A Novel. One volume, 16mo. Cloth, $1.00

"The Money-Makers" is a remarkable picture of American social and political life, designed largely as an answer to the much-discussed "Bread-Winners." It is written in an uncommonly vigorous style; there is a good deal of stirring movement; it satirizes many of the vices of the day; and presents a number of portraits the fidelity of which to certain outcomes of our social life will be generally recognized. "The Money-Makers" is from the hands of an experienced writer, whose *incognito* will be strictly preserved.

**ROSLYN'S FORTUNE.** A Novel. By CHRISTIAN REID. 12mo. Cloth, $1.25.

Christian Reid has been almost by common consent accorded the first place among the female novelists of the Southern States. "Her novels," says "Good Literature," "may, we think, be classified among the restful sort. Free entirely from the suspicion of sensationalism, they are also free from the opposite danger, dullness."

**DELDEE; or, The Iron Hand.** A Novel. By the author of "The House on the Marsh" and "At the World's Mercy." 12mo. Paper cover, 25 cents.

"The House on the Marsh" has been one of the most widely read of recent novels, and in this new work the author exhibits the same power in the management of a complicated plot and in the portrayal of dramatic incidents.

**NOBLE BLOOD.** A Novel. By JULIAN HAWTHORNE. 16mo. Paper cover, 50 cents.

"The personages and the incidents introduced are managed with that clear-sweeping and magnetic force which is one of the prime qualities of the author, now in the full flow of strength and prosperity. It will be read with interest by a large and perpetually expanding circle."—*The Telegram.*

"The *mise en scène* of the opening chapters is simply delicious; the genial, breezy, lovely bit of description is followed by a tale which, if little more than a story, is nevertheless an entertaining story, full of Irish humor, and leaving one with an impression that life after all is worth living and human nature worth loving."—*The Critic.*

**THE CRIME OF CHRISTMAS-DAY.** A Tale of the Latin Quarter. By the author of "My Ducats and my Daughter." 12mo. Paper cover, 25 cents.

**ALLAN DARE AND ROBERT LE DIABLE.** A Romance. By Admiral DAVID D. PORTER, U. S. Navy. Published in Nine Parts, price, 25 cents each. Now complete in two large octavo volumes. Illustrated. Paper covers, $2.00.

"Admiral Porter is the latest distinguished accession to the list of authors. He produces not a work on navigation but—a novel. Men of all professions are trying their hands at romancing nowadays. Admiral Porter need not be afraid of comparing his work with that of some professional novelist. The admiral excites the curiosity of the reader with a great deal of artfulness. The story has a mystery to which the author is leading up with much skill; he displays humor, touches of pathos, and a knack of sketching characters."—*New York Journal of Commerce.*

"All the well-known qualities of the successful romance are present in this one, and contribute to make it the great and most popular work of fiction of the year."—*Boston Sunday Globe.*

New York: D. APPLETON & CO., Publishers, 1, 3, & 5 Bond Street.